ALIAS™

AUTHORIZED
PERSONNEL ONLY

Also available from
SIMON SPOTLIGHT ENTERTAINMENT

ALIAS™

THE

SERIES

TWO OF A KIND?

FAINA

COLLATERAL DAMAGE

REPLACED

THE ROAD NOT TAKEN

VIGILANCE

ALIAS™

AUTHORIZED PERSONNEL ONLY

Files Compiled by Paul Ruditis

Based on the hit TV series
created by J. J. Abrams

 SIMON SPOTLIGHT ENTERTAINMENT
New York London Toronto Sydney

SIMON SPOTLIGHT ENTERTAINMENT

An imprint of Simon & Schuster

1230 Avenue of the Americas, New York, New York 10020

Text and cover art copyright © 2005 by Touchstone Television.

Unless otherwise credited, all photographs copyright © Touchstone Televisions and ABC, Inc.

Alias © 2005 by Touchstone Television. All Rights Reserved.

All rights reserved, including the right of reproduction in whole or in part in any form.

Designed by Lili Schwartz

SIMON SPOTLIGHT ENTERTAINMENT and related logo are trademarks of Simon & Schuster, Inc.

Manufactured in the United States of America

First Edition   10 9 8 7 6 5 4 3 2 1

Library of Congress Control Number 2004117771

ISBN-13: 978-1-4169-0215-7

ISBN-10: 1-4169-0215-5

CONTENTS

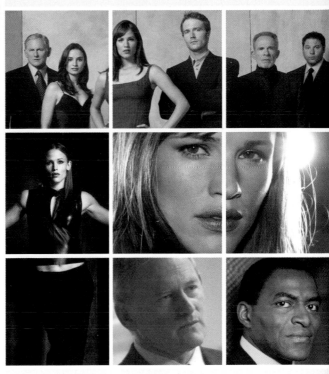

CLASSIFIED:

OMEGA 17
TOP SECRET

AUTHORIZED PERSONNEL ONLY

Authorized Personnel Only (APO) is a handpicked elite black ops team within the Central Intelligence Agency (CIA), led by Arvin Sloane. Concerned with the increased public scrutiny of the Agency and the resulting red tape, the CIA had been impeded in doing its job to the fullest. It brokered a deal with Sloane to set up a covert unit still governed by U.S. law but unhampered by the bureaucratic chain of command. Officially, APO is a unit that does not exist, comprised of team members that apparently have no CIA affiliation. Therefore, if any of them are captured or killed, the CIA will disavow any involvement.

Included herein are the top secret archived files of the APO unit. The following information provides all background necessary to understand the events leading to the formation of this unit and the missions undertaken during its first year in existence. The files are largely centered on the activities of the unit's central member, Sydney Bristow.

Any unauthorized disclosure is a violation of Section 23, Paragraph 5 of the Patriot Act.

APO Call Sign: Phoenix
ID Class: USS-CI-2300844
DOB: 4/17/74
Place of Birth: Charleston, West Virginia, USA
Family:
    Father: Jack Bristow
    Mother: Laura Bristow (aka Irina Derevko)
    Half Sister: Nadia Santos
    Aunts: Katya Derevko, Elena Derevko
Education: Master's in English Literature from
    University of Los Angeles
Languages: English (various dialects),
    Taiwanese, Mandarin, French, Hebrew,
    Japanese, Arabic, Italian, Russian,
    Hungarian, Uzbek, Urdu,
    and German

History with SD-6 and the CIA:

Sydney Bristow was approached to join what she believed was the CIA during her freshman year of college in December 1994. She did not accept the offer at first but continued to consider the idea. At the time, she did not love the subjects she was studying, had a lackluster social life, and was not speaking to her father. Ultimately, it was her curiosity to see if she could become a spy more than anything that resulted in her decision to accept.

Sydney started as an office assistant, working on the twentieth floor of the Credit Dauphine building in downtown Los Angeles. She assumed the bank had some affiliation with the CIA. After six months of evaluation, she was told that she was ready for "the Transition." This included eight months of training, tests, and what she later considered to be propaganda for the organization. She started with desk work, but moved to field ops within the first year. Before the transition she had never fired a gun or thrown a punch. It was during this time that she first heard the name "SD-6" in reference to a black ops division of the CIA. It was that division she was being trained to join.

Arvin Sloane, the head of SD-6, was personally involved in her recruitment into the organization. Though she was not aware of it at the time, Sloane had been a longtime family friend and had known her as a child. He had been out of the country for most of her childhood but had kept tabs on her. He later admitted that he always thought of her as a daughter, though he did not initially reveal how true he once believed those words to be.

Her actual father, Jack Bristow, was also a part of SD-6, but he had not initially been told of her recruitment. Once he learned of it, Jack strenuously objected to pulling her into that life, but it was too late to stop what was already in motion. With their relationship already strained, Jack did not reveal to his daughter that he also worked for the group. Sydney continued to work for SD-6 for seven years before she learned the true nature of the organization and of her father's involvement.

An SD-6 freelance operative killed Sydney's fiancé, Daniel Hecht, after she broke protocol and told him she was an agent of the CIA. It was an understandably shocking event, made even worse by the fact that she assumed the killing was carried out by an agency of the U.S. government.

Sydney was initially given a month off to mourn his death. After three months, it was clear that she was not planning to return to the group that had killed her fiancé. In spite of a warning from her partner, Marcus Dixon, that SD-6 would not let someone as deep in as Sydney leave so easily, she refused to change her mind.

One night, while getting into her car in a parking garage, Sydney suspected something was amiss. A red laser sight aimed at her proved her instincts correct. Sydney moved quickly, saving herself from the ensuing shot. The attack continued as she tried to escape the parking garage, forced to leave her car. Sydney managed to disarm the shooter as a sedan came screeching toward her. She grabbed the assassin's gun and aimed for the car, shocked to discover that her father was behind the wheel, urging her to get in.

It was at this time that Jack informed her that SD-6 was a mercenary organization with no ties to the CIA; it was part of the Alliance, the very organization she thought she was fighting. Even more shocking was that he was a member of that same organization.

With new resolve, Sydney approached the CIA as a walk-in and went back to work for SD-6 as a double agent in order to bring her fiancé's killers to justice. She convinced Sloane that she was a valuable asset to SD-6 and set out to dismantle the organization that had deceived her. CIA agent Michael Vaughn was assigned as her handler.

Sydney initially believed that she would be able to take down SD-6 in a matter of months, but she quickly revised that plan when she was shown just how far-reaching and influential the cell had become. She also learned that there was another mole in the organization who had been working to undermine SD-6 for years. It was her father.

Family History:

Sydney's involvement as a double agent has led to a much closer relationship with her father, Jack. He has often been the only person who truly understands the difficulties working undercover among people she considers friends. She had become estranged from her father following her mother's death in 1981 and was raised largely by a nanny. In spite of these circumstances, she used to believe that she had a seemingly typical childhood. This included an awkward phase around sixth grade, during which she recalls having big teeth, little eyes, and standing a foot taller than everyone else, which caused her to walk hunched over.

The estrangement between Sydney and her father naturally led to feelings of resentment toward him, since she never really understood why he was so distant. As it turned out, much of the reason for the distance was due to information Jack had learned following his wife's death. Only after Sydney found out the truth years later did she begin to have a better understanding of her father.

Sydney had always believed that her mother, Laura Bristow, died in a car accident coming home from the movies with her father. Further investigation as an adult led Sydney to believe that her mother's death was a result of her father's work in Intelligence. For a brief period she feared that he had been a double agent. She eventually learned that the accident was staged to fake her mother's death. Laura was a KGB officer, and her real name was Irina Derevko. Her marriage to Jack and even Sydney's own birth were merely part of the setup, a fact that devastated Sydney more than all the lies and deceit she had faced to date.

The presumed death of Laura Bristow affected Sydney's relationship with her father in ways she did not fully realize until years later. Jack had learned of his wife's betrayal shortly after her supposed death. As a result, he became obsessed with keeping Sydney from being hurt or betrayed. Jack's desire to keep her safe resulted in his enlisting her in Project Christmas, a program he had developed for the CIA that involved training qualified six-year-olds to become sleeper agents. Upon completion of the training, she was programmed to forget the experience, although the training stayed with her through adulthood and prepared her for life as a spy. Jack's original intention had been to bring her into the CIA, but Sloane's moves superseded Jack's plan when she was drafted into SD-6.

When Sydney learned of Project Christmas's existence, she first believed her mother had put her through the program. But her father's involvement eventually came to light and further complicated

their relationship. For all of his efforts to protect her from the dangers of his line of work, Jack just seemed to bring her in deeper with every precaution he took.

Years later Sydney learned just how close she had come to having a normal childhood with her family. The information was revealed while recreating Jack Bristow's life in 1981, as Sydney was hoping to obtain important information from her father, who was trapped in a hallucination as a result of radiation poisoning. Prior to her mother's supposed death, Jack had informed Laura that he was planning to resign from the CIA because he was tired of missing out on Sydney's life. However, Laura's subsequent death and the events surrounding it changed his mind.

Sydney had originally pursued graduate school in anticipation of a future in education because she believed her mother had been a teacher. When Sydney learned the truth about "Laura Bristow," she considered dropping out of school, but eventually decided to stick with it, realizing that her desire to teach was her dream, not her mother's. Her father was surprisingly helpful to her in making this decision. Even though she graduated following the downfall of SD-6, Sydney was not able to bring herself to leave the Intelligence business and pursue a career in education.

When Sydney realized that her mother was still alive, she became obsessed with finding the woman now known as Irina Derevko. Her father warned her against the mission, but Sydney was unable to let it go until she got some answers from the woman who had betrayed her family. The reunion did not go as planned. Derevko shot Sydney, though she later asserted that she did it only because they were being watched. Derevko claimed that wounding her daughter would at least have given her a chance to escape.

Derevko turned herself in to the CIA, but Sydney wanted nothing to do with her mother at that point. When Derevko insisted that she would provide the Agency with intelligence only through Sydney, her daughter relented. Slowly they formed a tenuous bond that strengthened over time. It was only after Sydney began to approach a normal relationship with her mother that Derevko seemingly betrayed her and the United States by escaping custody with an important artifact.

For almost a year afterward Derevko secretly worked with Jack to protect their daughter from a terrorist organization known as the Covenant. However, upon the fall of the Covenant, Sydney learned that her father had had her mother killed. At first Sydney refused to forgive her father. However, she eventually learned that the true betrayal came, once again, from her mother. Derevko had taken out a contract on Sydney's life. The only way that Jack could stop the hit was by killing Derevko, thereby nullifying the contract.

After learning the truth about the hit, Sydney still needed time before she could reconnect with her father. She did help keep the secret from her half sister, Nadia, to protect her from learning the truth about their mother. Eventually Sydney was forced to tell Nadia that their mother had tried to have Sydney killed, but Sydney soon learned that that wasn't quite the truth. The aunt whom she had never met before, Elena, was the one behind the hit.

Elena Derevko had created a duplicate of their mother while holding the real one prisoner to extract important information from her. Sydney was eventually reunited with her mother, though their time together was brief before Irina was forced back into hiding because she was still considered a fugitive.

Prior to discovering that her mother was still alive, Sydney learned that she was the "Chosen One," as depicted in the prophecy of Renaissance architect and seer Milo Rambaldi. The prophecy stated that the Chosen One would "render the greatest power to utter desolation." Sydney attempted to disprove the claim by breaking one of the conditions of her designation as the subject in the prophecy. And although there is some uncertainty regarding her role, the National Security Agency (NSA) still took her into custody and held her under National Security Directive 81-A, believing her to be a threat to national security until she was able to prove otherwise.

Further complicating the situation, Sydney learned of a second part of the prophecy referring to a "Passenger" with whom the Chosen One was destined to do battle. Only one of them would survive. As it turned out, this Passenger was a half sister Sydney had never known she had.

Presumably as part of her overall plan, Derevko had had an affair with Arvin Sloane while she was married to Jack. A daughter was born as a result of that affair, though only Derevko had known of the girl's existence. Soon after finding out the truth, Sydney was sent to find the girl, Nadia Santos, as she was the target of a Covenant plot. While protecting Nadia from the Covenant, Sydney was able to briefly get to know her sister. However, once the immediate crisis had ended, Nadia returned to her adopted home of Argentina.

Following the creation of the APO unit, Sydney was forced to go to her half sister for help with a mission. There was initial tension between the two, being that Nadia was the daughter of her despised enemy Arvin Sloane. Sydney slowly came around, knowing that Nadia could not be held responsible for Sloane and Derevko's past actions. When Nadia joined APO, Sydney opened up her home and asked her sister to move in. Though the pair continued to grow closer, they did so in the shadow of the fact that Sydney was hiding the truth about their mother's death from Nadia.

Personal History:

Though she was trained to compartmentalize her emotions, the duplicitous nature of Sydney's life affected her and everyone she loved. The hardest part about working undercover was lying to the people she cared about. But after considering what had happened to Danny, she ultimately decided it was a gesture of love to deceive her closest friends, Francie Calfo and Will Tippin, in order to keep them safe.

Sydney was forced to use her cover story as a bank employee for Credit Dauphine to explain many sudden absences and missed engagements when she was, in fact, on assignment. Despite her best efforts to keep her friends in the dark, they did suspect something was wrong on several occasions. But they usually attributed her behavior to Danny's death or to a possible new secret relationship.

Though Sydney was well practiced at keeping her secret, it hurt her when she had to miss out on things like shopping with Francie for her wedding dress. Sydney was able to be there for her friend when Francie left her fiancé and when she decided to open a restaurant. But even under the best of circumstances, Sydney could not keep an eye on Francie every minute of every day. And in a horrible act committed under orders from Sloane, Francie was murdered and replaced by a double by the name of Allison Doren.

Sydney continued to live with Allison for months, unaware of the fact that Francie was dead. When Sydney found out, she and Allison fought a vicious battle that ended with her home destroyed, Allison shot and left for dead, and Sydney disappearing for two years.

Her other closest friend from civilian life, Will Tippin, was also pulled into her undercover world when he tried to investigate Danny's death. Will's barely hidden love for Sydney often clouded their friendship, as she did not entirely share his feelings. His well-intentioned but misguided investigation into SD-6 ruined his career and nearly got him killed.

Though Sydney's father tried to prevent Will from discovering the truth, Will was shocked when he eventually learned Sydney's secret. He managed to accept the truth surprisingly well, more concerned about Sydney's well-being than anything. With his career in ruins due to a necessary cover-up, Will worked briefly as an analyst for the CIA before he was enrolled in the Witness Protection Program. Though Sydney was able to visit him on one rare occasion, and even share in a night of passion, Will became another close friend lost to her because of her work.

This sense of loss was certainly nothing new to Sydney and not solely a result of her work as a double agent. Early in her career at SD-6 she met and fell in love with Agent Noah Hicks. However, their relationship abruptly ended when he was reassigned to a deep cover assignment. For years Sydney thought he had left her without even saying good-bye. Hicks later claimed that he had sent her an encoded message explaining the departure, but she had never received it.

Years later the two reunited and found that they still had much in common, including the fact that they were both effectively double agents. Hicks, however, was not working for the same side. Regretfully, Sydney only learned the truth about Hicks's work after a masked man attacked her during a mission. The two fought and the masked man was fatally stabbed. When Sydney removed the mask, she saw that it was her former love.

Sydney also hated the fact that her friends at SD-6 did not know they were working against the same government they had pledged to protect. This was most evident in her feelings toward her partner, Marcus Dixon, whom she had met during her first tour of SD-6. Sydney and Dixon had been partnered for years and had the type of incredibly close bond necessary between two people often thrown into life-or-death situations. She was friendly with his family, though Dixon's wife and children believed her to be simply a colleague from Credit Dauphine. When SD-6's true nature was revealed, Sydney was devastated by the hurt that

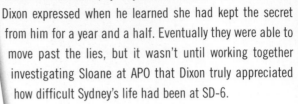

Dixon expressed when he learned she had kept the secret from him for a year and a half. Eventually they were able to move past the lies, but it wasn't until working together investigating Sloane at APO that Dixon truly appreciated how difficult Sydney's life had been at SD-6.

In spite of the lies and hidden agendas, Sydney was able to form real friendships with her coworkers at SD-6. One of the most trying times for her, in fact, involved the possibility of pulling her friend Marshall Flinkman out of SD-6 to come work for the CIA. Regretfully, the situation was complicated by a third party, but when SD-6 ultimately fell, Marshall was one of the first to sign up for duty at the CIA and easily overlooked the lies Sydney had been forced to tell.

After joining the CIA, Sydney began experiencing an attraction to her handler, Michael Vaughn, a feeling that was mutual. Their unrequited relationship continued for more than a year, as they were unable to act on their feelings until the fall of SD-6 was complete and they were freed from the code of conduct required of operative and handler. Aside from the natural complexities of working together and pursuing a relationship, the early stages of being a couple were complicated for numerous reasons. One of the larger stumbling blocks was when they both discovered that her mother had killed his father years earlier.

Nevertheless, they worked through everything together and for the first time in her adult life, Sydney was able to get close to someone with seemingly no secrets on either side. But their budding relationship abruptly came to an end upon Sydney's realization that Allison Doren had replaced Francie. The ensuing battle led to Sydney's disappearance for two years. When she resurfaced, having no recollection of anything that took place during her missing time, she was comforted by the fact that the CIA sent Vaughn to brief her, until she saw his wedding ring.

Missing Time:
Following her presumed death, Sydney was abducted and tortured by members of the Covenant. She underwent a horrific brainwashing program in an attempt to convince her that she was an operative known as

Julia Thorne. Sydney managed to resist the brainwashing, largely due to the programming she had received from her father as a child under the Project Christmas program. As part of the ruse to convince the Covenant that the brainwashing had worked, she was forced to kill an innocent man to prove her allegiance. Once the Covenant believed they had turned her, Sydney made contact with Director Kendall from the Joint Task Force on Intelligence.

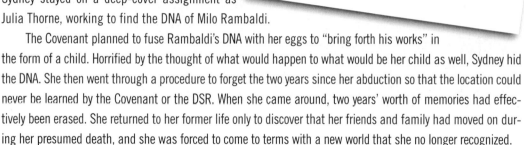

Although she wanted to let her friends and family know she was alive, Sydney soon discovered that the Covenant had them all under surveillance. Fearing for the safety of her loved ones, Sydney stayed on a deep-cover assignment as Julia Thorne, working to find the DNA of Milo Rambaldi.

The Covenant planned to fuse Rambaldi's DNA with her eggs to "bring forth his works" in the form of a child. Horrified by the thought of what would happen to what would be her child as well, Sydney hid the DNA. She then went through a procedure to forget the two years since her abduction so that the location could never be learned by the Covenant or the DSR. When she came around, two years' worth of memories had effectively been erased. She returned to her former life only to discover that her friends and family had moved on during her presumed death, and she was forced to come to terms with a new world that she no longer recognized.

During Sydney's two-year absence, Vaughn had fallen in love with and married Lauren Reed. At first Sydney was angered by the betrayal, but slowly came around to trying to be Vaughn's friend. It was difficult for both of them to pretend that they no longer had feelings for each other.

At a time when she had lost her closest friends and her lover, Sydney found solace in her friendship with fellow agent and neighbor Eric Weiss. This friendship was made especially difficult because Weiss was also Vaughn's closest friend.

Sydney and Vaughn were unable to contain their feelings for each other no matter how hard they tried. They eventually reunited after it was revealed that Lauren was a double agent working for the Covenant and Vaughn was forced to kill her to protect Sydney. Their relationship resumed, though both agreed to take things slowly in light of all that had happened.

The relationship seemed, at first, to be progressing too slowly, as they feared they were getting into a rut and weren't that exciting as a couple. Things soon changed as they took on the personal mission to determine the truth behind the death of Vaughn's father. Sydney was forced to lie to her father and Sloane while helping Vaughn in his search. She even covered up for him when he briefly went rogue. In the end the events served only

to strengthen their relationship. As a result Vaughn asked her to marry him. Sydney accepted, but as the two drove to Santa Barbara for a second attempt at a romantic trip—and possible elopement—everything went horribly wrong.

Psychological Profile:

Sydney is fiercely loyal to the people in her life. However, considering the amount of past betrayal experienced on behalf of her parents and Arvin Sloane, she is also cautious when given reason to suspect someone of clandestine activities.

Though Sydney has a respect for authority and a strong adherence to the rules, she has, on more than one occasion, gone rogue to protect herself and the ones she loves. One of the more prominent examples of this behavior was when she handed Sloane over to Sark, believing that in doing so she was sending Sloane to his death. Her motivation in going through with the exchange was to save Vaughn. This impulse to protect her loved ones guides many of the decisions she makes.

Sydney has endured various forms of torture, including tooth extraction, electroshock, and brain-washing attempts. Her ability to withstand these practices is in part the result of her training in the Project Christmas program, which included a fail-safe to protect its subjects from being turned. Sydney has been trained to fool lie detector tests—even one as advanced as a functional imaging test—and her spatial intelligence functions at extremely high levels. Sydney's one weakness is empathetic suffering. It is harder for her to watch others be tortured than it is for her to endure her own physical torture.

In recent years one of the largest influences on Sydney's behavioral patterns has been her dealings with Arvin Sloane. As the man is responsible for killing both her fiancé and her best friend and deceiving her into performing criminal acts, her hatred has motivated Sydney to seek revenge and stop him at all costs. Her feelings toward Sloane have been further complicated by his recent protestations of having "changed" and by her discovery that he was the father to her half sister. Sydney was backed into agreeing to join APO so she could help keep an eye on Sloane while in the conflicting position of working for him.

Sydney possesses a tremendous talent when it comes to adopting Alias personalities. She can easily adapt to almost any character and any situation. She also holds a talent for improvisation and is able to handle most situations she's thrown into with only minimal preparation. These extraordinary abilities help make her a first-rate operative.

APO Call Sign: Raptor
ID Class: USS-CI-2300682
DOB: 3/16/50
Place of Birth: London, Ontario, Canada
Family:
    Wife: Laura Bristow (aka Irina Derevko)
    Daughter: Sydney Bristow
Education: Doctorate, LAS
Languages: English, Russian, Chinese, Spanish, Arabic

History with the CIA and SD-6:

Jack Bristow was recruited into the CIA in 1970. He began his career working under Arvin Sloane in Washington, D.C. and was transferred to the Los Angeles field office in 1977.

Agent Bristow joined SD-6 with Sloane when the Alliance of Twelve was formed in 1991. He was one of only five agents in SD-6 who actually knew the truth behind the organization. Though it appeared that Jack was a servant to the cause, he was secretly working for the CIA to undermine SD-6 and the Alliance. His initial cover at SD-6 was as an airplane parts exporter at Jennings Aerospace. After his daughter learned of his affiliation with both agencies, Jack "transferred" to Credit Dauphine, where his cover became portfolio manager. The personal motive behind his transfer was so that he and Sydney could work more closely in their attempts to take down the organization.

At SD-6, Jack had high-level clearance and was usually in charge of the office when Sloane was out of the country. Sloane often called on Jack for high-security missions as well as for his ability to extract information from unwilling subjects. He was considered next in line to take Sloane's seat in the Alliance. This level of trust was important for his undercover work. In fact, Jack had worked for many years as a mole within the organization without even a hint of suspicion aimed in his direction. In his position, Jack was able to pass along information from SD-6 as well as tailor missions to benefit the CIA.

Jack was instrumental in maintaining his daughter's status as a double agent, providing cover for her actions and offering explanations after the fact to keep her safe when suspicions were aroused. This was most evident when he framed fellow SD-6 agent Anthony Russek for Sydney's suspicious activities. Using his level of clearance and directing op tech engineer Marshall Flinkman to ask certain technical questions, Jack managed to plant evidence indicating that Russek was the mole. The action saved his daughter, though Jack knew that he was sentencing Russek to death.

The suspicious behavior, however, did not go entirely unnoticed. As Sloane's closest confidant, Jack was the prime suspect in a mole hunt led by Ariana Kane. Little did Jack know that it was an even deeper setup, since Sloane had begun to suspect both Jack and Sydney of undermining the organization from within. Prior to the fall of SD-6, clues Sloane had left behind led the new head of the organization to learn of Jack's status as a double agent.

JACK WITH ARIANA KANE

Jack and Sydney had arranged for a pass phrase ("Take the surface streets, they're doing work on the freeway") to use as a warning in the event that one of them was compromised, so the other knew to flee. The only time the warning was used was when Jack was discovered as the mole in SD-6. The desire to save her father led Sydney to push harder for the plan to invade and ultimately destroy the organization.

Family History:

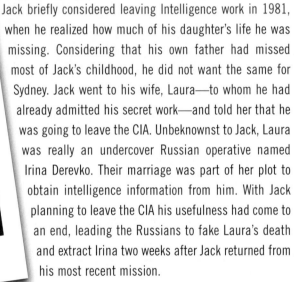

Jack briefly considered leaving Intelligence work in 1981, when he realized how much of his daughter's life he was missing. Considering that his own father had missed most of Jack's childhood, he did not want the same for Sydney. Jack went to his wife, Laura—to whom he had already admitted his secret work—and told her that he was going to leave the CIA. Unbeknownst to Jack, Laura was really an undercover Russian operative named Irina Derevko. Their marriage was part of her plot to obtain intelligence information from him. With Jack planning to leave the CIA his usefulness had come to an end, leading the Russians to fake Laura's death and extract Irina two weeks after Jack returned from his most recent mission.

Following Laura's death, Jack feared that she had been a double agent working for the KGB. Jack was blindsided by the news, especially when he was suspected of being in collusion with her. The FBI almost tried him for treason, and he spent twelve months in solitary confinement in a federal prison. During that time, a young Sydney was told that her father was away on business. Eventually he was exonerated and a classified FBI report cleared him of any involvement with the KGB. In spite of his reprieve Jack started to unravel and began drinking excessively and taking unnecessary risks. Jack never did leave the CIA.

His wife's betrayal led Jack to become obsessed with protecting Sydney as a child. Thus he subjected her to the Project Christmas training program he was developing for the CIA. The program was intended to train children as sleeper agents while they were still young and impressionable. Jack did not want his daughter to become a victim and adopted the responsibility of making sure that Sydney could think strategically and see through people's lies. Even though he tried to keep her as far away from his work as possible while she was growing up, Jack wanted to ensure that she grew to be as strong as she could be in an environment where one mistake could cost her life.

Once Jack found out that Sydney was in SD-6, he felt it might jeopardize his double agent status to reveal the truth to her, so he remained silent. It was a decision he ultimately came to regret. Eventually Jack was forced to reveal the truth to Sydney. At first she was hurt to find out about the secrets and lies, but she grew to understand why Jack had done some of the things he had done.

Working together to bring down SD-6 actually helped to heal their broken relationship. Jack's inability to open up to his daughter often led them into conflict but ultimately resulted in them coming together once they moved past whatever issue was at the heart of the problem. Though Sydney was understandably wary of her father as mounting evidence led to questions regarding his true affiliation to the United States, Jack and Sydney grew to trust each other enough that they were almost ready to handle a new threat to their relationship.

When Sydney told Jack that she suspected her mother was still alive, Jack wanted nothing to do with the investigation. However, to help prove the theory that Sydney was not the woman in Rambaldi's prophecy, Jack violated the trust of the CIA by breaking into Langley's classified archives to pull the operational file on Laura Bristow. He was surprised to learn that Arvin Sloane had been on the internal commission investigating Laura. Sloane had been aware of the fact that Laura had not died in the accident and he had kept the information from Jack for decades.

JACK AND IRINA DEREVKO

During SD-6's investigation into the identity of Alexander Khasinau, Sydney found a video in the core of the Man's supercomputer that showed an interview with Laura Bristow following her staged death. In the video her true identity was revealed as Major Irina Derevko. At first Jack refused to watch the video, but he eventually relented. Jack was equally heartbroken and angered to hear that she had spied on him for ten years in an attempt to learn about his work on Project Christmas. Even worse was the part where she called him a fool on the tape. Around this time, Sloane briefly pulled Jack off active duty to deal with the revelations.

When Derevko resurfaced and turned herself in to the CIA, Jack refused to even speak with her at first. When he did finally visit Derevko in her cell, it was to warn her against harming their daughter in any way.

The longer Derevko was in custody, the more Jack allowed himself to work with her. Their bond seemed to grow, and Jack even went to her for help in brainstorming ways to prove that he was not the mole in SD-6 during Kane's investigation. Even after they grew closer on a pair of joint missions, Jack never fully trusted Derevko—and with good reason. When Derevko eventually escaped with a valued Rambaldi artifact, Jack revealed that he had anticipated her move and had planted a tracker on her. It led Sydney to her mother before Derevko could remove it.

After her escape, Jack continued to keep in touch with Derevko unofficially through IM correspondence. He went to her for help protecting Sydney from the Covenant and accepted assistance from Derevko's sister Katya. Jack and Katya grew closer while they worked together to get Sydney out of a Vietnamese prison. Even though Katya ultimately proved to be working with the Covenant, it seemed that Irina Derevko could at least be trusted. However, Jack was surprised to learn that she had ordered a contract on their daughter.

Jack immediately requested CIA permission to kill Derevko before the contract on Sydney could be fulfilled. Jack found Derevko at the British Embassy in Vienna. After a brief conversation in which Derevko confirmed his suspicions, Jack put a bullet in her head. Though he knew that she had left him no other options, Jack regretted his actions every day following her death.

Jack tried to keep Derevko's death a secret from Sydney for her own benefit. Even when she found out about the murder, he refused to explain his reasoning, as he knew how difficult it would be for Sydney to find out that her mother had wanted her killed. Eventually she learned the truth on her own. That truth, however, turned out to be a lie.

Months after her death, Irina was seen very much alive as a prisoner of her sister, Elena Derevko. The woman whom Jack had killed was one of Elena's followers who had been put through the Project Helix doubling procedure. Jack led Sydney and Nadia on a mission to retrieve their mother and obtain her help in stopping Elena Derevko from unleashing Rambaldi's ultimate design. After giving him a punch in the jaw for his prior actions, Irina agreed to help. In the end Jack allowed her to go into hiding, knowing that she was wanted by the U.S. government.

As noted earlier, Jack's first and foremost responsibility is the protection of his daughter. Even during their time of estrangement he was looking after her behind the scenes. He had planned to help her and her fiancé escape when Danny was targeted by SD-6, and he arrived only minutes too late to save him. He then arranged to get Sydney out of the country when SD-6 had targeted her for refusing to return to work following Danny's death.

Though he hardly knew his daughter's fiancé, Danny, Jack took an active interest in her relationship with Agent Michael Vaughn. He warned Vaughn to stay away on several occasions, believing the man was not good enough for his daughter. However, through working together, Jack has grown to have a grudging respect for Vaughn. Jack eventually came around and gave his blessing to Vaughn when he asked permission to marry Sydney.

Personal History:

Jack used to be close friends with Arvin Sloane, sharing what they termed "an unsentimental patriotism and a similar devotion to their wives." Jack and Sloane seemed to be on parallel paths both professionally and personally until Sloane turned against his country. Even though Jack knew that Sloane had turned, he claims that their friendship did not truly end until the moment Sloane recruited Sydney into SD-6 over his objection.

When Jack later learned that Sloane had had an affair with Irina Derevko, he was surprisingly hurt by the betrayal that had occurred decades earlier. Even though Jack had learned by then to expect the worst from Sloane and Derevko in recent years, the affair happened at a time when Sloane was supposedly his friend and Irina was still thought to be his wife, Laura.

For a time it seemed that Jack was prepared to let Sloane die for the betrayal, as he withheld information that could have saved Sloane's life. However, it was all part of an overall plan that required Jack to rescue Sloane from lethal injection. Sloane then agreed to work with Jack to find the daughter who resulted from the affair. At the same time, Jack checked his medical records to confirm that he was Sydney's father. During the brief time of uncertainty, his feelings for her as a daughter never wavered.

Though Jack would never fully trust Arvin Sloane again, he did agree to work with the man to protect their daughters. After learning that Elena Derevko had had Sydney and Nadia under surveillance for years, the two fathers secretly teamed to locate Elena and stop her from whatever she had planned. Together they worked through APO to gather intelligence, and Jack even went so far as to use his own daughter in an attempt to gain needed information. But that was not the only secret the two men shared.

Jack had learned of the truth behind Sloane's creation of Omnifam to infect the world's water supply with a Rambaldi elixir. When Jack saw that Sloane had apparently repented, Jack remained quiet about the past actions. This silence nearly had global ramifications when Elena Derevko took up the plan where Sloane had left off.

Psychological Profile:

JACK WITH DR. BARNETT

Jack is especially talented at reading people and manipulating them to do what he wants. His forms of manipulation can be as subtle as playing to their egos or as obvious as strong-armed force. Some of his most skilled manipulations occurred when he positioned himself to head the Joint Task Force on Intelligence based on his knowledge of Irina Derevko.

Jack is considered an expert at anticipating the moves of both Arvin Sloane and Irina Derevko. Much of his expertise comes from the fact that the pair have repeatedly betrayed him, and he has learned not to trust either of them as a result. In point of fact, he considers himself to be like the pair in many ways. For one thing, he claims that the only thing that kept him from falling into the same obsession with Milo Rambaldi that Sloane and Derevko shared was the fact that he had Sydney to keep him from losing focus on what was important.

When Derevko turned herself in to the CIA, Jack was having a difficult time facing the realities of her betrayal of him so many years earlier. Sensing the problem, Sydney suggested that he see a counselor. Knowing he would refuse, Sydney had Director Devlin order him to speak with Dr. Judy Barnett for "trauma evaluation."

During their first session, Jack admitted to his fears of losing Sydney in a seemingly honest and open discussion from the heart. However, at the end of that first session, Dr. Barnett lauded him for being a master at deception. She noted that he had all of his subconscious "tells" under control so she would fall for his story. He was even smart enough to struggle over his words when describing his fear that Sydney's search for her mother could be seen as criticism of his role as a father. Barnett's analysis of Jack's destructive behavior was further supported by the shocking number of instances reported in his file of missions during which he had gone rogue. Dr. Barnett was most concerned that someone so skilled in deception could be best at deceiving himself.

Ultimately Jack admitted that his desire to keep Sydney and Derevko apart was because he was afraid of losing his daughter. Of course, he was referring to an emotional loss rather than a physical one. To ensure that Sydney did not fall for what he believed to be Derevko's manipulations, Jack set Derevko up to make it look as if she had lied about some intel in Sydney's mission to retrieve the bible of Derevko's organization. According to Derevko, the bible was in a house that was safe to enter. However, Jack had paid a freelancer to rig the foundation with Semtex so it would blow. He then tasked a satellite to the area to reveal the explosives. The presumed lie was enough to revoke Derevko's agreement with the CIA, effectively sentencing her to death.

Jack eventually admitted the truth to a Senate inquiry after Sydney found out what he had done. In open court, he claimed that when he looked at Sydney he saw the little girl who grew up to be an extraordinary human being and one of the finest agents he has ever known. He saw in her the promise of his redemption. Part of this admission was to contradict Sydney's belief that he considered her his greatest mistake and a permanent reminder of his fraudulent marriage. Turning himself in was his way to prove Sydney could trust him and that he loved her more than he could say.

As noted earlier, Jack's protection of Sydney is often the motivating factor in his actions, particularly those that are considered extreme. In one case, he killed double agent Steven Haladki when his leaked information put Sydney in jeopardy.

Following the presumed death of his daughter, Jack became obsessed with finding those responsible. He contacted the only person he felt he could trust: Irina Derevko. At the time, Derevko was number six on the CIA's Most Wanted list. Although Jack managed to discover that Sydney was alive, the National Security Council found out he was working with Derevko and questioned Jack's allegiance to the United States. He was made an example in an NSC power play and sentenced to solitary confinement. He was there for almost a year when Sydney resurfaced and obtained his release.

Jack defends every morally questionable thing he has ever done as being performed to protect Sydney. Ultimately, his protectiveness led to the execution of Irina Derevko when he learned she had put a contract on Sydney's life. He then tried to shield Sydney from the truth so that she did not have to live with the knowledge that her mother wanted her dead.

Jack has not thought twice about risking his own life to save his daughter's. During a mission to retrieve a coil from an experimental project in a nuclear plant in Siberia, Sydney was trapped in the test chamber as the reactor activated. Jack entered a reactor, risking a lethal dose of radiation to shut down the core and save Sydney's life. He then tried to cover up what he had done to further protect his daughter from a bitter truth: that he had effectively given his life for hers.

Jack was secretly suffering from a large-scale genetic mutation due to his actions protecting Sydney. Though he refused to share his problem with anyone at APO (swearing Marshall to secrecy), Jack believed he was seeking treatment from a former contact named Dr. Liddell. Unfortunately it was all a hallucination due to the poisoning. When Sydney learned the truth and found her father, she was forced to help act out his hallucination to find the real Dr. Liddell. During a reenactment of his life circa 1981, Jack revealed that he had been about to give up his CIA life for his daughter. Thanks to the information provided by Jack in his weakened state, APO located the doctor and found a cure.

ARVIN SLOANE

ID Class: 30408-00811
DOB: 10/31/50
Place of Birth: Brooklyn, New York, USA
Education: Doctorate in Linguistics,
   Master's in Finance
Family:
   Wife: Emily Sloane (deceased)
   Daughter: Nadia Santos
   Mother's Maiden Name: Bishop
Languages: English, French, Russian, Hebrew,
   Spanish, Arabic

History with the CIA and SD-6:

Arvin Sloane was recruited to the CIA in 1969. He rose through the ranks, performing his duties proudly as ordered. Early in his career, following a briefing at the White House, Sloane went out to get some air and was overwhelmed by how perfectly his life was going with both a successful, fulfilling career and a loving wife. Even though he was thoroughly happy, he could sense dark days ahead and that everything was going to go wrong.

As time went on, his involvement with the CIA turned into a negative experience as he lost faith in the organization. Years later his feelings of bitterness were compounded by finding out that his wife, Emily, was diagnosed with cancer. In spite of the dire news, he found it a comfort that he had known that darkness was coming.

SD-6 BRIEFING

Sloane and his wife befriended Jack and Laura Bristow during a happier time in the early 1970s. Neither Jack nor Arvin realized that Laura was a KGB operative by the name of Irina Derevko at the time. Following Laura's presumed death, Sloane was assigned to the CIA internal commission investigating the accident. While serving on the commission, he learned not only that Derevko was KGB, but that she was still alive. Sloane was ordered to keep that information from Jack; it was a secret he kept for more than twenty years.

Eventually Sloane became disillusioned and felt betrayed by the CIA. He believed that the American government was irredeemably corrupt. Jean Briault recruited Sloane into the Alliance when it was formed in 1991. He was appointed head of SD-6 and quickly brought Jack into the organization.

Sloane's tenure at SD-6 was marked by a fraudulent conspiracy on a grand scale, as he convinced dozens, if not hundreds, of employees that they worked for the U.S. government. Instead, they were part of what amounted to a terrorist cell operating within American borders. After a dozen years of lies, Sloane perpetrated an even greater fraud as he brought down the organization to further his own plans.

Family History:

Sloane's premonition of dark times proved all too true a few years later when his wife, Emily, became pregnant. The couple was overjoyed with the news that they were going to have a daughter and began to refer to her as Jacquelyn. However, because it was a high-risk pregnancy, they kept it a secret from even their closest friends. Sadly, Emily lost the baby. In her pain, she insisted that her husband never mention the name again. Sloane complied with the request, locking the secret away deep inside his mind.

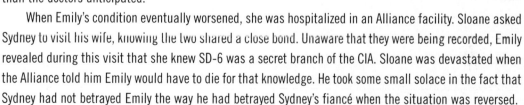

The darkness continued to deepen when Emily was diagnosed with lymphoma four years prior to the fall of SD-6. At the time the prognosis was that she had only six months to live. However, Emily defied the odds and survived for years longer than the doctors anticipated.

When Emily's condition eventually worsened, she was hospitalized in an Alliance facility. Sloane asked Sydney to visit his wife, knowing the two shared a close bond. Unaware that they were being recorded, Emily revealed during this visit that she knew SD-6 was a secret branch of the CIA. Sloane was devastated when the Alliance told him Emily would have to die for that knowledge. He took some small solace in the fact that Sydney had not betrayed Emily the way he had betrayed Sydney's fiancé when the situation was reversed.

Considering that the prognosis was grim for Emily anyway, Sloane arranged with the Alliance that she be allowed to live out her final days and let the cancer run its course. They granted his request. Shortly thereafter, he learned that Emily had gone into remission. His joy over the news was tempered by the fact that he knew the Alliance still wanted her dead. Sloane admitted the truth behind SD-6 to Emily. She was understandably angry that her husband was part of an organization that worked against the American government.

Sloane went to Alliance headquarters, demanding a seat in one of the empty chairs following the deaths of Jean Briault and Edward Poole. The Alliance surprised Sloane by having already voted to give him a place at the table—so long as he ended Emily's life. Sloane returned to his wife, who was still dealing

with her husband's recent announcement of having ties to the terrorist organization. As they shared a dinner, Sloane poured her wine that was supposedly laced with sodium morphate to fulfill his deal with the Alliance.

Sloane was made the newest full partner in the Alliance upon news of his wife's death. He was injected with a device that tracked his location and vital signs and also transmitted his conversations back to the Alliance.

Shortly after Emily's death, Sloane started to see hints that she was still alive. Someone was black-mailing him, claiming to have faked Emily's death and saying he was holding her hostage. In truth, it was all part of Sloane's plan to steal $100 million from the Alliance and bring down the organization, while he escaped with the money and all the Rambaldi artifacts they had collected. Sloane found a technician who could fool the device the Alliance had planted in him. Once the Alliance was no longer able to track him, Sloane killed the technician and disappeared for a brief time. Sloane was the one who had faked his wife's death, and he went to join her where she was living in secret on an island in the Philippines.

Emily eventually grew tired of Sloane's promises for a normal life when he was obviously still working outside the law, particularly in reference to his obsession with the works of Milo Rambaldi. After they moved into a new home in Tuscany, Emily went to the CIA with an offer to help bring him in, in exchange for the promise that he would not get the death penalty.

Shortly after Emily offered to aid in his capture, Sloane surprised her with his plan to sell off all his Rambaldi artifacts to Irina Derevko in order to save their marriage. In response, Emily silently revealed that she was wearing a recording device and that she had betrayed him to the CIA. The couple tried to flee their home, but during their escape, Emily was accidentally shot and killed by Marcus Dixon. Though Sloane was as much at fault for putting Emily in the situation, he swore revenge on Dixon. Sloane had a bomb planted in the car of Dixon's wife, killing her. He later admitted to feeling no satisfaction from the act, as he had killed the wrong person.

Decades earlier, Sloane had had an affair with Irina Derevko while she was posing as Laura Bristow. Sloane was surprised to find out recently that he had a child from that affair. Though his friendships were strained, Sloane enlisted the help of Jack and Sydney to find his daughter, who was indicated in a Rambaldi prophecy. They discovered that this daughter, Nadia Santos, was an agent with Argentine intelligence.

Sydney went undercover to find her and reunite Nadia with her father. The reunion was marred by Sloane's attempt to use Nadia in locating Rambaldi's ultimate artifact (see: *History with Rambaldi,* page 24). However, when the Covenant intervened in Sloane's experiment, he managed to do right by his daughter and set her free of the cruel procedure. Together they located the Rambaldi device.

Afterward Nadia returned to Argentina so she could spend some time adjusting to all that she had learned about her recently discovered family. Sloane eventually convinced her to join his newly formed APO unit, and she moved to Los Angeles. Nadia insisted that they take their relationship slowly because his obsessive behavior during their recent quest to locate the Rambaldi device coupled with his criminal history concerned her. In spite of these things, the two slowly began to bond as they worked together.

Personal History:

Arvin Sloane has few real friends in the world. Some of his closest allies were people he eventually betrayed, including members of the Alliance, SD-6, and the Covenant. Few people in his life have been as deeply hurt as Jack and Sydney Bristow.

SYDNEY AND SLOANE

Sloane befriended Jack during their time working together in the CIA. Though it was no surprise to Jack that a man like Sloane was capable of having an affair with "Laura Bristow," it was especially hurtful that it occurred before Sloane had turned to darker pursuits. The fact that Sloane was able to be so distrustful while they were still supposedly friends made the affair all the more painful for Jack when he learned of it.

That betrayal was nothing compared to the feeling Jack had when he learned that Sloane had recruited Sydney into SD-6 behind his back. Though Sloane and Jack argued over the decision when Jack found out, Sloane did not truly understand Jack's depth of anger until years later, when Jack informed him that this was the moment their friendship ended.

Sloane claimed to feel a fatherly love toward Sydney Bristow that often clouded his judgment regarding the suspicious behavior she exhibited at SD-6. On one occasion, when a trap was set to determine if she was a CIA mole, he actually set up a situation in which the CIA could have safely extracted her if her duplicity was revealed. However, his feelings for her did not stop him from going so far as to order her execution following her refusal to return to SD-6 after her fiancé's death or when specific evidence pointed to her being a mole.

Interestingly, Sloane felt no remorse for lying to Sydney and using her for years as an unknowing agent in illegal operations. On many occasions he assigned her tasks that he knew she would never have agreed to if she had known the truth about the organization for which she worked. Though this was true of all operatives within his organization, it was especially hurtful considering how much he claimed to care for her.

After the fall of SD-6, Sloane called Sydney to congratulate her on her graduation. He informed her that it was he who had provided the intel to take down the Alliance, claiming that his participation in the organization was simply a means to an end. He then warned Sydney not to come after him or he would have to kill her. At that point Sloane was on a hit list of thirty-five people in the world that CIA agents were allowed to assassinate. If Sydney were to kill him, she wouldn't even have been breaking the law.

History with Rambaldi:

Perhaps the single most life-defining aspect of Arvin Sloane's personality is his obsession with Milo Rambaldi and his collection of the prophet's works. This obsession began over thirty years earlier, when he joined the Army Corps of Engineers and was assigned to study a Rambaldi manuscript. His research led him to a man named Conrad, who set him on his journey to discover Rambaldi's endgame.

Sloane claimed to have a vision of an enterprise that would influence an existing world order he believed to be corrupt. He justified many of his more questionable actions through his search for Rambaldi and that ultimate goal. He sincerely hoped it would lead to a way to cure his wife of cancer as well as provide answers to the questions of life. During his time at SD-6, Sloane amassed more Rambaldi artifacts than any other SD cell. Afterward his dealings with Irina Derevko and Sark seemed motivated solely by his desire to complete his collection of Rambaldi artifacts.

Following the death of his wife, Sloane seemed to leave the Rambaldi project and journeyed to Nepal to meet with Conrad. His arrival was expected, and Conrad seemed to know that the death of Emily was foretold. He then showed Sloane a Rambaldi text that told him that he had a daughter and that she was part of Rambaldi's master plan. The revelation that he had a child was overwhelming, and Sloane returned to the Rambaldi project, hoping to use it as a means of finding her. Every move he made following the revelation was an attempt to locate his daughter.

What appeared to many to be his first true step in that new world-changing enterprise occurred after he had completed the Rambaldi project known as Il Dire and was rewarded with a message of peace. The device also indicated a DNA strand of a person Rambaldi had named "the Passenger." Sloane ran a DNA test and it showed that he was the father to that person. However, he kept this information a closely guarded secret for a year before it was revealed.

Publicly Sloane stated that it was only Rambaldi's message of peace that led him to an epiphany. He claimed to have suddenly seen the mistakes he had made and the pain he had caused his loved ones. He immediately turned himself in to the CIA, providing information that was used to dismantle more than two dozen terrorist cells.

Behind the scenes Sloane brokered a deal with a secret organization of government officials known as the Trust, promising to provide them with specific information and artifacts from his Rambaldi search. His willingness to cooperate, along with his secret agreement with the Trust, resulted in a pardon by the U.S. government.

Sloane moved to Zurich, where he started a world health organization called Omnifam. It is the third largest nongovernmental relief organization in the world. The company has helped feed almost three and a half million children worldwide, and their work on cancer has the potential to save millions of lives. It was later revealed that Sloane's true interest in creating Omnifam was far from humanitarian. He was secretly using the organization to gain access to water supplies around the world so he could inject a Rambaldi elixir into the populace. The initial plan had not worked because the substance was incomplete, and he eventually gave up on the pursuit, claiming to see the error of his ways. Unfortunately, another Rambaldi follower was later able to continue his work based on the groundwork he had laid.

As part of his pardon agreement, Sloane was also made a consultant for the CIA. He later brokered a deal with the Covenant in which he became a double agent for the CIA. However, the Covenant managed to frame him for being a CIA mole, throwing suspicion off the true double agent, Lauren Reed. Sloane's pardon was revoked, resulting in his being imprisoned and sentenced to death by lethal injection.

This ruse was quickly proven false, but Sloane remained in jail when secret dealings with Senator Reed came to light. Sloane convinced Jack to look into a clandestine government organization known as the Trust, with whom he had had previously worked, in the hopes that this proof would free him.

At the same time, Dr. Judy Barnett revealed Sloane's past affair with Irina Derevko to the CIA. As mentioned earlier, Jack was hurt by the betrayal and returned to Sloane, falsely claiming that he had found no information on the Trust. It appeared that Jack was willing to let Sloane die.

On the eve of his execution Sloane revealed his true motives to Sydney. He explained that once he had learned that he had a child who was part of Rambaldi's prophecy, he spent every minute looking for her. He had created Omnifam partly to gain access to medical databases that identified people through their DNA in hopes of finding his daughter. His main interest was to protect his child from the Covenant.

As the deadline for Sloane's execution approached, Jack slipped him a drug that would counter the effects of the lethal injection. He then teamed with Sloane to find his daughter. Sloane, however, double-crossed the CIA and stole his daughter, Nadia Santos, away to perform an experiment on her to find "Rambaldi."

Sloane was careful to use the proper amount of elixir on Nadia to force her into drawing an equation that would lead to Rambaldi. However, Lauren and Sark arrived and tried to force him to use more of the elixir, which could have caused brain damage. He did his best to protect Nadia when he realized she was in real jeopardy. When Sydney arrived with a CIA task force, Sloane used the opportunity to escape. He left Nadia safely with her sister.

Later Sloane met up with Nadia in the CIA safe house and convinced her that he was looking out for her best interests. She informed him that she had altered the equation during brief moments when she regained consciousness and had sent the Covenant to the wrong location. Together Sloane and Nadia went off to find Rambaldi's "Sphere of Life."

The journey ultimately took Sloane and Nadia to Siena, Italy, where they located the Sphere of Life in a cave that had been abandoned for five hundred years. Having reached what he believed was the final piece in the Rambaldi's puzzle, Sloane's obsession reached a fever pitch. He sent his daughter, who was the one prophesied to take the last part of the journey, across the cave's delicate glass floor that lead to the box holding the sphere. But when Nadia held the sphere and saw horrible visions of the future, she refused to bring it back across the glass.

When Nadia returned to solid ground, Sloane raged against her because the power of Rambaldi was poisoning his mind. Clouded with his obsession, Sloane believed that he could retrieve the sphere himself. But when he lifted the box from the pedestal, the glass floor gave way, dropping him into the pit below.

Nadia climbed down to the pit to retrieve her father, who was badly injured. While bleeding in the pit, Sloane re-evaluated his life and decided to end his Rambaldi journey for the sake of his daughter. He had Nadia contact Jack Bristow for extraction, intending to hand over the Sphere of Life to the CIA.

While brokering his deal to create APO, Sloane also agreed to work secretly with Jack to protect both Nadia and Sydney. Recent intel indicated that Elena Derevko had been keeping watch over the two girls for most of their lives. Sloane and Jack clandestinely maneuvered APO's work to learn Elena's whereabouts.

During that time Sloane learned that Elena had brainwashed an operative into thinking he was Arvin Sloane. The APO team managed to bring in the Sloane clone and learn Elena's true plan. She intended to bring forth Rambaldi's works and an end to civilization. Feeling guilty for his past actions on which Elena had built her plan, Sloane went rogue to try stopping her on his own. He ultimately reunited with his team and together they foiled Elena's plan. However, Sloane was forced to shoot Nadia to save her and Sydney from the conflict they were doomed to live out as the Passenger and the Chosen One.

Psychological Profile:

Arvin Sloane is known to be a master at manipulation. He has coldly ordered the execution of numerous operatives, including some of his own people, rarely expressing genuine regret. He has justified his actions in many ways, citing that most of the people he has betrayed over his lifetime deserved it. The one person he regrets having hurt is Jack Bristow. Sloane came to realize that his affair with Jack's wife wasn't worth betraying his friend.

Dealing with Sloane has been compared to playing a game of chess. It is not the next move that a player should be worried about, but the one that comes several moves down the line.

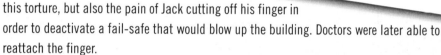

In addition to his emotional resolve, Sloane is able to withstand a great deal of physical pain and torture due to training Jack Bristow provided him. Sloane credits that training for his ability to undergo painful torture, such as what he experienced with the "Needles of Fire." During a takeover of the SD-6 offices, he endured not only this torture, but also the pain of Jack cutting off his finger in order to deactivate a fail-safe that would blow up the building. Doctors were later able to reattach the finger.

Though many were suspicious of his sudden change from villain to benefactor in light of Rambaldi's message of peace, Jack and Sydney flat-out refused to accept that it was true. This reaction hurt Sloane, who considered earning their forgiveness to be his final penance. Following the death of his wife, Sloane believed that they were all he had left. At Jack's suggestion, Sloane approached Dr. Barnett for counseling. Although he initially reached out to her, he ultimately refused to be counseled, but did begin a brief affair with the doctor.

Sloane continues to work on the side of the law and heads up the CIA's black ops APO unit. Though he maintains that he is a changed man, those who have been hurt by him in the past are not willing to believe him so readily. Most of the team under Sloane is in place to keep a watchful eye, ready to report him at the first sign of any infraction. Whether or not he has truly changed is still a question most people in his life ask every day.

MICHAEL C. VAUGHN

APO Call Sign: Shotgun
ID Class: USS-CI-2300708
DOB: 11/27/68
Place of Birth: Fleury, Normandy, France
Family:
Father: William C. Vaughn (deceased)
Mother's Maiden Name: Delorme
Wife: Lauren Reed (deceased)
Education: Master's in French Literature
Languages: English, French, Spanish, Italian

History with the CIA:

Michael Vaughn was recruited into the CIA in 1994 and was stationed in India for two years. His original call sign was Boy Scout, because on the first day of Clandestine Services Training he forgot his field manual. The instructor told him that this was his one screwup, and from then on he had better "be prepared."

Originally assigned as the handler for Sydney Bristow while he was a junior officer, Vaughn was soon pulled off the case in exchange for someone with more experience when it became clear how valuable an asset Sydney would be to the CIA. However, Sydney clashed with her new handler and insisted on being reteamed with Vaughn, since she trusted him. He was then promoted to senior agent at her behest.

Personal History:

Though Vaughn tried to keep his relationship with Sydney professional, the two shared a personal connection that was difficult to ignore. As they grew closer, Vaughn was warned by several people to maintain professional distance. This became increasingly difficult, and Vaughn found himself sharing more intimate moments with Sydney than typical in a working relationship. On their first Christmas working together, he gave Sydney an antique picture frame as a gift. The giving of gifts is not standard operating procedure for handlers.

The most vocal opposition to Vaughn's personal interactions with Sydney came from Agent Steven Haladki. Vaughn and Haladki had a tenuous relationship, based largely on mutual disrespect. Upon learning that Haladki had been reporting Vaughn's actions to his superiors, Vaughn confronted the agent and threatened him physically. Vaughn's best friend, Agent Eric Weiss, had to pull the two men apart. Following the confrontation, Vaughn was removed as Sydney's handler once again.

Shortly after the incident, word came through that SD-6 was under attack by agents of the Man. Vaughn insisted that something be done. Since the CIA could not confirm the attack, Vaughn went into SD-6 on his own. His initial attempts to pass on word to Director Devlin were thwarted by Haladki. Once Weiss realized what was happening, he went to Devlin and led a team in. Haladki reported Vaughn for going into SD-6 unauthorized, but Vaughn received only a slap on the wrist and was reinstated as Sydney's handler.

Initially Weiss also counseled Vaughn not to let his feelings for Sydney interfere with his work. Vaughn countered that he didn't know how to be Sydney's handler without letting it get emotional. When Sydney briefly considered leaving SD-6, Vaughn was torn between concern for her safety and pleasure over the fact that she suggested they go to a hockey game together, which was obviously intended to be a date. However, the infiltration of SD-6 by the Man's operatives reminded both Sydney and Vaughn of the importance of her work. Sydney remained at SD-6, and the pair decided to hold off on the hockey game until some future time.

Vaughn's feelings for Sydney motivated him to join her in an unauthorized mission to retrieve her friend Will Tippin when Sark abducted him. While Jack exchanged a Rambaldi artifact for Will, Sydney and Vaughn infiltrated a lab to destroy a Rambaldi device. Unfortunately, the device was far larger than they had anticipated. When Sydney destroyed the machine, an unidentified liquid came bursting out of it, flooding the lab. Sydney and Vaughn tried to flee the building, but an emergency door slammed shut, trapping Vaughn inside. He was caught up in the flood of liquid and was believed to have drowned.

As it turned out, Vaughn had used a screwdriver to undo a vent and escape the flood, only to be captured by Alexander Khasinau, the Man's second-in-command. Sydney later found Vaughn while on a separate mission and rescued him as he was about to undergo a mysterious surgery. She pumped him full of adrenaline to wake him so they could escape.

Later it was learned that the liquid from the Rambaldi device contained a virus that caused a fatal blood disorder. Although he showed no initial signs and was even presented with a clean bill of health, Vaughn later developed the disorder. As he lay in the hospital in critical condition, Sydney ran into his former girlfriend Alice and learned that the two were dating again. Pushing aside her jealousy, Sydney undertook another unauthorized mission to save him from a painful death by turning Sloane over to Sark in exchange for the antidote.

Although they could not act on their feelings, most of Vaughn's actions were still determined by his love for Sydney. When she was being held by the NSC, he made the connection that they could disprove the theory that she was Rambaldi's Chosen One if she managed to see the sky over Mount Subasio in Italy. He and Jack Bristow went to Devlin to get permission for a mission to break Sydney out of FBI custody.

The mission was a success on several fronts. Aside from possibly disproving the prophecy, the breakout also helped in developing a better working relationship between Vaughn and Jack Bristow. On several occasions Jack had expressed his displeasure with Vaughn's interest in Sydney, and he would continue to disapprove of Vaughn's behavior, but it was a start.

Though Vaughn was once again in his on-again-off-again relationship with Alice, he and Sydney continued to grow closer. On one occasion they attempted to have a public dinner together while on a mission in Nice. This was done at Weiss's urging, as he had undergone a change of heart over the matter due to a recent near-death experience.

Vaughn and Sydney's date suffered from regrettably poor timing, as it happened during Ariana Kane's investigation into Jack Bristow's activities at SD-6. Sydney was included in the surveillance and they were found out, which put Sydney's original mission in Nice in jeopardy. Luckily, they were able to take out Kane's agents before the men reported back, while Jack managed to implicate Kane in his own investigation. Though it all worked out, Vaughn and Sydney both regretted that they had put their mission in jeopardy over their personal lives. They once again had to admit to themselves that they could not start a relationship while working to take down SD-6. They did not know at the time how close they were to the end of the organization.

Soon after their failed date in Nice, Sydney received a valuable piece of intel that led the CIA to call for a well-orchestrated global raid on all SD cells and Alliance headquarters. With little time to spare, Sydney and Vaughn took a task force into SD-6, securing the facility and rescuing Jack from torture. Vaughn and Sydney had finally accomplished their mission. And as the smoke settled around them, they shared their first kiss.

Vaughn officially ended his relationship with Alice the next day. However, with Sloane still on the loose, Vaughn and Sydney had little time to truly enjoy being together. Their complicated work lives also continued to get in the way of their relationship. They both were equally embarrassed to find that Sloane had bugged Sydney's apartment and recorded their most intimate moments.

As their work continued to consume them, Vaughn and Sydney eventually realized they were not going to get a break unless they forced themselves to take it on their own. They planned a romantic weekend getaway to Santa Barbara, where Vaughn had intended to ask Sydney to marry him. He would never get the chance.

Vaughn was heartbroken to learn that, while he was planning his proposal, Sydney had died in a fire after being attacked by Francie's double, Allison Doren. After the funeral Vaughn left the country for six months to grieve her loss. He started talking to Sydney as if she were really beside him. One day she started answering as if she were in the room with him. Rationally, he knew that he was a "guy that spent his nights drinking and talking to his dead girl-friend," but he couldn't stop. He was so in love with her that it nearly killed him.

As the NSC wrapped up the case on Irina Derevko, Lauren Reed was brought in to depose the staff. She and Vaughn hit it off and began dating only nine months after Sydney's presumed death. Though it was a short mourning period, Vaughn needed to find a way to move beyond his grief. Lauren gave him that way.

They were wed at Lauren's family home in Virginia. Vaughn then left the CIA and pursued teaching French at the university level. He was trying to move on with his life when Sydney made contact. She was alive.

Even though Vaughn was no longer with the CIA, he was sent to Sydney's safe house in Hong Kong to help ease her back into her life. Although she had been gone for two years, for Sydney it was like she had seen him only yesterday. Vaughn was careful about filling her in on what she had missed, but she noticed his wedding ring before he could get too far. The news of his marriage did not go over well.

SYD, VAUGHN & LAUREN

Vaughn had already been thinking about returning to the CIA when Sydney was found alive. He was brought in to consult on a mission and was soon back for good. Things were tense between him and Sydney at the start, but eventually they were able to be friends. Their shorthand on missions proved invaluable on several occasions, a fact that was not overlooked by his wife, Lauren. And it wasn't long before old feelings began to resurface.

During a mission, Sydney was forced to stab Vaughn and leave him for dead in order to protect her cover and keep them both safe. She planted a tracking device on him so he could be retrieved. By the time Vaughn was found, he had lost oxygen when the stab wound collapsed a lung, resulting in tension pneumothorax. He was kept in an induced coma to minimize brain damage, and soon experienced a full recovery.

Although Vaughn was in love with his wife, he still had feelings for Sydney. Jack warned Vaughn that his kindness was killing Sydney and that he should distance himself. Vaughn tried but he couldn't do it, prompting him to wonder if he could be in love with two women at the same time.

Vaughn ultimately told Lauren that he didn't feel their marriage was working. He was about to begin a separation when her father died. This briefly reunited them until Vaughn realized that Lauren was a double agent working for the Covenant. Though he was enraged by the discovery, he was ordered to continue acting as if he didn't know the truth so the CIA could feed the Covenant information through Lauren. The ruse did not last for long, and Vaughn was caught and tortured by Sark. Lauren was supposed to kill him, but her residual feelings for him stopped her from finishing the job. A CIA task force eventually found him wounded but alive.

Vaughn was obsessed with finding and killing Lauren for betraying him. This was something that united him with Jack, while Sydney could not get behind the mission of revenge. His anger made him lose focus for a short time, but in the end he could not bring himself to kill her based solely on vengeance. This was a mistake; he let his guard down, which allowed Katya Derevko to stab him.

Vaughn's clearance was revoked pending an investigation into his rogue actions, but he broke himself out of the hospital—with Weiss's help—when he learned that Sydney's life was in danger. He rushed to her side in time to shoot Lauren to save Sydney.

The full depth of Lauren's betrayal did not hit until after she was dead. Vaughn then burned down the house they had lived in together, and his CIA clearance was held while he underwent a month of psych evaluations. At the end of that month, he resigned from the Agency.

His resignation, however, was part of the cover for him accepting a position in APO, where he continued to work alongside Sydney. He was still haunted by visions of Lauren, particularly the look on her face in the moment that he killed her. Though he knew she was evil, he also knew that killing her was wrong. Vaughn continued to deal with his issues over Lauren's death as he and Sydney agreed to take their relationship slowly.

Family History:

Vaughn's father, William "Bill" Vaughn, was a CIA agent who died while on a secret mission when his son was eight. The only way he could be identified was through his dental records. As an adult, Vaughn carried an old watch that had belonged to his father. When his father gave him the watch, it was with the comment that Vaughn could set his heart by it. The watch stopped the day he met Sydney.

Early in their working relationship, Sydney brought Vaughn a list of codes written in one of her mother's books decades earlier. He had it decoded and found that it was a list of aliases and handles of agents that were killed by a KGB operative. His father's name was on that list. Irina Derevko turned out to be his father's assassin.

It was difficult enough for Vaughn to accept the fact that Sydney's mother had killed his father. However, the situation was made immeasurably worse when he learned that Derevko was not only still alive, but she had turned herself in to the CIA. Though he refused to see the woman, Vaughn was eventually forced to speak with Derevko to obtain intel that would help Sydney during a mission. Derevko agreed to help, but only after he admitted his feelings for her daughter. He went on to explain that his feelings for Sydney were complex, and she admonished him for not sharing those feelings with Sydney.

Though Vaughn appeared to come around to working with Derevko, he secretly went through back channels to investigate her. He was hoping to discover proof that she was still the evil person who had killed his father. Due to his suspicious activities, counterintelligence began an investigation, and Vaughn admitted to Sydney what he had been doing. He was almost pleased to tell her he had found nothing incriminating on Derevko. This was shortly before Derevko escaped with an important Rambaldi artifact.

Vaughn was formally debriefed on his personal investigation. His security clearance was temporarily downgraded, but Jack convinced counterintelligence to keep Vaughn field-rated.

During this time Vaughn also learned that his father had died while working on a mission not sanctioned by the CIA. His father was a follower of Rambaldi and was protecting a little girl who had become known as the Passenger. Vaughn was charged with taking up his father's mission and keeping the Passenger safe. This was made difficult by the fact that the Passenger was believed to be a threat to the Chosen One, namely Sydney. It was later revealed that the Passenger was Sydney's half sister, Nadia.

A few months after Vaughn found out about his father's involvement with Rambaldi, he learned an even more startling secret. When his mother told him that his uncle was in poor health, Vaughn went to visit the man, whom he had not seen in a while. A nurse confused him with his father, Bill Vaughn, because his uncle often spoke of Bill visiting as if it were a recent occurrence. The nurse, Rosemary, later gave Vaughn a key that opened a bus station locker. Inside the locker was a journal written in Bill Vaughn's handwriting. The journal was dated through 1982—three years after his father's death. This clue set Vaughn on a search to find out if his father was still alive.

Vaughn's journey to find his father was complicated by lies and diversions secretly set about by Elena Derevko. The obsession to learn the truth pushed Vaughn to the edge, causing him to take great personal risks and nearly betray APO. Vaughn was guided to steal a piece of technology from a secret Russian project known as Nightingale. He did as instructed under the guise of an APO mission, but then went rogue. He took the device with him in hopes that the person feeding him information would accept it in exchange for the location of his father.

But that was only the first stage in the mysterious informant's plan. Vaughn was then instructed to take part in an assault team intending to steal a Rambaldi manuscript from a CIA convoy. Vaughn reluctantly joined the operation, unaware that Dixon was part of the convoy. When Vaughn was forced to shoot Dixon to protect the mission, Vaughn realized that he had been pushed too far and that his own father would never have allowed himself to turn on the government as he had. Luckily, Dixon had been protected by his bulletproof vest. In the end Vaughn realized that he was merely a pawn in the plans and that his father had truly died in the way that Vaughn had always believed.

Psychological Profile:

In his early days with the CIA, Michael Vaughn was very much the "Boy Scout" befitting his call sign. He was a loyal and trusted agent, rarely working outside of established parameters. The few times he broke the rules were in situations where his kindheartedness got in the way. In one such case he attended the funeral of a fallen operative. Though CIA agents are expressly warned not to show emotion at such events, Vaughn could not help but be reminded of himself when looking at the son of his fallen friend. He broke from the ranks to give the boy a hug.

Vaughn's more flagrant rule breaking tended to come during situations in which he was motivated to help Sydney. Though his reasoning was often based on his feelings for her, Vaughn also learned to trust her superior instincts and was willing to take risks based on her plans of action.

One area in which Vaughn's instincts often proved to be better than Sydney's was in regard to her father. Since he had emotional distance, Vaughn tended to be more suspicious of Jack's behavior than Sydney. In one case Vaughn was the first to raise alarm at Jack's actions in the Madagascar mission when he realized that Sydney's father had set up Derevko by lacing with explosives a building that was supposed to be safe for entry. When confronted, Jack simply replied that Vaughn's consistent short-coming was his naive sense of morality.

In recent months Vaughn's morality has been severely tested. Following Lauren's betrayal, he was moved to seek revenge by methods outside the law. Seeing a kinship in another betrayed husband, Jack even offered his assistance. The two men bonded over the shared experience of being hurt by women who supposedly loved them. This ability to see the darker shades of gray has been growing in Vaughn, to the point where he recently declared that, although he despised Arvin Sloane, he could not help but appreci-ate the man's ability to scheme. Furthermore, he even thanked Jack for killing Derevko, as he felt the woman deserved to die. Needless to say, Sydney has expressed some concern over his new attitude.

Vaughn's darker side came out fully in his quest to find the truth behind his father's death. But, as mentioned earlier, Vaughn eventually regained control of his life and came to terms with the fact that his father was, in fact, dead. In working to determine the truth, Vaughn and Sydney grew even closer. And, as the world nearly fell apart around them, Vaughn asked Sydney to marry him. She agreed.

As the pair was about to head off for their long-ago promised trip to Santa Barbara, the happy couple endured one last surprise. Vaughn began to admit that he had been lying to Sydney since the moment that they had met . . . that their original meeting back when she came to the CIA was a part of some greater plan . . . and that his name wasn't Michael Vaughn.

But before he could say any more, an SUV struck their car at full velocity, bringing a violent and abrupt end to the conversation.

APO Call Sign: Outrigger
ID Class: USS-CI-2300922
DOB: 8/14/55
Place of Birth: Minneapolis, Minnesota, USA
Family:
  Wife: Diane Dixon (deceased)
  Daughter: Robin
  Son: Steven
  Mother's Maiden Name: Forrest
Education: BA in Business from Sarah Lawrence College; Postgraduate Studies in computer science at MIT
Languages: English, Taiwanese, Sudanese (Dinka/Nubian/Beja), Hebrew, Arabic

History with SD-6 and the CIA:

Jack Bristow recruited former Marine Corp Force Recon specialist Marcus Dixon into SD-6 in 1991. Dixon's wife, Diane, believed that he was taking a job as an investment analyst at Credit Dauphine, but really he was receiving field ops training to become a secret agent. Dixon believed with all his heart that SD-6 was part of the CIA and that he was taking a job that would allow him to serve his country. He worked under this cloud of imposed ignorance for eleven years before he found out the truth.

Dixon eventually partnered with Sydney Bristow and now considers her to be one of his closest friends. Together they have gone on countless missions under a wide variety of aliases.

During their mission to recover the Rambaldi manuscript, he was shot by K-Directorate operatives and left for dead. Sydney was forced to call for extraction using her CIA call sign "Freelancer" rather than her SD-6 handle "Mountaineer." Dixon heard her use the call sign, but did not remember anything until he began to grow suspicious of Sydney's activities. Only then did he remember her using the call sign "Freelancer" when he had been shot. Dixon followed Sydney and caught her sneaking out of an SD-6 facility after having taken an unknown item. He questioned her about her activities, but she could not provide him with a sufficient response.

Dixon was forced to report Sydney's actions to Sloane. It broke his heart to do so, but he believed that he was doing it for his country. In the end Jack told Sloane and Dixon that Sydney had been on a secret mission under her father's orders. Though this was a lie, Dixon was relieved to learn that Sydney had not turned against SD-6.

Dixon's unwavering commitment to the belief that he was on the side of the CIA had unexpected consequences for SD-6. When their offices were infiltrated by operatives of the Man, Dixon found a way to contact the CIA through the computer system. Jack ordered him not to make contact, reminding him that SD-6 was a black ops division and the CIA would not acknowledge its existence under any circumstances. Dixon ignored the order and sent a message. He was later disappointed to find that Jack had been correct and no one came to help. At the time, he was not aware that Agent Vaughn did, in fact, answer his call and come to their aid.

Eventually Dixon learned the truth about SD-6 when Sydney asked him to tap into the computer system and confirm a code so the CIA could move in. Dixon was devastated by the news that he hadn't been working for the CIA all this time as he was led to believe. And the fact that his partner and close friend had known the truth behind SD-6 and had been lying to him for more than a year and a half was even more upsetting to him. Reluctantly, he went into the office and discovered that the code was correct, confirming what Sydney had told him. He immediately called his wife, Diane, to tell her he loved her. Then he sent the confirmation code that signaled the raid on SD-6 and all Alliance facilities.

Dixon was brought in for a debriefing and was eventually cleared of all charges. He received an offer to join the CIA but declined. He was so hurt by the deception that he told Sydney he never wanted to see her again.

Personal History:
When Dixon told his wife the truth about his job, she was devastated that he had kept this secret from her for all the years of their marriage. Diane briefly separated from him and told him that if he accepted the job with the CIA, she would leave him for good.

Although Dixon was effectively retired from intelligence work, Sydney went to him in need of information that only he could provide. He refused to help, saying that he wanted to put that part of his life behind him for the sake of his family. But when a former enemy took Sydney prisoner, Dixon had no choice but to go to her rescue—they had been partners for so long, and over the course of their shared history, he had grown to care for her deeply. The mission served to bring him into the CIA, though he was not sure what that meant for his marriage.

During a mission to capture Sloane, Emily got in the way, and Dixon accidentally shot and killed her. He was really broken up about the accident, particularly because Emily had always been kind to him and

Sydney. He planned to put in for reassignment to the Directorate of Intelligence, knowing he could get a safe job out of state as an analyst. He claimed that he'd be happy doing that so long as Diane and the kids were with him. Diane eventually began to understand the importance of Dixon's work and told him to withdraw the transfer. Just as it looked like Dixon and his wife were poised for a new beginning, Diane was killed in a car explosion—an act of revenge by Sloane.

Psychological Profile:

Dixon considered taking his life after losing Diane, but he realized that he could not do that to their children and went back to work only days after the funeral. Vaughn believed Dixon was self-medicating and reported him to Dr. Barnett. Dixon admitted to Sydney that he had been taking Vicodin to help with the pain, but had since stopped taking the pills. However, he was afraid that the drugs were still in his system and would show up on his mandatory drug test. He falsified the blood test to get a negative result. When the results came back, he asked Sydney keep his secret, forcing her to lie to her superiors. In the end Dixon admitted his actions, feeling guilty over the lie and the position he had put Sydney in.

Dixon suffered severe coping problems and anger management issues, and he refused to take any time off until Sloane was captured. He became aggressive and unreliable in the field. He attacked Will while he was under suspicion of being the double who had killed Diane. But with time, Dixon's anger subsided. To this day, however, he has nightmares in which he sees Diane almost every night.

During the two years that Sydney was presumed dead, Dixon was promoted to director of the Joint Task Force on Intelligence. Although he was aware of the fact that Sydney was alive and undercover, he was ordered to keep the information confidential when she returned. It finally gave him an understanding of how hard it must have been for Sydney to keep SD-6 a secret from him. Though in his position he was forced to work with Sloane, Dixon made it clear that he would never trust the man who had had his wife killed.

When Sydney returned to the Agency, she and Jack discovered that she was the one responsible for killing Andrian Lazarey during her missing time, and they eventually went to Dixon with the information. Although he already knew the truth, Dixon admonished them for keeping the secret, and then ordered that the information not be revealed to the NSC. But Lauren Reed made the connection and reported it to

Robert Lindsey, director of the NSC. Dixon was relieved of duty on the grounds of obstruction of justice and willingly conspiring to impede an international investigation. He took full blame for withholding the information so that his team could remain active under Lindsey.

Following Sydney's escape from NSC custody and Lindsey's assassination, Dixon was reinstated. He joined the team that was sent in to stop the Covenant experiment to revive Rambaldi by fertilizing Sydney's eggs with Rambaldi's DNA. Though they were under orders to bring back whatever they could find, Dixon told Sydney to torch the place.

The Covenant kidnapped Dixon's children, Robin and Steven, initially demanding the release of Covenant operatives in U.S. custody in exchange for their safe return. Steven was released in order to deliver a message to his father. Dixon temporarily stepped down as director of the Task Force and told Sydney that the real request was for him to break into Project Black Hole and steal a Rambaldi artifact. He asked for Sydney's help and she quickly agreed. Together they stole the object and made the exchange for Robin. Once the crisis was averted, Dixon returned to his position as director, thanks to Jack's help as well as unconfirmed assistance from Vaughn and Lauren. The team managed to successfully cover Dixon's involvement in stealing the artifact.

After the Covenant was destroyed, Dixon stepped down as director of the Joint Task Force on Intelligence, feeling a need to get back in the field where he felt he belonged. He quickly accepted a position with APO, though was stunned to learn that Sloane was head of the organization. Though he hated the idea of working with Sloane again, Dixon knew that he had to make sure the guy was kept in check. Dixon took his promise to watch Sloane very seriously, even going so far as to tap Sloane's phone and double-check all mission facts provided to him.

When Dixon believed he had evidence of Sloane's illegal activities, he approached Sydney with the information, and they took it to CIA director Hayden Chase. Though Chase was initially concerned with the steps Dixon had taken to track Sloane, she kept him on the case. In the end Dixon discovered that Sloane was working with Jack to stop the re-forming of the Alliance. Dixon was ordered to remove the phone tap and to ease up on the measures he was taking to keep tabs on Sloane. Though Chase was disappointed in Dixon's extreme actions, the mission did serve to bring the two closer together. Dixon began a secret relationship with his superior. They both eventually admitted that the clandestine weekend rendezvous weren't enough, and their relationship was ultimately revealed in the hospital while Dixon was recovering from being shot by Elena Derevko.

Dixon still refused to trust Sloane, for obvious reasons. No matter how many times Sloane insists that he has changed, Dixon will likely continue to keep an eye on the man who had him fooled for eleven years into believing he was working for the government. He has spent much time wondering how he could let himself be fooled for so many years while working at SD-6 and has since realized that the reason he was duped was that he never fully believed that anyone as evil and manipulative as Arvin Sloane could exist.

APO Call Sign: Merlin
ID Class: 30408-12650
DOB: 12/29/71
Place of Birth: Los Angeles, California, USA
Family:
   Wife: Carrie Bowman
   Son: Mitchell
   Mother's Maiden Name: Feldman
Education: PhD from CalTech in Robot Physics
Languages: English, Ewok

History with SD-6 and the CIA:

Marshall Flinkman was recruited into SD-6 in 1997 and eventually became head of op tech engineering. His mother, however, thought he ran a global IT service for Credit Dauphine. He would compose photos of himself in front of world landmarks so he could show his mom all the places he'd been, even though he had never been outside of southern California.

Though he didn't know it at the time, Marshall was almost responsible for blowing Sydney's cover as a double agent on a few occasions. When the CIA tapped into SD-6's server, Marshall discovered a worm and cut the hard line immediately. He reported the bandwidth leak to Sloane, who responded that it had only been a drill. He later discovered the piggybacked signal that was sent during Sydney's mission in Geneva and reported it, hoping that he didn't get anyone in trouble. That information led to Sydney being taken in under suspicion of being the mole. Later Jack used Marshall to manipulate the computers to provide a false lead, exonerating Sydney.

Marshall was not field rated until he was needed on a mission to infiltrate a secure server at a data storage facility in London in an attempt to access the Echelon satellite system. Because of the security in place, electronic devices could not be brought in, which meant the operative sent into the facility needed to know how to crack a program written in polymorphic algorithms. As Marshall was the only operative in SD-6 trained to do that, he was tasked to go on his first field mission with Sydney. This was also the first time he had ever left his home state of California.

Though he did not like to fly, he was excited about the mission and amazed to watch Sydney in action. He felt very protective of Sydney, since his job was to keep her safe by providing the technology and cover identities for her missions. During this particular mission he was hit with a tranquilizer before he could access the computer. It took a kiss from Sydney to rouse him so he could focus on the task.

Considering that Marshall has a photographic memory, there was no way Sydney could fake the information she had intended to give Sloane to access the Echelon system. Once the job was completed, the CIA had planned to abduct Marshall and bring him in with an offer to join the Agency. However, foreign operatives kidnapped Marshall first, and Dr. Jong Lee started to torture Marshall when he refused to help rebuild the Echelon system for them. Marshall gave in only when his mother's safety was threatened.

Marshall's compliance was only a ruse to give him access to the computer so he could get a message to SD-6. He worked for hours on a bogus system, knowing that he would be killed when the truth was revealed. Just as Marshall's duplicity was revealed, Sydney entered to rescue him. In turn, he helped them both escape by using the parachute he had built into the lining of his suit jacket due to his fear of flying.

Following the revelation that SD-6 was not an arm of the Central Intelligence Agency, he was debriefed and offered a position at the real CIA. He accepted, handling the situation as well as could be expected. After three years with the CIA, Marshall was crestfallen when many of his friends suddenly left the Agency for a variety of reasons. His depression turned to terror when he was arrested for misuse of government assets. Marshall was later relieved to learn that the arrest had been a ruse to bring him into APO, where he was reunited with his friends and coworkers. Though thrilled to be part of the old team, Marshall continues to struggle with the fact that he has to keep his work secret from his wife and is forced to spend a lot of time away from his family.

Personal History:

Marshall developed a crush on NSA agent Carrie Bowman but couldn't bring himself to ask her out. Instead, she asked him. Their first date was at a sushi restaurant. Marshall thought he had ruined the evening after developing an extreme case of flop sweat due to his discomfort in the unfamiliar dating situation. But apparently Carrie didn't mind, as they continued dating for two years until she became pregnant with his child. After he learned of the pregnancy, Marshall announced his intention to marry her, but Carrie refused, citing issues she had with the concept of wedlock.

However, when Carrie went into labor, she changed her views and insisted that she be married before the baby was born. Marshall quickly managed to get Eric Weiss ordained online, and he performed the ceremony while Marshall kept watch over a mission occurring simultaneously in Chamonix. Carrie gave birth to a baby boy they named Mitchell. Ever the proud father, Marshall can often be heard bragging about his baby's accomplishments and showing photos and videos to anyone who will watch.

Lauren Reed shot Marshall in the stomach while she posed as Sydney to infiltrate the Rotunda (the headquarters for the Joint Task Force on Intelligence). He managed to sound the alarm before blacking out. The wound was not fatal, and after a brief hospitalization, he returned to work.

Psychological Profile:

Marshall's mannerisms and speech patterns are somewhat offbeat, and even he describes himself as not much of a social person. His parents were agnostic, and Marshall believes they were inordinately empirical and logical to a point that he considered foolish. He had no Santa Claus or even Tooth Fairy when growing up.

Marshall likes prime numbers, has an interest in pop culture (with a varied taste in movies), loves to play the drums, and collects Pez dispensers. Making pop-up books helps clear his mind, and he used to keep an inflatable chair in his office because he found it therapeutic.

APO Call Sign: Houdini
ID Class: USS-CI-2300784
DOB: 4/17/68
Place of Birth: Los Angeles, California, USA
Family:
    Brother
        Mother's Maiden Name: Blumberg
Education: BS in Economics
Languages: English, Spanish

History with the CIA:

Eric Weiss, who was named after his great-great-uncle, Houdini, was recruited into the CIA in 1997. He was formerly a junior officer and transferred to the Joint Task Force on Intelligence along with his partner, Michael Vaughn. Weiss was one of the few members of the Task Force who remained with the Agency following the dissolution of the Covenant. When he learned that his former coworkers had all joined the black ops APO division, Weiss was also given the opportunity to join the organization, though he was slightly offended that he was picked last.

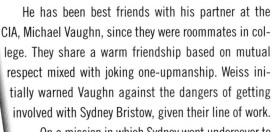

He has been best friends with his partner at the CIA, Michael Vaughn, since they were roommates in college. They share a warm friendship based on mutual respect mixed with joking one-upmanship. Weiss initially warned Vaughn against the dangers of getting involved with Sydney Bristow, given their line of work. On a mission in which Sydney went undercover to meet with Mr. Sark, her cover was nearly blown when Dixon showed up to intercept the meet for SD-6. As the exchange went south, Vaughn managed to secure Sark as Sydney fought off Dixon. Though Weiss warned Vaughn to stay with Sark, Vaughn went after Sydney to make sure she was not compromised. Due to the fact that Vaughn deserted his post, SD-6 obtained Sark. Weiss later covered for Vaughn with Director Devlin, taking the blame

for the loss of Sark. Weiss then told Vaughn to get over his feelings for Sydney, as they were affecting his work.

During a mission to intercept an exchange of the operations manual for Derevko's outfit, Irina Derevko shot Weiss in the neck. The wound was serious, and he was hospitalized and out of action for three months. Following what Weiss considered to be a near-death experience, he changed his opinion on Vaughn and Sydney's relationship. On their first mission together following his recuperation, Weiss encouraged Vaughn to ask Sydney out to dinner. Vaughn did as suggested, but the events of the evening ended up jeopardizing their covers.

Psychological Profile:

Eric Weiss has always exhibited fierce loyalty to his friends. When Vaughn was under investigation by CIA Counterintelligence, Weiss broke protocol and talked to Sydney about the situation. He then helped her locate Vaughn so that she could warn him.

Following Sydney's return from her two-year absence, Weiss's relationship with her strengthened. When she commented that what she missed most following her apartment fire was her first edition *Alice in Wonderland* that had burned, he replaced it for her with a third edition. (The first edition was too expensive.) He was her only friend left in the area and helped her move into a neighboring apartment. Easing her into accepting Vaughn's relationship with Lauren, he simultaneously counseled Vaughn in dealing with his conflicted feelings for Sydney.

Personal History:

Weiss did not have much luck in the arena of romance. He was once dumped by his girlfriend for a roadie at a Duran Duran concert, but redeemed himself in college after trying to impress a waitress named April First with his singing. Though his vocal talents were far from impressive, she had missed the performance—just seeing him carrying a guitar got her interested in him. He also expressed an interest in new agent Christine Phillips, though she did not return the feeling.

Weiss was immediately smitten with Nadia Santos when he first saw her at Sydney's door. An innocent flirtation began between the pair, though Vaughn warned his friend to take it slowly, as Weiss was known to fall hard and fast. He charmed her with his magic tricks and took her bowling, and the two started dating. Their relationship was made awkward by the fact that her father was his boss, Arvin Sloane.

Weiss was also ordained Exalted Minister of the Internet Church of Mammals and performed the marriage ceremony of Marshall Flinkman and Carrie Bowman.

NADIA SANTOS

APO Call Sign: Evergreen
DOB: 1981
Place of Birth: Moscow, Russia
Family:
    Mother: Irina Derevko
    Father: Arvin Sloane
    Half sister: Sydney Bristow
    Aunts: Katya Derevko, Elena Derevko
Education: Unknown
Languages: English, Spanish, Russian

Personal History:

Nadia Santos is the daughter of Arvin Sloane and Irina Derevko and is a half sister to Sydney Bristow. The result of an affair, Nadia was born shortly after Derevko returned to Moscow in 1981. Her father only recently learned of her existence. Nadia is believed to be the Passenger whose coming Milo Rambaldi prophesied.

Dr. Jong Lee experimented on Nadia as a young girl by using the Rambaldi elixir to try to get her to reveal the equation that would lead to Rambaldi's Sphere of Life. It is believed that CIA agent and Rambaldi follower William Vaughn (Michael's father) rescued Nadia from the painful experiments and brought her to the San Marcos orphanage run by Sophia Vargas, though the timeline of these events is unclear. At the orphanage Sophia changed Nadia's last name to Santos ostensibly to protect her.

While in the orphanage, Nadia saved another young girl from a child predator. Afraid she would get in trouble, Nadia fled the orphanage at age twelve for a life on the streets. During this time she befriended a boy named Cesar Martinez. The pair built a reputation as small-time criminals, stealing to survive. When Nadia was finally arrested in her late teens, she was wanted for over 130 crimes, ranging from shoplifting and burglary to grand theft and assault with a deadly weapon. A man named Roberto Fox visited her in jail with an offer to work in Argentine Intelligence, based on her impressive record.

While in jail, Nadia had a brief reunion with Sophia. After the discussion, Nadia decided to accept Fox's offer and was surprised to find that Cesar had also been invited to join Fox's organization. The two teens trained together while Cesar continued to make unwelcome advances on her. Nadia always politely rebuffed her friend, in part because she had developed feelings for the older Fox. Upon her graduation to the field, Fox and Nadia realized their feelings were mutual and made love. Soon after, Nadia realized that Fox was running an illegal operation under the guise of working for the government. Nadia confronted Fox and shot him for lying to her and betraying his country.

Six years later Nadia was on her first deep-cover assignment in a Chechnyan prison. As she lay in a hospital bed in the prison, she was found by a sister she never knew she had. Sydney freed Nadia from the prison and brought her to her father.

Sloane attempted to gain her trust as a father, but he ultimately kidnapped her and injected her with the same elixir she had been subjected to as a child, forcing her to reveal a Rambaldi design. This time, however, Sloane carefully monitored the serum to make sure she did not suffer brain damage. As she built a tolerance to the elixir, Sloane had intended to free her rather than risk her life, but Lauren and Sark arrived and forced his hand.

Sydney infiltrated Sloane's home with a CIA task force and managed to free Nadia and take her into protective custody. However, Sloane sneaked her out of a CIA safe house, working to regain her trust. Nadia admitted that she had altered the equation during brief periods in which she regained consciousness. She agreed to lead him to the location where "Rambaldi" could be found.

Nadia traveled with her father to a cave in Siena, Italy, in search of the Sphere of Life. Once the object was in hand, Nadia saw flashes of a horrific future in which she would do battle with her sister, Sydney. Overwhelmed by the imagery, Nadia refused to take the Rambaldi artifact out of its hiding place, a fact that angered her father because she was supposedly the only one who could remove it from the booby-trapped cave. Sloane, believing that he would also be able to remove the artifact, went for it and crashed through the cave's glass floor down to a pit below. Nadia rescued her father, who claimed to have had an epiphany when he lay broken and bloodied. He swore to give up his Rambaldi obsession for his daughter.

Once their search for Rambaldi ended, Nadia chose to return to Argentina, where she left the intelligence business in light of her recent experiences. During that time she used every resource available to her to learn about her father's past. Her departure was short-lived, however, as Sydney soon approached her for help with a mission involving former contacts of hers. Nadia willingly gave over information but refused to help any further. However, when Sydney was taken prisoner, Vaughn asked for Nadia's assistance again. This time she agreed.

SYDNEY AND NADIA

Nadia infiltrated the organization of a former contact and rescued her sister. After completing the mission, she decided to move to Los Angeles and join APO so she could learn more about her family. She moved in with Sydney. When she asked about their mother, Sydney took Nadia to Moscow to visit Irina Derevko's grave. Once she learned the sketchy details of her mother's death, Nadia swore she would seek revenge on the person who killed her. She was unaware of the fact that Jack had killed Derevko in order to save Sydney.

Nadia underwent a standard psych evaluation when she formally joined APO. Jack volunteered to conduct the interview and was very impressed with the results. The test showed that her ability to adapt to sudden changes in protocol and handle adverse situations was exceptional. In fact, the results were much like her sister's.

Following the test, Jack informed Nadia that he had received intel indicating that an operative named Martin Bishop had been responsible for her mother's death. Coincidentally, Sydney was on a mission infiltrating Bishop's organization at the time. Nadia joined the mission and killed Bishop in a mistaken act of revenge.

Nadia continued to grow closer to her father and her half sister as she acclimated herself to life in Los Angeles. She began a flirtation with Eric Weiss, and the two started dating. Her life finally seemed to be moving forward in a positive direction. It wasn't until she learned about her role as the Passenger that a cloud began to form—Rambaldi's prophecy foretold that she would one day battle her own sister to the death.

Nadia was shot and left for dead by Anna Espinosa. Doctors induced a coma to protect her higher brain functions while her friends and family held vigil over her. When it was learned that she possibly had important intel on the location of Anna, Jack Bristow was forced to pull her prematurely out of her coma, which could have caused permanent damage to Nadia. Luckily, she came out fine.

Nadia secretly visited her aunt Katya in prison to learn more about her mother since Sydney and Jack were reluctant to speak in depth about Irina Derevko. When Katya nearly killed herself in order to get a message to Sydney, Nadia was horrified to see firsthand the lengths to which the Derevkos would go to get what they wanted. Soon after, Nadia learned that Irina had put a hit out on Sydney's life and that Jack had ended Irina's life to stop it from happening.

Though she was shocked and angry by the admissions, Nadia eventually understood the position in which Jack had been. It was likely easier to accept since this realization came at the same time she learned that her mother was still alive.

Nadia and Sydney rescued their mother from Elena Derevko. At first Nadia wanted to wait to tell Irina who she was, but Irina figured it out on her own. The two shared a brief, yet long-awaited, reunion before they had to go save the world.

As part of the team sent in to stop Elena Derevko from unleashing a global epidemic of violence, Nadia was infected with a Rambaldi substance that caused her to lose her grasp on reason. She attacked Sydney and tried to kill her. Her father, Sloane, was forced to shoot Nadia to stop her. Nadia was alive, but doctors kept her under sedation until the day they could hopefully find a cure for her condition.

HAYDEN CHASE

Director Chase is responsible for overseeing the creation of APO. She tapped Arvin Sloane to lead the black ops division and personally recruited the original central members. Sloane was an obvious though controversial choice for the director position, given his extensive underworld connections. However, Chase purposely neglected to tell the other members of the unit the full truth behind the leadership of the organization until most of them had signed on and reported to duty. As there was concern over putting Sloane in charge of APO, she tasked Sydney, Jack, Vaughn, and Dixon with keeping an eye on their supervisor and making sure that he operated within the bounds of the law.

Chase is still field rated, though she has not been active in the field for twelve years. She has a direct management style and allows for operatives to work outside normal parameters so long as they do not abuse their position. A single woman, she recently began a relationship with Marcus Dixon.

MEMBERS OF THE JOINT TASK FORCE ON INTELLIGENCE

CENTRAL INTELLIGENCE AGENCY (CIA)

A United States government agency charged with gathering information on foreign governments and groups that engage in terrorism or organized crime. The CIA also engages in counterintelligence by identifying, neutralizing, and/or manipulating the intelligence activities of other countries.

Ben Devlin: Former director of the CIA.
Hayden Chase: Director of the CIA

Dr. Judy Barnett: Psychiatrist charged with evaluating the mental and emotional state of all CIA operatives and assisting with any personal crises they may experience. She has an undergraduate degree from Yale and a medical degree from Columbia; she performed her internship at Massachusetts General. She spent three years studying Arvin Sloane for her postdoctoral dissertation. Although she knew most of his past transgressions, she failed to maintain her professional distance and allowed him to seduce her. Their brief relationship ended when she believed he had used her to access CIA files. Barnett has counseled several members of the current APO team.

Steven Haladki: Former senior officer in the CIA and officer in the FBI. Haladki seemed to make it his mission to interfere with the operations of Vaughn and Sydney. It was later discovered that he was a double agent working for the Man. Deceased.
Will Tippin: Former analyst. (See: *Civilians*, page 72.)

CIA AGENTS

Saeed Akhtar: CIA contact in Kashmir. Deceased.

Jane Banks: Hypnotherapy specialist.

Craig Blair: Senior officer.

Burnett: Computer specialist.

Chapman: Ops specialist.

Cohen: Low-level officer.

Vicki Crane: Tech specialist.

Davenport: Senior officer. Formerly Michael Vaughn's superior.

Hank Foster: Counterintelligence threat analyst.

Kellogg: Commando. Part of the team that infiltrated the Hensel Lab. Deceased.

Paul Kelvin: Infiltrated SD-6 impersonating biotech engineer Jeroen Schiller.

Virginia Kerr: Hypnotherapy specialist.

Pietr Klein: Undercover scientist working out of Germany. Deceased.

Lloyd Kretchmer: Senior officer. Handler for Jack Bristow.

Seth Lambert: Senior officer who temporarily replaced Vaughn as Sydney's handler.

Jim Lennox: Agent investigating Project Helix who was caught and tortured. The first person to have a duplicate made through Project Helix.

Logan: Commando. Head of the team that infiltrated the Hensel Lab. Deceased.

Rick McCarthy: Technical specialist.

Dr. Doug Nicholas: Head of the team that investigated the Rambaldi virus.

O'Neil: Desk guard at CIA storage facility.

Christine Phillips: Low-level officer.

Phillips: Low-level officer.

Pollard: Low-level officer.

Ulrich Rotter: Agent working undercover as German scientist. Kidnapped by the Covenant and offered in exchange for Sark.

Rudman: Technical operative.

Richard Schmidt: Agent working under diplomatic cover at the Rabat Embassy.

Dr. Siegal: Leader of CIA group therapy sessions for agents who have experienced lost time.

Lucques Trepanier: Specialist in creating false identities.

Emma Wallace: Agent investigating Project Helix who was caught and publicly executed. Deceased.

Jonah Wilcox: Commando.

Mitchell Yeager: Counterintelligence threat analyst brought in to investigate Vaughn when he was under suspicion of being a double agent.

FEDERAL BUREAU OF INVESTIGATION (FBI)

The primary investigative branch of the U.S. Department of Justice. The FBI investigates crimes dealing with the safety and security of the United States, collecting intelligence on individuals or groups considered dangerous to national security.

Kendall: Former director of the FBI as well as former director of the Joint Task Force on Intelligence. It was later discovered that he was actually a member of the Department of Special Research, working undercover as director of the FBI. (See: *DSR*.)

NATIONAL SECURITY AGENCY (NSA)

An agency of the United States Department of Defense with the role of ensuring the security of U.S. information systems, as well as gathering undisclosed information from other countries.

Frederick Brandon: Deputy director of the NSA. Deceased.

Carrie Bowman: Special Projects agent and MENSA member. While working alongside CIA op tech engineer Marshall Flinkman, the two started dating. After two years together, Carrie became pregnant, though she refused to marry Marshall due to issues she had with the concept of wedlock. When Carrie went into labor, she altered her opinion on the institution of marriage and insisted they be wed immediately. Following a brief ceremony officiated by Weiss, Carrie gave birth to her son, Mitchell Flinkman.

DEPARTMENT OF SPECIAL RESEARCH (DSR)

KENDALL

An "off the books" agency within the NSA created during World War II to investigate Nazi interest in the occult. After the war, an executive order was signed empowering the agency to investigate fringe science, including parapsychology and remote viewing.

Kendall: Director of the DSR. Kendall had been undercover as director of the FBI while leading the Joint Task Force. He was responsible for keeping Sydney under deep cover in the Covenant as Julia Thorne during her two missing years. Though she told him to promise her that he would not reveal what had happened during that time, Kendall was forced to break that promise. After months of manipulations from the Covenant, Kendall knew that Sydney needed to learn the truth so that she could stop them from merging her DNA with Rambaldi's to create a prophesied child.

Brodien: Junior CIA officer unlucky enough to be teamed with Sydney Bristow on the staged mission that ultimately led her to publicly resign from the CIA. In light of his actions revealing Sydney's flagrant disregard for protocol, he was promoted to the DSR, where the formerly green agent was quickly hardened by his experiences. He was the last surviving member of the team sent in to stop Elena Derevko from activating Rambaldi's ultimate device. He did not survive the mission. Deceased.

Project Black Hole: Secret DSR facility storing the U.S. government's collection of Rambaldi artifacts.

NATIONAL SECURITY COUNCIL (NSC)

A part of the executive office of the president of the United States, the council serves as an interdepartmental cabinet on defense, foreign policy, and intelligence matters. Members include the president, the vice president, and the secretaries of state and defense. The council supervises the Central Intelligence Agency.

Robert Lindsey: Senior director of the NSC. Deceased.

ENEMIES OF THE STATE

THE ALLIANCE OF TWELVE

Known simply as "the Alliance," the organization was a board consisting of twelve men plying the spy trade for profit. Some of the members were from the private sector, but most were former intelligence officers. They started the company together in 1991 to trade intelligence in a new form of organized crime with a special interest in

collecting Rambaldi artifacts. Their organization was divided into a dozen "SD" cells around the world. Each cell was active in global terrorism for over a decade until the CIA, working with numerous foreign intelligence organizations, managed to bring down the entire operation. Little did the CIA realize at the time that the takedown of the Alliance was initiated internally by one of its own members: Arvin Sloane. Recent reports indicate that former Alliance members are working to rebuild the organization.

KEY ALLIANCE OPERATIVES

Tambor Barcelo: Head of security.

Jean Briault: Alliance member and friend to Arvin Sloane. He was killed by Sloane after being set up by Edward Poole. Deceased.

Alain Christophe: Leader of the Alliance.

Miles Devereaux: Former member of the Alliance and head of operations at SD-6.

Ariana Kane: Head of counterintelligence who investigated Jack Bristow's activities following the extortion plot involving Emily Sloane. She had an affair with Jean Briault, which was the basis of Arvin Sloane's plot to frame her for the extortion when, in fact, he was behind the entire scheme to obtain $100 million from the Alliance. Presumed dead.

Edward Poole: Head of the British arm of the Alliance (SD-9) with ties to the Man. Poole deceived Sloane into believing that Briault was working for the Man in a plot to convince the Alliance not to declare war on the Man's organization. Deceased.

SD-6

"Section Disparu" (Cell 6) translates to "the section that does not exist." Alain Christophe coined the term. SD-6 was an agency of the Alliance under the leadership of Arvin Sloane. The office was located on sublevel 6 of the Credit Dauphine building in Los Angeles. SD-6 recruited agents based on the false information that it was a black ops arm of the CIA charged with "the retrieval and study of

intelligence, both military and industrial, throughout the world, that is critical to the superiority and survival of the United States of America."

SD-6 was one of a number of private agencies of the Alliance that traded in weapons, drugs, and intelligence. The Alliance used covert means to undermine world governments and industry in its attempts to take over the world. Over the twelve years of its existence, SD-6 made over $400 million for the Alliance, plus another $300 million from various transactions with arms dealer Ineni Hassan. It acquired more Rambaldi artifacts than all the other SD cells combined.

FORMER SD-6 AGENTS AND ASSOCIATES

Douglas: Low-level agent.
Leonard Dreifuss: Known as the go-to guy for transport, he bankrolled SD-6 operations from Geneva.
Karl Dryer: Op comm analyst brought in for emergencies.
Gregory Fisher: Assigned to get Sydney into an asylum in Romania. Deceased.
Anthony Geiger: Briefly replaced Sloane as head of SD-6 right before it was disbanded. Deceased.
Steven Gordon: Senior officer.
Grey: Torture specialist.
Mokhtar Hammouda: Former Egyptian commando and SD-6 contact in São Paulo. Deceased.
Noah Hicks: Deep-cover agent. He was secretly a freelance assassin known as the Snowman and was formerly involved with Sydney. Deceased.
Eloise Kurtz: Agent tasked by Jack Bristow to impersonate Sydney's alias, Kate Jones, to mislead Will Tippin during his investigation. Deceased.
Dr. Mallaska: Worked at the SD-6–operated Angel of Mercy Hospital.

Rebecca Martinez: Alias of agent sent in to determine if Will Tippin was still a threat.

Calvin McCullough: Senior partner and head of the Psychological Warfare and Operations division. He oversaw questioning, administered lie detector tests, and performed psych evaluations. Sloane, owing him a favor, tipped McCullough off to the pending takedown of SD-6 by the CIA, allowing the man to evade capture. McCullough managed to stay underground for several years, working for Elena Derevko on a procedure to create a near duplicate of Arvin Sloane. Once APO caught up with McCullough, he took his own life rather than provide much needed intel.

Anthony Russek: Senior officer who transferred from Jennings Aerospace. Jack Bristow framed him as the SD-6 mole to protect Sydney. He had a wife and an infant daughter named Gabrielle. Deceased.

Kyle Wexler: Deep-cover agent. Deceased.

FTL

An Asian organization similar in function to SD-6, FTL also had an extensive collection of Rambaldi artifacts that were stolen by Sark for the Man. Once the agency was infiltrated, its agent roster was compromised, and its network crumbled within hours of the attack.

Quan Li: Former head of FTL. Killed during a raid led by Sark. Deceased.

K-DIRECTORATE

A Russian terrorist organization similar to FTL and SD-6, K-Directorate also had an interest in the study of Rambaldi. Agents of the Man effectively destroyed the organization after Sark killed the leader of K-Directorate.

Anna Espinosa: A Cold War baby born in Cuba and raised in Russia, Anna Espinosa is a personal enemy of Sydney Bristow. She was the go-to officer for wet work and active measures at K-Directorate and went freelance after the organization crumbled. Espinosa specializes in close-quarter kills by means of strangulation, edged weapons, and guns. It was considered her "signature" to remove the right index fingers of her victims. Espinosa also excels at high-level theft and security breach. "Black Widow" was one of her former call signs.

Espinosa spent six and a half years on Interpol's Most Wanted list and was presumed dead until recently. She resurfaced working freelance for the Cadmus Revolutionary Front, but she was more interested in taking over the operation. Her plan failed when she was double-crossed by Sark and taken into custody.

Ilyich Ivankov: Former head of K-Directorate. Deceased.

Lavro Kessar: Second-in-command at K-Directorate until his promotion following Ivankov's death.

THE TRIAD

A loose coalition of organized crime entities dealing mainly in drugs and prostitution, the Triad has made a significant foray into weapons in recent years.

THE MAN

The Man was an alias used by Irina Derevko. Prior to turning herself in to the CIA, Derevko headed an intelligence organization that garnered one of the largest Rambaldi collections in the world by stealing artifacts from other agencies involved in spycraft.

Aliases: Laura Bristow, the Man
DOB: 3/22/51
Place of Birth: Moscow, Russia
Family:
    Husband: Jack Bristow
    Daughters: Sydney Bristow, Nadia Santos
    Sisters: Yekaterina (Katya) Derevko,
      Elena Derevko
Education: Master's work in English Literature
    (as Laura Bristow)
Languages: English, Russian

History with the KGB and CIA:

Alexander Khasinau recruited Irina Derevko into the KGB in 1970. For a woman to be asked to serve her country at that time in Russia meant she would be guaranteed a future beyond anything she could have anticipated. She excelled at the job and quickly rose to the rank of major.

Her superior, General Cuvee, assigned her to steal documents from a ranking member of the CIA. Of the agents selected, she chose to seduce and marry Jack Bristow, having particular interest in his development of the Project Christmas program. Going by the name Laura, Irina Derevko masterfully manipulated her situation, calculating every detail right down to fulfilling his desire to start a family, although she did show signs of remorse for bringing into the world a daughter destined for a life of espionage. Derevko briefly considered killing her daughter soon after the birth.

Derevko's work as an undercover agent for the KGB resulted in the deaths of twenty CIA operatives, including the father of Michael Vaughn. Secret orders were hidden within the pages of books Jack brought back to her from his trips abroad.

Personal History:

While still under the alias of Laura Bristow, Irina passed along a first-edition copy of *Alice in Wonderland* to her daughter. It was Sydney's most prized possession, partially because it reminded her of the mother she thought she knew—the one who was a teacher, inspiring Sydney to pursue grad school and follow in her footsteps.

Derevko claimed there were times that the illusion of her marriage seemed real, particularly following Sydney's birth. And although she later claimed that those feelings were gone, they did seem to resurface on several occasions during her interactions with Sydney as an adult.

In 1981 Derevko faked her death in a car accident with the help of Igor Sergei Valenko, who was operating under the guise of FBI agent Bentley Calder. In a briefing with Khasinau and Valenko following her extraction, Derevko was recorded discussing how she had spied on Jack for ten years and considered him a fool. Her files were classified Omega 17 by the FBI, meaning they were highly classified.

It was not learned until later that Derevko gave birth to a daughter shortly after she disappeared. The girl, Nadia, was the result of an affair between Derevko and Sloane. The KGB took the child away from her and subjected Nadia to various experiments and tortures, hoping to learn the location of Rambaldi. Luckily, Vaughn's father rescued the girl and put her in hiding to keep her safe.

History as the Man:

Derevko later headed an organization under the guise of her other alias, "the Man." She was once again working with Khasinau, although this time he reported to her. She first made her presence known by staging simultaneous raids at SD-6 and FTL headquarters. The raid on FTL netted her all of FTL's Rambaldi artifacts and led to the destruction of that organization. Her mission into SD-6 was unsuccessful and served only to alert SD-6 and the CIA to her presence.

For several months she was able to hide her identity behind the moniker of the Man. Most intelligence agencies believed Khasinau to be the Man. However, Derevko revealed herself when her daughter was taken prisoner. Upon their reunion, Derevko shot Sydney in the shoulder, though she later claimed that she had done so for her daughter's protection. Khasinau was watching, and Derevko figured wounding Sydney was the only way to facilitate her escape—she was able to buy her some time and still maintain her position of leadership.

History in CIA Custody:

Derevko killed Khasinau, disappeared with "the bible"—the operations manual for her organization—and hid it. She then turned herself in to the CIA, informing them that she would provide them with intel only if she could deliver it directly to her daughter. Vaughn noted that Derevko was a certifiable Rambaldi expert and knew more about the inner workings of global organized crime than any other person being held by the United States.

Derevko worked out a barter system for herself, exchanging information for personal items and creature comforts. Her first request was for a pair of earrings that were supposedly given to her by her mother when she graduated the academy at age twenty-one. The earrings were checked for illegal devices and nothing was found. However, after Derevko escaped, she sent a message back to her daughter through the earrings in Morse code. The message said, "Truth takes time."

Though Derevko was willing to work with the U.S. government, she was selective in the intelligence she shared. Although all of her information was suspect, she was just beginning to gain her daughter's trust when a valuable piece of intel she had given Sydney proved wrong. Sydney was sent in to retrieve the bible from a house in the woods that Derevko had indicated was safe to enter. When Sydney arrived, she discovered—with Jack's help—that the place was rigged with explosives. Following this betrayal, Derevko was transferred to Camp Harris for unrestricted interrogation. The breach also invalidated her agreement with the CIA, and she was sentenced to death.

Derevko pled guilty to all eighty-six counts of espionage against her and received the death penalty. Jack later admitted to setting her up, but since her agreement had never been binding, the plans continued for her execution. Sydney resorted to extreme measures to keep her alive, kidnapping and blackmailing a U.S. senator to have her mother's immunity agreement honored.

After a while, Derevko relented in her insistence on dealing only with Sydney and agreed to work with Jack as well. She and Jack also realized that they were technically still married. They continued to grow closer and went on a mission together with Sydney to infiltrate a prison where Derevko had once been held. Though the mission started out with much bitterness between Jack and Irina, they were working together successfully by the end.

After the fall of SD-6, Sydney tried to quit the Agency to begin a normal life with Vaughn. But the CIA threatened that if she quit, she would no longer be able to see her mother. Derevko warned Sydney that if she made the decision to stick with her job based on that threat alone, then she was a fool, and Derevko would refuse to see her again if that was the case. However, Sydney realized the importance of her work and remained of her own accord.

Derevko accompanied Jack on another mission to smoke out Sloane. It finally seemed that they had grown to trust each other, and they shared an evening together. Jack agreed to remove a tracking device from her to protect her cover. And the very next day she used her advantage and escaped, along with a stolen Rambaldi manuscript.

It turned out that Jack had not put his trust in her after all and had replaced the tracking device with a passive transmitter. As Derevko began her Rambaldi search anew, the CIA tracked her to a biotech firm in Stuttgart and sent Sydney and Vaughn in after her. Derevko saved Sydney's life by making sure she left the building before it exploded.

Sydney eventually caught up with her mother one last time. It was then that Derevko informed her daughter that she, Sydney, was the one named in Rambaldi's prophecy. Before escaping, Derevko also admitted that she loved Sydney.

History as a Free Agent:

During the period in which Sydney was missing, Derevko worked with Jack via instant messages to help locate their daughter. At the time, Derevko was number six on the CIA's Most Wanted list. She sent in her sister Katya to help once Sydney resurfaced. But as soon as Jack pressed her for information on the Passenger, she cut off communication for good.

Recently Jack learned that Derevko had put a hit out on Sydney, and he had her killed to protect his daughter. Once Derevko was dead, the contract on Sydney's life was terminated. Unaware of that information at the time, Sydney saw to it that her mother was buried in a mausoleum in Moscow, three blocks from the home in which she grew up.

That, however, was not the end of the story.

Unbeknownst to Jack and Sydney, Irina Derevko had been replaced by a follower of Elena Derevko who had been willing to give her life for the cause and had undergone the Helix protocol to become an exact duplicate of Irina. The real Irina Derevko was a prisoner of her sister. Elena subjected Irina to a litany of tortures, finally breaking her sister to get necessary information for completing Rambaldi's endgame.

Irina remained a prisoner until her two daughters freed her. Without being told, Irina recognized her

daughter Nadia and the pair shared a warm reunion. Irina's reunion with Jack Bristow was more tepid, but she eventually forgave him for supposedly killing her.

Irina joined the team sent to stop Elena from activating Rambaldi's ultimate device and causing worldwide devastation. The mission was a success, and Irina killed her sister as punishment for her ordeal. Before the CIA came to extract the team, Jack allowed Irina to escape. As she left, Irina told Sydney that she would be watching over her daughter.

DOB: Unknown
Place of Birth: Possibly Galway, Ireland
Family:
    Father: Andrian Lazarey (deceased)
Education: Unknown
Languages: English, French

History as a Mercenary Spy:

Sark originally came onto the scene under the employ of the Man and was the leader of the team responsible for bringing down FTL. In trying to identify Sark's origins, SD-6 analyzed his speech patterns and found that though his grammar and syntax gave away nothing, his latent vowels suggested he had spent a considerable amount of time in Ireland, most likely Galway.

It was later learned that Sark was a descendent of the Romanov family of Russia and son to Andrian Lazarey. Sark was abandoned by his father and sent to school in England at a very young age. He believes his upbringing made him more self-reliant and, perhaps, prematurely ambitious. Upon Lazarey's presumed death, Sark inherited $800 million.

During his time working for the Man, Sark ran several missions and attempted to broker deals to collect various Rambaldi artifacts. His most notable deal occurred when he shot and killed the head of K-Directorate while attempting to retrieve the Rambaldi manuscript.

Sark was captured by SD-6 in Denpasar, on the island of Bali. Known for routinely switching alliances, he showed his preference for civilized interrogations over a bottle of wine as opposed to torture. He appeared willing to work with any enemy, as his loyalty shifted based on his own self-interest. Sark agreed to help SD-6 trap the Man, but he managed to use the mission he was on as a means to escape. He then had a blood transfusion to remove the nonlethal radioactive isotope Sloane had slipped him for tracking purposes.

After the death of Alexander Khasinau and Irina Derevko's disappearance, it appeared that Sark had taken over their organization, although some suspected that he was still working under Derevko's orders. On several occasions Sark tried to sway Sydney Bristow to work for his organization. Though Sydney refused, she did agree to work with him in exchange for an antidote to save Michael Vaughn from a Rambaldi virus. The deal required Sydney to turn Sloane over to Sark, at which time she expected her employer would meet his death. Instead, Sark brokered a deal with Sloane, offering a piece of unknown information and an offer to share resources in the Rambaldi hunt.

Aware that SD-6 was not part of the CIA, Sark acted as if he had been given a pardon in exchange for his intel, and he was sent on a mission with Sydney almost immediately after joining the team. But Sark was ultimately on a different mission, and he provided Sydney with the necessary information for the CIA to take down the Alliance and SD-6.

After SD-6, Sark continued to team with Sloane and was behind the placement of Allison Doren in Sydney's life as Francie Calfo's double. He and Allison had dated prior to the doubling procedure and continued their relationship afterward as well.

Sark helped arrange for Derevko's escape from U.S. custody and fell into the role of her second-in-command. After they worked with Sloane in an attempt to obtain the Il Dire Rambaldi artifact, Derevko eventually gave up Sark, who was captured by the CIA. Sark quickly offered to assist the CIA, noting—again—that his loyalties were flexible.

Sark was held in custody for two years while he provided valuable intel. Once it was believed he had been "bled dry" of all usable information, Robert Lindsey arranged to exchange Sark for a CIA hostage being held by the Covenant. It turned out to be a setup in which Lindsey was hoping to capture Covenant operatives. The mission failed and Sark got away.

It had been assumed that the Covenant wanted Sark so they could kill him for his involvement in the death of the brother of Ushek San'ko, a high-ranking official in the organization. As it turned out, San'ko knew that his brother's death had been accidental, but he still felt some kind of amends needed to be made and extorted Sark's $800 million inheritance from him. Sark willingly turned over the money, since he hadn't even known that it was his to inherit, and agreed to join the Covenant.

During his time with the Covenant, Sark kidnapped his father, Andrian Lazarey, when the man resurfaced. Considering that his only memories of Lazarey were of an abusive father who abandoned him, Sark had no problem torturing the man in an attempt to find out information on the Rambaldi Cube. After Lazarey was rescued, Sark was fine with the Covenant's assassination of his father.

As a Covenant operative, Sark was quickly disillusioned by the way he was treated as a foot soldier when his money was bankrolling its operations. He attempted to stage a coup with Lauren Reed, hoping to take over the organization by killing off the cell leaders. Lauren went along with the plan but betrayed Sark to McKenas Cole, the Covenant's second-in-command. In the end Cole was pleased with the result of the plan since it saved him the trouble of dealing with the cell leaders who had recently been named in information obtained by the CIA. As a reward, Cole appointed Sark and Lauren as the heads of the North American cell.

Sark and Lauren's partnership quickly took a romantic turn as they continued to work together to locate the Passenger—that is, until he was captured by the CIA during a raid on the Rotunda, during which Lauren escaped. Vaughn tortured him for information regarding Lauren's location, even breaking Sark's nose. Sark played on Vaughn's emotions, but he eventually gave up the information. Later he shared even more vital information with Sydney while she was disguised as Lauren. Sark remained in U.S. custody while his broken bones healed.

Agents of APO later approached Sark when they learned that operatives of the Covenant had formed a new organization known as the Cadmus Revolutionary Front (CRF). After a brief negotiation, Sark agreed to help APO, citing that his time spent in prison had given him a sense of purpose. One of the conditions of his agreement was that he be given the opportunity to see the body of Lauren Reed to confirm that she was dead. As Vaughn took him to the morgue, Sark revealed that he did truly love Lauren and was deeply saddened by the loss. Sark did keep his word and worked with APO to capture Anna Espinosa, who had been working with the CRF. Once his agreement was fulfilled, Sark used the opportunity to escape. He is still at large.

Alexander Khasinau: Highly decorated former KGB general. He was Irina Derevko's senior officer during her time working undercover as Laura Bristow.

Khasinau was long rumored to be a powerbroker for the Russian mafia in its affairs with rogue states and in the international arms bazaar. He was initially believed to be the Man, but it was later determined that he was Derevko's second-in-command. Following the collapse of the organization, Derevko killed Khasinau in a move to protect the organizational bible for her operations before turning herself in to the CIA. Deceased.

THE COVENANT

A loose affiliation of Russian nationalists comprised of former Central Committee members and retired KGB that functioned much like an organized crime family. At one time there were six leaders of Covenant cells scattered around the globe. Each cell leader wore a watch containing access keys to their respective headquarters. Operatives Julian Sark and Lauren Reed worked together to assassinate those six cell leaders in an attempt to ascend within the organization. The plot worked and the pair were named co-leaders of the North American cell.

The Covenant was made up of avid Rambaldi collectors. Their primary mission was to fuse Rambaldi's DNA with eggs taken from the Chosen One, Sydney Bristow. Following her battle with Allison Doren, the Covenant kidnapped Sydney and subjected her to months of torture and indoctrination, trying to brainwash her into believing she was an operative named Julia Thorne. Once they believed she had been turned, the Covenant set her on the track of locating Rambaldi's DNA. They did not realize that the process of turning her had not worked, and Sydney managed to hide the DNA before having its location—and two years of her life—erased from her memory.

Undaunted, the Covenant spent months manipulating Sydney into remembering her missing years and relocating Rambaldi's DNA. Once they managed to do that, the Covenant stole the DNA and began the process of fusing it with eggs they had surgically removed from Sydney while she was in their custody. The Joint Task Force on Intelligence managed to shut down the operation and destroy the lab before the experiment was complete.

The Covenant continued to work to find Rambaldi's greatest prophecy. The search was unsuccessful, largely due to the efforts of Sydney Bristow and Michael Vaughn. The Covenant fell apart shortly after the capture of Sark and the death of Lauren Reed. However, former operatives have recently formed the Cadmus Revolutionary Front in an effort to continue the mission.

The truth behind the Covenant, however, took more twists and turns as the APO team worked to solve a new mystery surrounding renewed interest in Rambaldi's works. Contrary to original belief, the Covenant never truly fell. The person behind the Covenant only led the CIA to believe that it had taken down the organization. However, she was still working behind the scenes to bring Rambaldi's master plan to fruition. The Covenant was still alive under Elena Derevko.

ID Class: USS-NS-9376655
DOB: 12/5/76
Place of Birth: Virginia, USA
Family:
    Father: Senator George Reed (deceased)
    Mother: Olivia Reed

History with the NSC and the Covenant:

Lauren Reed was born in Virginia and grew up in London. Her father was Senator George Reed. Lauren was recruited into the National Security Council in 2000. She was part of the team that brokered Sloane's pardon in exchange for information and his agreement to come on as an intelligence consultant. Lauren was assigned to be Sloane's liaison until Sydney replaced her at Sloane's request. Though she had wanted to become field rated, her father had determined that it was too dangerous and made sure it didn't happen. Lauren had been unaware of this fact until Sloane told her.

Lauren deposed the Task Force staff during the wrap-up of the investigation into Irina Derevko's escape. During that time she developed a relationship with Michael Vaughn, though it was later discovered that her motivation for getting closer to him was because she was working for the Covenant. Vaughn fell in love with her and they were wed at her parents' farm in Virginia.

Lauren was assigned as NSC liaison to the Task Force following Lindsey's departure. She headed up the investigation into Andrian Lazarey's death. Initially she was unaware that members of the CIA, including her husband, were thwarting her investigation and keeping the secret that Sydney had been the murderer. When Sark gave Lauren the information she was looking for, she immediately informed her superiors.

VAUGHN & LAUREN

Natural tensions existed between Lauren and Sydney, but Lauren was given an opportunity to prove to her husband that her personal feelings could be put aside when she was asked to serve as an observer during Sydney's interrogation following the revelation that she had killed Lazarey. She used the request to assure Vaughn that there was nothing to worry about regarding Sydney's incarceration. But when she was asked to file a false report for the White House, Lauren quickly learned that Syd was in danger. However, she was instrumental in abetting Sydney's escape from prison.

Following the cover story that she had been kidnapped by the Covenant along with Sydney, Lauren reported back to Lindsey to provide Sydney more time to investigate her missing years. To enforce the charade, she had to allow Sydney to rough her up so it looked like she had been held and beaten by the Covenant.

Though it appeared that Lauren was coming around, this was all part of a plot to use Sydney to find Rambaldi's DNA. While working for the Covenant undercover at the NSC, Lauren assassinated Andrian Lazarey shortly after it was learned that he was still alive.

Then Lauren partnered with Sark to kill the heads of the Covenant cells in a power play. The coup failed when Lauren reported the activity to McKenas Cole, second-in-command at the Covenant. Their actions did, however, strengthen the Covenant when the CIA obtained the Doleac Agenda, an operational file that revealed the identities of the now dead cell leaders. They were selected to lead the North American cell of the organization as a reward.

During this time the CIA began to suspect that there was a mole in the Task Force. Lauren first attempted to frame Sloane for the information leak, but that was quickly proved false. She also worked to strengthen her bond with Vaughn in light of learning that her husband and Sydney had shared a kiss. At the same time, Vaughn suggested they should separate. The solution to both of her problems presented itself when Sark developed a plan that she should frame her father, Senator Reed, and kill him so Vaughn would stay with her in light of the "tragedy."

LAUREN AND OLIVIA REED

Though Lauren had a largely estranged relationship with her father, she could not bring herself to kill him. But her mother, another Covenant operative, was able to carry out the murder in Lauren's place. Following Lauren's inability to act, combined with repeated failures, her position within the Covenant began to degrade. Arms dealer Kazari Bomani was planning to silence Lauren, but Sark killed Bomani first. His actions were possibly motivated by his feelings for Lauren, as they had begun an affair.

Eventually the CIA found out that Lauren was the mole when Vaughn discovered a disguise she had used to kill a CIA resource. Lauren quickly learned that they were on to her. She and Sark took Vaughn hostage and tortured him for information that he refused to give. Lauren had been instructed to kill Vaughn, but she let him live, and he was ultimately recovered by the CIA.

Disguised as Sydney Bristow, Lauren entered the Rotunda and stole information regarding the Passenger. During her escape, she shot Marshall Flinkman, and injured several agents when explosives she had planted were detonated.

Lauren continued to track the Passenger, and her search ultimately led to a dig site in Palermo. Sydney Bristow infiltrated the site. The two fought, but Lauren managed to get the upper hand. Just as she thought she had won, Lauren was shot and killed by her husband, Vaughn. Deceased.

Kazari Bomani: One of the largest arms dealers in Africa until Sloane's testimony put him away. The Covenant secured his release, at which time he kidnapped Sloane, intending to kill him. But in the end he agreed to work with Sloane. Bomani led the Covenant's mission in obtaining Rambaldi artifacts. Deceased.

KAZARI BOMANI

McKenas Cole: Former SD-6 freelancer who was abandoned during a mission to destroy the Shali Oil Pipeline. Cole was captured by the Russians and tortured. Eventually he went to work for the Man and led a commando raid on SD-6. He was captured by the CIA, but eventually managed to secure his release from federal custody. He went on to the position of second-in-command at the Covenant.

McKENAS COLE

Olivia Reed: Wife of Senator Reed and mother to Lauren. She killed her husband and framed him as the Covenant's mole in order to protect Lauren. Olivia also oversaw the decrypting of the Rambaldi manuscript containing clues for the Passenger.

OLIVIA REED

Allison Doren: Her parents believed their daughter, a result of the Russian version of the Project Christmas program, died in a bus accident. She was the second recipient of the Project Helix doubling program, which genetically altered her appearance to make her look exactly like Francie Calfo in order to obtain intelligence directly from Sydney. Allison was in a relationship with Sark, prior to as well as after the doubling procedure. She took Francie's place, ingratiated herself

ALLISON DOREN

into Sydney's life, and seduced Will Tippin. While undercover Allison kept Sydney under surveillance and planted the bomb that killed Dixon's wife. When her cover was threatened, Allison framed Will for treason, even though she had developed feelings for him—despite herself. When her cover was blown, Allison tried to kill Will, though he survived.

During a fight with Sydney, Allison was shot three times. However, a Rambaldi serum helped nurse her back to health and made her nearly invulnerable. During a mission with Sark to retrieve the Rambaldi Cube, Allison encountered Will once again. There was a struggle in which he stabbed her and left her for dead. Possibly deceased.

Yekaterina (Katya) Derevko: Sister to Irina Derevko. Undercover as a Russian military officer, she helped Jack and Sydney on several occasions, forming a brief relationship with Jack. It seemed that she was working with the Covenant in trying to obtain the Passenger. However, it is likely that that was a ruse to flush out the true leader of the Covenant.

KATYA DEREVKO

Katya is presently incarcerated at the Quantico Women's Detention Center. For most of her incarceration her sole visitor was Nadia Santos, who was hoping to learn more about her mother, Katya's sister, Irina. Katya is highly allergic to chocolate and went into anaphylactic shock from a piece of candy as a means of impressing upon Nadia the importance of passing a message along to Sydney. Sydney reluctantly went to visit her aunt. Katya informed her niece that Irina did not put the hit on Sydney and directed her to information on the true culprit. She also provided Jack Bristow with necessary intelligence on the person behind recent Rambaldi-inspired illegal activities and the woman behind the Covenant.

Elena Derevko (aka Sophia Vargas): Sister to Irina and Katya, and the true mastermind behind the Covenant. Elena was one of the KGB's foremost assassins. Under the code name Sentinel, she was responsible for the murders of countless diplomats and politicians. In the course of her work she earned the reputation of being the cruelest of the Derevko women. Elena disappeared almost thirty years earlier, when she broke all ties with the KGB and her family. It was rumored that she and Irina had had a falling out.

The KGB, CIA, and Irina Derevko all tried looking for Elena, but to no avail. A year earlier, Jack received a tip from an old associate. It led him to one of Elena's safe houses in Warsaw. There he found files on Sydney and Nadia indicating that Elena had had them under surveillance for well over a decade.

ELENA DEREVKO

During the time Elena was missing, she was living under the guise of Sophia Vargas, head of the orphanage where Nadia had been taken. Though it appeared she was taking care of Nadia, Elena was actually working to prepare the girl for her future role as prophesied by Milo Rambaldi.

Elena continued to work behind the scenes, nearly orchestrating Vaughn to deliver a piece of Rambaldi technology to her. She also created an almost duplicate version of Sloane to hide her activities. She briefly re-entered Nadia's life as Sophia to gather necessary intel to break into the DSR facility and piece together Rambaldi's ultimate device.

Elena's goal was to bring about the end of mankind as it was known and re-engineer the evolution of the species. The plan failed when the APO team consisting largely of her family members stopped her. Irina ended her sister's life. Deceased.

Ned Bolger: U.S. Army Corporal, Serial #11-27-62, from Torch Lake, Michigan. Underwent an experimental procedure in which he was brainwashed to believe he was Arvin Sloane, to the point where the real Sloane's memories were actually implanted into his head. APO subjected the fake Sloane (known informally as Sloane clone) to another experimental procedure hoping to secure the location of an orchid that was integral to Rambaldi's ultimate plan. The procedure was successful in finding the information, but it drove Bolger mad in the process.

WILLIAM D. TIPPIN

DOB: 3/8/73
Place of Birth: Austin, Texas, USA
Family:
    Father: Robert Tippin
    Mother: Patsy Tippin
    Sister: Amy Tippin
Education: BA in Print Journalism

Personal History:

Will Tippin is one of Sydney Bristow's dearest friends, and for much of their friendship he was entirely unaware that she was a spy. He worked as a city reporter for the *Los Angeles Register.* Seated at the metro desk, he wrote on many subjects, including more than two dozen articles on restaurants that gave him insight into health department ratings and code requirements. He also received the Caplan Award for his story on migrant worker Luis Maroma. Around this time, he had a brief relationship with Jenny, an intern at the paper.

Though Will was not on the crime beat, he approached his editor asking to cover a story on the murder of Danny Hecht. After collecting an intriguing amount of information, he was given the go-ahead. Several times Sydney asked him to stop pursuing the story, but Will couldn't stand to see her hurting and thought that finding the truth behind the murder would help. For months he investigated, getting closer to the truth about SD-6, never realizing the danger until he was in too deep.

History with the CIA:

Fearing for Sydney's safety, Jack Bristow teamed with Will to find the identity of the person who had been leaking information about her. Their search led them to Alexander Khasinau. While on a mission, Sydney discovered Will in Khasinau's custody and rescued him. As he slowly came out of a drug-induced haze, Will was shocked to find out the truth about his close friend. Eventually he began to understand the difficult life that she had to lead.

Will was abducted from a CIA safe house, and Sark brought him to Dr. Jong Lee to be tortured and questioned about the Circumference. Will did not know anything about the Rambaldi text, but he was returned to safety in an exchange arranged by Sydney and Jack. Before being exchanged, Will was able to exact some revenge on his torturer by injecting Dr. Lee with a drug that caused paralysis.

During the time Will had gone missing, a friend at the paper brought the article Will had written to the editor, with instructions from Will to publish it if anything happened to him. Once his story was published revealing the clandestine organization known as SD-6, Will's life was once again in danger. Jack set up a cover story to discredit him, making him out to be a drug addict who had made up the story. Will was arrested and pleaded guilty to a felony charge of heroin possession. Forced to go along to save his own life, he was fired from his job and sentenced to community service.

WILL AND VAUGHN

Will had to move in with Sydney and Francie for a time because he could not afford his own place. After working at Francie's new restaurant, Will went to Vaughn for a job. Unfortunately, Vaughn could not officially hire Will because of his fictitious arrest. However, Vaughn was able to use his discretionary fund to commission Will to do some freelance analysis for him. His work proved so good that he was given permission to be hired as an analyst of classified documents once he passed the Milgram-Reich Allegiance test. His cover was as an employee at a travel magazine called *Trade Winds*.

Shortly after Will began a relationship with Francie, she was secretly murdered and replaced by an operative working for Sloane and Sark. A woman named Allison Doren had undergone a procedure, known as Project Helix, that made her an exact duplicate of Francie. Will continued the relationship not knowing that his girlfriend was really Allison. When the CIA began to suspect that the double created by Project Helix had infiltrated their organization, Allison framed Will. He was taken into custody but was quickly proved innocent.

WILL & SYDNEY

Eventually Will realized that Allison was Francie's double. He called Sydney to warn her, and then Allison attacked him and left him for dead. Will managed to survive and was sent into Witness Protection as a construction foreman named Jonah living in Wisconsin.

Sydney reconnected with Will when she was trying to learn what had happened to her during her missing two years. She was hoping to connect with a former contact of his when he was working for the CIA. Together they tracked down his contact, which led Sydney to a container holding Rambaldi's DNA. During the mission Will had the chance to fight and presumably kill Allison.

Over the course of their friendship, Will had nursed a slight crush on Sydney, but his feelings went largely unreturned except for a quick kiss that went no further. As Sydney and Vaughn grew closer, Will did his best to let go of his feelings for her. However, when they reunited while he was in Witness Protection, the two shared one night together and decided to part, leaving some things unsaid.

FRANCIE D. CALFO

DOB: 1/3/75
Deceased: 1/26/03
Place of Birth: Sacramento, California, USA
Education: MBA student at the University of Los Angeles;
      withdrew to open her own restaurant

Personal History:

Francie Calfo was Sydney's best friend and roommate. Francie cared deeply about her friend's well-being and was often vocal about her displeasure with Sydney's overwhelming cover job at Credit Dauphine. On several occasions she counseled her friend to quit, citing that Sydney's work life was too demanding; she spent so much time away "on business" that she barely had time for her friends, not to mention a relationship. Francie originally suspected Sydney's frequent absence and obsession with work had to do with lingering feelings over Danny's death.

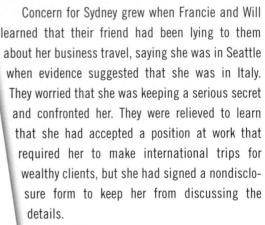

Concern for Sydney grew when Francie and Will learned that their friend had been lying to them about her business travel, saying she was in Seattle when evidence suggested that she was in Italy. They worried that she was keeping a serious secret and confronted her. They were relieved to learn that she had accepted a position at work that required her to make international trips for wealthy clients, but she had signed a nondisclosure form to keep her from discussing the details.

Francie had been dating Charlie Bernard for four years when she started to suspect that he was having an affair. Her suspicions eventually proved correct, but not before she had agreed to marry him. Sydney managed to convince them to postpone an impromptu Vegas wedding, and Charlie finally admitted his infidelity. This led Francie to end the relationship. Despite her feelings of anger and pain given the circumstances of their breakup, she continued to wear her engagement ring, clinging to the perfect relationship she thought she had had. Finally, she managed to remove it the day Sydney was able to take off her ring from Danny.

Francie worked as a caterer and party planner as she studied for her MBA. After leaving school she opened a restaurant in the Silverlake section of Los Angeles. She hired Will to help her with the opening when he found that she was relying on criminal types to help push through the necessary paperwork for liquor licenses and such. The restaurant opening was well attended and the place became quite popular, making a profit within the first six months.

As her restaurant was starting to take off, Francie's personal life took a positive turn as well when she and Will shared a kiss. Unsure initially of what this meant, Francie decided to pursue a relationship with him to find out how they would be as a couple. Her happiness came to a sudden, unexpected end when Allison Doren killed her and assumed her identity. Deceased.

Charlie Bernard: Former fiancé of Francie Calfo. He was a law school graduate who passed up an offer to work at the Flemming Letterman law firm to pursue an interest in singing. Francie ended their relationship when she learned he had been seeing another woman while they were dating.

Daniel (Danny) Hecht: Medical student and fiancé of Sydney Bristow. He was assassinated by SD-6 when the agency learned that Sydney had revealed to him her status as an agent. Deceased.

Emily Sloane: The wife of Arvin Sloane. She held a degree from the London School of Economics and worked at the State Department. Emily was originally given only six months to live after being diagnosed with lymphoma, but after three years of treatment, she went into remission. When the Alliance learned that she knew about SD-6, Arvin Sloane created an elaborate ruse to fake her death and protect her from harm. It did, however, require him to cut off one of her fingers as evidence that she was still alive. (The finger was supposedly sent to him by an unknown individual who was holding Emily hostage.)

Once her husband left the Alliance, she and Arvin settled into a villa in Tuscany. She soon learned that he was still involved in his former life and went to the American Embassy requesting to speak with Sydney Bristow. Emily brokered a deal in which she agreed to turn in her husband in exchange for his life being spared, but later changed her mind when he expressed his willingness to give up his criminal pursuits for her. During the operation to obtain Arvin, Emily was accidentally shot by Marcus Dixon as she and her husband were trying to escape. Deceased.

Diane Dixon: Wife of Marcus Dixon, mother of Robin and Steven. Diane believed that her husband was an investment analyst. Following the revelation that he was working for what he had believed to be a secret branch of the CIA, she separated from him for a time, upset by all the years of deception between them. At first she felt that she no longer knew her husband, but she grew to understand and appreciate the importance of his job. Sloane had her murdered in retaliation for his wife's accidental death. Deceased.

Robin Dixon: Eldest child of Marcus and Diane Dixon. She was kidnapped by the Covenant and exchanged for a Rambaldi artifact.

Steven Dixon: Youngest child of Marcus and Diane Dixon. He was kidnapped by the Covenant but released with a private message for his father.

MILO RAMBALDI

Born in Parma, Italy, in 1444, Milo Rambaldi was the chief architect for Pope Alexander VI. The inventor seemed to have a psychic vision of the future, and some consider him to have been a prophet. Rambaldi's designs were so advanced that the people of his time simply thought he was insane. He was excommunicated for heresy and sentenced to death for suggesting that someday science would allow people to know God. Milo Rambaldi died in 1496, though some believe he still lives to this day.

After Rambaldi's recorded death, his workshop was torn apart and his sketches were traded and sold for next to nothing. In the following five centuries, his work was scattered throughout the world. No one is exactly sure how much of it is left.

On some of his drawings, Rambaldi listed part numbers of actual technology not manufactured until today. A Russian historian happened upon one of his earlier designs, which looked like a transistor. SD-6 later acquired one of his notebooks. Analysis indicated that it contained a rudimentary schematic for a transportable vocal communicator: a cell phone. Rambaldi spent the last ten years of his life working on a project with technology beyond anything that has ever been seen.

The Rambaldi Eye is the symbol of the Magnifique Order of Rambaldi. It is stamped on his artifacts and tattooed on the hands of his followers. It is believed that the symbol may refer to the Chosen One (Sydney) and the Passenger (Nadia). Irina Derevko believed that the two outer symbols referred to Sydney and Nadia and the inner symbol was the item over which they would do great battle.

Prior to the finding of the Rambaldi (or Di Regno) heart, the U.S. government had verified forty-seven Rambaldi predictions. He had not been wrong once.

Rambaldi wrote that a man would come along and discover the true meaning of his work and, in doing so, change the world. Arvin Sloane believed that he was that man. He believed that Milo Rambaldi's collection of artifacts and texts all led to one ultimate mission that could lead to the betterment or the destruction of mankind . . . or both. Though some believed that a few of the leads were sheer folly, many of the following items played integral roles in obtaining Rambaldi's ultimate goal.

THE CIRCUMFERENCE (AKA THE MULLER DEVICE)

The Muller Device, first constructed by Oskar Muller, was based on a Rambaldi design known as the Circumference. It is a metal instrument with a red ball that hovers between two metal conductors. When the device is shut down, the ball turns to liquid. Though the original Muller Device was small enough to be held, there have been other, considerably larger, versions of the device as well.

The Circumference included a set of instructions on how to use the device, which has been described as a kind of battery. The instructions were written on a seemingly blank page with text that

was revealed by applying a Rambaldi solution to the parchment. The liquid from the large device built by Derevko carried a virus that caused a blood coagulation disorder. Subjects exposed directly to the liquid would eventually be infected, though the virus was entirely undetectable until the first sign of infection—bleeding from the fingernails. The nervous system would then be poisoned from the feet up. The resulting paralysis would affect the nerves that control the ability to breathe, and the patient would eventually suffocate. Death was inevitable unless the patient received a serum created from a blood derivative used to make a genetic-specific antidote for the victim.

For more on the Muller Device, please refer to items listed at the end of this catalog.

Related Medical Note: Reports indicate that Rambaldi also developed a lifesaving serum used in treating serious wounds. This serum was used on Allison Doren to heal three bullet wounds to her chest, and after months of rehabilitation she was fine. Later the serum protected her against new bullet wounds.

EQUATION FOR ZERO-POINT ENERGY

Underground caverns carved into the symbol of Rambaldi (the Rambaldi Eye) were located in Siberia. In the center of the sub-glacial caverns was the Rambaldi Music Box. The music box was designed on the premise that every musical note has a corresponding frequency, so any musical piece could be expressed as a series of numbers. The music box required a code to play the tune. Encoded within the tune the music box played was an equation for zero-point energy: a fuel source. The military applications alone for such a discovery would be unlimited.

SELF-SUSTAINING CELL REGENERATION SAMPLE

Many of Rambaldi's studies focused on immortality. One such example of his experiments was found in a small yellow flower kept inside an egg-shaped artifact. Preliminary analysis indicated that the flower was somewhere between four and six hundred years old. The container required power from six pluto-nium cores to be opened. It is believed to be Rambaldi's proof of endless life.

RAMBALDI-DESIGNED NEUTRON BOMB

Rambaldi's designs also led to the creation of a neutron bomb. It is made of an intricate combination of old gears and coils structured around state-of-the-art circuitry. With a capacity of one hundred million watts, it is a high-energy pulse weapon that raises the body temperature of its victims to over two thousand degrees, so they literally melt from the inside out. It works like a microwave, exciting water and fat molecules and converting them into atomic motion (heat). Since water and fat do not exist in inorganic materials, they are left unaffected. There is no defense against that kind of energy. It can go through walls, steel, concrete. The energy can also knock out computer circuitry, so if it were aimed at the sky it could bring down planes.

THE CHOSEN ONE AND THE PASSENGER

Rambaldi's most important work centered on his prophecies of the Chosen One and the Passenger. Research into the prophecies revealed the Chosen One to be Sydney Bristow, while the Passenger is her half sister, Nadia Santos. It was also prophesied that "The Passenger and the Chosen One shall battle. Only one will survive."

MACHINE CODE SKETCH

As early as 1489 Milo Rambaldi was writing machine code. An entire sequence was written on the back of two sketches—one possessed by SD-6 and the other in a private collection. Once the two codes were combined, it was learned that they were written in a compression scheme. The codes were decrypted to list a longitude and latitude in Malaga, Spain, that led to the Sol d'Oro.

SOL D'ORO ("THE GOLDEN SUN")

A gold disk made of synthetic polymers, the Sol d'Oro was found in a stained-glass window in a five-hundred-year-old church in Malaga, Spain.

RAMBALDI CLOCK

The clock, based on one of Rambaldi's designs, was built by clockmaker Giovanni Donato, the only man who ever collaborated with Rambaldi. Well ahead of its time, the clock has a margin of error of less than one second per decade, even though keeping time was not its sole purpose. The clock has a date on the back: August 16, 1523. It is the one date in history when absolutely nothing of note occurred. When the clock is combined with the Sol d'Oro and set to 12:22 GMT (Greenwich Mean Time), it reveals a star chart

in the disk. The only spot on Earth with that exact view of the stars on that date was discovered to be the southern slope of Mount Aconcagua in Argentina.

RAMBALDI MANUSCRIPT

Found at the Argentine coordinates determined by the Rambaldi clock, the leather-wrapped manuscript was located in a pit covered by a door marked with the symbol of Rambaldi.

The forty-seventh page of the manuscript was written in an invisible ink that could only be revealed by using a special liquid. When the paper was treated with this substance, the image of a woman bearing a resemblance to Sydney Bristow emerged. And the prophecy reads:

"This woman here depicted will possess unseen marks, signs that she will be the one to bring forth my works, bind them with fury, a burning anger, unless prevented. At vulgar cost, this woman will render the greatest power unto utter desolation."

The prophecy mentioned three specific physical anomalies: DNA sequencing, platelet levels, and the size of her heart. Sydney matched all three. The prophecy also noted that "this woman without pretense will have had her effect never having seen the beauty of my sky behind Mount Subasio. Perhaps a single glance would have quelled her fire."

It was believed that once Sydney saw the sky above Mount Subasio, she would be able to disprove the fact that she was the woman in the image. Despite successfully accomplishing this task, Sydney is still believed by many to be the Chosen One of Rambaldi's prophecy. The truth remains unclear.

RAMBALDI LIQUID

An ampoule originally obtained by SD-6 contained a liquid that reveals hidden writing on page forty-seven of the Rambaldi manuscript. It was stored in a small gold box that bears the symbol of Rambaldi.

PROPHECY CODE KEY

The code key for decrypting the prophecy was a series of words and numbers written in the picture frame of a painting of Pope Alexander VI that had been stored in the Vatican archives.

RAMBALDI CUBE/RAMBALDI'S DNA

A piece of human tissue—still vital—was found inside an artifact known as the Rambaldi Cube. The name etched inside the box is Milo Rambaldi, suggesting that it was a sample of his DNA. Twelve keys were required to open the vault that housed the cube for centuries in a cave in Namibia. Andrian Lazarey devoted his life to finding those keys. He finally located all the keys with Sydney's help during the time she was posing as Julia Thorne. Together they located the cube.

Once it had been found, the Covenant intended to follow Rambaldi's instructions to combine his DNA with the eggs of the Chosen One to effectively produce his offspring. Sydney, however, hid the cube once again to make sure they did not follow through with the plan.

RAMBALDI'S STUDY OF THE HUMAN HEART

This Rambaldi text, a study of the human heart, is assumed to be part of the prophet's larger project—that is, his obsession with immortality. Rambaldi had drawn the DNA profile of a man living today, Proteo Di Regno, on his manuscript, and that DNA was also a code key to decrypt page ninety-four. The page had a list of predictions, including:

September 7, 1812: The bloodiest battle in Napoleon's war with Russia.
June 28, 1914: The assassination of Archduke Ferdinand, which led to World War I.
August 6, 1945: The bombing of Hiroshima.

The list went on to predict other historical events. It also included a date only a few days away. At that exact time Arvin Sloane was in Nepal, where a former contact named Conrad gave him a secret message referring to the Passenger. It was located in a wooden box with the symbol of Rambaldi carved in it.

THE DI REGNO HEART

This Rambaldi device is in the shape of a human heart with a small spinning ball in the center. The heart had been inside the body of a Rambaldi follower named Proteo Di Regno until he was killed in order to obtain the heart. There was no record of Di Regno ever having received a heart transplant—as outlandish as that would have sounded at the time—and it is unclear if the Rambaldi heart was keeping him alive. The Di Regno heart was used to power Il Dire.

IL DIRE ("THE TELLING")

Rambaldi's true goal was found in a construct that was effectively a puzzle. Each of the forty-seven artifacts that were used in the construction of Il Dire generated its own unique magnetic field. Those fields determined where in the overall design the pieces fit. The final device printed out a message with one word: Peace.

Sloane traced back the etymology of the word "peace" to its Greek origin, *eirene,* which is also a derivation of the name Irina. According to Sloane, there were eight yards of blank parchment scroll before the message appeared. However, when the Covenant reconstructed Il Dire, there was a considerable amount of writing on the first part of the parchment. It was later revealed that Il Dire sketched the DNA pattern of the Passenger.

PUZZLE BOX

The puzzle box is a gold box with the name "Irina" inscribed on it. Project Black Hole had the box for two years and couldn't figure out how to open it. According to Sloane, something inside the box could hurt Sydney.

There is a legend that Josef Stalin made the greatest effort to open the box, which was believed to have remained unopened since the time of Rambaldi. It was rumored to contain "the Passenger," initially believed to be a strain of a plaguelike bioweapon capable of killing millions. Stalin sent teams of archeologists around the globe in search of the key to opening the box.

As legend has it, a discovery was made in 1941 in the Karoo desert of South Africa, where a map carved into a disk of red-tinted crystal was found. The etchings in the crystal were believed to be a guide to the key that opened the box. Unfortunately, the archeologists were obsessed with gaining sole credit for the discovery and turned on one another. The men killed each other, and the desert reclaimed them and the map.

When the Covenant found the key and opened the box, they discovered that Sloane had somehow managed to store the Di Regno heart inside.

RAMBALDI KALEIDOSCOPE

This item was in Project Black Hole's archives. It contains pieces of loose colored glass reflected by mirrors set at angles that create patterns when viewed through the end of the tube. In this case the pattern is made up of three crystals, all of which are required to read the map properly. Sloane had already collected two of the crystals. The third had recently been recovered in the Karoo desert. The map reveals a landscape found underwater off the coast of Japan.

PUZZLE BOX KEYS

Located in underwater caves, these four disks worked as keys that fit into the puzzle box to open it. It is believed that Rambaldi followers fortified the cave over the centuries.

THE HOURGLASS

The hourglass was not important to Rambaldi's overall design except for the green liquid stored inside. When the Hourglass was broken, the liquid spilled out and coalesced into a solid ball.

RAMBALDI EEG MACHINE

The ball created by the Hourglass liquid was then inserted into the center chamber of a Rambaldi-designed electroencephalograph— a wooden ring with spokes and a pen. Once the ball was placed in the chamber, it acted as a battery for the device. When placed over parchment it sketched the brainwave pattern of the Passenger— Nadia Santos.

THE PASSENGER

Reference to the Passenger was first discovered on the manuscript page Conrad (see: *Noted Rambaldi Experts,* page 92) showed to Sloane on the date prophesied by Rambaldi. The manuscript is known as the Restoration. It is written in a code for which the CIA has the code key.

Rambaldi prophesied that there would be a person, a "Passenger," who would be capable of serving as a direct conduit to him. The text contained a formula for an elixir. According to Rambaldi, when injected the elixir would bring an altered state of consciousness, allowing the Passenger to channel a message rumored to be the key to Rambaldi's endgame.

The elixir worked only on the Passenger. It stored a muscle memory and was filled with protein strains. When injected, the fluid moved to the cerebral cortex and triggered the Passenger to execute a prerecorded series of noncognitive activities—in this case, drawing. The toxicity level of that much protein being forced into the cerebrum could carry harmful side effects, including brain damage and ultimately death. When she was injected with the elixir, the Passenger, Nadia, wrote out an equation in pre-Galilean algebra in the shape of the Rambaldi Eye. It led to a set of coordinates where the Sphere of Life was believed to be located. The Sphere of Life is a vessel in which Rambaldi was able to store what was believed to be his consciousness . . . his essence . . . his soul.

THE SPHERE OF LIFE

More than Rambaldi's essence, the Sphere of Life was the final component in the fulfillment of Rambaldi's life's work. It was housed in a secret cave in Siena, Italy. The Sphere of Life was kept in a box that sat on a pedestal in the center of a glass floor imprinted with the Eye of Rambaldi. Only the Passenger could cross the floor and retrieve the sphere. However, when she touched the sphere, Nadia was filled with horrifying visions of the future. When she refused to take the sphere from the pedestal, Sloane attempted to remove it himself. The moment he took the sphere from its pedestal, the glass floor shattered, dropping him into a pit below.

Sloane survived the fall, and upon re-evaluating his life, he turned the Sphere of Life over to the U.S. government as part of his deal to create the APO unit.

TRANSFORMING COIL

A piece of technology of unknown origin that was part of the experimental Nichtengall (Nightingale) procedure for altering human DNA. The coil was integral for the creation of the final large-scale version Rambaldi device (previously known as the Muller Device). The coil acts as a containment stabilizer in the Rambaldi construct. Without the coil the device is incapable of withstanding its own power output.

HYDROSEK

A water contaminant developed by the Indonesians that could wipe out entire ecosystems. It is unclear how this chemical is directly linked to Rambaldi.

LADY SLIPPER ORCHID: *PAPHIOPEDILUM KHAN*

The rarest of all orchids, it was initially thought to be extinct. The bloom was brought back to Italy from China by Marco Polo as a gift from Kublai Khan. The monks of the Mont Inferno Monastery of the Vespertine Order in Umbria, Italy, used a chemical from the flower in their experiments to breed the aggression out of a class of bees with an exceptionally venomous sting. The process made the bees very hard to antagonize as they chose productivity over aggression. However, the activation of a handheld version of the Muller Device managed to instigate the bees' aggressive tendencies, turning them into killers.

The chemical from the orchid, when combined with other Rambaldi substances and distributed to the population by way of the water supply, can alter human DNA to make the species "mutate" into either peaceful or aggressive beings.

THE VESPERTINE PAPERS

Rambaldi texts referring to the Lady Slipper Orchid, rumored to have been destroyed during World World II.

THE VADE MECUM

A Rambaldi text detailing a set of instructions for how the pieces fit together to create Rambaldi's ultimate device. Professor Lazlo Drake was the only person in possession of a translation of the text. Short of his death, he would only provide the translation once all the artifacts were in one person's possession.

IL DILUVIO (THE FLOOD)

Rambaldi imagined a moment when the world would be cleansed and when everything would begin anew. Il Diluvio was the ultimate Rambaldi manuscript containing the application for Rambaldi's formula for re-engineering the evolution of the human species. Some believe that the plan dealt with changing human nature itself and vanquishing "evil" for the ascendancy of "good." Adding the formula containing the rare Lady Slipper Orchid to a water supply would cause the brain chemistries of all who drank the water to alter to expand humanity's capacity for qualities like empathy and harmonic coexistence.

In the wrong hands, the formula, in combination with a huge version of the aforementioned Muller Device could trigger mass violence and aggression. Some believed that this was Rambaldi's ultimate goal: to see how humanity reasserted itself after the end of civilization as it was known.

Elena Derevko attempted to see out that dream, beginning her work in Sovogda, Russia, and creating the situation in which the Chosen One and the Passenger faced off. As Rambaldi wrote: "When blood red horses wander the streets and angels fall from the sky, the Chosen One and the Passenger will clash . . . and only one will survive."

The prophecy did not reach full fruition since Sloane intervened. Nadia—the Passenger—was infected by the altered water supply. She was about to kill the Chosen One—Sydney—when Sloane shot his daughter to stop her. The wound did not kill her, but Nadia was being kept under sedation until a cure could be found.

In the end Sydney did fulfill her personal prophecy as the Chosen One by taking down the "greatest power" and saving the world.

NOTED RAMBALDI EXPERTS

GIOVANNI DONATO

The only known person to have collaborated with Milo Rambaldi, Giovanni Donato, was believed to have died in 1503. However, Rambaldi was rumored to have made him a promise that he would live an impossibly long life and even revealed to him the date of his foretold death. A man by the same name was located recently and thought to be a descendant of the famed clockmaker. When Sydney brought the clock to him, Donato fixed it and then uttered the words, "The clock is fixed. Now it's over." He was then shot and killed. Some believe that this was the original Giovanni Donato, living out Rambaldi's prophecy. Deceased.

CONRAD

A westerner living with Nepalese monks, Conrad initiated Sloane's Rambaldi quest thirty years earlier. He later helped guide Sloane to the next phase of his journey following Emily's death. Conrad was killed while attempting to escape from Sark. As he lay dying, he revealed to Sydney that the Passenger was her sister. Deceased.

ANDRIAN LAZAREY

Member of the Romanov family and absent father to Julian Sark, Lazarey was a notable Rambaldi expert whom the Covenant wanted dead. (He also served as a contact for CIA analyst Will Tippin under the name St. Aidan.) Sydney, acting under the alias of Julia Thorne, informed him of the Covenant's plans to have him offed. Together they staged his death and began working with each other to locate the cube containing Rambaldi's DNA. When they finally found the cube, his hand was caught in a trap. Julia had to cut it off so he could free himself before he was killed by a cave-in. He was later abducted and tortured by his son and eventually assassinated. Deceased.

DR. VIADRO

Doctor for Nadia Santos, who was tortured to give up the location of the Passenger. He attempted to shoot Sydney to protect the Passenger, but was shot by Vaughn first. Deceased.

TOSHIRO TAKENADA

A wealthy collector from Kyoto.

ANFRENE DAUSSAULT 'NGUMBE

A dilettante with far more money than vision (according to Sloane).

LAZLO DRAKE

Former Professor of European history specializing in the Renaissance. He built his reputation on the discovery of the Vade Mecum, a manuscript that basically described how Rambaldi's creations were to be assembled to bring forth his final prophecy. Drake was the self-appointed gatekeeper of the instruction booklet for Rambaldi's endgame, until Elena Derevko murdered him and took the text. Deceased.

THE TRUST

A secret government organization interested in Rambaldi artifacts and responsible for Sloane's pardon.

SENATOR GEORGE REED

Senator from Virginia and member of the Intelligence Committee. He was part of the team that secretly brokered a deal with Sloane, saving him from prosecution in exchange for Rambaldi artifacts and information. Married to Olivia and father of Lauren, he was unaware that both were members of the Covenant. Senator Reed attempted to cover up for Lauren's activities when he found out, hoping to make up for years of neglect. Unbeknownst to the senator, his daughter had come to kill him but could not pull the trigger. His wife, Olivia, did the work instead. His death was initially ruled a suicide, as planted evidence pointed to him being a Covenant mole. Deceased.

MARLON BELL

Director of the Department of Justice, who oversaw the execution of Arvin Sloane.

For more information on notable Rambaldi experts, see: *Department of Special Research, page 52; Arvin Sloane, page 20*; and *Irina Derevko, page 58*.

MISSION ARCHIVES

OBJECTIVE: Identify and obtain the Muller Device

Arvin Sloane opened his mission brief reporting the death of Oskar Muller, a man considered by many to be a modern-day alchemist. In the month following his passing, there was great interest among the multinational intelligence organizations in recovering Muller's notebooks and experiments. None were found.

Antonio Quintero, a mole in FTL (a Chinese intelligence organization) had made contact with SD-6 two weeks earlier providing information that one of Muller's plans had surfaced. It was at the Cultural Affairs building in Taipei (a known FTL cover station). Quintero uplinked the plans to SD-6. The plans were written in Demotic, a simplified form of Egyptian hieratic writing. A brush pass was then scheduled for Quintero to provide the actual plans, but the agent did not show. It was assumed that his cover had been compromised.

The mission objective was to case the east wing of the Cultural Affairs building based on Quintero's notes, locate the lab where the plans were being held, and return to SD-6 with the information. There was no plan for retrieval at the time due to the risk following the loss of Quintero.

Agents Sydney Bristow and Marcus Dixon went in, disguised as guests at a party in the Cultural Affairs building annex. Dixon faked a collapse to create a disturbance while Sydney sneaked past guards into an unauthorized section. She searched the building and confirmed the existence and location of the plans. Upon Sydney's return to the party, a man wearing a suit and glasses discovered her coming out of the unauthorized section. He demanded an explanation. Sydney broke into tears, claiming that she was simply looking for a bathroom and didn't want to get in trouble with her boss for being in the wrong place. The man let her go.

This was the final mission Sydney Bristow undertook while still believing that SD-6 was a branch of the CIA. Prior to the mission Sydney had told her fiancé, Danny, that she was a CIA operative. He did not react well to the news that she had been keeping such a huge secret. As he was trying to cope with the truth, Danny left a drunken message on her answering machine while she was on her mission. SD-6 Security Section picked up the message and, under the direction of Arvin Sloane, hired a freelance assassin to take care of the breach.

Sydney returned home to find that Danny had been murdered. His bloodied body had been left in their bathtub.

LOCATION: Taipei, Taiwan
ALIAS: Employee of Modira Plastics

UNAUTHORIZED MISSION J535-B:

At first Sydney refused to return to SD-6 following Danny's death, until she realized that her decision had put her life in danger. Arvin Sloane would not allow someone with her clearance to ever leave the organization. Knowing that she now needed to prove her continued allegiance to SD-6, Sydney took on the personal mission to retrieve the Muller Device as the first part of a larger plan.

Sydney contacted her friend Will Tippin, asking to borrow his sister's passport and a credit card, unable to explain to him that she was planning to expense a flight back to Taipei. She took that trip under the guise of Amy Tippen so that SD-6 could not track her. Sydney infiltrated the Cultural Affairs building by scaling the wall and entering through an airshaft. Once inside, she was captured and tortured for information by the man in the suit and glasses whom she had run into during her first visit to the embassy.

Sydney managed to escape the torturer and retrieved the Muller Device. The item was a metal arm with a floating red ball that turned to liquid when the device was deactivated. She fought her way past security and fled the building.

Sydney returned to SD-6, dropping the Muller Device on Sloane's desk before requesting an additional week off for midterms. She then approached the CIA as a walk-in, offering to assist in the takedown of SD-6.

LOCATION: **Taipei, Taiwan**
ALIAS: **Amy Tippin**

OBJECTIVE: Locate and obtain Russian nuclear device

SD-6 MISSION E631-A:

SD-6 intercepted an internal memo from GRU (Russia's military intelligence agency) headquarters indicating that several files pertaining to the Soviet-American nuclear arsenal during the Cold War were missing. Further intel indicated that Kazimir Shcherbakov and Luri Karpachev—two mid-level administrators at the CRC in Moscow—were planning to sell unidentified documents to Abul-Hasayn Navor, a military attaché from Sudan. Based on the timing of the meet, it was assumed that those documents were the stolen files. Sydney and Dixon were tasked with preventing the transaction and retrieving the stolen files.

The meet was scheduled at the Banya Club in Moscow. Dixon went in impersonating Navor, to conduct the meet and secure the files. Meanwhile, Sydney, in the guise of a hotel maid, broke into Navor's hotel room in the Bryusov Gazetny Hotel to intercept the money intended for the buy.

Sydney took out Navor's guard with a sedative and found the case with the money. As she opened it, another of Navor's guards entered the room. Sydney flung the open briefcase at him and the pair fought. Sydney took out the guard, but Navor interrupted when he heard the commotion. He was quickly dispatched with a second sedative.

As the dust settled, Sydney noticed that something was wrong. The money that had fallen out of the case was fake: What had appeared to be piles of francs were actually stacks of white paper with a single franc note on top. The meet was a setup.

With no money for the exchange, Sydney shifted gears by stripping into a second alias in a tight blue party dress. She went to the Banya Club, where she saw Dixon—posing as Navor—in negotiaions with the Russian men. Because they did not have the payoff, Sydney and Dixon attempted to switch the disks in a brush pass. The pass was a success, but Dixon's cover was blown in the process. He and Sydney had to fight their way out of the club.

CIA COUNTERMISSION:

Sydney carried out the SD-6 assignment and retrieved the disk, then performed two brush passes at the airport. The first one was done at the gate, where she passed the disk to her handler, Agent Vaughn. He took the disk into a back room, where it was duplicated. The duplication process took longer than expected, and Vaughn was worried that they would not make it for the second pass. As soon as the disk was ejected, he hurried through the airport, making the final switch at the airport curb moments before Sydney rode away. She had successfully made her first dent in the strength of SD-6.

LOCATION: **Moscow, Russia**
ALIASES: **Maid at the Bryusov Gazetny Hotel;**
   club patron at the Banya Club

SD-6 MISSION E631-B:

The disks obtained in Russia referred to Doomsday Six, an operation during the Cold War wherein six fully armed nuclear missiles were smuggled into and buried in the United States. In December 1989 information on the operation was disclosed to the U.S. government and the bombs were promptly recovered.

Information retrieved from the disk once it was decrypted revealed that there was a seventh missile that had remained undisclosed. SD-6 linked the missile to a man named Milovich Ivanov in Buckingham, Virginia. Sydney was sent to that location to find Ivanov. Instead she found his grave. A patch of dead grass covering the plot indicated that there was something other than a body lying below.

Sydney dug up the grave using a shovel stolen from the caretaker's shed. There was no body inside the casket, though. It was the seventh nuclear device. And it had been activated when she opened the box.

With only two minutes to disarm the device, Sydney reacted purely on instinct. Instead of contacting the CIA, she frantically called the one person she knew could help: Marshall Flinkman, SD-6's head of op tech engineering. With his help she was able to disconnect the timer with eleven seconds to spare.

CIA COUNTERMISSION:

Sydney was instructed to sabotage the SD-6 mission by falsifying her report, indicating that she had failed to locate the device. When she contacted Marshall for help in disarming the detonator, she failed in her countermission objective. Vaughn was angry over the break in protocol, but Sydney insisted that she had no alternative in the time allotted and convinced him to let her get the nuke back from SD-6. Vaughn informed Sydney that SD-6 had sold the device to arms dealer Ineni Hassan, and Sydney was sent to retrieve it.

As she had previously met Hassan on business through SD-6, Sydney broke into his facility in Cairo under a burka that obscured her identity. She retrieved the plutonium core from the device. The delicate radioactive material was in her hand when she heard a gun cocked by her ear. It was Hassan.

Knowing she was as good as dead, Sydney flung the core into the air, distracting Hassan so she could take him out. She tore the gun from his hand, cracked him in the skull, and caught the core in midair as Hassan fell. She then escaped the facility with the core.

To facilitate their undercover work, Jack Bristow informed Sloane that he had told Sydney he worked for SD-6. Once that part was public, Jack then covered for Sydney while she was away in Cairo. He told Sloane that she was having trouble adjusting to the fact that her father had secretly been part of the organization the entire time she worked there. It wasn't entirely a lie.

LOCATIONS: **Buckingham, Virginia, USA;**
   Cairo, Egypt
ALIAS: **Woman in burka (CIA countermission)**

OBJECTIVE: Locate the Sol d'Oro Rambaldi artifact

SD-6 MISSION E632-A:

Sloane had been negotiating with Eduardo Benegas to purchase a Rambaldi sketch when Benegas suddenly withdrew the piece without explanation. Considering SD-6's interest in the works of Milo Rambaldi (and specifically, Sloane's interest as well), Sydney and Dixon were sent in to retrieve the sketch. It was believed to have a message written in a Rambaldi version of machine code—an electronic language that did not exist in Rambaldi's time.

The sketch was secured in a lockbox in a vault at Benegas's Madrid auto museum. K-Directorate was in possession of the key to that lockbox after their operative—and Sydney's personal enemy— Anna Espinosa had stolen it. Sydney was concerned to hear that Anna was also on the case.

Sydney and Dixon attended an event at the auto museum posing as guests. Dixon placed a sonic wave emitter on a glass display, causing it to shatter, while Sydney slipped out of the gallery during the disturbance. She first went to bypass the security cameras, where she discovered that Anna Espinosa had beaten her to it. Sydney piggybacked on K-Directorate's signal and braced herself for the inevitable confrontation with her enemy.

Sydney reached the vault first, but K-Directorate jammed the frequency on her

lock descrambler. Sydney could only stand by and watch as Anna took the lockbox. Dixon terminated the jamming signal so she could follow Anna out of the building. After a violent fight, Anna made her escape by climbing a ladder up the side of the building. As she was about to hit the roof and be gone for good, Sydney squeezed off a single shot from Dixon's gun. She hit the strap of Anna's carrying case, tearing it away and dropping the lockbox at Sydney's feet.

CIA COUNTERMISSION:

Agent Vaughn had the CIA station chief in Barcelona prepped for a dead drop of the code. As a backup plan Sydney would encrypt the code on a Radiohead MP3 and download it on audio galaxy. Since the lockbox was impossible to open, Sydney could not carry out either countermission.

LOCATION: **Madrid, Spain**
ALIAS: **Auto show attendee**

SD-6 MISSION E632-B:

The lockbox retrieved from Madrid was rigged to destroy the document inside if it was opened by anything other than the key that was in K-Directorate's possession. Seemingly at an impasse, Jack Bristow was brought in for his expertise in game theory. Sydney wanted to infiltrate K-Directorate, but Jack noted that every scenario along those lines was too dangerous for his daughter. Instead he suggested a safer course of action that put Sydney once again face-to-face with her sworn enemy. Sydney and Anna were scheduled to meet in a stadium in Berlin to bring the case together with the key and open the box jointly.

The stadium was divided down the middle under tight security by both SD-6 and K-Directorate. If either agent deviated from the game plan, she would immediately be taken out. Sydney and Anna were instructed to open the case, read the code, and exit without further action.

Sydney and Anna both entered the stadium and met in the middle of the field. Together they opened the case. Inside, acid immediately began pouring onto the page as a fail-safe. They had only moments to memorize the code before it disintegrated. Sydney quickly set to committing the long code to memory. It was assumed that Espinosa was able to do the same.

CIA COUNTERMISSION:

Due to the high-profile nature of their work, Vaughn was relieved as Sydney's handler in exchange for a more senior officer: Agent Lambert. Lambert's first instruction was for Sydney to plant a tracking device on Anna during the meet. Sydney refused, as she considered it a ridiculously risky op. The meeting was orchestrated under incredibly tight security. Attempting to plant a bug on Anna would put Sydney's cover—and her life—in jeopardy. Due to Lambert's ill-advised plan, combined with his condescending attitude and careless protocols, Sydney insisted that if Vaughn was not on the other end of her earpiece by the time of the meet, she would give the CIA nothing.

As Sydney prepped for the meet, she confirmed that the newly promoted Vaughn was watching via satellite from a two-hundred-mile orbit above. Once the code was obtained, Sydney went radio silent on Dixon and gave the code to the CIA.

LOCATION: **Berlin, Germany**
ALIAS: **None**

SD-6 MISSION E633-A:

Using the coordinates translated from the code on the Rambaldi sketch, SD-6 sent in a team to Athens. Those coordinates turned out to be a false lead that K-Directorate also followed. At least the mission had been successful at confirming that Anna had also memorized the code.

It was later determined that the code was written in a compression scheme. Once the code was decrypted taking the scheme into account, the coordinates revealed a different destination. Sydney was sent to a five-hundred-year-old church in Malaga, Spain, to obtain an artifact known as the Sol d'Oro (Golden Sun). The object, a glass disk, was hidden in a stained-glass window.

As Sydney secured the disk, she turned to find Anna Espinosa beside her. They fought for the disk. At first Anna got the upper hand, promising to give Sydney a painless death. But Sydney managed to turn the tables and fight Anna off. Sydney took the disk, leaving Anna alive and handcuffed to a rail in the church, much like Anna had left Sydney in a mosque a year earlier.

The disk was taken to SD-6, where it was analyzed. Marshall reported that, incredibly, it was made of synthetic polymers roughly five hundred years before their invention.

LOCATION: **Malaga, Spain**
ALIAS: **None**

OBJECTIVE: Provide protection for humanitarian Dhiren Patel

SD-6 MISSION E633-B:

SD-6 received intel indicating that Luc Jacqnoud of the group Zero Defense was planning an attack on the United Commerce Organization (UCO) Ministerial Conference in São Paolo. Sydney and Dixon were sent to Morocco to monitor a meeting between Jacqnoud and an unknown client. Their objective was to identify the client and prevent any transaction from taking place.

Upon landing in Morocco they connected with SD-6 agent Mokhtat Hammouda. Since Jacqnoud's meet was scheduled to take place in a local marketplace, Sydney went in disguised as a shopper. She used a parabolic microphone to record the conversation while Dixon and Hammouda observed over video monitor, attempting to ID the client. Sydney was forced to abort when she recognized one of the guards from a previous mission.

The guard eventually recognized Sydney as well and gave chase while his partners discovered the mission base. Sydney and Dixon managed to escape, but Agent Hammouda was killed in action. Sydney had a difficult time accepting the fact that a good man had died unaware of the fact that he was actually working for the wrong side.

Jacqnoud's client was later identified as Malik Sawari, an industrial demolition specialist. His latest creation was the BLU-250, an explosive commissioned by a Swiss corporation to blow out mountain ranges for the production of high-speed trains. During the meeting the men noted that Dhiren Patel was going to be the "delivery man." This seemed impossible, since Patel was winner of the Edgar Peace Prize and one of the world's foremost humanitarians.

CIA COUNTERMISSION:

Sydney shared the information obtained from the meeting and sought counsel from Vaughn to deal with Hammouda's death. He told her never to allow the resentment of her work to overwhelm her. And that if she ever needed him, she had his number.

LOCATION: **Morocco**
ALIAS: **Kate Jones, traveling with Mindspring**
    Learning Tours

SD-6 MISSION E633-C:

Based on the information obtained during surveillance of the meet between Jacqnoud and Sawari, it was assumed that noted humanitarian Dhiren Patel could not possibly know that he was assigned to be the "delivery man." Zero Defense was obviously planning to send a message to the UCO Conference by way of a bomb planted on Patel somehow. Sydney and Dixon were tasked to locate Patel, recover the weapon, and safeguard the UCO.

In São Paolo, Patel was drugged and openly kidnapped in front of the entire conference. Only Sydney and Dixon realized what was going on, because the kidnappers carried an unconscious Patel out on a gurney, loading him into an ambulance. Sydney followed the ambulance to a warehouse. She watched as the bomb was surgically implanted in his body.

Sydney was made by the same guard who had recognized her in Morocco. She was forced to flee the building without Patel. The humanitarian was returned to the conference, unaware that he had a bomb inside his body.

Dixon kidnapped Patel while Sydney stole another ambulance with the proper equipment to conduct an unscheduled emergency surgery. Dixon carefully cut into Patel to remove the bomb as Jacqnoud chased them through the streets of São Paolo. Since the bomb was on a remote, Sydney needed to keep distance between Jacqnoud's vehicle and Patel. Once the bomb was removed, Dixon threw it out of the ambulance. It exploded under Jacqnoud's car.

CIA COUNTERMISSION:

It was assumed that SD-6 has no interest in safeguarding the conference and that there was an ulterior motive to its plan. Sydney was under instruction to identify the minister member that SD-6 was really trying to protect, presuming that he was an Alliance operative. Events prevented her from obtaining the identification.

LOCATION: **São Paulo, Brazil**
ALIAS: **Conference attendee**

OBJECTIVE: Obtain prototypes of the Hensel vaccine

SD-6 MISSION E634-A:

Jeroen Schiller, a leading biotech engineer with Hcnscl Corporation in Berlin, had been in communication with SD-6 for two months. He was willing to trade information on Hensel's development of a vaccine capable of resisting all biological weapons in exchange for safe passage into the United States. Sydney and Dixon were instructed to find Schiller and download the vaccine formula from Hensel's computers. Since the last documented photo of Schiller was taken in 1975, SD-6 had tech perform an age progression on the photo to give them an idea of what Schiller might look like today.

Sydney entered the offices of Hensel Corp. and located Schiller. She immediately downloaded the information from his password-protected computer and handed him a gas mask. Knowing they could not get Schiller out unnoticed under the building video surveillance, Dixon then administered a tranquilizing gas through the Hensel Corp. to knock out anyone who could stop them.

CIA COUNTERMISSION:

The CIA asked Sydney to perform a switch with Schiller and turn CIA agent Paul Kelvin over to SD-6 in his place. Due to the high-risk nature of this switch, she requested permission to inform her SD-6 partner, Marcus Dixon, of the truth behind the organization and her double agent status. The request was denied.

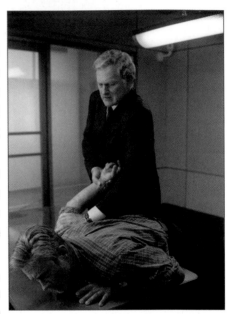

Since she could not bring Dixon into the loop, Sydney was forced to adjust their mission. She changed the rendezvous point with Dixon, explaining that she was being followed. As Dixon moved to the new meeting point, Sydney made the switch.

Kelvin, under the guise of Schiller, was brought to SD-6, while the real Schiller was taken to a CIA safe house. Kelvin then gave SD-6 access to a Web site with some information on the vaccine. Once SD-6 downloaded and ran the programs from the site, they also downloaded a worm into the SD-6 mainframe, giving the CIA backdoor access to the entire system. In the meantime CIA questioning of the actual Schiller was not going as planned. The man refused to speak to anyone other than Arvin Sloane.

Vaughn tried to convince Schiller that Sloane was a fraud, but the man refused to believe he was currently in CIA custody. In desperation, it seemed the only way to convince him was to fly him to Langley. But events at SD-6 indicated that Kelvin did not have time for the CIA to do that.

Agent Kelvin came under suspicion because he could not tell Sloane the location of the lab where prototype inhalers were being manufactured. Sloane was going to have Jack force the information from the man, even though Jack knew Kelvin had no idea of the answer. It was only after Sydney laid out the situation— and told her personal story—to Schiller that he agreed to cooperate.

She fed the information to her father, which he in turn gave to his friend, Kelvin. To make the situation believable, Jack had to torture his friend to make it look like "Schiller" was reluctantly giving up the information when Kelvin repeated the location back to Jack.

LOCATION: **Berlin, Germany**
ALIAS: **Rhine-Kom computer specialist**

SD-6 MISSION E634-B:

Information collected by SD-6 in conjunction with information obtained from Schiller revealed that the vaccine had been perfected and was being manufactured into inhalers at a plant in Badenweiler. Sydney and Dixon were sent to break into the plant, steal the inhalers, and blow up the building. According to Sloane, Hensel was producing supplies for a neo-Nazi terrorist faction. This was only a cover story to justify their actions. As far as SD-6 was concerned, the mission was a success.

CIA COUNTERMISSION:

While in the building, Sydney swapped out the real inhalers with fakes. She then met up with a CIA commando team to give them the real ones. The head of the team, Logan, was already impressed with Sydney, as he had heard good things about her from Vaughn. Following their brief exchange, Sydney went to defuse the bomb that Dixon had planted. Believing they were safe from harm, the CIA team stayed behind to hack into the facility's computers and investigate what other projects Hensel had in development.

After she disarmed the bomb, Sydney rendezvoused with Dixon, intending to leave the area once the bomb "malfunctioned." She was not aware of the fact that Dixon had rigged a secondary detonator. When the explosion did not occur, Dixon activated the second trigger and blew up the building. Logan and three other operatives died in the explosion.

LOCATION: **Badenweiler, Germany**
ALIAS: **None**

OBJECTIVE: Obtain a Rambaldi manuscript

While investigating former FTL sites, an SD-6 recovery team found a musical birthday card left behind by the Chinese organization. Later a similar musical card was found at another recently abandoned FTL station. Analysis studied the music samples and found an identical pattern of numbers buried in the higher frequencies. It was believed to be a code.

Determined to crack the code, Sloane ordered an SD-6 commando team to storm an FTL ship that was carrying plans for their latest code machine. From information gathered on the ship, SD-6 discovered that there were only eight machines in existence that could read the code buried in the music.

One of the devices was located at the Hobbes End Gallery in London. The owner, John Smythe, was an affiliate of FTL. Sydney and Dixon were sent in, posing as a French couple looking to buy art. Dixon kept Smythe busy with a tantalizing offer to purchase the entire showing, while Sydney broke into his office to steal the code machine. As she left the office, Sydney tripped the motion sensor, alerting security. Dixon could only watch as a guard left the gallery for Smythe's office.

Trapped in a hallway, Sydney took the only escape route open to her. She lifted herself up into the pipes in the ceiling and hung a few feet above the guard as he made a sweep. One of the hot pipes Sydney was holding began to scald her hand, forcing her to carefully shift to another pipe while the guard was still in the hall. Once he finally moved past, she dropped to the floor and returned to Dixon with the small code machine in her purse.

CIA COUNTERMISSION:

While in Smythe's office, Sydney planted a passive listening device. To avoid detection, the bug would work only when hit with a beam from an orbital satellite. She then delivered the code machine to SD-6 with the intention that the CIA would later take any information it provided off the SD-6 network server, using their tap into the system.

LOCATION: **London, England**
ALIAS: **Wife of a wealthy Frenchman**

SD-6 analysis determined that the decoder stolen from John Smythe created encryptions based on a DNA sequence. Since the birthday cards were addressed to the recently deceased leader of the FTL cell in Rabat, Gareth Parkashoff, the codes were believed to be based on his DNA. But only one person knew the location of Parkashoff's body: Martin Shepard, the assassin who killed Parkashoff. At the time, Shepard was locked down in a mental institution in Budapest.

Martin Shepard was a freelance agent who had been programmed to kill on command and forget the details afterward. In fact, he wasn't even aware of the fact that he was an assassin. But the programming was breaking down, and Shepard was starting to see images of his crimes.

Not knowing what was happening to him, he checked himself into the Mangalev Asylum. Sydney was teamed with SD-6 agent Gregory Fisher, who posed as a doctor admitting her into the sanitarium. They were both unaware that K-Directorate also had agents in the asylum under the leadership of a Dr. Kreshnik.

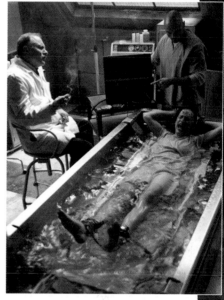

While Sydney made initial contact with Shepard, Dr. Kreshnik killed Fisher. He then tortured Sydney, hoping to learn if she had extracted the location of Parkashoff's body from Shepard. Sydney was forced to feign an alliance with Kreshnik so he would set her free to continue building her relationship with the unstable Shepard.

Ultimately, she was able to break through Shepard's programming. But the man was hardly prepared to accept the truth. Sydney helped him deal with the revelation and the pair escaped the asylum. Shepard gave her the location of Parkashoff's body and Sydney got him to a CIA safe house, while reporting to SD-6 that he had died during their escape.

CIA COUNTERMISSION:

Sydney relayed the information to SD-6, and once they translated the code, she reported their findings to the CIA.

While in a safe house, Shepard admitted to Sydney why he had come to recognize her. He was the assassin hired by SD-6 to kill her fiancé, Danny Hecht. Sydney was jolted by the news, but she could not really blame Shepard, since he had no control over his actions.

Sydney helped him go into hiding while lying to SD-6 about his death. She was then left to deal with what she had learned.

LOCATION: **Bucharest, Romania**
ALIAS: **Asylum patient, Miss DiCamillo**

SD-6 MISSION E636:

Using Parkashoff's DNA, SD-6 decoded the FTL message and learned of a Rambaldi artifact dig taking place in Tunisia. An SD-6 advance team was sent in for recon, but FTL had already recovered the object and sent it for analysis to the Department of Engineering Science at Oxford University. It was assumed that FTL had no idea they had found a Rambaldi artifact, since they sent it to civilians for analysis.

Sydney went undercover, attending a reception at the university as FTL agents were posing as security guards. She was surprised to find that Anna Espinosa, from K-Directorate, was also in attendance. They were both going after the artifact.

Sydney told Dixon to contact university security to let them know someone was trying to break into the lab, knowing it would also alert FTL. Even though it put Sydney's mission in jeopardy, she had to make sure Anna did not get the artifact. Sydney reached the lab first and shorted out the lock so Anna would not be able to enter after her. The K-Directorate operative could only watch through the bullet-proof glass as Sydney made off with the artifact: a five-hundred-year-old clock.

LOCATION: **Oxford, England**
ALIAS: **Molly Zerdin, scout for the Rubin Institute
  looking for grant candidates**

SD-6 MISSION E637-A:

Initials found on the Rambaldi clock indicated that it was built by a clockmaker named Giovanni Donato. He was believed to be the only man who ever collaborated with Rambaldi. Since the clock did not work, Sydney was instructed to take the device to a clockmaker, who was assumed to be a descendant of the original Donato. During the course of the mission it became evident that there was a possibility—no matter how improbable—that the man she went to see was the original Giovanni Donato.

Donato was able to get the clock working again, but it required another piece to reveal its true purpose. As they were wrapping up, Donato was shot and killed. The bullet had been meant for Sydney.

Anna Espinosa and K-Directorate operatives had arrived to take the clock, but Sydney managed to get away with it.

LOCATION: **Mexico City, Mexico**
ALIAS: **Christina Auriti with Auriti Antiquities**

SD-6 MISSION E637-B:

Marshall Flinkman concluded that the Sol d'Oro (Mission E633-A) and the Rambaldi clock worked together to display astronomical coordinates. Those coordinates, in conjunction with the date inscribed on the back of the clock, directed SD-6 to Mount Aconcagua in the Andes Mountains.

Sydney and Dixon were dispatched to the coordinates to dig for a Rambaldi artifact. Before they left, Dixon pulled Sydney aside to let her know how proud he was of her. He wanted her to know that he was impressed by the courage she displayed in her commitment to returning to the job after Danny's death. And once again Sydney was reminded that she was keeping the truth about SD-6 from her partner and close friend.

At the coordinates, they found a hatch bearing the Rambaldi eye symbol. It opened into a pit where a Rambaldi manuscript had been stored. Due to interference from the surrounding mountains, they were cut off from communication with SD-6. Sydney descended into the pit and found the manuscript when Dixon warned her over the communicator that they had company. He started to tell her to get out of the pit, but his words were cut off by gunfire. The next thing she heard over her headset was the voice of Anna Espinosa.

Sydney tried to race out of the tunnels, but Anna intercepted her. The two fought as Sydney attempted to scale the long ladder up out of the pit. Anna managed to overpower Sydney, taking the manuscript and dropping Sydney down into the pit below. When Sydney revived, she ascended the

ladder to find that the K-Directorate operatives had left Dixon behind, bullet-ridden and dying.

CIA COUNTER MISSION:

Sydney was instructed to photograph the artifact using a still camera with digital signal uplink to a geosynchronous keyhole satellite, but Anna interrupted before Sydney could complete the mission.

(continued on page 114)

Arvin Sloane first became suspicious of the Bristows when Jack began to cover for Sydney while she was on missions for the CIA. Her behavior had changed during her SD-6 missions as well. He questioned her for moving a pickup point during the mission to retrieve Jeroen Schiller from Hensel Corporation. The suspicion only intensified when Schiller proved to be evasive with his answers. Of course, Sloane was unaware that "Schiller" was actually a CIA operative and a friend to Jack. Though suspicious of Sydney's actions, Sloane was reluctant to believe that she would ever betray him.

When Marshall discovered a bandwidth leak in the SD-6 computer system, Sloane told him it was only a drill. In reality, Sloane was concerned by the leak and what it indicated. He confirmed that it was an intentional leak and suspected there may be a mole at SD-6. Alliance leader Alain Christophe suggested that there might be more than one.

At the time, Sydney realized that she was being followed and confronted Sloane, who explained that it was simply a result of stepped-up security. Sloane then brought in Karl Dryer to perform a functional imaging test on Sydney. The test monitored variations like blood flow inside the brain. It was far more difficult to deceive than a standard lie-detector test.

Vaughn had to help her prepare for the test and she passed. However, Dryer was still suspicious. He told Sloane that Sydney's responses were too perfect. Dryer threatened to go to the Alliance with his suspicions that Sydney was the mole, but Sloane defended her.

Sloane then set up another test, sending instructions to have Sydney killed when she made a dead drop in Denati Park. The information was intentionally sent over the bugged server. If Sydney were to be pulled out before the drop, it would have indicated that she was working with whoever intercepted the information. Jack realized the intel was a trap and told the CIA to hold back as Sydney made the drop. Vaughn was upset over the risk to Sydney's life based solely on Jack's instincts. But Jack insisted there was a greater risk in acting rashly.

Sydney made the drop without incident, but Dryer was still suspicious. He was also concerned because Sloane's plan would have revealed Sydney as the mole, but it also provided a means for her to escape unharmed.

After learning from Vaughn about the save at Denati Park, Sydney thought she was in the clear . . . until SD-6 took her into custody and threw her in a holding cell. During a recent mission in Geneva, SD-6 had picked up an extra comm signal. It was the one she used to contact the CIA to share intel. Though they could not pick up the voices on the signal, the mere fact that it existed was enough to prove that she was working with another agency.

Sloane had Agent Anthony Russek sent into the cell to try to get Sydney to confess to being the mole. She refused to say anything, even when Russek told her his own family was threatened because he had been on the Geneva mission with her. As she was about to be taken for torture to extract the information, Sloane suddenly released her.

Sydney later learned that Jack had manipulated Marshall to go into the SD-6 server to check something for him. Jack had previously accessed the server to provide falsified information indicating that Russek was the mole. Marshall brought the information to Sloane as Jack had planned. As a result, Sydney's name was cleared . . . but Russek was killed.

Though Sydney was relieved to be in the clear, she was upset to learn the lengths to which her father had gone to save her. Even though Russek was one of the few agents who knew the truth behind SD-6, it did not make the situation any easier to handle. And it added a new strain in Sydney's relationship with her father.

(continued from page 111)

With Dixon near death and no way to communicate with SD-6, Sydney was forced to risk her cover to save her friend. She used the uplink to call for a CIA extraction. As she said her call sign, "Freelancer," into the communicator, Dixon stirred. He again lost consciousness, with Sydney unaware of whether or not she had been compromised.

LOCATION: **Argentina**
ALIAS: **None**

OBJECTIVE: Locate Ineni Hassan and obtain "the Package"

SD-6 MISSION E638-A:

The U.S. government had recently frozen the funds of international arms dealer Ineni Hassan. In response, Hassan hired men to stage a bank robbery with the real purpose of transferring his money so he could access it. These events indicated to SD-6 that Hassan was no longer willing to work with the government and planned to become an illegal arms dealer. At least that was Sloane's story.

In truth, this mission was payback in response to a misunderstanding Sydney had unwittingly orchestrated. Believing that Sydney was a disguised operative working for SD-6 when she stole the plutonium core from the Russian nuclear missile in Mission E631-B, Hassan later sold ten Stinger aircraft missiles to SD-6 so they could fortify their base in Oman. Hassan took the money but failed to deliver. SD-6 wanted to steal the money back to send a message to all their business associates.

Sydney was tasked to infiltrate a party thrown by Hassan's accountant, Logan Gerace, and steal Hassan's offshore account number, then dead drop the information at Denati Park. With Dixon still in the hospital, Sydney went in alone. She parachuted onto the grounds of Gerace's villa and crashed the party. Even though she was not on the guest list, Sydney was able to make her way through the guests and collect Gerace's fingerprint off a glass. The alarm system was biometric, and his fingerprint would access the system for her. She then entered his study and downloaded the information off his computer. Once she left the party, Sydney made the drop at Denati Park, unaware that her life was potentially in grave danger (see: *File Insert, SD-6 Mole Hunt,* page 112).

CIA COUNTERMISSION:

The CIA wanted to bring Hassan to justice as well as having SD-6 get his money. Sydney was told to share the account number with both SD-6 and the CIA, so the CIA could tag the accounts and see how SD-6 spent the money.

LOCATION: **Tuscany, Italy**
ALIAS: **Guest at Gerace's party**

SD-6 MISSION E638-B:

Information taken from Gerace's computer did not reveal Hassan's account number, but it did lead SD-6 to a safety-deposit box in a Geneva bank that held that information. Because Dixon was still recovering, Sydney was sent in to infiltrate the bank with Agent Anthony Russek. While Russek listened in from a surveillance van, Sydney obtained access to the safety-deposit boxes while under an alias. Then she tranquilized the bank employee, broke into the box, and retrieved the account number: D6135C7E.

CIA COUNTERMISSION:

Using a CIA transmitter along with her SD-6 link to Agent Russek, she read the account number to SD-6 and the CIA simultaneously. She did this unaware that SD-6 picked up the piggybacked signal, throwing her cover into jeopardy.

LOCATION: **Geneva, Switzerland**
ALIAS: **Christiana Stephens from
    Dryburgh Diamonds**

SD-6 MISSION E639-A:

Using Hassan's account number, SD-6 seized most of his assets and effectively smoked him out of hiding. Signal intelligence picked up a number of communications originating from a private resort island off the coast of Kenya.

Steven Driscoll, a former UK military adviser turned self-employed ID forger, lived on that island. SD-6 suspected that Driscoll had created new documentation for Hassan. Sydney was sent to find Driscoll and ascertain Hassan's new identity.

CIA COUNTERMISSION:

While on the island, she broke into Driscoll's room and discovered that Hassan had not only gotten a new identity (in the name of Nebseni Saad), but he had also undergone surgery to get a new face. She was instructed to share Hassan's identity with the CIA but tell SD-6 that the mission was a failure. Though she carried out the countermission, SD-6 later obtained the information from another source.

LOCATION: **Semba Island, Kenya**
ALIAS: **Victoria King, daughter of industrialist**
 Martin King

CIA MISSION E639-B:

Once SD-6 had the location of Ineni Hassan, Jack Bristow was sent in to kill the man. The CIA counter-manded his mission and charged him to fake Hassan's death and offer him a new ID in exchange for his client list. But the mission went south and Hassan's men took Jack prisoner.

Sydney asked for—and was given—permission to go in after her father. But as she infiltrated the grounds of Hassan's hideout, she was also taken prisoner.

Hassan, believing Sydney to simply be another SD-6 operative, ordered Jack to kill Sydney to prove his shifted loyalty. As Jack took aim with his gun, he managed to blink a Morse code message to his daughter. Together, Sydney and Jack overpowered the guards and took Hassan hostage. With his coerced assistance, they managed to escape the grounds. They brought Hassan to the CIA, after fak-ing evidence of his death for SD-6.

LOCATION: **Havana, Cuba**
ALIAS: **None**

SD-6 MISSION E640-A:

Believing Hassan to be dead, SD-6 tracked a flurry of activity from Hassan's second-in-command, Minos Sakkoulas. He was pre-sumably looking to take over Hassan's work. SD-6 intercepted a call indicating that Sakkoulas was planning to sell an arms device known as "the Package." Sakkoulas kept the specs on the Package in the vault of Club Panthera, his nightclub in Athens. Sydney was sent in to retrieve the specs from the club along with Dixon, who had recently recuperated and had no memory of Sydney using her "Freelancer" call sign on their earlier mission.

While Dixon accessed club security, Sydney made contact with Sakkoulas under the guise of wanting to work at his club, intending to get herself access to his office. However, Sakkoulas had other plans for the comely job applicant. He took her to his den to wait there while he met with a client, locking her in the room with a guard.

CIA COUNTERMISSION:

Sydney was tasked to scan the specs on the Package for the CIA and provide SD-6 with phony ones. When she failed to gain access to Sakkoulas's office, Dixon went in and retrieved the specs. Sydney took out the guard and went for the lock, insisting to Dixon that she could finish the job. But by the time she made it out of the office, Dixon was already downloading the information. She failed to scan the specs for the CIA.

LOCATION: **Athens, Greece**
ALIAS: **Potential club dancer**

CIA MISSION E640-B:

Following the failed countermission in Greece, Hassan informed the CIA that the Package (an EM refractor used to cloak missiles) was being held with his weapons stockpile in a silo in Crete. Sydney requested permission to go in and steal the device, since she had failed to obtain the information in Greece. Vaughn, however, was concerned with her going away on another undercover mission so soon after her trip to Cuba. It was too large a risk of her cover with SD-6.

To deal with any potential concerns from SD-6, Sydney had her father suggest the mission to Sloane. Acting as if he had learned the Crete information from a source, Jack fed the location to Sloane, who then tasked Sydney with the assignment. When she arrived at the silo, however, she learned that Hassan had double-crossed the CIA by supplying a false password that tripped an anti-intruder device. The room Sydney was in filled with gasoline. And a spark was set to ignite the room in exactly one minute.

Hassan offered to provide the code to disarm the fail-safe—for a price. He wanted his wife and son taken safely out of Argentina to join him in hiding. With his hand forced, Vaughn had CIA director

Devlin sign off on the deal. But when Sydney had the code, Sakkoulas interrupted. She fought past the man and took the Package moments before the gasoline ignited and blew up the building. Sakkoulas died in the explosion.

LOCATION: **Crete, Greece**
ALIAS: **None**

OBJECTIVE: Take back SD-6 from forces of the Man

SD-6 MISSION E641:

After recently finding out that her deceased mother was not the woman Sydney had always thought she was, Sydney had second thoughts about continuing her work with the CIA and SD-6. Her family history of spies, double agents, false loyalties, and a lifetime of secrets had grown to be too much. That, coupled with her growing feelings for Vaughn, led Sydney to make the decision that she was ready to quit SD-6 and the CIA. Little did she know that at the same time, events were conspiring against her to keep her in that life.

Commandos under the lead of former SD-6 operative McKenas Cole infiltrated the offices of SD-6 and took the agents hostage. Claiming to work for an unknown enemy called the Man, they attempted to break into the SD-6 vault to retrieve a Rambaldi artifact in the form of an ampoule of liquid. With the office in emergency fail-safe mode, anyone who tried to access the vault without the proper identification would set off four sets of C4 explosives, destroying all evidence of SD-6 and killing everyone inside.

At the time of the lockdown, Sydney and Jack were in the elevator to the subterranean offices, discussing her recent decision to resign. He was very much against the action, knowing it would endanger her life and the lives of her friends. Suddenly the elevator stopped. When no one answered the emergency phone, Jack knew they needed to get out of the elevator in a hurry. Under lockdown, the elevator would be recalled to SD-6 and open automatically. They would be caught inside.

Jack and Sydney escaped the elevator moments before it opened to Cole's men. Jack informed Sydney of the security precautions. They would have to manually disconnect the bombs themselves to ensure the safety of their friends and coworkers.

To stop the bombs and slow Cole, they needed equipment from Marshall's workshop. As they obtained the materials and set about their plan, Cole realized there was someone in the building working against him. Jack was forced to reveal himself so Sydney could continue. Luckily, she wouldn't be alone for long.

Thinking the CIA would intervene, Dixon sent a message to Langley, which was routed to Agent Vaughn. CIA director Devlin denied Vaughn permission to take a team in without verification, so he went in alone and found Sydney. Together they attempted to finish the job of disconnecting the bombs with the help of a British agent who had already infiltrated Cole's team. The agent, Toni, was killed during the subterfuge, and Sydney was forced to turn herself in to save the lives of the hostages.

Creating a distraction with a minor explosion, Sydney and Jack managed to take back the office. But Vaughn had not had the time to disconnect all the explosives. The only way to deactivate the fail-safe was with Sloane's fingerprint. Since Sloane was in shackles and could not be released before the explosion, Jack was forced to cut off Sloane's finger and use it to deactivate the system.

SD-6 was left under the impression that Cole escaped with the ampoule, but the CIA took him into custody ouside of SD-6's offices and obtained the Rambaldi liquid. And Sydney was once again reminded of the importance of her work. In spite of her feelings, she decided to remain at SD-6 while continuing to work for the CIA.

LOCATION: **Los Angeles, California, USA**
ALIAS: **None**

The Search for Laura Bristow

A fter reading her father's CIA files, Sydney was curious about pages missing from Case 332-L, regarding an Agent Calder. Vaughn discovered that there was no record of Case 332-L anywhere in the CIA files. He also learned that Agent Bentley Calder was FBI. The only reason they could come up with for the FBI interest in Jack was that some time in the past he had been under investigation for selling secrets.

Disturbed by this revelation, Sydney decided to investigate further, starting by meeting with Calder's widow. Mrs. Calder told Sydney that her husband died in a car accident in 1981. That was the same year as Sydney's mother, Laura Bristow, died. Sydney recognized Calder's photo and compared it to the newspaper article about her mother's death. The article included a photo of the postman who had been involved in the accident. It was the same man.

Sydney had always believed that her mother died when her parents were coming back from the movies. She had been told a postal worker fell asleep at the wheel, causing the accident. Now she suspected that the crash hadn't been an innocent accident at all. The FBI investigation into her father could have resulted in her mother's death.

Sydney and Vaughn continued looking into the mystery. Eventually this drew interest from Jack. When he realized what was going on, Jack provided Sydney with an FBI report signed by the deputy director under President Carter. It cleared Jack of having any involvement with the KGB. He claimed the accident was his fault, however, because the FBI was after him.

The investigation seemed to be over until Francie spilled lemonade on a book that had belonged to Sydney's mom. Sydney found a Cyrillic code hidden in the wet pages. It was one of the books that Jack had brought back for Laura from his trips abroad. Sydney assumed he was using the books to bring secret instructions. When the list was decoded, it was found to be a list of aliases and handles of agents who had been killed by an unknown foreign agent, believed to be KGB. Vaughn's father was one of the agents on that list.

Sydney and Vaughn believed that Jack had been the double agent. Knowing how much this revelation hurt Vaughn, Sydney agreed to take the information to Devlin.

However, Jack showed up at the meeting with other high-ranking officials to finally reveal the entire truth.

Jack apologized for making it a public display, but he thought it would be best to present the information in front of those already in the know. He then explained that the codes in Laura's books were KGB instructions. But it was Sydney's mother who was the foreign agent.

Sydney was rocked by the revelation and nearly quit SD-6 and the CIA in light of the news. However, she managed to stay on as she came to terms with her deceased mother's past.

As the investigation into Rambaldi intensified, Sydney was taken into FBI custody for questioning. The CIA—particularly Jack and Vaughn—were not happy with the way things were progressing and helped her escape so she could disprove a Rambaldi prophecy. While escaping, Sydney drove her getaway car off a pier and survived by breathing air from a tire. She then realized that her mother could have done something similar and was possibly still alive.

Knowing the CIA had classified her mother's files and would not give her access, Sydney went to the only person she could for help: Arvin Sloane. She later learned that Sloane was on the CIA commission investigating Laura Bristow's death. He had known that she was, in fact, alive for all these years, but he was under orders not to tell Jack.

Once Sloane learned that Alexander Khasinau was believed to be the Man, he focused Sydney's search there because Khasinau had been Laura Bristow's superior at the KGB. Sydney obtained a data core belong-ing to Khasinau that contained a video taken after her mother supposedly died. The video included Alexander Khasinau and the man known as Bentley Calder. They were in the process of debriefing Laura, whose real name was Irina Derevko.

Having visual confirmation that her mother actually did survive the crash gave Sydney a renewed sense of purpose in finding the woman. Sydney continued to search for the Man, knowing that he would lead her to her mother. Little did she realize how direct a connection there was between the two.

No matter how much she said she wanted to find her mother again, Sydney wasn't prepared for the reality. During the eventual mother-daughter reunion, Derevko pulled a gun and shot Sydney.

OBJECTIVE: Identify the Man and determine the meaning of Rambaldi's prophecy

SD-6 MISSION E643-A:

SD-6 learned that rival organization FTL had been attacked at the same time SD-6 was taken over by McKenas Cole. FTL's agent roster was compromised and their entire network crumbled within a couple of hours. An unidentified young man who also worked for the Man's organization led the raid. Following the destruction of FTL, it was believed that the Man had amassed a large number of Rambaldi artifacts.

Communiqués between K-Directorate and the Man's people were intercepted, indicating that the two organizations were offering to share Rambaldi information in a meeting set up through K-Directorate go-between Brandon Dahlgren. Sydney and Dixon were instructed to plant a listening device on Dahlgren to pick up the meeting information.

Dixon entered the Regal Casino—Dahlgren's year-round home—under the guise of Darian Buchanan, a delegate from the Jamaican Parliament. Security flagged him as a high-stakes player and escorted him to the private gaming suite where Dahlgren regularly played. Meanwhile Sydney entered the casino disguised as an employee and tapped into the surveillance system to aid Dixon in his game. Using the information she gathered by watching his cards, they forced the betting so that Dahlgren eventually had to bet his college ring. Dixon then switched it with a bugged duplicate before losing the hand and returning the ring.

LOCATION: **Las Vegas, Nevada, USA**
ALIAS: **Regal Casino cocktail waitress**

SD-6 MISSION E643-B:

After learning that the meeting between K-Directorate and the Man would take place in Moscow, Sydney and Dixon were sent to record a video of the meet and obtain a positive ID on the Man. Using a high-tension wire, Sydney crossed from a neighboring building to record the meeting from outside the window, five stories off the ground.

Meeting attendees included the head of K-Directorate, Ilyich Ivankov, and his lieutenant, Lavro Kessar. The Man did not participate, but he did send the operative who had led the raid against FTL, now identified as Mr. Sark.

Sark made an offer to buy the Rambaldi manuscript Anna Espinosa had stolen in Argentina (Mission E637-B). When Ivankov refused to sell, Sark killed him and reiterated his offer to Kessar. During the surveillance, Sydney knocked a piece of the concrete edifice to the ground, alerting the guards. Under fire, Sydney cut the line and swung down to the street, where Dixon picked her up and took her to safety.

CIA COUNTERMISSION:

Sydney double-recorded the meeting using a flash memory card compatible with the SD-6 fiber-optic camera she used to monitor events. The card was left in the seat pocket of seat 15C of the plane she took back to the United States and was picked up by CIA agents.

LOCATION: **Moscow, Russia**
ALIAS: **None**

SD-6 MISSION E644:

After Ivankov's body was shipped to K-Directorate headquarters, SD-6 believed that the Man was holding Lessar hostage in exchange for the Rambaldi manuscript. Sydney and Dixon were sent to intercept the exchange of the manuscript in Tunisia.

The manuscript was being kept on a boat off the coast. Playing the role of a stranded boater, Sydney obtained access to the K-Directorate boat. From there it was a simple matter of taking out the guards and stealing the manuscript. The escape off the boat would have been simple as well, had she not been interrupted.

Dixon was keeping watch from the shoreline. He informed Sydney, via comm, that Sark had arrived for the exchange, effectively cutting off her avenue of escape. With no other option, Sydney simply took the K-Directorate boat and departed.

CIA COUNTERMISSION:

As in Argentina, Sydney was asked to photograph the manuscript for the CIA. Once the photos were examined, it was found that page forty-seven was blank. According to CIA sci-tech, of the few Rambaldi documents they had previously recovered, the forty-seventh page was always significant. The CIA needed to obtain that page.

Sloane had taken the manuscript home because he wanted to show it to Sydney. His wife, Emily, had invited Sydney and a guest for dinner. The CIA tasked her with switching the blank page with a fake and planting a bug in Sloane's home office. All this was to be done while Sloane was in the house. Jack got himself invited to the dinner and helped make the exchange.

LOCATIONS: **Golfe de Gabes, Tunisia; Los Angeles, California, USA**

ALIAS: **None**

SD-6 MISSION E645-A:

SD-6 intercepted a communiqué from Sark informing the Man of the loss of the Rambaldi manuscript. The call was traced to Rio de Janeiro, and Sydney was sent in to obtain surveillance photos of the Man. Once those photos were obtained, SD-6 was able to identify the Man as Alexander Khasinau, a highly decorated former lieutenant colonel of the KGB.

LOCATION: **Rio de Janeiro, Brazil**

ALIAS: **None**

CIA MISSION E645-B:

Using the liquid found in the ampoule recovered from SD-6, the Department of Special Research had revealed the hidden text on page forty-seven. They used a code key reverse-engineered from previous work to reveal "the prophecy." The page showed a picture of a woman bearing a striking resemblance to Sydney.

Rambaldi's prophecy read: "This woman here depicted will possess unseen marks, signs that she will be the one to bring forth my works, bind them with fury, a burning anger, unless prevented. At vulgar cost, this woman will render the greatest power unto utter desolation."

Based on this information, the DSR, in conjunction with the FBI, subjected Sydney to invasive testing, hoping to disprove their theory that she was the woman in the drawing. The CIA was concerned that this line of testing would not solve the issue, and they realized that it was also possible that the code key was incorrect.

According to DSR files, the actual code key was stored in the Vatican archives. To save herself from endless testing and unknown experiments, Sydney and Vaughn broke into the Vatican archives, hoping to find the key and disprove the translation. They accessed the archives by posing as employees of the Department of Water and Power and went in through the basement of a neighboring building. The code key was located in the frame of a painting of Pope Alexander VI. Once the key was passed along to the DSR, it only managed to confirm what the agency already believed to be correct.

Sydney was taken into custody for questioning.

LOCATION: **Vatican City**
ALIAS: **Italian DWP worker**

CIA MISSION E646:

The FBI seemed to be planning to hold Sydney indefinitely for questioning. Aside from the fact that she was, ridiculously, being held for a prophesied crime she was supposed to commit, every passing hour she was gone put her cover at SD-6 in jeopardy. When the FBI refused to share information with the CIA, Vaughn made a discovery on his own.

According to the text of the prophecy, the woman mentioned would never have "seen the beauty of [Rambaldi's] sky behind Mount Subasio." Jack and Vaughn convinced CIA director Devlin to secretly support a mission to break Sydney out of FBI custody so she could prove she was not the woman in Rambaldi's prophecy.

As Sydney was being transferred from the Moorpark Federal Building to a safe house, CIA operatives extracted her from FBI custody. Vaughn provided her with a getaway car and a disguise. She was scheduled to meet a plane to take her to Italy. But before she could reach the plane, local police identified her and gave pursuit.

At the end of a car chase that her friends were watching on TV, Sydney was forced to drive off a pier to avoid capture. To survive underwater, she used air from the car tire to breathe until she believed it was safe to surface. During that time, she realized how similar the situation was to her own mother's death and came to the conclusion that it was possible the woman was still alive.

Sydney contacted her father and told him her suspicion. He did not want to discuss the issue, partially because the FBI was still after Sydney and she had to get out of the country. Sydney finally met up with the plane that took her to Italy. Once she saw the sky over Mount Subasio, she radioed for extraction. It was sufficient evidence for the FBI to release her.

LOCATION: **Mount Subasio, Italy**
ALIAS: **None**

SD-6 learned that Khasinau had recently converted $250 million of assets into cash. SD-6 deep-cover agent Kyle Wexler had acquired evidence of the transaction on a microchip and had scheduled a brush pass at the Russian Embassy in Vienna. When Sydney complained about being sent on a mission that would distract her from the search for her mother, Sloane explained that Khasinau was formerly Laura Bristow's superior. Finding Khasinau could lead to Sydney's mother.

Sydney went in to make the pass while Dixon kept her under surveillance. She attended a masquerade ball at the embassy but was surprised to learn from a second undercover operative that Wexler's cover had been blown and Khasinau's men had already killed him. This information came from Wexler's partner, Noah Hicks. Sydney was even more surprised to find that Hicks was involved, as she had not seen him since their relationship ended years earlier.

Agent Hicks led Sydney to Wexler's body. Suspecting that Wexler had swallowed the chip before he died, Noah cut into the body and found it lodged in the esophagus. As it was likely that Noah's cover was also blown, Sydney was forced to extract him. Dixon did not agree with this course of action. Aside from the fact that it was not part of their mission protocol, Dixon was concerned that Sydney was not thinking clearly because of her past relationship with Noah.

CIA COUNTERMISSION:

To inform the CIA of what was found on the chip.

LOCATION: **Vienna, Austria**
ALIAS: **Party attendee**

SD-6 MISSION E647-B:

Analysis of the chip indicated that Alexander Khasinau had bought two Westbury 23 supercomputers, capable of making five hundred trillion calculations per second. This type of computer was believed to be ideal for simulating theoretical design and possibly revealing the overall plan for Rambaldi's ultimate project. Sydney and Noah Hicks were sent in to retrieve the core from the cryogenic chamber where it was kept.

The computer core was stored in an underground bunker at a temperature of at least halfway to absolute zero, which was cold enough to freeze a person's skin in under a minute, even if only a millimeter of flesh was exposed. Sydney and Noah were able to infiltrate the bunker posing as lost American hikers. Once inside, they took out the guards and broke into the room storing the core.

While Sydney was in the cryochamber, another guard stumbled across the fallen security officers and sounded the alarm. This provided enough of a distraction for one of the lab techs to pull the lever controlling the chamber's mechanical arms. The arm hit Sydney's faceplate, causing tiny cracks in the glass . . . and letting in the subfreezing air.

As Sydney began to freeze, Noah was able to bypass the fail-safe to get her and the core out of the refrigerated room. They rushed out of the building, taking out guards as they went.

Following the mission, they were instructed to wait at a safe house for extraction. The two shared an evening of passion before Khasinau's men found them. Sydney and Hicks were forced to call for extraction half an hour earlier than planned. They escaped on a motorcycle, followed by Khasinau's men. When the

gas tank was hit, they radioed for immediate extraction. Failing all options, Sydney aimed the motorcycle at the pursuing Humvee and rode directly for it. As they took their suicide drive, an SD-6 helicopter dropped a rescue harness. Sydney and Noah hooked themselves into the harness and were pulled away moments before the vehicles collided.

LOCATION: **Arkhangelsk, Russia**
ALIAS: **American hiker**

SD-6 MISSION E648-A:

Analysis found nothing of substance on the computer core stolen from Khasinau, though there was an item of personal interest to Sydney. It was a piece of video of Laura Bristow shortly following her presumed death. The video revealed that Bentley Calder, the FBI agent who supposedly died in the accident with her, was alive—and he wasn't just FBI. He had also been a KGB double agent named Igor Sergei Valenko. Further investigation revealed that he had more recently done business with a financial office in Cape Town.

Sydney went to her father to enlist his help in getting Sloane to assign her and Noah on a mission to learn more. Neither Sloane nor Dixon were in favor of Noah returning to the field so soon, as there were some unanswered questions about Noah's loyalty. But Sydney insisted that he work with her.

Together they infiltrated the computer facility housing the financial records. The facility's security system was two-tiered, with sound and motion detectors. Marshall provided an active noise control device to dampen all sounds in the room. Sydney was lowered from above to hold a wireless modem to the server, so Noah could hack into the system from his laptop computer above. As she hung in the air, the rope began to slip. With the computer distracting him, Noah did not see that Sydney was about to fall to the ground and trip the alarm.

As Sydney continued to slip closer to the floor, she tried to yell out, but the sound dampener blocked her voice. Luckily, Noah saw the rope and grabbed it before Sydney hit the floor, pulling her back up to the rafters. They had seemingly been successful at downloading information that would lead to Valenko and ultimately Khasinau.

LOCATION: **Cape Town, South Africa**
ALIAS: **None**

SD-6 MISSION E648-B:

Although the mission in Cape Town was successful in downloading Calder's information, when Sydney and Noah returned to SD-6, they learned that everything had been wiped from the computer. This was presumably the result of security measures taken at the computer facility. However, Marshall was able to reconstruct the data from Noah's computer, which indicated that Calder maintained a private residence in Australia.

Upon returning from their mission, Noah asked to go on another deep-cover assignment. Since they had been growing close again, Sydney was understandably upset that he would just abandon her again. But Noah explained that he had no intention of taking on the assignment. He was quitting SD-6 and planning to disappear. He asked Sydney to go with him, but she wasn't ready to leave her life that way.

As Noah left, Sydney and Dixon were tasked with taking a team to infiltrate Valenko's home and grab him. When they arrived, they found that Valenko was dead. An assassin named the Snowman had killed him. And the Snowman was still in the house.

The masked assassin attacked Sydney. They fought and she stabbed him in the struggle. As he lay dying, Sydney discovered that the Snowman was Noah Hicks.

LOCATION: **Mackay, Queensland, Australia**
ALIAS: **None**

CIA MISSION E649-A:

Sydney developed a plan to draw out Khasinau by faking a leak that there was another ampoule filled with the liquid that revealed Rambaldi's invisible ink on page forty-seven of the manuscript. To provide a basis for the leak, Sydney and Vaughn broke into the Kherefu Art Museum to steal several Rambaldi artifacts.

Vaughn posed as an insurance agent supervising the museum security with a power shutdown. Once the power was out, Sydney accessed a vent leading to the vault where the Rambaldi artifacts were kept and she stole them. The intention was to just borrow the artifacts and return them later through back channels. The CIA then spread the rumor that another ampoule was among the items stolen and was available for purchase on the black market.

LOCATION: **Algiers, Algeria**
ALIAS: **Insurance agent for Fine Arts Coverage**

CIA MISSION E649-B:

Once Khasinau learned of the ampoule, he made contact with the undercover operatives and set up a meeting for a buy. Under the alias of a member of a fundamentalist group (with her face hidden behind a head covering called a niqaab), Sydney met with Sark, Khasinau's envoy, to make the exchange. To ensure that Sark bought the scam, she allowed him to test the real liquid, then planned to switch it with the fake when they sealed the deal. The fake ampoule contained colored water and a radioactive isotope the CIA could track via satellite. But the CIA was not aware that SD-6 had also learned of the meeting and sent Dixon in to obtain the ampoule.

Dixon interrupted the transaction before Sydney could make the switch. She fled while Vaughn subdued Sark and retrieved the ampoule. Dixon gave chase, and Sydney was forced to fight against her SD-6 partner. She managed to escape without her cover being blown when Vaughn intervened. However, SD-6 was able to capture Sark before he could be taken into CIA custody.

LOCATION: **Denpasar, Bali**
ALIAS: **Member of the Rislak Jihad,**
   an Islamic fundamentalist group

SD-6 MISSION E650:

Sark provided SD-6 with intel that he had a scheduled meet with Khasinau to give him the liquid that could reveal a new page of Rambaldi text. Sark was given a counterfeit ampoule that he was to pass along to Khasinau during the meet. At the same time, Sydney was tasked with obtaining a recording of Khasinau's heart signature. Dixon then used the recording to bypass security in Khasinau's office and steal the Rambaldi page, replacing it with a counterfeit.

CIA COUNTERMISSION:

Sydney was to exchange the Rambaldi page with a fake one on the way to the extraction point and deliver the fake to SD-6. While Dixon was stealing the original, she saw that Khasinau was holding her friend Will Tippin. Unaware that it was part of her father's unauthorized mission, she broke Will free from Khasinau's men and was forced to reveal her cover to her friend. In the ensuing fight, Sydney was unable to make the switch of the Rambaldi page.

LOCATION: **Paris, France**
ALIAS: **Club singer Abella Bernier**

UNAUTHORIZED MISSION E651:

Will Tippin was kidnapped from the CIA safe house, and Sydney, Vaughn, and Jack undertook an unauthorized mission to save him. Sark offered up Will in exchange for the stolen Rambaldi page and the solution required to make the text visible. To make this exchange, Sydney and Jack were forced to betray both SD-6 and the CIA.

To get to the blank Rambaldi page, Jack accessed Sloane's computer to retrieve the pass code to a secret SD-6 off-site lab, where the code changed hourly. At the same time, Sydney recorded a conversation with Sloane so they could piece together the code using his voice.

While her father stole the liquid ampoule from the CIA holding facility, Sydney broke into the lab to steal the Rambaldi page. At the time, she was not aware of the fact that Dixon had grown suspicious of her actions. He finally remembered her using the "Freelancer" call sign in Argentina and began an investigation on his own. When Sydney came out of the SD-6 lab, Dixon was waiting for her with many questions. She did her best to cover for her actions, but he remained suspicious.

Once Sydney, Jack, and Vaughn had the page and the liquid, they used it to reveal that the blank page referred to a Rambaldi artifact known as the Circumference. It was a set of operating instructions for a device that the Man had built from the same design as the Muller Device (SD-6 Missions J535-A and J535-B). Knowing that they could not allow the device to be activated, Jack planned to make the switch for Will, while Sydney and Vaughn broke into Khasinau's lab to destroy the device.

The switch went as planned, but the break-in did not. Sydney discovered that Khasinau's device was much larger than Muller's. When she destroyed it, the giant red ball turned to liquid and flooded the facility. Sydney was taken prisoner, while Vaughn was trapped in the flood and left behind.

When she awoke, Sydney learned the true identity of the Man: Irina Derevko, the woman she knew as her mother, Laura Bristow.

After a brief reunion, Irina shot Sydney in the shoulder and left her to consider sharing the information on who had sent her. Sydney escaped by using items found in the room and fought her way free.

The mission effectively destroyed Khasinau and Derevko's headquarters in Taipei and exposed members of their organization. Jack took credit for the mission with Sloane, which answered Dixon's questions about Sydney's actions in protecting their cover. But Vaughn was still missing and presumed dead.

LOCATIONS: Los Angeles and Santa Barbara, California, USA; Taipei, Taiwan
ALIAS: Club patron

SD-6 MISSION E652-A:

Jean-Marc Revet was a member of the French National Assembly and one of the financiers behind Derevko and Khasinau's outfit. He was believed to be the key to finding their location now that the Man's organization had been dealt a powerful blow with the destruction of the Circumference device.

Sydney and Dixon were sent in to his private estate during a party. As Dixon kept watch outside the estate, Sydney gained access to his home office and planted a bug on Revet's phone line so SD-6 could monitor his conversations.

CIA COUNTERMISSION:

Sydney added a CIA delay transmitter to the wire that Marshall had designed. The delay allowed the CIA to monitor all of Revet's communications while controlling what SD-6 heard.

During the mission, Sydney recognized a man from the Taipei operation. She suspected that he could lead her to information on Vaughn, so she followed the man down to an operating area, where she found Khasinau about to cut into Vaughn in some strange experiment. After Khasinau left the room, she revived Vaughn and they escaped.

LOCATION: Cap Ferrat, France
ALIAS: Party attendee

CIA MISSION E652-B:

Information retrieved from the bug in Revet's office indicated that Khasinau was scheduled to meet with an operative to retrieve the bible. This was an operations manual for Derevko's organization that included information on contacts, weapons, tech inventory, and objectives. It was information that Khasinau and Derevko could use to rebuild their organization. The operative had grabbed the book in Taipei and kept it safe.

Sydney went to Barcelona with the CIA team to stake out the meeting place. Once they observed

Khasinau they moved in, attempting to secure him and seize the bible. As soon as the team went in, a sniper began firing, killing Khasinau's operative and injuring Agent Weiss. Derevko was the shooter.

During the ensuing melee, Sydney followed Khasinau, hoping to retrieve the bible. As she had him cornered, Derevko came in and held Sydney at gunpoint. Derevko aimed her gun at Sydney, but then killed Khasinau instead. She then made her daughter get down on the ground. But Derevko did not hurt her daughter; she just took the bible and escaped.

Following the mission, Irina Derevko turned herself in to the CIA.

LOCATION: **Barcelona, Spain**
ALIAS: **None**

OBJECTIVE: Obtain Rambaldi's equation for zero-point energy

SD-6 MISSION E653-A:

SD-6 learned that Khasinau was dead and suspected that Derevko was in hiding. Knowing that Derevko used blackmail extensively in her operation, Sloane sent Sydney and Dixon to break into the vault of Derevko operative Mohammad Naj and retrieve a disk containing blackmail material on various high-profile subjects.

Dixon used a computer interface through the phone system of the Moroccon hotel in which Naj lived. Once in the system, Dixon planted the alias Beatrice Cunelli in the reservation system. According to the computer, she was booked into Naj's suite, so the concierge simply gave her the key. While Sydney was in Naj's suite, she tripped an alarm, alerting Naj to the break-in. Dixon disabled the elevator, trapping Naj and his bodyguard, and they managed to get out with the disk. Once back at SD-6, Sloane forwarded the disk to Alliance headquarters in London.

CIA COUNTERMISSION:

Though SD-6 knew Derevko was in hiding, they were unaware of the fact that she was in CIA custody. Naturally, Derevko's surrender did not sit well with either Sydney or Jack. When Derevko stated that she would share information only with her daughter, Sydney refused to speak with the woman, even though she may have had useful information on the current mission.

Vaughn instructed Sydney to perform a brush pass inside the hotel with Agent Richard Schmidt. The agent was waiting on the third floor to scan the disk, analyze what was on it, and make a bogus copy close enough to the original to fool Sloane. The plan would have worked had there not been a secondary alarm trigger on the safe.

(continued on page 135)

Will Tippin's Investigation into the Death of Danny Hecht

When Will Tippin failed to get a clear answer from Sydney on why she borrowed his sister's passport and credit card, he began to look into Danny's death as a means of helping Sydney heal from the tragedy. He discovered that the night Danny was killed, he was booked on a flight to Singapore. Sydney explained that Danny was scheduled to attend a medical conference, but she was surprised by the news herself.

WILL & SYDNEY

Later it was revealed to Sydney that her father had bought the ticket so that Danny and she could escape to safety, since Sloane had put a hit on her fiancé. Jack had been only minutes too late to save Danny.

Will continued the investigation, attempting to obtain photos from the traffic cameras around Danny's apartment. But he discovered that all the cameras in a one-mile radius around the building were out that night. He also learned that Danny was not booked at a conference in Singapore. Additionally, a woman who had purchased the seat next to Danny also had not shown for the flight. Her name was Kate Jones.

Will tracked Kate down and scheduled a meeting with her. She told him that she and Danny were having an affair. Will didn't believe the lie because he had already obtained Social Security records indicating that Kate Jones had died in 1973. Kate fled the meeting.

Using her license plate number, Will found that the woman's real name was Eloise Kurtz. He eventually got her to admit that she had been paid to lie to him. When he went to her apartment to meet, he found it had been cleaned out. Unbeknownst to Will, Jack Bristow had sent in Eloise Kurtz to mislead Will, but Sloane had her killed because she was made.

Will found a pin in Kurtz's car that had what appeared to be a government-issue bug inside that was still active. He tried to contact the person on the other end of the bug. Eventually a disguised voice got back to him with instructions that led to an audiotape of Kurtz's murder.

Will took the tape to an audio engineer to examine, and they found reference to SD-6 in the recording. A computer search revealed a reference to SD-6 in the transcripts of a lawsuit against David McNeil, a businessman who developed an encryption program. McNeil was imprisoned for larceny after trust, and his lawyer, Stoller, told Will that McNeil's wife killed herself under mysterious circumstances. McNeil believed that SD-6 had ruined his life because he had refused to sell them the encryption program. But McNeil feared for his daughter's safety and refused to help Will.

Will gave up the investigation, fearing that it was too dangerous, but the mysterious

voice from the bug sent him an envelope with a key inside. The key opened a locker containing the autopsy report on McNeil's wife, indicating that her death was not a suicide.

Once he knew his daughter was safe from SD-6, McNeil agreed to cooperate. He told Will that his software had a backdoor program that sent information on anyone who used it back to the server at his old company. The files revealed forty-two companies that used the software, and all had retired CIA operative Alain Christophe as a board member.

After reviewing videotape of Will's meeting with McNeil, Sloane wanted to have him killed. Jack promised to take care of the situation himself. He then kidnapped Will (while masked) and threatened him to get off the story or else his friends and family would die. Will did as he was told, angering McNeil, whose daughter had been sent into hiding. Jack and Sloane were eavesdropping on the conversation and called off the hit on Will.

After some time, the voice contacted Will, saying that he had enough on SD-6 to publish and that one of the men who had kidnapped him was Jack Bristow. Will went to his associate, Abby, and gave her an envelope with his story and instructions to publish it if anything happened to him. After he confronted Jack about SD-6, Jack teamed with Will to find the identity of the mysterious voice.

Jack instructed Will to set up a meeting, enticing the voice by saying that he knew about the Circumference. This was a lie. The meeting was set for Paris, where Jack gave Will a drug to counteract the effects of truth serum and provided a transmitter so he could record the person's actual voice. It turned out that the mysterious voice belonged to an agent of the Man.

While on a separate mission, Sydney saw that Will was in jeopardy and rescued him from the Man's operatives, revealing her secret. While Will was in protective custody, Sark kidnapped him and took him to Taipei to question him on the Circumference. He was tortured by Dr. Jong Lee but exacted his revenge on the man by pumping him with a paralyzing drug. He was then brought to Jack in exchange for a page of Rambaldi text.

At the same time, the *L.A. Register* printed Will's story because he had been missing for several days. The only way to keep him safe, Jack told him, was to discredit him. Will was soon found in a crack-house raid, nursing a heroin addiction. He claimed that he made up the whole story about SD-6 up as a ploy for attention. He was fired from the paper and put on probation, serving one hundred hours of community service.

(continued from page 132)

Considering that Derevko probably did have useful information, Vaughn went to meet with the woman who had killed his father. Following a tense exchange, Derevko warned him that there was a fail-safe: Sydney needed to pull the fire alarm beside Naj's safe before she opened it. Considering the source, Sydney did not trust the intel and proceeded as originally planned. Moments after the safe was open, an alarm sounded. Derevko had been telling the truth.

Sydney managed to get out with the disk, but Dixon intervened before she could make the brush pass. Sydney returned to the CIA and immediately went to see her mother.

LOCATION: **Rabat, Morocco**
ALIAS: **Beatrice Cunelli, rich tourist**

CIA MISSION E653-B:

Confused and angry, Sydney tried to maintain a strictly professional relationship with Derevko, asking what was on the blackmail disk. Derevko suggested that SD-6 would first go after Petr Fordson, but she refused to tell Sydney why. The exchange was brief, but Derevko insisted that Sydney should trust her simply because she was Sydney's mother.

CIA files on Fordson revealed that his company had contracted with the Pentagon a year earlier to manufacture a terahertz-wave camera to be placed in a satellite. Once in orbit, the camera could see through solid matter to a depth of a hundred meters. A month earlier, Fordson had failed to make delivery, claiming production problems. It was believed that prior to turning herself in, Derevko was in the process of setting up a deal for Fordson to give her the camera in exchange for material she had on him.

Sydney and Vaughn were sent to break into Lasgrove Industries to obtain the camera. They infiltrated the office building through the rooftop restaurant. Sydney was set to enter the lab during the guards' change of shift, which would give her five minutes to complete the mission. Vaughn surveyed the situation from the bar, where he found Sloane arriving to meet with Fordson.

As the meeting moved to the balcony, Sydney went over the rail on a high-tension wire and dropped to the fourteenth floor, entering the building through the window using a laser cutter. She then broke into the lab, took the camera, and went back out the window and down to the ground floor, managing to avoid Sloane in the process.

When Sydney returned to the building housing the Joint Task Force on Intelligence, she learned that Derevko refused to provide any information on the T-wave camera. She did, however, ask that congratulations be passed to her daughter for the successful mission. This enraged Sydney. She immediately went to Derevko's cell and told her that as far as she was concerned, her mother had died decades earlier. They would interact only when necessary. There would be no personal anecdotes. And Derevko was to refer to her as Agent Bristow.

Derevko agreed to the terms, knowing that she would have the chance to connect with her daughter again.

LOCATION: **Helsinki, Finland**
ALIAS: **Restaurant patron**

SD-6 MISSION E654-A:

The camera stolen from Lasgrove Industries turned out to be an early prototype. The real Lasgrove Industries terahertz-imaging camera was scheduled to be launched into orbit by the Asiatic Space Agency. Their latest client was the person who had assumed control of Derevko's organization in her absence: Sark.

Sydney was sent in to infiltrate the launch site, posing as a corporate buyer, and then install an SD-6 circuit board on the satellite to learn what Sark was looking for when the camera was sent into orbit. Sydney gave Dixon access to the computers by calling him through a landline while in the building. He then hacked into the security surveillance feed and cut it for five minutes during the launch.

Sydney tranquilized her guide and entered the launch site via a street luge through the two-mile-long exhaust ducts. She had to clear the area before the launch, otherwise the flame from the rocket thrusters would kill her.

Suspicious due to the fact that the video system was experiencing a glitch, Sark ordered the launch to be moved up. Sydney barely had time to hook up the circuit board and escape on the luge as a ball of fire chased her.

CIA COUNTERMISSION:

Sydney actually installed an alternate circuit board that allowed the CIA to piggyback on SD-6's signal.

LOCATION: **Sri Lanka**
ALIAS: **Joanna Kelley from Euro-Teledyne Corporation**

SD-6 MISSION E654-B:

An intercepted feed from the satellite carrying the terahertz-imaging camera pointed to a twenty-square-mile area of Siberia with underground caverns that coalesced into the symbol of Rambaldi (the Rambaldi Eye). In the center of the subglacial caverns was a metal object that SD-6 wanted to acquire before Sark got it.

Dixon and a support team established a perimeter around the cavern to guard all possible approaches, while Sydney went in to retrieve the item. During the mission, Dixon tracked incoming operatives, but no one could get a visual. The incoming targets were swimming in under the ice. Firing through the frozen ground, they took out SD-6 agents Cooper and Novak. Dixon realized his target was under the ice and killed the operative. Since Sydney had gone radio silent, he could not warn her that danger was coming her way.

CIA COUNTERMISSION:

According to Derevko, the object Sark was after was the Rambaldi Music Box. Encoded within the tune played by the music box was an equation for zero-point energy: a fuel source with unlimited military applications. The music box would not play without the proper combination, which Sark was working on deciphering.

While he had been kidnapped, Will witnessed Sark working on something on his laptop. Under hypnotherapy, Will recalled seeing a list of names: Dostoyevsky, Nabokov, Tolstoy, and Chekov. It was some kind of cipher text. Derevko translated the cipher text into numbers to give Sydney the combination.

While on the mission, Sydney went radio silent with Dixon, explaining that the ice formations looked sensitive to sound. She then plugged the combination into a keypad on the device and played the tune for the CIA to record. She then sprayed the box with a corrosive chemical agent so SD-6 couldn't get it. As the box disintegrated, Sark entered the cavern, holding a gun on her.

Since the box was ruined, Sydney slid the useless artifact to him. While he was distracted, she threw her ice axe, embedding it in his leg. He fired at her, weakening the ice, and she fell through into the subzero water. The ice froze over in seconds, trapping her.

Underwater, Sydney found the dead operative and used his machine gun to break through the ice and escape. Dixon pulled her out of the water, saving her from hypothermia.

LOCATION: **Siberia, Russia**
ALIAS: **None**

OBJECTIVE: Re-establish mission to retrieve the bible (a continuation of Mission E652-B)

SD-6 MISSION E655-A:

An SD-6 team was sent to the Falkland Islands to recover the music box from Sark. They obtained the device, but confirmed that it was corroded. While on the mission they also found operative Claus Richter. Sloane believed that Derevko gave the bible to Richter to hide.

Richter was taken to an SD-6 holding cell for interrogation. He seemed sick, but he had been screened for every type of possible infection. Nothing was found, yet the man was clearly dying. The first sign of illness was bleeding from the fingernails. Jack bargained for information by offering the man morphine. Richter admitted that the location of the bible was too remote to describe. He had designed a map to lead Derevko to the book.

Sydney was sent in to the Russian FAPSI Library to recover the map to the bible. Richter had hidden it in a first-edition copy of *War and Peace.* While she was in the library, Sark interrupted her mission. Sydney tripped the alarm to alert the guards to their presence as a distraction. As the guards arrived, Sark got a look at the map before Sydney was able to take it. But with security on full alert, she was trapped inside the building with no means of escape.

CIA COUNTERMISSION:

Sydney was instructed to provide the CIA with the real map and give SD-6 a fake that would lead them to the middle of the Sunken Forest.

While looking to escape the facility, Sydney recalled that her mother had said something about secret passages. With time running out, Sydney instructed Vaughn over the comm to get Derevko on the line. Vaughn raced to Derevko's cell, where she detailed a secret passage out of the building. Sydney used an activation switch for a private security door in the office of General Vitali Simonov. The passage exited in Lenin's tomb, depositing her safely on the streets of Russia.

LOCATION: **Moscow, Russia**
ALIAS: **Major in the Russian army**

CIA MISSION E655-B:

CIA techs attempted to decipher the map, but Vaughn suggested that Derevko might be able to do it faster. Sydney, who had been softening to spending time with her mother, mentioned that Derevko had a request. She wanted a pair of earrings returned to her, as they had been a gift from

Sydney's grandmother. The CIA checked the earrings and granted the request in exchange for the information.

Derevko noted that the map led to coordinates in Madagascar, near Sambava (latitude minus fourteen degrees, twenty-six minutes, longitude forty-nine degrees, fifty-seven minutes, and twenty seconds). According to Derevko, the building was clean—no explosives or anti-intrusion systems.

Sydney and Vaughn were sent in to retrieve the bible. As they were about to enter the building, Jack ordered the satellite tracking the mission to scan for infrared, not trusting Derevko's intel. It seemed his suspicions were right, because the satellite detected explosives underneath the building. If Sydney and Vaughn had entered, they would have been killed.

Sark arrived moments after the mission was aborted. Unaware of the explosives, he sent his men into the building and it exploded. The bible was presumably destroyed in the explosion.

Derevko's agreement with the U.S. government was nullified by the fact that she had provided potentially deadly false intel. This was nothing compared to the personal betrayal Sydney felt. However, Jack later admitted to setting Derevko up based on his fear of losing his daughter.

LOCATION: **Madagascar jungle**
ALIAS: **None**

OBJECTIVE: Obtain information on the Triad's next-generation weapons

SD-6 MISSION E656-A:

SD-6 learned that Niels Haider had been murdered in Vienna. The bold nature of the hit—midday with complete disregard to civilians—indicated that it was the work of the Triad, the organization for which Haider worked. It was assumed that they killed one of their own operatives because they discovered he was selling intel to SD-6. In his last communication to SD-6, Haider said that the Triad was engaged in a plot to "develop and deploy sixteen next-generation weapons."

Testing of the unknown weapons was advancing ahead of schedule in an abandoned bomb shelter underneath the Magistrate's Bureau in Budapest. Sydney and

Dixon were sent in to access the facility and identify the nature of the weapons. Sydney was to infiltrate the building and retrieve the specs and test data off the central server, then proceed to the R&D lab and take photographs of the weapons. There she would log on to the computer and disable the firewall, so that SD-6 could hack in and directly download the specs for the weapons. But the surprising nature of the weapons altered the plan.

CIA COUNTERMISSION:

Sydney was instructed to give Dixon a dummy IP address, while uploading the actual intel to the CIA. This proved more difficult from both a practical and emotional standpoint when Sydney saw the sixteen next-generation weapons. As an instructor watched, sixteen children sat in a classroom setting . . . each putting together a gun while blindfolded. The children *were* the weapons.

LOCATION: **Budapest, Hungary**
ALIAS: **Young woman researching her family tree**

CIA MISSION E656-B:

Sydney was tasked to bring in Valery Kholokov, the man behind the Triad's program training children to be sleeper agents. He was the instructor she had photographed with the children. Sydney led a strike team to retrieve him from his home in Buenos Aires, and he was brought in for questioning to find out how many other kids he had trained.

The information gathered on the Triad training program revealed that the best spies have certain traits, such as proficiency with numbers, three-dimensional thinking, and creative problem solving. These abilities are evident in children as young as five years old.

Every first grader in the European Union takes a standardized test. A few years earlier the Triad had acquired the company that did the testing. They added a series of questions to locate children with those traits. This year twenty-eight children were indicated. Their parents were sent letters inviting them to participate in a monthlong achievement program. Sixteen accepted.

Given that six-year-olds acquire knowledge at an incredible rate, the group was taught the basic skills of marksmanship, linguistics, and visual and verbal cue recognition within a period of weeks. At the end of the month, the Triad sent the children home with the intent to contact the test subjects at some point in the future and send them into the field. Before the children were sent home, their memories were reset so they remembered nothing but that the experience was extremely satisfying. The children Sydney photographed were put under surveillance so the CIA would know if the Triad ever contacted them.

While in Kholokov's house during the strike mission, Sydney noticed a three-dimensional puzzle. Though she did not recognize the puzzle, she was able to put it together in a matter of seconds. Later she learned under hypnosis that she had been put through a similar training program when she was a child. It was a CIA program known as Project Christmas. The supervisor on the project was her father.

LOCATION: **Buenos Aires, Argentina**
ALIAS: **None**

OBJECTIVE: Identify and find a cure for the Rambaldi bioweapon

SD-6 MISSION E657:

A routine medical workup revealed that Sark's operative Claus Richter may have been exposed to a virus before he was picked up (Mission E655-A). His body had a concentration of flu antibodies at a thousand percent above normal levels, and his symptoms were similar to Ebola—notably massive hemorrhaging—only this virus worked by breaking down bonds between cells. He suffered an ugly death. Based on what was learned, SD-6 surmised that Sark was developing a bioweapon synthesized from a virus that had never been seen before.

SD-6 uncovered a charter agreement indicating that Sark had rented a medically equipped 727 to transport three patients presumably suffering from the same virus to a private hospital in Geneva. The hospital was one of Sark's business fronts. SD-6 believed he had assembled a team to study the virus.

At the same time, Jack and Sydney were experiencing another difficult period in their relationship. Based on information Vaughn discovered, Sydney recently came to the conclusion that Jack had set up Derevko during the mission to retrieve the bible. The tension was compounded by Sydney's recent discovery through hypnotherapy that Jack had put her through his Project Christmas training as a child. Sloane noted the distance between the two, though he was unaware of the cause. In an attempt to bring father and daughter closer together, Sloane sent Sydney and Jack on a mission to infiltrate the medical facility and acquire the virus research.

Jack was admitted into the hospital as a patient in need of a kidney transplant, while Sydney accompanied him, fittingly, as his daughter who had agreed to donate her kidney. They tranquilized the operating staff and posed as doctors to gain access to the basement-level quarantine facility. After using tranq guns (continued on page 143)

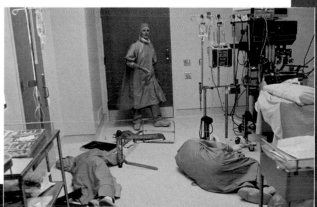

Investigation into the Russian Sleeper Agent Program

While looking over a set of test questions administered in Russia designed to identify children who would make good agents, Vaughn realized how similar they were to questions found on American standardized tests. Considering a rumor during the Cold War about Soviets raising sleeper agents, he felt it bore investigation. Using his discretionary fund, Vaughn hired Will Tippin to find out if any of the questions ever appeared on standardized tests in the United States over the past twenty years.

Will looked up the test and found no matches for the questions. However, the tests from 1982 were missing. The Educational Testing Service didn't have a hard copy or a disk available, so he asked his former coworker Abigail Finch for help. She managed to obtain a copy of the test from the Department of Education. He soon realized that the test was a fake, as the information on it was from 1983.

Will contacted Henry Fields, the designer of the original test. Fields claimed that he didn't put any questions about spatial reasoning on the test because there was no statistical utility in asking first graders a question that only one in ten thousand could answer. However, when Fields retrieved an old hard copy of the 1982 test from his files, Will found it had the question, "How can rainbows be seen only when the sun is behind the observer?" Fields claimed that it wasn't one of the questions he had sent ETS, which suggested that someone had altered the test between the proof stage and when it was administered. The test was given to more than five million children in thirty-three states.

Will reported back to Vaughn, but Devlin had already ordered a halt to the investigation. However, when Devlin learned the number of children who had taken the test, he sent the information on to the FBI. Will continued to investigate without pay and found that forty children received a perfect score on the test.

The FBI had been trying to find out the same information but hadn't come up with anything yet. Will explained that this was probably because the tests from 1982 were missing from the Testing Service archives. Devlin approved Will to continue the research and become a CIA analyst once he passed the Milgram-Reich Allegiance test.

(continued from page 141)

on the workers, Sydney took blood from the man identified as Patient Zero. In the man's weakened state, he mistook Sydney for Derevko, since he was one of the Man's employees.

As Sydney drew his blood, the patient's vitals fell below preset warning levels, which alerted the doctors. Jack and Sydney managed to escape with the files. Further research indicated that Derevko had deliberately ordered Sark to expose some of their operatives to the virus in order to study it.

CIA COUNTERMISSION:

Based on the blood samples brought back from Geneva, the CIA believed that Derevko's Rambaldi device destroyed in Taipei was the source of the virus. It was feared that Sydney and Vaughn may have been infected due to their contact with the device. After a round of testing, it was determined that both were free of the virus.

The relief over the results was short-lived when Vaughn started bleeding from the fingernail. He was exhibiting the first sign of infection.

LOCATION: **Geneva, Switzerland**
ALIAS: **Marion Harrison**

CIA MISSION E658-A:

Vaughn reported that he was showing signs of the virus. Though he was instructed to stay where he was, Vaughn ignored the doctor and went to see Derevko, suspecting that she might have a clue to the cure. Her information, however, came with a price. She insisted that he tell her how he felt about her daughter. Vaughn collapsed shortly after leaving Derevko.

Derevko informed Sydney that there was an antidote for the Rambaldi virus. It could be found at a former Soviet training base for nuclear submarine personnel, currently run by

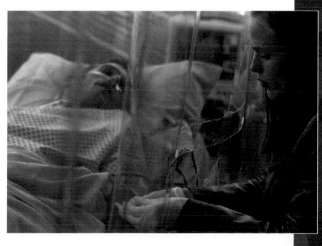

Derevko's operatives, including Sark. The serum was a blood derivative requiring blood from the patient to create a genetic-specific antidote for the particular patient. After Sydney drew Vaughn's blood at the hospital, she ran into his ex-girlfriend, Alice. Sydney was surprised to learn that the two had started dating again.

Sydney pressed on with the mission to Estonia. The assault team launched a Zodiac two miles up the coast and dropped Sydney in as close as they could. She swam the rest of the way, using propulsion jets. Once at the facility she needed a security pass code to use the serum generator. She was supplied with a handheld computer to jack into the system. The computer had a satellite link that allowed the CIA to access the system and provide her with the code she needed (pass code: 2664729).

Further research into the system revealed that the generator was connected to the central security system, meaning that if Sydney used the generator for the antidote she would alert security. Director Kendall instructed her to abort the mission, but she ignored the order and started the device, putting the facility on alert. Sydney was trapped in a room with a ceiling lined with sprinkler heads rigged to disperse ammonia fluorochloride, a chemical used to decontaminate metals and concrete. It could also eat away at organic materials, including her skin.

Sark turned on the sprinkler heads, spraying her with the acidlike substance and then offered a deal. Sydney was instructed to bring Arvin Sloane to Sark—and presumably to his death. At that point Sark would give her the antidote. Kendall refused to approve the mission.

LOCATION: **Paldiski, Estonia**
ALIAS: **Facility employee**

UNAUTHORIZED MISSION E658-B:

Knowing that Vaughn did not have much time, Sydney took on a personal mission to deliver Sloane to Sark. Knowing she could not do it alone, she went to her father for help. Jack warned that sending Sloane to his death in this manner would not be the same as killing someone in self-defense. This type of premeditated murder would stay with her. When Sydney insisted that she was going through with the plan, Jack agreed to assist her.

Sloane was staying at the Nayoshi Ginza in Tokyo for a meeting with the head of the Alliance. Sydney contacted Sark to arrange the turnover the night before Sloane's Alliance meeting. Jack met with Sark's associate in the United States to get the antidote once Sydney had turned Sloane over to Sark. Posing as a geisha, Sydney tranquilized Sloane, then convinced the Ginza workers that he was sick. Sark sent in an ambulance to pick up Sloane and had his operative turn over the antidote to Jack. The antidote was administered and Vaughn's life was saved, potentially at the cost of Sloane's.

Sydney later learned that Sark did not have Sloane killed. Instead he offered a partnership with

SD-6 to work together in solving Rambaldi's true aim. Since the majority of the operatives in SD-6 believed they were working for a branch of the CIA, Sloane brought Sark in under the guise of having brokered a pardon for the man. This angered Dixon, while only Sydney understood the full truth.

LOCATION: **Tokyo, Japan**
ALIAS: **Miko, a geisha**

OBJECTIVE: Prevent Sark from activating six nuclear missiles

SD-6 MISSION E659-A:

Zoran Sokolov was a freelance mercenary who had extensive dealings with Mr. Sark. Sokolov had recently asked if Sark would be interested in obtaining a set of communication codes used by Uzbekistan ground forces along the border. With the codes, extremist rebels in neighboring Tajikistan could track Uzbek troop movements and plan terrorist attacks, gravely destabilizing U.S. allies in Asia. (This was Sloane's cover story, used to hide the fact that the codes served a different purpose.)

Sydney and Dixon were sent in to make contact with Sokolov, posing as Sark's associates, then purchase the codes and bring them back. The codes were in a computer in a case stolen from a colonel in the Uzbek army. Sokolov didn't originally know that the colonel's fingerprint was required to open the case, or it would detonate a self-destruct mechanism inside. When he found out, Sokolov had the colonel assassinated so they could get the print. It was then just a matter of getting access to the body.

Sydney was brought into the morgue posing as a dead woman. Using a microchip provided by Sokolov, Dixon linked to the computer to locate the body of the colonel. He relayed the information to Sydney, who copied the man's fingerprint with a scanner. Security was alerted when Sydney's "body" was found missing. She fought her way out and posed as security to escape.

CIA COUNTERMISSION:

Once Derevko learned of the codes' existence, she immediately requested to be freed from captivity for forty-eight hours. She even offered to agree to a Special Forces escort to counter the SD-6 mission personally, but she would not tell Sydney what the codes were for because she did not trust the CIA. Kendall did not approve.

As a result, Sydney's countermission was to dead drop a copy of the codes when she got back, so the CIA could figure out what the codes were really for.

LOCATION: **Uzbekistan**

ALIASES: **Sark's associate; cadaver**

CIA MISSION E659-B:

It was discovered that the codes given to SD-6 were control codes for six portable nuclear warheads that the Uzbeks had admitted went missing six months earlier. The CIA learned that Sark had electronically sent the codes to an unknown third party. Knowing the obvious risk of having terrorists in control of nuclear weapons, Kendall was forced to make a deal with Derevko for her help.

In exchange for receiving a pillow and a blanket, Derevko gave up the location of the warheads. They were in Kashmir, under what used to be a maximum-security prison. It was now the stronghold for a mercenary group known as the People's Revolutionary Front. It appeared that Sloane and Sark had partnered with this organization.

As the mission was top priority, this time Derevko was released to stop Sark and the People's Revolutionary Front. Sydney and Jack accompanied her on a mission to disable the nuclear devices. To

ensure that she did not escape, Derevko was fitted with an explosive necklace that Jack could set off if she tried to get away.

The unrest in Kashmir had caused both Pakistan and India to seal their borders, so the team boarded a train in New Delhi and got off as they were passing through the eastern tip of Kashmir. They parachuted out of the train on a bridge and met with their CIA contact, Saeed Akhtar. He provided the op tech they would need to get into the building and took them to the prison. En route they were ambushed by soldiers of the People's Revolutionary Front. Saeed was killed and the Bristow family was held prisoner.

Using the explosion of Derevko's necklace as a distraction, the team fought free of the soldiers and stole their weapons. At the same time, the CIA intercepted a communication indicating that the rebels planned on activating the nukes the following day at 1700 hours.

Having lost their contact and supplies, the team met with one of Jack's contacts in Srinagar. They obtained a truck that took them part of the way to the facility but were forced to walk the final ten miles. After clearing a minefield, they accessed the prison.

Midmission the Indian government found out that the Pakistani rebels had acquired nukes. As a result, the Indians planned on launching an air strike against the facility in twenty-four hours. Vaughn went through back channels, trying to get the Indian government to call off the strike. He did not succeed, but General Arshad gave him a chopper, a pilot, and a head start to get the team out.

To find the nukes, the team had to split up to enact different parts of the mission. Jack and Sydney completed their roles, but when it was time to reconvene, Irina arrived with guards and her former superior, Gerard Cuvee. She claimed she was caught and had to turn them in or they'd all be killed. She managed to free Jack and Sydney so they could make contact with the CIA. Kendall ordered them to head for the extraction point immediately, but Jack refused to leave without Irina.

At that point, Sydney and Jack learned that the nuclear devices were not intended as weapons. They were all after a Rambaldi artifact: an egg-shaped container. Cuvee was using the plutonium cores to open the container, which revealed a small yellow flower. The artifact was proof that Rambaldi mastered self-sustaining cell regeneration in his efforts to create endless life. Irina took the flower as the air strike hit the facility. The team also managed to obtain the plutonium cores to the nuclear devices.

LOCATION: **Muzaffarabad, Kashmir**
ALIASES: **Daughter in the Godson family;**
 Indian woman

OBJECTIVE: Protect the Echelon satellite system

SD-6 MISSION E661-A:

The Echelon satellite system is a web of satellites designed to monitor global data traffic. Phone calls, faxes, and e-mails from around the world are filtered through a program capable of flagging keywords on an NSA watch list. It scans two million conversations an hour and has been very successful at identifying threats to national security.

Sark provided intel indicating that Gerard Cuvee might have acquired the ability to access the Echelon system through an access terminal he had stolen from the NSA. It was being kept in a front company in Paris. Cuvee believed that Sark betrayed him in Kashmir, and he was likely planning to move the terminal to an undisclosed location. A surveillance team intercepted an operations log indicating that an armored transport had been scheduled for a pickup. Sydney and Sark went in to intercept the convoy en route and bring the terminal to SD-6.

Sydney accessed the city's traffic control network, while Sark followed the armored car, disguised as a police officer. Sydney caused a backup, then took out the armored car, while Sark dealt with the escort vehicle. The terminal was not in the armored car, however. It was with one of the operatives in the escort vehicle. Sydney went after the operative on foot and obtained the terminal.

CIA COUNTERMISSION:

On the return flight, Sydney installed a secure deletion program to the terminal that wiped the hard drive clean under the guise of a fail-safe when Sloane opened it. SD-6 assumed that Cuvee had installed the fail-safe.

LOCATION: **Paris, France**
ALIAS: **Land surveyor**

SD-6 MISSION E661-B:

SD-6 intercepted a call to a data storage facility in London that catered to high-end corporate clients. It was considered likely that Cuvee had duplicated the Echelon software and had it stored on a secure server so he could reverse-engineer a new terminal. The facility was wired with electronic counter-measures, and the computer was secured via military-grade encryption. Any radio contact or decryption device would have been detected, which meant that only someone who knew how to crack polymorphic algorithms could access the terminal. Since Marshall was the only agent qualified to hack into

the server without aid of an electronic device, he was assigned his first field op.

Box seats were arranged for Sydney and Marshall at Royal Albert Hall behind the seat of Thatcher Powell, Cuvee's head of IT security. Sydney drugged his drink so he would sleep through the first act. At that point she stole his access card to the server room.

Sydney's client status got her past the

desk guard. Then she and Marshall infiltrated the third floor, which Cuvee had leased. As they approached the server rooms, guards tranquilized Marshall, but Sydney took care of them. While trying to stay awake, Marshall accessed the system and downloaded the file. They were back at the opera by intermission, when Powell awakened to find his access card was still in place.

CIA COUNTERMISSION:

Considering that Marshall has a photographic memory, Sydney knew they could not fake the information when they returned to SD-6. Failing other options, the mission plan was to pull Marshall out of SD-6. When Sydney and Marshall returned from London, he was to be taken into protective custody and brought to Langley for an extensive debriefing. He would then be given the option to work for the CIA. The mission was aborted when an unknown third party kidnapped Marshall before the CIA got to him.

Before being captured, Marshall had e-mailed Cuvee's copy of the Echelon access program to SD-6.

LOCATION: **London, England**
ALIAS: **Marie Robinson from Jennings Aerospace**

SD-6 MISSION E662-A:

When SD-6 downloaded the program Marshall had e-mailed, they discovered that Marshall's e-mail had been broken up into packets of data and routed to SD-6 via Internet service providers around the world. There was a malfunction and several data packets were not transmitted. Without them, SD-6 could not access Echelon. The error occurred in a government-operated facility in Ho Chi Minh City. Sydney and Dixon were sent there to retrieve the data packets.

Sydney entered the Ministry of Culture and Information under the guise of giving a presentation for a front company. Once the attendees were rendered unconscious via a high-intensity pulsed strobe light, she retrieved the ID of La'an Nguyen, which gave her access to every room in the ministry. The data packets were supposed to be on the hard drive located in the server room, but the hard drive was not there.

As it turned out, the hard drive was in for repairs in another room. Knowing that Sydney had only a limited amount of time before the people she had been giving the presentation to would wake, Dixon said that he would go for the hard drive. Sydney insisted that she could make it, but Dixon beat her to the room and found the drive.

CIA COUNTERMISSION:

Sydney was instructed to download the data packets and swap them out with corrupted data. When Dixon obtained the drive, Sydney had to abort the switch.

With the data information, SD-6 would be able to access the Echelon system. However, the process required them to hack into the system through an access port "back door." Since Derevko was the only one who could locate that back door, she was given access to a computer to close the port before SD-6 could get in. The back door was found at an overlap point between Echelon and Russia's SORM system. She was able to close it before SD-6 could access the system.

LOCATION: **Ho Chi Minh City, Vietnam**
ALIAS: **Nina Bailes from Tech-Sky Industries**

SD-6 MISSION E662-B:

Marshall was coerced into helping Cuvee's operatives reconstruct the Echelon data. Cuvee's operatives included the man in suit and glasses whom Sydney had encountered in Taipei (Mission J535-A). Marshall signaled SD-6 through the computer, and Dixon was able to trace him back through the IP address. Sydney, knowing there was no extraction team, informed Sloane that she and Dixon wanted to go in themselves. He had no choice but to sanction the rescue operation.

Once at the building, Dixon piggybacked onto the surveillance feed and found Marshall in a storage room on the forty-seventh floor. Dixon locked down the elevators and secured all access doors to keep the guards away. All Sydney would have to deal with were the guards in the room.

Meanwhile, instead of designing the program to access Echelon, Marshall had been stalling for time until his duplicity was discovered. He was about to be executed for his deception when Sydney arrived to rescue him. Unfortunately, security was alerted and they were trapped in the room on the forty-seventh floor. Though Sydney was out of options, Marshall had their solution, thanks to his fear of flying: A parachute he had hidden in the lining of his jacket enabled them to escape out the window.

LOCATION: **Mexico City, Mexico**
ALIAS: **Rave girl**

OBJECTIVE: Acquire the Triad's quantum gyroscope missile guidance system

SD-6 MISSION E663:

Karl Schatz, a Triad courier, was known to be transporting a prototype quantum gyroscope missile guidance system to Berlin for mass production. The system was capable of transforming a seventies-era

Scud missile into a precision-guided munition with a range and lethality equivalent to a cruise missile. Sydney and Dixon intercepted the device en route in a simple pickpocket operation carried out at the security screening area of the airport.

CIA COUNTERMISSION:

Once Sydney obtained the prototype, she was to separate from Dixon for their flights home. She met up with the CIA team in a utility room at the airport so they could duplicate the gyroscope. Since the duplication process would take several hours, there was some time to kill. Believing they were safe from prying eyes in a foreign country, Vaughn and Sydney took Weiss's advice and went out for what quickly became a romantic dinner. But just as quickly it turned into something else entirely.

They were observed having dinner by operatives of the Alliance who were trailing Sydney as a part of an ongoing mole hunt at SD-6. Though they were able to take out the operatives before Sydney's cover was blown, she was forced to abort the countermission and deliver the real prototype to avoid suspicion.

After Sydney returned to SD-6 and learned that the mole hunt had been called off, she determined that it was safe to give them the fake prototype and return the original to the CIA. But she and Vaughn agreed that they could not take such a risk again.

LOCATION: **Nice, France**
ALIAS: **Punk/Goth girl**

OBJECTIVE: Take down SD-6 and the Alliance

CIA MISSION E665-A:

The team was called into headquarters for an emergency briefing. It was obvious that something was up, but none of the agents knew the purpose of the meeting until Kendall made the announcement to a shocked room. The Joint Task Force on Intelligence had intercepted communications that revealed Sloane had been MIA for five days. The Alliance had already replaced him as head of SD-6.

When Sydney went into SD-6, Sark mentioned that Sloane's replacement, Anthony Geiger, was bragging about tapping into Sloane's secret files on Server 47. Neither Sydney nor Jack knew of this server, but Sydney suspected that it might be a weakness they could exploit. She believed it was a central Alliance computer that would provide names of the Alliance partners, locations of their offices, and everything they would need to take down the organization.

The CIA tracked Server 47 to a 747 purchased by the Alliance in 1998. The interior of the plane was retrofitted to contain a secure server with a satellite uplink. Gils Macor oversaw the operation on the plane, which landed only for refueling. Macor and his bodyguards traveled with the server at all times.

Twice a week at alternate airports in England and Spain, a high-end escort agency dropped off a new "friend" for Macor. In Barcelona, Sydney boarded the plane as the newest "friend." Once she was alone with Macor, she forced him to help her access the terminal in his private bedroom. She transmitted the contents to Vaughn. They had everything they needed to take down the Alliance and SD-6.

Sydney was forced to fight her way off the plane, taking out Macor and his guard. The pilot was shot during the fight and Sydney had to parachute out of the plane before it went crashing into the ocean.

LOCATIONS: **Barcelona, Spain; airspace over
   the Atlantic Ocean**
ALIAS: **High-end escort**

SD-6 MISSION E665-B:

The information taken off Server 47 suggested that it was time to take down SD-6. Each SD cell used a code that changed weekly to operate its security system. The current codes were listed in the information received from the server. Jack was sent in to SD-6 to confirm the actual code. If it matched the code they had, it would confirm that the rest of the intel was real. Unbeknownst to the CIA, however, recent intel had come to Geiger's attention suggesting that Jack was the mole. As soon as he entered SD-6, Jack was taken into custody.

With Jack compromised, Sydney could not go in either. As a result, she was forced to reveal the truth to Dixon about SD-6. Though she wanted to help him deal with the shocking news, there was simply not enough time. She asked him to confirm the code for her before it changed. When Dixon left her, it was unclear whether or not he was going to perform the task.

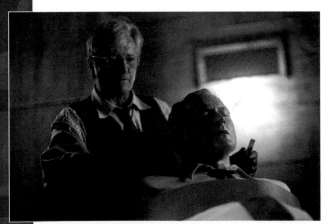

Dixon went into the office, still numb at the idea that he had been working against the U.S. government for over a decade. He managed to confirm the code, but before he contacted Sydney, he gave his wife, Diane, a call to tell her he loved her. When Dixon sent the code for confirmation, he knew that his life would be changed forever.

Once the code was confirmed, the CIA, in conjunction with the FSB, BAP, MI-5, and the Shin Bet, conducted a simultaneous raid of all
(continued on page 155)

Arvin Sloane managed to bring down one of the world's largest criminal organizations, a feat no government organization had succeeded in accomplishing. His plan was deceptively simple, but it required numerous willing—yet unknowing—participants to set it in motion.

The first part of Sloane's plan was to extort $100 million out of the Alliance to bankroll his future endeavors. He did this following the supposed death of his wife, Emily. When the Alliance believed that Sloane had ended her life, they made him a partner in the organization, injecting him with a tracking device and giving him a new level of access to the organization.

Shortly after his ascension to partner, Sloane created a scheme to make it appear that he was being blackmailed by operatives who had kept Emily alive and taken her hostage. A series of events including a traced phone call from a B&B where Emily was registered, a wineglass containing a drug to counter the effects of the poison he had used on his wife, and a sighting of her on the street made it appear that someone was playing with him. SD-6 investigated every step along the way, supporting his belief.

After Emily's casket was exhumed and found empty, Sloane went to the Alliance to bring them into the loop. He was then contacted by an unknown individual claiming to have Emily. When he asked for proof, the person sent him Emily's ring finger in a box. Forensics showed that it had been cut off while she was alive. The individual called back demanding $100 million in bearer bonds in exchange for her safe return.

Sloane warned the Alliance that someone had obviously infiltrated their secure communications. The best way to find out how was to put a tracking device in with the bearer bonds. When Sloane made the exchange, instead of finding Emily, he received a photo of her with a bullet through her head. Moments later the tracking device on the bonds went dead.

Ariana Kane, head of Alliance counterintelligence, was sent in to investigate the extortion plot. She began her investigation with Jack. Due to the intense scrutiny he was under, Jack had the CIA manufacture hard evidence to cover his tracks over the past several months.

In spite of his precautions, Kane found brain matter on the gun Jack had checked out the day Emily was killed. The gun had been used to kill Steven Haladki after Jack

learned that the CIA agent was working for the Man and had relayed information that had placed Sydney's life in danger. The tests proved it was Haladki's DNA, but this did not explain why Jack did not report the murder. Jack told Kane that he reasoned it was best to keep quiet about killing CIA agents for security purposes.

Kane asked for his cell phone to make sure the phone's SIM card corresponded with the locations he was supposed to have been. Vaughn made a duplicate SIM card and they did a brush pass to replace it. However, the ink on the card blurred, giving it away as a fake. Her agents were called in to get Jack, but he escaped.

Jack worked with Derevko to review the investigation files and find a way out of this situation. They realized that Ariana Kane was linked with Jean Briault, the Alliance member Sloane had killed. There was also evidence that the day Sloane turned over the $100 million in bearer bonds, Kane opened an account in Monaco. The money appeared briefly in that account before being switched to another. Jack was in the server room tracking the money and e-mailed this information to Sloane. But he was taken into the SD-6 "conversation room" before he could confirm that Sloane had gotten the message.

Sloane interceded before Jack could be harmed. Later Jack and Irina wondered about Sloane's motives, since he had been the one who requested Kane for the investigation. In the end Kane was found guilty of a crime that Sloane had committed.

Bringing about the end of the Alliance was a simple matter of passing along the necessary information to Sydney Bristow. After having discovered that Jack and Sydney were double agents, Sloane had the Alliance's tracker disabled so he could disappear. Then Sark passed along intel to Sydney that led her to the computer server that bore all the Alliance's information. As the CIA worked to take down the Alliance, Sloane relaxed on a beach with Emily, who was very much alive.

(continued from page 152)

known Alliance facilities, bringing down the entire organization. Sydney rescued her father from a likely execution. And, in the end, Sydney and Vaughn shared a genuine kiss.

LOCATION: **Los Angeles, California, USA**
ALIAS: **None**

OBJECTIVE: Locate information on and destroy Project Helix

CIA MISSION E664-A:

CIA agent Emma Wallace was killed in a very public execution in Berlin. She had been working on a deep-cover assignment trying to gain the trust of Dr. Renzo Markovic, a former R&D scientist who had been developing new classified technology. He had already received preliminary bids from several terrorist organizations. Another operative the CIA had in place, Jim Lennox, was presumed dead as well. His last transmission indicated that Markovic was heading to the Sirena del Sol Resort where he conducted his research.

Sydney was sent in to the resort to seduce Arden Kezek, Markovic's chief of security, so he would follow her into a trap. Vaughn injected him with a cardiotoxin that would cause a heart attack within an hour. Vaughn supplied the antidote after Kezek led them to Agent Lennox—who was still alive—and downloaded the information on Project Helix.

LOCATION: **Cayo Concha, Dominican Republic**
ALIAS: **Resort patron**

CIA MISSION E664-B:

Project Helix was found to be a breakthrough in next-generation molecular gene therapy. It referred to a new procedure whereby a patient's face and body were shaped to identically resemble someone else in a doubling process that altered the physical appearance of the patient on a genetic level. The only way to distinguish between the real person and the double was through an ocular scan. A flaw was deliberately put in the iris to help differentiate the duplicate.

Sydney and Lennox went to a train yard to download the schematics on the sequencer used in the procedure. During the mission a man claiming to be Lennox made contact with the CIA. When he arrived at the train yard he did, indeed, prove to be an exact duplicate. The CIA knew that Markovic had performed the initial Project Helix procedure on himself, but it was unclear which version of Lennox was the real one and which was Markovic.

Not knowing which man was her ally, Sydney had to disarm both operatives and take them into custody. She revealed the fake Lennox when he turned his gun on her, trying to stop her from destroying the device that would return his identity. The real Lennox then killed Markovic, and they destroyed the Project Helix technology to ensure that no one else went through the procedure.

Information from the Project Helix files indicated that the sequencer had been used twice, but it did not reveal the identity of the second subject. Sydney was unaware that under orders from Arvin Sloane, the second subject of Project Helix—Allison Doren—had already killed and replaced her best friend, Francie.

LOCATION: **Poland**
ALIAS: **None**

OBJECTIVE: Capture Sloane and secure the release of Neil Caplan

CIA MISSION E666-A:

With the fall of SD-6, Sydney announced her intention to resign from the CIA. Although Sloane was still on the loose, she reasoned that her main goal had been accomplished. He was only a small part of the Alliance and that enemy had been destroyed. Since she was about to graduate, Sydney was ready to start a new phase of her life. That is, until Sloane called her with congratulations, telling her that it was he who had provided the intel to take down the Alliance and warning her to keep away from him or he would have to end her life.

Enraged by his audacity, Sydney went back to the CIA and put off signing her resignation until Sloane was taken in. Her first opportunity came with a new mission.

Sloane and Sark had kidnapped mathematician Neil Caplan and his wife and son. Caplan specialized in a branch of mathematics known as knot theory, the study of geometric objects and how they fit together. Considering that all Alliance facilities had been raided but the CIA hadn't found a single Rambaldi artifact, it was assumed that Sloane must have moved everything to a secure location. They suspected he was using Caplan to help assemble a Rambaldi device.

Following his debriefing, Marshall signed on with the CIA, reasoning that he thought he'd been an agent for them all along. He was able to recover a few fragments from the RAM drive on Sloane's database. It indicated that Sloane had checked the address of a cybernetics specialist named Holden Gendler before wiping all stored information. This led the CIA to the dead man who had removed Sloane's Alliance implant prior to his own demise.

From there the CIA found information that Sloane had chartered a C-123 out of Shipman Airfield to transport "the artifacts." The airfield was operated by a transatlantic smuggling cartel. Sydney accessed the airfield undetected to find the flight data recorder of the plane Sloane chartered, which tracked him to his location.

LOCATION: **Mojave Desert, California, USA**
ALIAS: **None**

CIA MISSION E666-B:

Sydney and Vaughn followed information from the flight recorder to Switzerland, where Vaughn met with one of his contacts and learned that Sloane had hired local mercenaries for a job. The team infiltrated the operation and found Caplan's wife and child, though the mathematician remained missing. Marshall then tracked the incoming calls on one of the operative's phones to Sloane's cell phone. He was at the AMPCORP bank.

Sydney and Vaughn intercepted Sloane at the bank, but he informed them that the place was rigged with C-4, and he would set it off if he was not allowed to leave. He took Sydney as his driver, while Vaughn worked to defuse the C-4. Once the explosive was defused, Sydney was instructed via comm to take Sloane in. Sydney informed him that he was on a CIA hit list, meaning that if she killed him she wouldn't even be breaking the law. Unfortunately, she didn't get the chance.

Sloane threw open his door, but he wasn't intending to jump. Sark was in a van behind them. He had the van pull up beside Sydney's car, shearing off the open door. Sydney tried to shake off the van, but a bodyguard held her at gunpoint. As the vehicles continued down the road, Sark pulled Sloane into the van and escaped.

LOCATION: **Zurich, Switzerland**
ALIAS: **None**

CIA MISSION E667-A:

A CIA asset outside Kandahar reported seeing someone matching Sloane's description in the company of men loyal to Amhad Kabir, a Pashtun warlord who worked with the Taliban. The CIA was interested in finding Kabir, hoping to learn the purpose of that meeting. Unbeknownst to Kabir, Sloane had had Dixon infiltrate Kabir's compound a year earlier to steal a shipment of missiles. Being that Dixon had information on Kabir's compound, Sydney asked for help in finding the man. Dixon, however, was still hurting from the fact that she had been hiding the truth from him for so long. He refused to get pulled back into the spy life and would not help her.

Examining other options, Will Tippin provided analysis indicating that Kabir's ex-wife, Alia, held a bitter hatred toward him. Sydney was sent in to the Vatican Embassy in Mexico City to convince Alia to reveal the location of her ex-husband's compound.

While Sydney tried to meet with Alia, Echelon picked up the keywords "terrorist," "weapon of mass destruction," and "Rambaldi" at coordinates matching Sydney and Vaughn's location. Sensing danger, Weiss instructed them by comm to get out immediately. But Alia refused to leave with her. Sydney was forced to knock Alia unconscious to carry her out of the building. Vaughn drove them out of the area as the satellite picked up a massive explosion behind them. Weiss said it was obliterating everything on radar, but from Sydney and Vaughn's perspective, nothing appeared out of the ordinary at all.

When they returned to the embassy church, they found that sixty-two people had been incinerated by a mysterious device that left the building intact. It was assumed that Sloane provided this demonstration to kill Kabir's ex-wife. Suddenly Alia was much more willing to help. The CIA released information that she was killed in the attack in exchange for her agreeing to turn over the location of Kabir's compound.

LOCATION: **Mexico City, Mexico**
ALIAS: **Old Mexican woman**

CIA MISSION E667-B:

Sydney parachuted into Kabir's compound to steal the neutron bomb that was determined to be a Rambaldi device. As she worked her way into the building, she was caught before she could signal for the tactical unit. The unit could not go in after her for fear that the weapon would be used against them.

With their options exhausted, Vaughn approached the one person who had previously been in the compound: Dixon. The former agent reluctantly agreed for Sydney's sake. Together they infiltrated the compound, obtained the Rambaldi device, and rescued Sydney. When they returned, Dixon accepted a position within the CIA, unsure of what it meant for his marriage.

LOCATION: **Kandahar, Afghanistan**
ALIAS: **None**

CIA MISSION E668-A:

Intel revealed that Sark had killed Luri Karpachev, a high-level arms dealer in Russia. Derevko listed Karpachev among former contacts when the NSA debriefed her. When his body was found without a wallet, Derevko noted that he kept the key card to his home safe. She assumed Sloane was looking for a Rambaldi manuscript that Karpachev had sold in 1993 to Ilya Stuka. The manuscript was a study of the human heart.

Derevko suggested she could meet with Stuka to find out about the manuscript. Then she could arrange a meet with Sloane to make the exchange, so the CIA would be able to grab him. Though Derevko had been working more agreeably with the CIA, the idea of releasing her was a risky proposition. The only way Kendall would allow the mission was for Derevko to be injected with a subdermal tracking device, with Jack holding the receiver so he could track her movements at all times.

Derevko and Jack teamed up for the mission. She met with Stuka and learned that he had traded the manuscript to an opium dealer named Chang in Hong Kong.

LOCATION: **Bangkok, Thailand**
ALIAS: **None**

CIA MISSION E668-B:

Based on Derevko's intel, the State Department requested Chang's palace to be added to a list of sites being inspected by the United Nations. The visits were routine verification of treaty compliance. Irina and Jack entered the building posing as inspectors and sedated a captain they were going to "interview." They then broke into the library, stole the manuscript, and returned to the Joint Task Force headquarters with it.

LOCATION: **Hong Kong, China**
ALIAS: **Jack and Irina pose as UN inspectors**

Word that Derevko was interested in selling the manuscript reached Sloane through back channels. Sark set up a meeting to discuss the purchase of the Rambaldi manuscript using Derevko's old e-mail address. Knowing the mission would be risky and there was a possibility she would not return, Derevko told her daughter she loved her and said her good-byes. Sydney reassured her mom that she would be coming back, though Sydney did not realize that that wasn't quite Derevko's intention.

The plan was that Irina would go to meet Sark with two Delta Force guards. She would not have the manuscript with her but would tell him it was close by. Sloane would pick her up while the CIA tracked her on satellite back in L.A., and Jack would be waiting with a helicopter several blocks away. When the call was made, the team would surround the vehicle and ambush Sloane.

Irina was concerned that Sloane might find the tracker. She convinced Jack to remove it from under her skin. When he was finished, Jack and Irina could not deny that their bond had once again grown in the months they had spent working together. They shared a kiss and fell into bed together.

The next morning a car arrived with Sark, not Sloane, inside. After a brief exchange, Irina got into the car. As the CIA tracked the car, they suddenly lost the downlink to the satellite. Kendall called Delta team in to stop the car. But when they reached it, the car was empty. When they realized they had been duped, Jack was instructed to activate the tracker. He was forced to admit that he could not do that because he had removed it at Irina's request. Realizing what was going on, Jack told Kendall to get the Rambaldi manuscript immediately. When it was retrieved, Kendall found that it had somehow been replaced by a fake.

As the CIA came to terms with its failure, Sark brought Derevko to Sloane. She handed him the stolen Rambaldi manuscript.

LOCATION: **Panama City, Panama**
ALIAS: **None**

OBJECTIVE: Learn what Derevko, Sloane, and Sark are planning, and take them into custody

Jack Bristow was given operational control of the task force based on his intimate knowledge of fugitive Irina Derevko and his long-standing written record of accurate predictions regarding his former wife. As it turned out, Jack had removed the tracking device Marshall had implanted, but unbeknownst to Derevko, he switched it with a passive transmitter. So even if Sloane performed a bug sweep, they wouldn't pick up anything until it transmitted. Once the signal went active, base ops tracked Derevko to Stuttgart. Sydney and Vaughn were sent in to confirm Irina's signal and move in only after she led the CIA to Sark and Sloane.

Derevko was tracked to Brucker Biotech, the German equivalent of the Human Genome Project. Marshall hacked into the CCTV system and relayed the feed to the team. They saw Sark enter the building, but he took out a surveillance camera, causing the CIA to lose the feed. Minutes later they also lost the signal from Derevko's transmitter. She had obviously discovered the tracking device.

Fearing they would lose two of the three targets, Sydney and Vaughn were sent into the building. They located Derevko, but she led them on a chase that took them outside. The building exploded moments later. Derevko had managed to save their lives before she and Sark disappeared again.

Analysis indicated that Brucker sponsored genetic research, specifically the mapping and sequencing of human chromosomes. It was rumored that they had catalogued the DNA of millions of private citizens. It was possible that Derevko was interested in the information because it would allow them to access genetically targeted viruses, though the CIA was not sure if that was the true reason she had accessed the building.

LOCATION: **Stuttgart, Germany**
ALIAS: **None**

CIA MISSION E669-B:

Emily Sloane—previously believed to be dead—suddenly walked into the consulate in Florence. She told the duty guard that she wanted to cooperate with the CIA and that she would talk only to Sydney Bristow.

After the initial shock of learning that Emily was alive, Sydney flew to Italy to meet with her. Emily offered to help turn her husband in, but only after the CIA promised in writing that it would not sentence him to death. Though Sydney was reluctant to agree to that plan, she knew it was their best chance at obtaining Sloane.

Emily was wired with a transmitter when Sloane returned to their Tuscan villa with Derevko and Sark. As the CIA listened in, Sloane told Emily that he was giving up everything for her. He was planning to lead a normal life. Suddenly the transmitter went dead. Emily had removed the wire.

Fearing that Sloane had found the wire, Sydney insisted that her team storm the building. Once inside, Sydney went after her mother. She shot Derevko, forcing her mother to abandon the disk case she had been holding so she could escape.

As they ran to a waiting helicopter, Dixon fired at Sloane but hit Emily. Derevko pulled Sloane away from his wife and they escaped in a helicopter with Sark. Sydney was heartbroken to find that Emily was dead.

LOCATIONS: **Florence, Italy;**
Tuscan countryside, Italy
ALIAS: **None**

UNAUTHORIZED MISSION E670-A:

Failing any other leads on Derevko and Sloane, Sydney contacted Elsa Caplan, hoping to find more information on her still-missing husband (Mission E666-A). When Elsa refused to help, Sydney dug deeper into the Caplan history and learned that over the previous year, three phone calls had been made to their residence from a Russian Intelligence operative named Grigory Ivanov. At first Sydney suspected that Neil was working for Russian Intelligence. Concerned for her husband, however, Elsa admitted that she was the spy.

Seven years earlier Elsa had been ordered by Russian Intelligence to seduce and marry Neil. Her objective was to keep tabs on his work. She was given a tracking device to implant in his arm. It had a secondary purpose in that it was designed to release fifteen milligrams of cyanide into his bloodstream two days after it was activated. The CIA had intercepted information

meant for Elsa, indicating that the implant was active. She effectively committed treason by admitting the truth, but Elsa insisted that she loved her husband and wanted him back.

To find Neil Caplan, Sydney needed to obtain an SVR locating device to home in on the implant in his arm, but Jack ordered her to give up the search. Considering how similar the Caplans' story was to Jack's life with "Laura Bristow," he did not trust Elsa. However, Sydney went against Jack's orders, obtained the code from Elsa to locate the implant, and went to meet with Morgan Nikovich, a black market contact who dealt in SVR contraband. He sold her an SVR tracking device.

LOCATION: **Moscow, Russia**
ALIAS: **Russian cowgirl**

UNAUTHORIZED MISSION E670-B:

Sydney made contact with Vaughn and gave him Caplan's location in Saria, Spain. Vaughn met her in Saria and the two planned to infiltrate the building in which Caplan was being held.

Sydney and Vaughn fought their way through the guards and found Neil Caplan. Sydney removed the implant, calmly explaining that his wife was a Russian agent. Caplan revealed that he already knew this. He worked for the NSA. They may have lost Sark in the process, but they were able to reunite a family.

The mission was also successful in that they were able to download the DNA database Caplan decrypted from the computer he was working on. It provided them with a lead on Sloane and Derevko. Though she was ultimately victorious, Jack still took Sydney to task for disobeying his orders.

Although things were tense between Sydney and her father, other parts of her personal life seemed to be coming together. Dixon happily told her that he would be staying in Los Angeles. His wife, Diane, had come to terms with his work, so he had rescinded his recent transfer request. As Sydney and Vaughn went out to dinner with the Dixons, it appeared as if their lives were finally getting on track. But it was after dinner that everything went horribly wrong.

As Dixon watched Diane drive off, her SUV exploded, killing her instantly. It was Sloane's payback for Emily's death.

LOCATION: **Saria, Spain**
ALIAS: **None**

OBJECTIVE: Locate and obtain the Rambaldi Heart

CIA MISSION E671-A:

While the CIA had been in possession of the manuscript that was ultimately stolen by Derevko, the pages were catalogued and copied. Marshall analyzed a page devoted to Rambaldi's study of the human heart. Drawings on the page turned out to be specific strands of DNA that, when strung together, provided a DNA fingerprint for Proteo Di Regno, a private citizen currently living in Panama City.

The DNA also acted as a code key to decrypt page ninety-four of the Rambaldi manuscript. The page listed times and dates of horrific historical events, including a date forty-eight hours in the future with no prediction attached. Until the moment specified by Rambaldi had come and gone, the operations center was put under the jurisdiction of the NSA by order of the National Security Directive.

Sydney and Dixon were sent to bring Di Regno in, but they arrived after the man had been killed and his heart removed. They noted that Di Regno bore the mark of Rambaldi on his hand. At the crime scene Sydney found a piece of a latex glove presumably used by the murderer. They were able to take a partial print off the latex.

LOCATION: **Panama City, Panama**
ALIAS: **None**

CIA MISSION E671-B:

Marshall was able to find a match for the fingerprint. It belonged to Emilio Vargas, a freelance assassin specializing in interrogation and wet work. Sydney and Dixon went in posing as members of the Triad looking to hire Vargas. Once they got him alone, they forced answers out of him. Dixon's interrogation turned incredibly brutal, as he was still grieving over his wife's death and needed to extract Sloane's location.

Vargas admitted he had killed Di Regno for the heart. He explained that it wasn't a real heart, but rather a machine that was now in a truck on its way to Cartagena.

LOCATION: **Guadalajara, Mexico**
ALIAS: **Triad operative**

CIA MISSION E671-C:

The truck was tracked to the Estrella Shipyard. Sydney, Vaughn, and Dixon went in with Delta Force to determine whether the heart was a weapon or explosive of some kind. By the time they reached the empty truck, there were only twenty minutes before the prophesied deadline. If they were unable to locate or determine the nature of the device, NSA deputy director Brandon had been given permission to initiate secondary protocol and rig the yard with enough C-4 to destroy everything in the area.

Dixon found the man who took possession of the heart and threatened him with a C-4 explosive. Dixon ignored all orders to disarm the weapon as time clicked down. The man indicated that the shipment was in Container 246-B as time ran out. But the bomb did not go off. Dixon had previously cut the primer cord, rendering the C-4 harmless.

Once they located the heart device, it was clear that it was not a bomb, although its real purpose was uncertain.

LOCATION: **Cartagena, Colombia**
ALIAS: **None**

OBJECTIVE: Learn the identity of the second subject of Project Helix

CIA MISSION E672-A:

Due to some damning evidence, Will Tippin was under investigation for being the second duplicate created using the Project Helix technology (Missions E664-A and E664-B). Sydney, however, refused to believe that her friend was guilty of spying on her and being the one who planted the bomb that killed Diane Dixon for Sloane. Based on analysis Will had been working on regarding the second double, Sydney and Vaughn searched for Hans Jurgens, the scientist who invented the computer imaging equipment for Project Helix.

The task force acquired surveillance of Jurgens in Berlin, where he was tracked to a local sex club. Sydney entered the club playing the role of a dominatrix. She and Vaughn blackmailed Jurgens for the information, threatening to show his wife pictures of him with Sydney.

Jurgens told them that the computing power required to model a person's entire genome was tremendous. During the doubling process, Markovic had to be connected to an off-site computer facility (a server farm). If they could access those servers, they could find the identity of the second double. Jurgens did not know the location of the farm.

LOCATION: **Berlin, Germany**
ALIAS: **S&M bondage queen**

CIA MISSION E672-B:

With help from an unknown source, Will managed to escape custody. While in hiding, he contacted Sydney and told her that his prior research indicated Markovic had a farm in Marseilles. It was probably the server farm they were looking for. After evidence arose to suggest Will's innocence, Jack quietly (without Department of Justice approval) sent Sydney and Vaughn with a team to infiltrate the server farm.

Considering the chief of security held a kill switch that enabled him to wipe clean all of their data at any sign of attack, Sydney's first objective was to enter the security room to get hold of the kill switch so the team would have time to upload the file. But Derevko was on site and had beaten Sydney to the punch. Derevko erased the file; however, she also transferred a copy to a secure location. She offered it to Sydney in exchange for something to be determined at a later date. Derevko left with the promise that she would be calling on Sydney soon.

When the CIA later accessed the file, they learned that Will's DNA did not match that of the person who had been doubled.

LOCATION: **Marseilles, France**
ALIAS: **None**

OBJECTIVE: Learn the nature of the Rambaldi device Sloane was assembling

CIA MISSION E673-A:

Derevko contacted Sydney with information that there had been a break-in a month earlier at the NSA facility storing the Rambaldi artifacts. Everything was taken, except for the newly acquired Rambaldi Heart. Sloane had the other twenty-three artifacts, meaning that he would be able to put together Rambaldi's ultimate device.

Derevko provided the address for Sloane's warehouse of Rambaldi artifacts. The team went in to raid the building, but

Sydney realized, too late, that it was a setup. At the same time, Jack had been sent to retrieve the heart from the NSA facility, but he was kidnapped and the heart was taken while in transit.

LOCATION: **Zurich, Switzerland**
ALIAS: **None**

CIA MISSION E673-B:

Derevko contacted Sydney again, saying that she did not know the boxes that were supposed to contain the Rambaldi artifacts had been switched. She then told Sydney where Sark could be located and that he knew where Sloane was holding Jack. Sydney followed the intel and found Sark at Club Välsmakande. Stating that his loyalties were flexible, Sark easily gave up Sloane's location in Mexico City. Sark was then taken into custody.

LOCATION: **Stockholm, Sweden**
ALIAS: **Club patron**

CIA MISSION E673-C:

Using Sark's access codes, Sydney took Alpha Team into the building where Sloane was holding Jack. She disabled security on the floor and arrived just as Sloane completed putting together the Rambaldi device known as Il Dire. He finally had a major piece of the Rambaldi puzzle that he had been searching decades for.

At the same time, they realized that Derevko was also in the building. Dixon located Jack, while Vaughn went after Sloane and Sydney chased her mom. Derevko led her daughter to the roof. Seemingly cornered, Derevko admitted that Sydney was the one in Rambaldi's prophecy. Then she jumped off the roof. Sydney raced to the edge to find that her mother had been tied to a bungee cord. She managed to escape.

When Sydney reunited with Vaughn, she learned that Sloane had also gotten away with the Rambaldi device.

LOCATION: **Mexico City, Mexico**
ALIAS: **None**

The Presumed Death and Return of Sydney Bristow

Sydney returned from the mission in Mexico City to enjoy an evening with her roommate, Francie. While they were relaxing, Sydney found that she had a voicemail message from Will. She was horrified to hear that he suspected Francie was the double from the Project Helix program. And when she went for a spoonful of coffee ice cream, which the real Francie hated, Sydney confirmed the suspicion and went for her gun.

The double, Allison Doren, realized Sydney was on to her and attacked. While the two fought, Sydney found a bloodied Will in the bathtub. She feared he was dead but had no time to confirm it as Allison continued the attack. Sydney managed to shoot the faux Francie three times before falling unconscious.

Sydney awoke two years later having no memory of the missing time. The world was a different place for her. Dixon was CIA director of the Joint Task Force on Intelligence. Marshall was about to have a baby with Carrie Bowman. Will had gone into the Witness Protection Program. Francie was dead. Sydney's father was in prison. Sloane was walking free. And Vaughn had gotten married.

OBJECTIVE: Recover stolen schematics for CIA spy drone

CIA MISSION E301-A:

As Sydney waited for answers to what had been happening over the past couple of years, the CIA continued with the day-to-day business at hand. Weiss reported to Dixon that they had lost contact with one of their operatives. A train heading to Avignon was boarded and all the passengers were killed. The hijackers obtained a computer smart card from the body of passenger Scott Kingsley, who had designed a spy drone for the CIA that could fly undetected by radar. The CIA feared that the drone could be modified and turned into a delivery system for biological or chemical weapons. Kingsley was en route to Avignon to deliver the schematics, but they were on the stolen smart card. The group responsible referred to itself as the Covenant.

Based on the conversation Sydney overheard between Dixon and Weiss, she pretended to recognize Kingsley's name and a reference to a Covenant outpost in Paris. She needed some answers, and she knew the only way to get them was by getting back into the mix, even if she had to lie to do it.

Agent Weiss led the operation into the Covenant facility but was open to any warnings Sydney may have had due to her supposed familiarity with the building. The team quickly came under attack, and Dixon ordered them to abort the mission. As they attempted to leave the building, the team was killed except for Weiss and Sydney. It had obviously been a trap.

Upon their escape from the building, Sydney admitted to Weiss that she had faked the memories, hoping to find some information on her missing time. He suggested that she go see Arvin Sloane. The former head of SD-6 had been pardoned by the government and set up a relief organization called Omnifam. Though Sydney did not believe for a second that Sloane had repented, she had little choice in the matter. Most of her contacts had dried up in the past two years. And with her father currently in prison, she felt utterly alone.

LOCATION: Paris, France
ALIAS: None

UNAUTHORIZED MISSION E301-B:

Sydney reluctantly made contact with Sloane. After an uncomfortable reunion, he revealed that the man she saw in charge of the operation in Paris was a former Russian MVD (from the Ministry of Internal Affairs) and high-class hit man named Gordei Volkov. Using information from one of her few remaining old contacts,

Sydney learned that Volkov was scheduled to make the delivery in Prague. Sydney hit Volkov's vehicle hard and fast and retrieved the smart card. Volkov died, falling on his own knife during their fight.

Sydney then returned to the Rotunda, threatening to destroy the smart card unless the NSC released her father immediately.

LOCATION: **Prague, Czech Republic**
ALIAS: **None**

OBJECTIVE: Recover an abducted CIA scientist

CIA MISSION E302-A:

Two agents, Pietr Klein and Ulrich Rotter, were working undercover at Leizug Aerospace when they were forcibly taken from the facility. The CIA received an audio file from an unidentified organization claiming responsibility for the abduction. There were coordinates in the file leading to a designated location where they would find a package. The CIA believed it was the work of the Covenant.

Sydney volunteered to retrieve the package, though Dixon would rather have sent Weiss so that Sydney could have some time before going back into the field. Sydney found the box and swept it for explosives. Once she determined it was clean, she opened it and found the severed head of Pietr Klein. A piece of paper was wedged in his mouth. It was the Covenant's list of demands, written in Russian.

LOCATION: **Munich, Germany**
ALIAS: **None**

CIA MISSION E302-B:

Per the list of demands, the NSC authorized trading Sark for Ulrich Rotter, the remaining CIA scientist being held by the Covenant. NSC director Robert Lindsey justified the transaction by claiming that after spending two years in custody, Sark had been bled dry of information and was no longer a useful asset. Intelligence provided by Arvin Sloane also indicated that Sark was responsible for the death of a high-ranking member within the Covenant, which suggested that their intent in making the exchange may have been revenge. Dixon agreed to authorize the trade.

Sydney and Weiss accompanied Sark to the exchange point in the desert. Once the exchange was initiated, Sark and Rotter were released simultaneously just as a group of incoming vehicles, including a Delta Force chopper, threatened the exchange. The NSC announced that it had countermanded the operation. Lindsey was using the CIA agents as bait. The ruse failed, and the Covenant got away with both Sark and Rotter.

LOCATION: Sonora Desert, Mexico
ALIAS: None

CIA MISSION E302-C:

A satellite was tasked to track the Covenant sedan carrying Sark and Rotter once it left the desert. The passengers were followed to a nightclub in Frankfurt known for selling top-of-the-line synthetic drugs. Analysis believed it was a Covenant front. It was assumed that the club owner, Otto Edel, would know where Rotter was being held.

Sydney infiltrated the club and demanded information from Otto by holding a syringe with an air bubble to his neck. He told her the location of the alarm terminal that protected the sub-basement, but he did not know the code. Sydney used a code descrambler, but Vaughn, who had been brought in to monitor from the Operations Center, realized that the alarm required the code to be translated into a password. He decrypted the code and gave her the password "Top Hat." Once the system was deactivated, the team moved in and retrieved Rotter.

Prior to the mission, Vaughn, who had left the CIA after his marriage so he could move on with his life, was reinstated in the CIA. Though Sydney was having a difficult time adjusting to their new relationship in light of his marriage, she was working toward healing. However, this became increasingly difficult with the addition of the new NSC liaison, Lauren Reed . . . Vaughn's wife.

LOCATION: Frankfurt, Germany
ALIAS: Former Harvard biochem major turned
   drug dealer

OBJECTIVE: Obtain or destroy the Russian Medusa antisatellite pulse weapon

CIA MISSION E303-A:

At 4:47 p.m. Moscow time, Russia's early warning system was activated. They assumed it was an incoming missile, but it was actually a satellite that had fallen from orbit and crashed into Gorky Park. As a result of the perceived attack, the Russian president activated his nuclear briefcase, initiating a countdown to a prelaunch sequence. With two minutes to spare they attained visual ID and scrubbed the launch. Ten minutes later Echelon picked up a call from a secure line between Sark and former Russian colonel Boris Oransky. It was not a coincidence.

Oransky had been dishonorably discharged in 1996 from Russia's military space command and went to work for a privately held French contractor, the owner of the satellite that had fallen to Earth. It was initially unclear why he brought down his own company's satellite, but during the call he and Sark discussed meeting to move on to "phase two."

Sark was tracked to Mexico City, where he was kept under surveillance. Sydney and Weiss were sent in to record Sark and Oransky's meet in a marketplace. Under disguise, Sydney had to get in close to the meet to observe what the men were looking over. She heard them refer to "Medusa" and saw a photo of the location—a three-mile radius around the Kremlin. But her proximity to the private conversation garnered unwanted attention from Oransky. Sydney was made.

The meeting ended abruptly. Oransky took a hostage while Sark fled. It was a standoff until Marshall tapped into Oransky's comm and overloaded his operatives' earpieces. Sydney saved the hostage, but Oransky got away.

LOCATION: **Mexico City, Mexico**
ALIAS: **Senorita in a poncho**

CIA MISSION E303-B:

Information found on the SD-6 database revealed that Medusa was an antisatellite pulse weapon. Once operational, it could cripple a network of satellites, making the government blind to potential attack. The device would beam a microwave at one satellite in the chain, which would then relay the pulse across the entire network.

It was determined that the falling satellite in phase one of Sark and Oransky's plan revealed Russia's nuclear attack protocols, including the location of the bunker housing Medusa. Sark and Oransky were likely prepared to steal the device.

The Russians claimed to oppose antisatellite weapons and were not about to admit having one. Therefore, the CIA had to access the bunker where Medusa was stored and prevent it from being stolen.

Considering that Sloane had a relationship with the science ministry, they used him to get Sydney and Vaughn into the building by attending an awards banquet as members of Omnifam. By the time they sneaked out of the party, Sark and Oransky were already in the process of stealing Medusa. Sydney and Vaughn were forced to destroy Medusa by rigging the generator and blowing up the entire sublevel. They escaped through a vent only moments before the explosion would have incinerated them. Sark escaped, but Oransky died in the explosion.

LOCATION: Moscow, Russia
ALIASES: Sabina Milan from Omnifam;
　　　　　Russian soldier

OBJECTIVE: Prevent the Covenant from releasing a newly developed bioweapon

CIA MISSION E304-A:

A four-man team broke into a French epidemiology lab that performed cutting-edge vaccine research on viruses like West Nile, HIV, and Ebola. They took four vials containing strains of Ebola. A fifth was damaged during the heist, infecting one of the team members. That man, Laszlo Bogdan, was taken into custody.

The French handed Bogdan over to the CIA, as they shared in the American government's desire to learn more about the Covenant. Sydney helped question the man, who was an expert in cracking high-end security systems. He mentioned that a second job was being planned. The stolen chemicals were not going to be used until after that job, because the Covenant was planning on using the items to modify the virus.

Freelancer Simon Walker was leading the team for both jobs. His team included Javier Parez, Avery Russet, and the now deceased Laszlo Bogdan. Echelon picked up Walker looking for a replacement for Bogdan. Sydney went in undercover as the replacement. She was tasked to place a tracking device on whatever they stole so the CIA could follow it to the Covenant. As she went in to meet Walker for the first time, she was surprised to learn that he already knew her . . . under the name Julia Thorne.

Assuming Walker had met her during her missing years, Sydney had no choice but to play along. Apparently they had something approaching an intimate relationship, and he seemed to think of her as a killer. She was accepted into the team after succeeding at a test stealing a diamond necklace from Princess Demetria of Greece.

LOCATION: **Seville, Spain**
ALIAS: **High-class freelance specialist . . .**
    then Julia Thorne

CIA MISSION E304-B:

Walker questioned Sydney about a surveillance photo of her with Vaughn. She claimed that Vaughn was her supplier. Since he was listening in, Vaughn immediately called Marshall and had him work up a file for a fictional Vaughn. When Walker checked into Vaughn's credentials, he found enough to back up what Sydney had told him. Walker bought her cover story and then detailed their plan for the heist.

The team was set to hit a storage facility run by the disease control ministry, thirty-five miles outside Saragosa. To get in they had to disable the power, which triggered an off-site security response, giving them five minutes to get the package and get out. Once the safe was open, Sydney had only one minute to remove the canister inside before the safe would self-destruct.

The target was an artificial pathogen. When combined with the pathogen stolen the week before, the Covenant would be able to genetically tailor a biological weapon for specific targets—a designer bomb that would be effective against only the people of their choosing. The heist was a success.

During the heist Vaughn was discovered on watch, and it almost compromised Sydney's cover. She was forced to stab him and leave him for dead to keep Walker from killing him. Before his body was dropped down a gully, she managed to put a tracer on him so he could be found. The tracer had been intended for the case storing the biological weapon. Though Sydney managed to save Vaughn's life, she lost the case.

Sydney broke into Walker's room to steal the case while he was out celebrating. However, Sark had come to collect early. He got away with the pathogen. The Covenant now had what they needed to create the biological weapon.

LOCATION: **Saragosa, Spain**
ALIAS: **Julia Thorne**

CIA MISSION E305-A:

At 4:30 GMT an imaging satellite picked up a heat signature of a small aircraft flying a tactical profile. The National Reconnaissance Office tracked it to a maximum-security facility in the Ural Mountains, where it flew multiple passes, deploying some kind of biological weapon. Echelon intercepts between the responding emergency teams indicated that the entire prison population of three hundred guards and five hundred prisoners died within minutes.

There was, however, one survivor: Kazari Bomani, the largest arms dealer in Africa. Sark broke the man out during the hazmat cleanup. It was believed that the Covenant was able to tailor the bioweapon to kill everyone except the person whose genetic profile was encoded into the virus.

Because Sloane had been the one who provided intel that led to Bomani's arrest, Lauren and Sydney went in to meet with Sloane to see if he had a lead. It was a difficult pairing, since Lauren still blamed Sydney for the injuries Vaughn sustained when she stabbed him to protect him from Walker.

As Sydney and Lauren signed in at Sloane's conference building, they saw him pull up in a town car. Before they could greet him, Covenant agents intercepted and kidnapped him. Sydney and Lauren gave chase, but Sloane's kidnappers got away with him.

LOCATION: **Mexico City, Mexico**
ALIAS: **None**

CIA MISSION E305-B:

Sloane was released by Bomani shortly after his kidnapping, beaten and bruised. He informed Lauren that he had told Bomani what he had been planning to tell the CIA: that his contacts within the Yakuza (the Japanese mafia) had developed the first AI computer virus. The virus could probe networks, analyze systems, and then write itself, creating its own subviruses. In the wrong hands it could crash markets, destroy banks, shut down transportation, and bring military installations to a halt.

Sloane gave the CIA the information so they could go in and disable the virus first. If they destroyed it, Bomani would know Sloane had tipped them off and would kill him. In effect, Sloane became a double agent working for the Covenant, while presumably staying loyal to the CIA.

Bomani and Sark were planning to infiltrate a Yakuza-run casino in Osaka where they would download the virus from a secure server. Sydney was instructed to go in first and disable the program. Marshall would provide Sydney with a program to rewrite the virus and render it unusable. Since he could not do that without seeing the code, he had to go along on the mission.

Once they were in the back room of the casino, they used a password Sloane had provided to access the computer. Marshall downloaded a copy of the virus, then rendered it unusable as Sark and Bomani arrived. Syd and Marshall hid, as Sark accessed the system and transferred a copy of the unusable virus to their server.

LOCATION: Osaka, Japan
ALIAS: Girlfriend of a high roller

OBJECTIVE: Obtain the Russian launch-control console-interface device

CIA MISSION E306-A:

Someone posing as a Russian defense official approached hardware engineer Robert Lange and asked him to create a device that could be taken into any missile silo and interface with the launch control console. Once the device was built, Lange learned that the man who had hired him wasn't actually Russian defense; he was a Covenant representative. Lange went on the run to prevent the Covenant from getting what he had invented.

Sloane provided intel that Lange was scheduled to meet Heinrich Strauss at Club Delphi in Milan to pick up new identity papers. Sydney and Vaughn were sent in to get to Lange before the Covenant did. Since Lange had undergone massive plastic surgery, they had to scan for facial reconstruction to identify the man. They found Lange at the exact same moment that (the still living) Allison Doren had trained a laser sight on him. Sydney pushed him out of the way, but Lange fled.

Sydney managed to catch up with Lange, but she was too late. Allison had extracted Lange's tooth and killed him before Sydney could stop her. Allison knocked Sydney unconscious and escaped.

The camera previously used to identify Lange had stored an X-ray of the man's face. It showed that the missing tooth held a radio frequency identification chip. It was believed that Lange used the transmitter to open a high-security lock that would otherwise self-destruct.

LOCATION: Milan, Italy
ALIAS: Club patron

CIA MISSION E306-B:

Sydney instructed Sloane to set up a meeting with Sark and Allison to let them know that their travel plans to retrieve Lange's device had been compromised. He then offered assistance in revising their arrangement. Once they told him where they were heading, Sloane set up a plane for the following morning.

When Allison's plane landed, Sydney and Vaughn tracked her to an abandoned hotel. Allison retrieved a case from inside a hotel room wall just as Sydney arrived. The two fought and Sydney shot Allison.

Allison was sent away in an ambulance that never got to its destination; the ambulance crashed and the attendants and guard were killed. Sydney suspected that Allison survived the shooting, thanks to the Rambaldi medication that had saved her life when Sydney shot her two years earlier.

The CIA was able to retrieve the device before Allison disappeared.

LOCATIONS: Prague, Czech Republic; Sofia, Bulgaria
ALIAS: None

OBJECTIVE: Destroy the Chinese-built maser

CIA MISSION E307-A:

Sloane informed the CIA that Sark had given him a mission to locate, copy the specs, and corrupt a Chinese-built maser. A maser is a microwave that gets focused into a pinpoint beam, similar to how light gets focused into a laser. When the maser is mounted on a satellite, it can kill people from space, making the cause of death look like tissue damage, heart failure, or a brain hemorrhage—as if the victim died of natural causes.

Sloane was scheduled to attend a charity function hosted by the Chinese government at one of their ministries. The Covenant had acquired intelligence that China had a working maser unit and intended to mount the device on one of its satellites as part of an assassination program. The Covenant tasked Sloane to steal the maser's operating system, which was in the Chinese defense minister's office. The CIA assigned Sydney to go along, obtain the system from the minister's office, corrupt the maser, and pass the faulty data to the Covenant. She did not enjoy the thought of going on a mission with the one man she despised more than anyone else in the world.

Using a remote-controlled car with optical camouflage, Marshall was able to deactivate the building's alarm system from base ops. Then Sydney gained access to the minister's office and attached a motherboard to the EPROM chip. She connected the computer with Marshall, who accessed the maser's operating system and corrupted it.

LOCATION: Beijing, China

ALIAS: Christina Myers, executive assistant to Arvin
Sloane

OBJECTIVE: Reconstruct Sydney's memories of the past two years

UNAUTHORIZED MISSION E307-B:

Following the previous mission, Sloane gave Sydney a possible clue to her missing years. The day she was found in Hong Kong, Sloane received a letter in his office written in Sydney's handwriting. Inside there was a code. Jack used a cipher text that Derevko had devised to break the code, indicating that Sydney should go to an address in Rome: 1124 Piazza Barberini, a penthouse apartment belonging to Julia Thorne.

Vaughn learned that Lauren had discovered that Sydney was Julia Thorne and had told the NSC. He warned Sydney and arranged a charter jet to take her to Rome before she could be taken in for the murder of Andrian Lazarey, a Russian diplomat she was believed to have killed. Sydney explored the apartment, finding things that were familiar from images she had been having in dreams. She also found a bottle of pills with a prescription for Julia Thorne.

The NSC raided the apartment and took Sydney into custody. Dixon was immediately removed as director of the Task Force for withholding information from the NSC on Sydney's presumed involvement in Lazarey's death. The Rotunda was placed in lockdown as the NSC took control.

LOCATION: **Rome, Italy**
ALIAS: **None**

UNAUTHORIZED MISSION E308:

With Sydney in NSC custody and Dixon removed from duty, Jack and Vaughn teamed up to break Sydney out of the holding facility. They asked Sloane to help make it appear as it if were an action by the Covenant.

Jack broke into the FEMA building to download blueprints of Camp Williams, an unacknowledged NSC detention center used for the interrogation of suspected terrorists whose captivity the government would not admit. As Jack left the building, security came after him, firing. Sloane pulled Jack into the van and took the bullet. Jack performed the operation to remove the bullet from Sloane when they got back to his storage facility.

To get into Camp Williams, they also needed access codes. After Marshall failed to obtain the codes for them, Lauren offered to help. She had become disillusioned by Lindsey's off-the-books NSC actions while interrogating Sydney. Jack met with an old contact named Brill to put together a tactical team. Lauren used an override system on security, placing it within five inches of the central control station.

Inside the facility, Sydney had been subjected to torture and questioning. The NSC found a coded message taped to the underside of a desk in the apartment in Rome. They insisted that Sydney decrypt it, but she refused. Later, fearing for the safety of a prisoner she had befriended named Campbell, Sydney gave up the message. It was a set of coordinates. Campbell was a setup, however. He worked for the NSC.

Lindsey then informed Sydney that they were proceeding with a dangerous neurostimulation procedure in order to learn more about her forgotten years. Once the procedure was complete, they expected to know more about the Covenant as well as leaving Sydney in a mental state in which she could never tell anyone about what happened.

As they were prepping for the procedure, the strike team entered the building and freed Sydney. She told her father that she had given Lindsey incorrect coordinates. The real coordinates pointed to a strip of desert near the San Andreas Fault. There Sydney and Jack found a buried metal box encasing a human hand with the Rambaldi symbol tattooed on it.

LOCATION: **Southern California, USA**
ALIAS: **None**

UNAUTHORIZED MISSION E309:

To protect Jack and Vaughn's cover, Lauren returned to Lindsey claiming that she had been taken by the Covenant and that Sydney was still being held hostage in exchange for the Rambaldi device known as Il Dire. Sloane then contacted Lindsey and confirmed that the Covenant was responsible for the breakout. Vaughn and Jack went in saying that they were investigating her disappearance. They had set up a paper trail replete with rental cars and airline tickets.

Lauren gave Lindsey a cell phone that supposedly came from the Covenant, along with the instruction to hit redial at 6:30 that evening. He did as ordered and made the deal for the exchange. Lindsey then contacted Sloane about putting a hit on Sydney to have her taken out during the exchange. Lindsey wanted to make sure she would never tell anyone about what he had put her through at the NSC detention facility.

Meanwhile Sloane had made contact with Dr. Brezzel, a researcher to whom Omnifam had given a grant to develop a noninvasive therapy for treating long-term severe amnesia, using a combination of synthetic and organic drugs. The doctor agreed to perform the procedure on Sydney.

Dr. Brezzel monitored Sydney while she was in an REM state, giving her a verbal cue over headphones so she became lucid. Once she was aware of being in the dream state, her objective was to pick up the thread of her last memory (before the missing time) in as much detail as she could. In the dream she remembered being taken away by some men following the fight with Allison Doren. She then went on a tangent where she saw the name St. Aidan. Sydney's health was at risk during the procedure, and Brezzel was forced to abort.

At the same time, Lauren had Marshall run a DNA analysis on the hand Sydney and Jack had found buried in the desert. He couldn't find a match in the available data banks. He did run some other forensics tests and found that whoever the hand belonged to had been alive as recently as four months earlier, when it was removed. Using the Kremlin's database, Marshall then matched the hand's DNA to Lazarey, which suggested that Sydney did not kill him.

Sydney insisted on going back into the dream, where she fought with a double of herself who told her to trust Lazarey. She then saw Will Tippin, who made another reference to St. Aidan, suggesting that he might know something. Out of the dream, Dr. Brezzel informed Sydney that memories had been removed with a precision that suggested that she was a willing participant.

LOCATION: **New Haven, Connecticut, USA**
ALIAS: **None**

UNAUTHORIZED MISSION E310-A:

Once Jack obtained Will Tippin's location from Witness Protection, Sydney went to meet him. Will informed her that St. Aidan was a contact of his when he worked as a CIA analyst. He went through his old routine to get in touch with the man and they set up a meet. When St. Aidan arrived, Sydney was hiding, but she could see it was Andrian Lazarey, missing hand and all.

Lazarey tried to end the meeting, but Will stopped him by mentioning Julia Thorne. Just as Lazarey asked if they had been to Graz and found some unknown item, Sark intervened and abducted Lazarey.

LOCATION: **Warsaw, Poland**
ALIAS: **None**

UNAUTHORIZED MISSION E310-B:

Sydney managed to figure out where in Graz she would have hidden the object Lazarey mentioned during her missing time. She discovered a safety-deposit box in the Hotel Verlustzeit that was registered with a long-term storage contract to Julia Thorne. Sydney then looped the surveillance cameras, and she and Will went to break in to the box. They quickly learned that they were not the only ones after the box.

Sark and Allison Doren arrived soon after, having tortured the information out of Lazarey. They cut into the back of the safety-deposit box and took the item inside mere moments before Sydney could grab it.

Will and Sydney split up. Will took on Allison and stabbed her, while Sydney fought Sark and retrieved the metal box he had taken known as the Rambaldi Cube. Upon close examination, Marshall discovered a piece of human tissue that was still active, along with the name Milo Rambaldi etched inside the box.

LOCATION: **Graz, Austria**
ALIAS: **Member of a rock band**

UNAUTHORIZED MISSION E310-C:

Completing the ruse established in Mission E309, Sydney prepped to make the exchange with Lindsey—she would be released from custody in exchange for the Rambaldi device Il Dire. Sloane hired a team that appeared to work for the Covenant to pick up the device. As soon as they left the area, Sydney would drive to a separate location to meet Lindsey. Sydney was concerned that Sloane would take the device, so she secretly had Weiss track it for her.

During the exchange, a sniper shot and killed Lindsey—the same sniper he had asked Sloane to hire to kill Sydney during the exchange. It was Sloane who altered the plan, and although he denied involvement in the assassination plot, Sydney knew better. When she got to him, she discovered that there was nothing in the box but junk. Sloane explained that Lindsey was the one who was deceiving them with the machine parts, not him. Once again, Sydney did not believe him, though she couldn't do anything about it.

LOCATION: **Los Angeles, California, USA**
ALIAS: **None**

CIA MISSION E311:

Once the full Task Force was back in place following Lindsey's death, Director Kendall abducted Sydney and filled her in on her missing years. The Rambaldi Cube had been stolen, and he was taking her to the Project Black Hole facility, hoping to work with her to retrieve it. Luckily, Marshall had placed a tracer on the Rambaldi Cube, and they traced it to Patagonia, where the Covenant was planning to fuse Rambaldi's DNA with Sydney's eggs to create a form of "second coming."

Dixon led a team of commandos into the facility, believing the fertilization was to happen that night. Although Kendall wanted everything brought back for analysis, Dixon gave Sydney permission to destroy the entire lab and its contents.

During the raid they found a beaten Lazarey and took him back to Los Angeles for medical attention. En route he mentioned "the Passenger," but Sydney did not know what he was talking about. As they moved into the hospital a sniper killed Lazarey. At a later date it was discovered that the sniper was Lauren Reed.

LOCATION: **Patagonia, South America**
ALIAS: **None**

Sydney Bristow's deep-cover assignment as Julia Thorne

Any unauthorized disclosure is a violation of Section 23, Paragraph 5 of the Patriot Act.

SYDNEY'S FUNERAL

It was believed that Sydney Bristow had died following her fight with Allison Doren. There was a fire in her apartment, and a charred body was found with matching DNA. After nine months Director Kendall received a phone call from Sydney. She was in Rome and said that she had escaped from the Covenant and wanted to come home. Kendall met her at a safe house in Tuscany, where Sydney told him everything, starting with her fight with Allison.

She was knocked unconscious during the fight and woke up days later, strapped down in the back of a van under the supervision of Oleg Madrczyk, a Covenant torture specialist. He told her that they had unearthed Francie Calfo's body and burned it in the apartment. When a body is burned badly enough, the DNA they test is in the teeth. The Covenant had extracted pulp from Sydney's teeth and injected it into Francie's, thus ensuring the false ID.

Sydney was injected with a neurotoxin causing temporary paralysis and was forced to watch her own memorial with her mouth taped so she could not call out for help. At one point, she was inside a van mere feet away from Vaughn.

From the funeral Oleg took her to a Covenant facility near St. Petersburg. He spent months trying to break her using sensory deprivation, electroshock, and other cruel methods of torture. Oleg drugged Sydney and withheld food from her for weeks, but she resisted. This went on for six months. At about that time, Oleg thought he had made a breakthrough. Once he thought she believed she was Julia, the Covenant gave her a test. She was instructed to kill a man named Lazarey as a show of her allegiance to the organization.

TESTING SYDNEY

Sydney, however, had not been broken. Her training from Project Christmas contained a fail-safe to protect its subjects from being turned. She was effectively hardwired to stand up to some pretty intense efforts at brainwashing. However, she did have to kill a man to secure the Covenant's trust that the torture protocol had worked, trading his life for her own.

When Sydney contacted Kendall, he tried to convince her that she couldn't go home. Ignoring his advice, she went to see Vaughn. It had been only nine months since her presumed death, and she was surprised to see that he appeared to be with another woman already. Sydney was going to confront Vaughn when she noticed some men watching his place.

Knowing Vaughn would be in danger if she showed up, she went back to Kendall, who revealed that he was not FBI, but really an agent of the DSR. The Covenant, which U.S. Intelligence knew little about at that time, was working on some kind of Rambaldi project. Kendall tasked Sydney to go undercover as Julia Thorne to learn what they were up to.

In Algeria she met Simon Walker and worked with him in the search for the cube that housed Rambaldi's DNA sample. They pursued a variety of leads, with Sydney reporting back to Kendall every step of the way.

Simon located Andrian Lazarey, a Russian diplomat who was devoted to studying Rambaldi and finding the cube. Sydney went to Lazarey the night before she was supposed to kill him, and they struck a deal to fake his death.

Sydney fed the Covenant false leads while she and Lazarey were working for the DSR to find the cube. It took her nine months, but she found it buried in a cave at the Fish River Gorge in Namibia. A mile-long trek brought her to an elaborate vault that housed the cube. Lazarey had devoted thirty years of his life to acquiring the twelve keys to the vault. Each one had a name on it that corresponded to a keyhole in the wall. Once the vault was opened, Lazarey's hand was stuck in a trap as the cave started to collapse around them. Sydney was forced to cut off his hand, and they escaped with the cube.

The agreement Sydney had with Kendall was that after the cube was found, they would let Lazarey disappear and Sydney would deliver the cube to Kendall, but she never showed. Instead she sent a DVD explaining that she couldn't go along with the plan. Sydney knew that the end purpose was to fuse her eggs with Rambaldi's DNA to give birth to a child. She hid the cube and went to see a man who had done long-term research on how the brain stored short- and long-term memory. She didn't want to know what happened to the DNA, so she went through a procedure to make her forget . . . everything.

OBJECTIVE: Extract Covenant defector

CIA MISSION E312:

The CIA received word that a Covenant operative wanted to defect. In exchange for his extraction and immunity, the high-ranking official offered to turn over everything he knew about the Covenant.

Sydney and Vaughn were sent to North Korea to meet with the defector in the Gai-Li marketplace. But once the CIA plane was in North Korean airspace, the pilot and copilot died under suspicious circumstances. Vaughn took the controls as the plane came under attack by heat-seeking surface-to-air missiles, which forced Sydney to shut off the engines. Vaughn dropped the plane into a nosedive and they escaped the missiles before initiating a crash landing.

Assuming it was the work of the Covenant, the Joint Chiefs ordered Dixon to stand down on any rescue mission, given the tenuous relationship the United States had with North Korea. Unofficially, Dixon had no intention of resting until Sydney and Vaughn were found. In the meantime Jack contacted Irina via computer for assistance. She sent her sister, Katya, in to help.

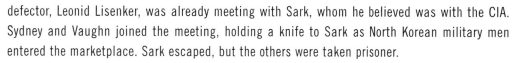

As the Korean military arrived, Sydney and Vaughn blew up the plane, then continued to Gai-Li. There they found that the defector, Leonid Lisenker, was already meeting with Sark, whom he believed was with the CIA. Sydney and Vaughn joined the meeting, holding a knife to Sark as North Korean military men entered the marketplace. Sark escaped, but the others were taken prisoner.

A Korean colonel tried to get Vaughn and Sydney to talk, but they refused. Lisenker, however, was more than willing to confirm that they were CIA agents and fill the Koreans in on anything they asked so he could live. As the Koreans prepared a firing squad for Vaughn and Sydney, the pair of former lovers shared a kiss. They were then taken out to be shot.

As the colonel counted down to fire, one of the guards jumped the trigger, taking out his compatriots and saving Sydney and Vaughn. Their savior was a contact of Katya's. He made sure they got safely out of the country.

In the meantime Katya's price for her assistance was for Jack to assassinate Sloane. Jack quickly accepted the mission, but Katya called him off moments before he killed his former friend.

LOCATION: Gai-Li, North Korea
ALIAS: Swiss insurance adjuster

OBJECTIVE: Obtain the Doleac Agenda

CIA MISSION E313-A:

When Lisenker had decided to defect, he hid a microdisk at a Covenant chalet with a copy of the Covenant playbook, known as the Doleac Agenda. It detailed operational plans for the six Covenant cells, including the names and headquarters of the cell leaders. Sydney and Vaughn were sent to plant a hidden camera on a rock face beside the chalet so the CIA could inspect the property. The chalet was owned by an arms dealer and former contact of Lisenker.

LOCATION: **Chamonix, France**
ALIAS: **None**

CIA MISSION E313-B:

Based on information obtained from the infrared camera, all indications pointed to the fact that the chalet's security Lethal Response System (LRS) was the work of Toni Cummings, a former thief who turned her talents from cracking security systems to designing them.

Once they got a lock on Cummings's location, Sydney and Weiss went in posing as clients to obtain specs on the chalet's LRS—a system that is illegal in most countries. As they were not certain that

Cummings had designed the security system, they first needed to confirm that it was her work and then persuade her to detail the countermeasures she had put in place at the chalet. Once confirmed, Cummings provided the information and schematics in exchange for the promise that she would be treated well while in custody.

LOCATION: **Athens, Greece**
ALIAS: **South African diamond miner**
    Rebecca Davidson

CIA MISSION E313-C:

According to Cummings, the Lethal Response System was a half-mile-long tunnel that served as the way into the chalet. Her schematics indicated that the LRS comprised three separate zones: automated sentry guns, electrified zones, and motion-triggered acid spray. Jack was brought in for the mission so he could execute an uplink while Sydney and Vaughn infiltrated the chalet.

Once the uplink was activated, Marshall tapped into the security network and severed the kill-zone's diagnostics from the main alarm system so the guards didn't know the team was there. They needed to get through the LRS, into the wine cellar, and back again in five minutes.

When Sydney and Vaughn reached the first tunnel in the LRS, they used inflatable Kevlar balls to attract the sentry guns, which locked onto the balls and kept firing until they ran out of ammunition. The next zone was supposed to be armed with 150,000 volts of electricity. However, it was set to 500,000 volts, which their rubberized neoprene suits could not protect against. If they touched the walls or ladder they would be fried immediately.

Sydney and Vaughn used a rope to lower themselves into the tunnel, careful not to touch the electrified walls or ladder. Once in the lower-level tunnel, they sprayed sealant to keep an acid spray in the final section from raining on them.

The Doleac Agenda was encrypted on a microdot that Lisenker had injected into the cork of a bottle of Château Margaux 1953. It took a moment for them to find the right bottle. While they were in the wine cellar, security was alerted. Sydney took the bottle and they escaped through the tunnels, making it out and past the guards with Jack's help.

Regrettably, all named Covenant leaders were found dead by the time the Doleac Agenda was obtained. Though it was unknown at the time, Lauren and Sark had killed the leaders in a failed attempt to take over the Covenant. However, their actions ultimately were beneficial to the Covenant, as they rendered the Doleac Agenda useless to the CIA. As a result they were named coheads of the North American Covenant cell.

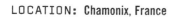

LOCATION: Chamonix, France
ALIAS: None

OBJECTIVE: Obtain the new plasma charge technology

CIA MISSION E314-A:

The CIA intercepted a burst transmission that indicated an operative of Shining Sword, a fundamentalist terror network based in the Philippines, had acquired a plasma charge and was shipping it to one of their European cells. The transmission included specs indicating that the device was only six inches in diameter but very powerful. It could easily take out several city blocks.

The CIA traced the transmission to a digital storage facility in Vancouver, where the Shining Sword operative maintained his database. The company, Digi Stash, was a self-storage facility for digital files with state-of-the-art firewalls that could not be hacked into unless someone on the inside opened a port.

Sydney and Vaughn went to the facility looking to lease vault space. Once they were inside, they uplinked with Marshall, looking for information to intercept the bomb. When they hacked into the system, they found that someone else at the facility was in the process of infecting the system with a virus. They were forced to disconnect before the virus affected the CIA's copy of the information.

Upon exiting, the vault manager opened fire on Sydney and Vaughn, though he was begging someone not to make him shoot. After they took cover, they came out to find the manager dead. They went after the mystery assailant, but lost her.

LOCATION: **Vancouver, British Columbia, Canada**
ALIAS: **A radio astronomer**

CIA MISSION E314-B:

Marshall was able to learn from the recovered data that a freighter was scheduled to dock in Lisbon with the plasma charge. Sydney and Vaughn were sent in with an explosives sniffer to find the charge. Once on the ship, masked operatives attacked them. Sark was unmasked and forced Vaughn to drop his gun to protect Sydney. Sark and his unidentified partner tried to escape. Vaughn went after Sark, while Sydney followed the unidentified woman.

Vaughn caught up with Sark, but he activated the bomb to get free. With Marshall's help over the comm, Vaughn deactivated the bomb, but both Sark and the woman escaped.

LOCATION: **Lisbon, Portugal**
ALIAS: **None**

CIA MISSION E315-A:

Bomb designer Daniel Ryan blew up the Wicklow National Bank building to demonstrate his latest product to the Covenant. He set up the bomb, then called the authorities to give them time to evacuate the building and bring in the bomb squad. It was likely that he wanted the bomb squad to prove there was nothing that could be done to disconnect the upgraded version of the plasma charge. That proof came at the cost of two innocent bomb squad lives.

Ryan indicated that negotiations with the Covenant would be exclusive for forty-eight hours, at which time he would detonate a second bomb—targeted against America—to elicit bids from hostile terrorist groups. If interested, the Covenant was instructed to make contact with him at a pub in Belfast. Instead, the CIA made contact, then drugged and kidnapped him.

According to recent Covenant defector Lisenker, Ryan always did business with the Covenant from room 305 in the Commodore Hotel. The CIA built a replica of the hotel room and the floor to convince him that he was doing business with the Covenant, and Sydney went in as his new contact. Ryan was suspicious when his usual contact did not arrive, but his concerns were diminished when he ran into Lisenker in the corridor. Ryan agreed to their terms but added the condition that he would deal only with Sark. Lisenker knew that Ryan had never met the man, which allowed Vaughn to enter posing as Sark.

Ryan planned the exchange. An associate of his would carry the disk with the information on Nuage Air Flight 212 from Rome to Paris. Twenty minutes outside of Rome, Ryan's associate would come and sit next to "Sark" and the transfer would be made. Once the associate met with Sark, he would call off the second demonstration. The problem was that the associate would be looking for the actual Sark.

The CIA then used the frequency Ryan had originally broadcast from to relay the information to the Covenant to get Sark on the plane.

LOCATIONS: **Belfast, Northern Ireland; Los Angeles, California, USA**
ALIAS: **Covenant agent Emma Warfield**

CIA MISSION E315-B:

Sark got on the plane as planned, but the contact did not arrive. After pressing Ryan for information, Sydney realized that the meeting was staged to get Sark on the plane. It was a setup.

Vaughn was instructed to take Sark into custody, while Sloane informed Sydney that the Covenant killed Ryan's brother, Christopher. Actually, it was Sydney who had killed him, to prove she believed she was Julia Thorne. And now a bomb had been planted on the plane to kill Sark in a very public act of revenge.

Vaughn found the bomb in the baggage compartment. It had a barometric sensor with a trigger device based on altitude. If the plane descended, the bomb would detonate. Marshall suggested

tricking the bomb into thinking it was still at 18,000 feet by encasing it in an airtight, temperature-controlled bubble after it was removed from the fuselage and the motion sensor was deactivated. Vaughn used Sark to help disconnect the bomb, and they put it in a cooler.

Ryan pretended to agree to disarm the bomb, but once he realized that Sydney was the woman who had killed his brother, he activated it via cell phone instead. He also activated the bomb in Marshall's office that Vaughn had brought in following Mission E314-B. Considering that the bombs were activated by a phone call, Marshall extrapolated that the detonator must have been on a cellular network. If he could find the right signal, he might be able to reverse-engineer the deactivation protocol and shut down both bombs. But it would take time.

Knowing how tight the time was, Jack turned an interrogation into murder as he killed Ryan. He then brought Ryan back to life with a defibrillator. Jack took this course of action to prove that Ryan wasn't as prepared to die as he thought he was. Ryan gave up the codes to deactivate the bombs, and Sark was taken into custody.

LOCATIONS: On board a plane outside Rome, Italy;
    Los Angeles, California, USA
ALIAS: None

OBJECTIVE: Locate "the Passenger"

CIA MISSION E316-A:

While Sark was being extradited to the United States, his plane made an unscheduled landing in the middle of the desert. The passengers found inside were dead and frozen, indicating that Sark had parachuted out at altitude, leaving the plane depressurized. It landed on autopilot.

Moments after the discovery, Sark called Dixon to inform him that the Covenant had Dixon's children. In exchange for the children, the Covenant demanded the release of five men who had been apprehended in the past year and were currently in CIA custody.

Suspecting that Sark had bailed over Arizona, Marshall tasked Echelon to focus on a two-hundred-mile radius around the estimated drop point. The satellite intercepted a burst of Covenant communications from a warehouse in Nogales. After examining the options, Dixon ordered a tactical mission.

(continued on page 193)

I t was believed that the Covenant had intercepted CIA intelligence regarding the meet with Covenant defactor Leonid Lisenker in North Korea. Suspecting the intel had come from an internal source, Jack was assigned to run point on the investigation into a possible leak.

All information concerning Sark's extradition to the United States was being strictly compartmentalized within the Task Force. When he escaped, it proved that the intel had come from the inside. Jack had  Marshall pull up the server logs for the classified FAA database. They found that it was accessed from an outside IP address under Dr. Barnett's account. Marshall tracked the IP back to Omnifam and Sloane was arrested.

During the investigation, Marshall picked up Sark on the plane's voice recorder responding to someone with the phrase, "Not if I see you first, love." Later Jack heard Lauren use the same phrase with Vaughn. Further investigation into Lauren's recent travel and activities suggested that she may have been the mole.

Jack presented Senator Reed with a paper trail that—although not definitive proof—made a strong case for Lauren being the mole instead of Sloane. Neither the NSC nor Central Intelligence had authorized Lauren's most recent flights. Sixty percent of those flights coincided with dates and locations where verifiable Covenant activity occurred.

Later, when Jack returned to meet with the senator, he found the man dead, an apparent suicide after having admitted to being the mole. Lauren's explanation for her recent activities was that her trips had all been under her father's orders. She attempted to resign, but Dixon did not accept her resignation. With her mother's help, Lauren had masterfully covered up her actions.

In going through the senator's personal effects, the CIA discovered evidence that Sloane had been consulting with him on Rambaldi artifacts for the past two years. In direct violation of his pardon agreement, Sloane had handed over Rambaldi artifacts to Reed. In light of this revelation, the CIA revoked his pardon and he was sentenced to death.

Sloane told Jack that Senator Reed had recruited him to work for a secret organization within the U.S. government known as the Trust. Reed indicated that they were interested in Sloane's knowledge of Milo Rambaldi. He made an agreement that if Sloane would work with the Trust, Reed would secure his pardon. Sloane said he had lived up to his side of the bargain and asked Jack to prove that the group existed.

Jack met with a contact who indicated that the Trust did exist, and he later confirmed that Sloane had been telling the truth. However, after Jack learned of Sloane's past affair with Derevko (when she was still believed to be Laura Bristow), he did not reveal what he had learned about the Trust. It seemed that he was effectively allowing Sloane to die. However, this was later revealed to be part of a larger plan.

In the meantime Sydney approached both Vaughn and Jack with her suspicions that Lauren was the mole. During a mission to meet a Covenant freelancer named Cypher, Sydney thought she had seen Lauren kill their contact. At first Vaughn refused to believe her, but he later searched Lauren's things. He found the wig and a gun she had used to kill Cypher.

Vaughn told Jack and Sydney about his discovery. Jack instructed him to act like nothing had changed, so they could track Lauren and the Covenant's search for the Passenger. In the meantime the Agency was secured, limiting Lauren's access to classified documents.

(continued from page 190)

The warehouse was a trap and the children were not in the building. Even though it was an obvious trap, Dixon refused to leave the building without his children. Finally Sydney was able to convince him to leave. They escaped moments before the building exploded.

LOCATION: **Nogales, Mexico**
ALIAS: **None**

UNAUTHORIZED MISSION E316-B:

Dixon's son, Steven, was released with instructions to give his father a cell phone. The moment the two were reunited, a call came in from the Covenant, who admitted to feeding the CIA Echelon intercepts using his children as bait. Dixon reported back to the Task Force that the Covenant now insisted on the release of ten prisoners. At least that was what Dixon was instructed to say.

Dixon, however, received other instructions. The Covenant wanted him to use his personal access codes to steal a Rambaldi artifact from the NSC storage facility, Project Black Hole. Dixon approached Sydney for help. She could not turn her friend down.

At the facility, Sydney took out a perimeter guard while Dixon entered through the front door and gained access to the security console. He shut down security at a steam vent, so Sydney could enter wearing a neoprene hot suit to keep her from being scalded. When she got into the warehouse, she found that the artifact in Lot 45 had been taken to analysis. The artifact turned out to be a gold puzzle box with the name "Irina" written on it. Sydney exited with the box.

LOCATION: **Nevada, USA**
ALIAS: **Dune buggy rider**

CIA MISSION E316-C:

Sloane indicated that the Covenant was close to locating the key to activate the puzzle box. He suspected that the contents of the box could harm Sydney.

At the same time, Dixon came under suspicion with the DSR for stealing the artifact. Lauren and Vaughn knew that they had to cover for their friend. They had Marshall interfere with the surveillance team that was sent in after Dixon during the exchange so that Dixon would not be found.

Once the exchange was made, Sark was about to fit Dixon's daughter, Robin, with a collar containing a lethal cardiotoxin to give him time to escape. Dixon would have two minutes to disarm the device before the compound was injected into his daughter's system. The team was horrified that Sark would put an innocent young girl in that situation.

Sydney told Sark to use her instead. Sark gave in and put the collar on Sydney, warning that if they tried to stop him, he could trigger the poison remotely. Sark was allowed to leave while Jack disarmed the device.

LOCATION: Los Angeles, California, USA
ALIAS: None

CIA MISSION E317-A:

Vaughn received intel from a contact in Mexico detailing a map that would lead to a key that opened the puzzle box taken from Lot 45 in Project Black Hole. It was rumored that inside that box was a bioweapon known as the Passenger. The Covenant followed the legend to a crystal map in the Karoo desert. Surveillance indicated that Bomani was at the site, using Omnifam trucks equipped with global positioning transponders.

Sloane provided Sydney with the codes to track Bomani's movements via satellite. Marshall traced the trucks to the Russian consulate in Gaborone, where the consulate general, Petr Berezovsky, was known to have strong ties to the Covenant.

During a state event, Sydney and Vaughn had to access the second floor, where Sark and Bomani were analyzing the map. Using a recording device and a voice construction software program, Sydney obtained the password "Mockingbird" (in Russian) from Berezovsky to access the elevator to the second floor. Vaughn joined her with the reconstructed voiceprint to get to the crystal, but they triggered a silent alarm and had to fight their way past Sark and Bomani and their operatives to escape with the crystal.

LOCATION: Gaborone
ALIAS: Polina Alexander, Russian couture designer

CIA MISSION E317-B:

Using a Rambaldi artifact in conjunction with two previously obtained crystal disks, the map to locate the key was revealed. But Marshall could not locate the map's landform anywhere on the globe. Following Sloane's suggestion, a search of topography with oceanic mapping revealed the location— the Yonaguni Rock Formation off the coast of Okinawa. There they would find four disks that would open the Rambaldi Puzzle Box.

Sydney and Vaughn swam to an underwater Rambaldi cave and found the disks. While they were in the cave, they were out of radio contact and did not know that four operatives, including Bomani, were coming in after them. They fought themselves free of the operatives, but Bomani stole the keys and escaped.

LOCATION: Sea of Japan
ALIAS: None

CIA MISSION E318-A:

A large-scale cyberterrorist attack, originating from a server in Berlin, was launched. It infected servers throughout Europe and Asia and estimates indicated that it would consume over half of all global Internet bandwidth within twenty-four hours.

The virus targeted medical facilities, hospitals, laboratories, and universities. Given the CIA's presumption that the Passenger was a bioweapon, it was assumed that the Covenant was launching a precursor attack, possibly trying to shut down all treatment facilities. Once they had control of the Passenger, it would be unstoppable.

The virus code had all the trademarks of a computer hacker operating out of Berlin known as Cypher. Sydney and Vaughn were sent in to identify Cypher, confirm that he had created the worm, and shut it down. Considering that Cypher used a PDA with a unique code, Marshall programmed a wireless sniffer that sought him out.

When found, Cypher explained that the worm was not originally designed to attack medical facilities, but he was shot and killed by a mysterious sniper before he could say more. He did turn over his flash drive files to Vaughn. But when they tried to uplink the information to Marshall, they found that the files on Cypher's flash drive were completely wiped in a manner that suggested intentional sabotage.

Marshall was able to partially reconstruct the files along with the source code and learned that the worm was actually collecting information—the destruction was only a side effect. The Covenant was looking for something in those medical files. Marshall tweaked the source code so it wouldn't destroy any more data and rerouted the information to the CIA servers so they would receive whatever the Covenant was after.

It was later discovered that Lauren was the assassin who was responsible for killing Cypher and wiping the flash drive.

LOCATION: Berlin, Germany
ALIAS: Goth computer hacker

CIA MISSION E318-B:

Marshall eventually learned that Cypher's worm was designed to cross-reference genetic databases, searching the globe for the DNA of a specific woman. The worm came up with ten matches for the same DNA, which suggested they were aliases for the same woman. Medical records revealed that this woman had always been treated by the same physician: Dr. Robert Viadro. Sydney and Vaughn were sent to meet with the doctor.

When they entered the doctor's home, they found signs of a struggle. They then came under attack by men with Rambaldi tattoos on their hands. Sydney and Vaughn took out the operatives and eventually found the doctor in his panic room. He had been tortured, and he admitted to betraying the Passenger.

Viadro recognized Sydney as the Chosen One in the prophecy. He pulled her gun and tried to shoot her to protect the Passenger, but Vaughn shot him first. Though he was their only lead, the doctor was able to provide a surprising revelation before his death: The Passenger was a person whom the doctor was willing to die trying to protect.

LOCATION: **Milan, Italy**
ALIAS: **None**

CIA MISSION E319-A:

An Echelon intercept indicated that the Covenant had kidnapped someone who could help the CIA find the Passenger. A convoy was in the process of transporting him across western Rajasthan. Sydney and Vaughn went in to intercept the convoy and take the man into custody. He turned out to be the man who started Sloane on his Rambaldi quest: Conrad.

Sark shot Conrad as Sydney and Vaughn tried to break him free of the truck in which he was being held. Before Conrad died, he told Sydney that the Covenant had obtained "the Restoration" and that the Passenger had been compromised. He further explained that the Passenger was Sydney's sister and her destiny. Sloane later confirmed that he had learned two years before that he had a daughter from a past affair with Irina Derevko. That daughter was the Passenger.

LOCATION: **Thar Desert, India**
ALIAS: **None**

CIA MISSION E319-B:

Having discovered that Lauren was the Covenant mole, the CIA planted information with her that they had found the location of a document known as the Restoration and were going in to get it. They also said that in anticipation of receiving the document, Project Black Hole was delivering the code key necessary to read it. Marshall created a fake code key for Lauren to copy, knowing she would take it to her handler, who presumably had the document they were looking for. Sydney and Vaughn followed Lauren to a meeting with her mother, discovering that the Restoration was in their family home.

Vaughn was livid that his wife had not only betrayed him, but their country as well. He wanted to end their marriage, but he was ordered to continue the facade, as it could work to the CIA's benefit. Using their couples counseling session as a setup, Dr. Barnett suggested that Vaughn go with Lauren to visit her mother. During the trip Vaughn accessed the family safe, found three pages of Rambaldi text, and scanned them for the CIA. He was nearly discovered but used his more amorous side to distract Lauren. Sydney shut down the comm they were on as Vaughn and Lauren began to make love.

LOCATION: **Richmond, Virginia, USA**
ALIAS: **None**

CIA MISSION E319-C:

Using the real code key, Marshall was able to translate the scanned documents, which detailed a Rambaldi artifact known as the Hourglass. It had recently been sold at auction to a man named Masa Raidon, who ran the Yakuza's U.S. shipping business out of San Pedro. He owned a Yakuza stronghold in Little Tokyo, where he was holding the Hourglass.

According to the Rambaldi manuscript, the Hourglass would reveal the location of the Passenger only to her father, meaning Arvin Sloane. But the Justice Department refused to postpone Sloane's execution, since he was charged with going against the terms of his pardon agreement. Because Sloane was her only link to finding her sister, Sydney tricked her father into admitting that he had information that could clear Sloane. She then forced him to promise he would use the information to stop the execution as she prepared for her mission.

Sydney accessed the Yakuza stronghold and, with Marshall's help, bypassed security. However, there was a motion detector set on random sweep that wasn't on the building schematics. When she learned mid-mission that Sloane's execution was going forward, she heedlessly rushed in, setting off alarms and taking the Hourglass. With Vaughn's help, Sydney fought her way out, trying to make it in time to stop the execution. She was too late.

Sydney was furious with her father. But it was later revealed that Jack had slipped Sloane a drug that would counteract the effectiveness of the lethal injection. He brought Sloane back to life to help find the Passenger.

LOCATION: **Los Angeles, California, USA**
ALIAS: **Club patron**

CIA MISSION E320-A:

According to Jack's contact, the Trust had a cold storage vault at the Smithsonian. The vault was secured by a five-key retinal system that corresponded to the five members of the Trust. Since Jack and Sloane had only been able to confirm the identity of Marlon Bell, DOJ division director, Sloane suggested that a visit from the dead would unearth the other four.

Upon seeing Sloane alive, Bell summoned his fellow members of the Trust. Sloane then crashed that meeting. He recorded each Trust member's retina and uplinked them to Jack, who in turn transmitted the images to Sydney's PDA. She then used the recordings to open a security door in the Smithsonian and retrieve another Rambaldi artifact that was soon discovered to be an EEG.

Sloane smashed the Rambaldi Hourglass and the green liquid inside congealed into a ball. When that ball was placed in the center of the EEG, it created a drawing of a specific brain wave—the brain wave that belonged to the Passenger.

LOCATION: Washington, DC, USA
ALIAS: Shannon Girard, dinosaur expert

CIA MISSION E320-B:

The Department of Defense (DOD) had developed an experimental satellite network of remote encephalography, allowing it to locate people by reading brain waves from orbit. One of Jack's contacts at the DOD uplinked the Rambaldi EEG reading to the defense satellite network. It gave them a location in a labor camp for female prisoners in Chechnya. That was where they would find the Passenger.

The prison's central database listed the identity of the Passenger as Talia Kozlov. However, this was an alias. The Passenger turned out to be an Argentinean Intelligence agent named Nadia Santos.

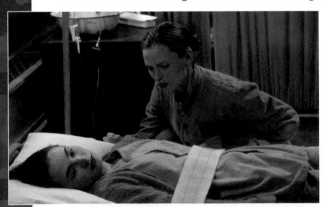

Sydney infiltrated the prison and found her sister in what appeared to be a catatonic state. As Sydney tried to escape with Nadia, the guards stopped them. During the ensuing fight, Nadia revealed her catatonia to be a ruse and joined in. They escaped and got Nadia to a safe house where Jack and Sloane were waiting.

As Sloane and Nadia met for the first time, Sark and Lauren burst into the safe house with a tactical team. They searched the premises and found that Sloane had disappeared with Nadia in the commotion. Jack and Sydney were infuriated to hear that Sloane had set them all up.

LOCATION: **Chechnya**
ALIAS: **Chechnyan prisoner**

CIA MISSION E321-A:

The signal-intelligence post in Manila intercepted an encrypted phone call between Arvin Sloane and a well-known underworld fixer. Sloane requested that vials of fluid be recovered from a bunker facility called Novgorod 21. Contacts at Project Black Hole indicated that the facility had been inactive since the 1980s, when it was the center for Soviet Rambaldi research.

Sydney and Vaughn were sent in to penetrate the bunker and plant a tracking device on the liquid to lead them to Sloane. They quickly discovered that the place had already been largely cleaned out of the fluid. They were able to uplink the facility records, however. The records included video of a young Nadia being pumped full of the elixir in a painful experiment.

While in the facility they tripped an alarm, which sent in Russian guards. Unbeknownst to Sydney, they were being led by her aunt, Katya Derevko. Katya tranquilized her own men, instructing Sydney and Vaughn to take the guards' uniforms so she could escort them out of the bunker. Once they escaped, she told Sydney that as a little girl, Nadia was taken from the facility before she could finish the project they had been working on. She was being used to transmit a message from Milo Rambaldi.

LOCATION: **Novgorod, Russia**
ALIAS: **None**

CIA MISSION E321-B:

Reviewing the video obtained from the bunker, Marshall and Sydney recognized the man working on Nadia as the same man who had tortured them both previously (Missions J535-B and E662-B). He was identified as Dr. Jong Lee, the lead scientist in charge of conducting Russia's Passenger experiments.

The NSA used electronic intercepts to track Lee's recent communication. It appeared that he had met with Sloane in Zurich at least twice in the past four months, most likely to help him procure Rambaldi fluid. Dr. Lee was presently located in a Cuban bioweapons facility. Sydney and Vaughn were sent to Havana to find out everything they could about the Passenger experiments and Sloane's current location.

Lee indicated that Nadia's drawings, induced by the special elixir, were supposed to lead them to "Rambaldi," but he didn't know exactly what that meant. Vaughn tortured Lee with acid to try to find out where Sloane was. The doctor insisted that he did not know. At that moment Sydney became more concerned with Vaughn than any information Lee might possess. She feared that Vaughn was becoming obsessed with finding Lauren through any means necessary so he could punish her for her betrayal.

LOCATIONS: **Havana and Cienfuegos, Cuba**
ALIAS: **Shipwreck survivor**

CIA MISSION E321-C:

While tracking Sloane's financial records, Jack found a large payment to Dayton Electrical, which had subcontracted to do work in, among other places, Chamonix. Suspecting that this was a front company for Toni Cummings, he paid her a visit in custody, offering a reduction in her sentence if she helped find Sloane. Cummings countered with a request to get out with time served. It was granted.

Cummings admitted to designing a system for Sloane two years earlier, but she didn't know where it was built. Marshall computed a list of all the equipment Cummings specified as being necessary to build the security program she designed for Sloane. The program scanned multiple databases for any shipments of that gear, leading them to a house outside of Kyoto. Cummings insisted that she go along, because Sloane had had her give him seven variables for the system. She wouldn't know which one he used until she accessed the on-site junction box.

In Kyoto the team quickly took the house. They were surprised to find Sark and Lauren in the residence. After a brief shoot-out, Vaughn went after Lauren instead of remaining with Sydney to secure Nadia. Sloane's guards nearly killed Sydney, but Nadia saved her.

Lauren, Sark, and Sloane got away, but the CIA obtained some of the drawings and text that Nadia had done while under the influence of the Rambaldi elixir administered by Sloane.

LOCATION: **Kyoto, Japan**
ALIAS: **None**

CIA MISSION E322-A:

Lauren Reed infiltrated the Task Force headquarters disguised as Sydney Bristow. She then uploaded the information on the Rambaldi equation that Nadia had been channeling through her drawings and corrupted the database. When Marshall interrupted, she shot him in the stomach. As he fell, he managed to sound the alarm. This, however, did not stop Lauren. She had already planted explosives throughout the Rotunda. When the alarm sounded, Sark set off the bombs. He watched via video monitor as sections of the Rotunda exploded, injuring numerous agents.

Sark was captured, and he eventually told Vaughn where to find Lauren. However, Vaughn decided not to report the information and went after Lauren alone. But he could not bring himself to kill her. In a standoff, Katya Derevko knifed him and left him for dead.

Vaughn was found by a CIA task force and brought to a hospital. Meanwhile Lauren had a man complete the analysis of the Rambaldi drawing, revealing a location in Palermo.

Sydney disguised herself as Lauren in jail and got Sark to reveal where he had backed up the Rambaldi equation. The CIA then input the information and found the Palermo location.

LOCATION: Los Angeles, California, USA
ALIAS: Lauren Reed

CIA MISSION E322-B:

Sydney found Katya at a dig site in Palermo and learned her aunt was working with the Covenant. Sydney knocked the woman unconscious and took a shot at Lauren. But the site foreman got in the way of the bullet.

Her cover blown, Sydney went on the offensive, and she and Lauren fought. Lauren told her that they were both pawns in the same game, but at least Lauren knew who controlled her. She indicated that Sydney needed to know the truth about all that had happened to her. That proof could be found in a numbered vault at a bank in Wittenberg.

Having broken out of custody at the hospital, Vaughn arrived just as Lauren was about to kill Sydney. He shot Lauren instead. As she died, Lauren revealed the vault to Sydney as number 1062.

At the same time, Nadia sneaked out of the safe house to meet with Sloane. She admitted to altering the equation at moments when the fluid wore off, meaning the Palermo dig site was a ruse. She then led Sloane to the real site where they would find Rambaldi's essence.

LOCATION: Palermo, Italy
ALIAS: None

Following Lauren's directions, Sydney accessed vault number 1062 at the bank in Wittenberg. Inside she found a file—classified, highest level. The file contained evidence of Irina Derevko being a security risk. None of it was new information, but there was a copy of an official request from Jack Bristow asking for authority to execute Irina Derevko.

LOCATION: **Wittenberg, Germany**
ALIAS: **Bank vault purchaser**

OBJECTIVE: Provide cover for joining APO

CIA MISSION E401-A:

Sydney and CIA junior officer Brodien were sent to Shanghai to retrieve surveillance photos from deep-cover agent Strum. Based on a tip from an unauthenticated source, Sydney believed Strum's cover was blown. Though not part of her orders, Sydney planned for an extraction without realizing it was a trap. When Sydney contacted Strum, the communication led their enemy directly to him. Strum was killed as a horrified Sydney listened in.

The killer then back-traced the radio signal and went after Sydney and Brodien. Knowing they were made and that the killer was looking for a pair of operatives, Sydney broke protocol once again. She dressed up Brodien like a club kid and split from him, so they could escape the building by walking right past the people searching for them. Once outside, Sydney stole a motorcycle and rode off with Brodien. Though the mission was a failure, they managed to escape with their lives.

Upon returning to the CIA, Brodien filed a complaint against Sydney due to her unauthorized and unorthodox behavior. She was brought in for an inquiry and effectively demoted to the mailroom. Outraged, she quit the CIA.

(continued on page 204)

Authorized Personnel Only

Sydney was looking for a fresh start after some of the more recent tragedy in her life. The opportunity seemed to present itself in an offer from Director Hayden Chase to join a newly formed elite black ops team. Sydney gladly accepted the challenge, excited about the future, without realizing how much it would resemble her past.

After publicly resigning from the CIA, Sydney met with Chase in the newly reopened CIA offices that would now make up the top secret home to the unit known as Authorized Personnel Only (APO). There Sydney learned that the handpicked team included her former partner, Marcus Dixon; her former lover, Michael Vaughn; and her recently estranged father, Jack Bristow. But that was nothing compared to the shock of learning who would be running the operation: Arvin Sloane.

As part of an exchange in which Sloane turned over an important Rambaldi artifact, he had been asked to put together a unit that would not be constrained by the same red tape that so often got in the way of the CIA's work. He chose the best in the field: people he had worked with—and worked against—before. But the U.S. government was not totally blind to Sloane's past. His original team of Sydney, Jack, Dixon, and Vaughn was charged with the uncomfortable job of keeping an eye on Sloane while they followed his orders.

(continued from page 202)

The above failed mission and subsequent inquiry were all a cover for her to "leave" the CIA so she could join the black ops APO team.

LOCATION: **Shanghai, China**
ALIAS: **Club girl**

OBJECTIVE: Locate and obtain Roman Vadik

APO MISSION E401-B:

Sydney accepted her first APO mission while still dealing with the shock of learning that the black ops team consisted of her friends and family while under the leadership of her enemy Arvin Sloane.

Sloane reported that Uri Komarov, formerly the lead scientist of Russia's Nuclear Science Unit, had disappeared with the only viable sample of Aurine-X11, a deadly and highly unstable isotope. Signal intercepts revealed that Komarov had a meeting scheduled on a train traveling between Belarus and Latvia. It was assumed he intended to sell the isotope. The CIA had no authority to act on the intelligence. That's where APO came in.

APO intercepted the protocol of the meet with the unknown buyer. The mission objective was twofold: Sydney was to recover Komarov and the isotope, while Vaughn identified the buyer and sold him a bogus isotope. The fake was outfitted with a tracking device so Langley could follow the buyer back to his base of operations and grab him there.

On the train, Sydney used seduction to get Komarov to open his carrying case for her, since the rightfully paranoid scientist was known to rig his transport devices with self-destruct mechanisms. At the same time, Vaughn met the buyer, a man named Tamazaki who supposedly worked for Roman Vadik. The exchange was going well . . . until Tamazaki thought he recognized Vaughn. He ended the meet, calling in one of his men to take care of Vaughn.

Vaughn fought free of the thug and warned Sydney via comm that he had been made. Sydney grabbed the isotope and made her way to their rendezvous point in the luggage area. She too was made and was forced to fight for her life, nearly being thrown from the train in the process. Vaughn arrived in the car and pushed the operative out the door while Sydney pulled herself back inside.

Though they lost Tamazaki, they did manage to take one of his guards into custody and retrieve the isotope.

LOCATION: **Belarus**
ALIAS: **Elsa**

APO MISSION E401-C:

The previous mission was also successful in determining the identity of the buyer as Roman Vadik, a man who was already twenty-sixth on the CIA's Most Wanted list. Vadik was responsible for the deaths of thousands. Some of Sloane's unnamed personal contacts confirmed that Vadik was cooperating with known terrorist cells in planning a major attack within the next six months. The CIA wanted Vadik taken in.

The year before, a foreign agent working on infiltrating Vadik's operation had made good progress in getting closer to the man. Sydney was sent to Argentina to debrief her, since she had a personal connection with the agent—it was her half sister, Nadia Santos. Nadia confirmed that no one dealt directly with Vadik, and she had never seen the man herself. Everyone worked with his lieutenant, Kazu Tamazaki.

Tamazaki considered himself a modern-day samurai. He had been arrested five years earlier trying to steal a famed sword from the Hasunaga Asian Museum in London. Following the meet in Belarus, Tamazaki went underground. He could not be located. Knowing of his interest in the samurai, Sloane suspected that the only way to fish him out was by going after the Shintaro Sword. It was the most famous samurai sword outside of Japan and the reason for Tamazaki's arrest years earlier. Sloane suggested that they fake a theft of the sword so they could offer it up to Tamazaki. Considering that the museum storing the sword was one of the most secure in the world, Dixon said that there was only one man for the job: Marshall Flinkman.

Soon after, Marshall was "arrested" for misuse of government assets because he had plugged a video game console into a monitor at work. This was all a ruse for bringing him into APO. Marshall was thrilled to be working with his old friends again, though he was a little concerned that Sloane was also there.

The team went to London, where Sydney and Vaughn climbed to the museum roof while Dixon and Marshall watched from a surveillance van. Vaughn tapped into museum surveillance while Sydney broke in to steal the sword. Unfortunately, their well-laid plan did not go off as easily as intended.

The team drugged the food delivered to the security guards so they would be unconscious during the break-in. Unfortunately, one of the guards did not eat that evening. As Sydney worked with Marshall's devices, carefully removing the sword from the pressure-sensitive base, the guard approached the room on his rounds. When he arrived at the sword display, he instantly noticed that the sword was missing, but he did not immediately realize that Sydney was hanging above him on a wire.

Sydney dropped down on the guard, knocking him out. Though it seemed she was in the clear, she could only watch as his soda bottle rolled to the sword platform and triggered the alarm. The security system immediately locked down the museum, and the police were called in.

Sydney managed to escape the building, but her route to rendezvous with the team was blocked. Just when it seemed there was no escape, Jack sped up in a car to rescue her. Sydney—still angry over learning that he had recently killed Derevko without explanation—did not want to get into the car. She eventually got inside, though she was not happy. When pressed to explain his secretly coming on the mission, Jack simply explained that the exit plan lacked redundancy.

LOCATIONS: **Argentina; London, England**
ALIAS: **None**

APO MISSION E402-A:

Dixon reestablished communication with a former contact—a fence he expected Kazu Tamazaki would contact regarding the sword. A meet was quickly set up, as Tamazaki was very interested in obtaining the stolen item.

In preparing for the meet, Jack and Marshall paid a visit to the operative Sydney and Vaughn had captured in Belarus, suspecting he would have information on Vadik. In exchange for protection, the guard revealed that Vadik and Tamazaki were the same man. This important piece of information changed the nature of the mission. It went from a simple meet to a grab.

Tamazaki insisted that the woman who stole the sword make the delivery, forcing Sydney on the assignment. Since she was allowed one backup, Sloane assigned Jack to her in an attempt to help the father and daughter get past their recent issues over Derevko's untimely death.

Tamazaki made contact with Sydney via phone. He instructed her to enter a tunnel that would take her into the Alves building across the street from her location. She would then go to the tenth floor for the meet. It was only when Sydney was isolated in the tunnel that the rest of the team realized the building didn't have a tenth floor. But it was too late. Sydney had been kidnapped.

LOCATION: **Rio de Janeiro, Brazil**
ALIAS: **Sword thief**

APO MISSION E402-B:

Knowing that Nadia had intel on Tamazaki's holdings in Rio, Vaughn contacted her for help with a rescue. Though initially reluctant to get back into the Intelligence game, Nadia didn't hesitate once she

heard her sister was in jeopardy. She told Vaughn that Tamazaki used to run an operation near the Catedral Metropolitan. Since she had the best chance of getting inside based on her past cover assignment, she offered her assistance there as well.

Jorge Calvo was the cover man for Tamazaki's Rio holdings. He knew Nadia as Elana Kelsey, a courier for the Tres Rios gang. Using that cover, Nadia reestablished contact and gained access to the building where Sydney was being tortured by suffocation through a mask flooded with water. When Tamazaki had seen that it was Sydney he was to meet with for the sword, he made the assumption that she was there for a different reason. He wanted to know how she had found out about the contract he previously had on her life. But Sydney didn't know what he was talking about.

Nadia rescued Sydney before she could learn more about the contract that Tamazaki had been paid to handle . . . or why it was canceled. Tamazaki interrupted the rescue attempt and tried to take out Nadia, but Jack arrived. Knowing he was outnumbered, Tamazaki fled with the Shintaro Sword. But Sydney still wanted answers.

Sydney gave chase. The two fought, and Tamazaki was impaled by the sword. As he lay dying, Tamazaki admitted that it was Irina Derevko who had taken out the contract on Sydney's life.

Sydney was having difficulty coping with the emotions tied to learning that her father had killed her mother to save her. At the same time, her half sister decided to move to Los Angeles to be closer to her family. When Nadia asked about their mother, Sydney took her to Derevko's grave in Moscow. As they stood together in the mausoleum, Nadia swore vengeance on their mother's killer . . . not knowing it was Jack.

LOCATIONS: **Rio de Janeiro, Brazil;**
   Moscow, Russia
ALIAS: **None**

OBJECTIVE: Retrieve the stolen Valta computer

APO MISSION E403-A:

The Valta computer was stolen in broad daylight as it was being transferred to NSA headquarters. The Valta represented cutting-edge technology that would revolutionize information gathering from satellite networks. If it fell into the wrong hands, it could be used to spy on anyone in the world. A new terrorist group out of Germany known as the Baden Liga financed the theft by transferring three million euros to an untraceable account in the Bahamas. APO was tasked to find out who was behind the theft.

Sydney and Marshall entered a bank in the Bahamas under the guise of opening a private account. The names of all account holders were stored exclusively in the bank manager's personal biometrically protected safe. Dixon and Vaughn created a distraction by brawling in the bank. When the bank manager left his office to deal with the disturbance, Sydney and Marshall accessed the safe by using the handprint and retinal scan they had surreptitiously obtained from the manager. Once the safe was open, they retrieved the name attached to the account number to which the money had been transferred. The thief who took the Valta was a man named Martin Bishop.

LOCATION: **The Bahamas**
ALIAS: **Claudia Maria Vasquez DeMarco**

RPO MISSION E403-B:

Intel indicated that Martin Bishop had not yet received his second payment for delivery, meaning he still held the Valta. APO agents needed to get to him before he could make delivery. Bishop was a British expat living in Spain. He specialized in acquiring high-risk, high-reward military targets. He was also known to be a cold-blooded killer. Rumor had it that he killed his wife in order to spend more time with his mistress. The Valta was to be recovered or destroyed, and CIA tactical units were on standby to complete the mission once the computer had been located.

APO tracked Bishop to an estate one hour outside of Malaga, Spain. Since his computer could not be hacked from the outside, Sydney had to get inside the compound. Knowing his weakness for women, she went in as a damsel in distress fleeing her past. She had to be careful, though, since his weakness for women had a tendency to end violently.

Since, for safety reasons, Sydney could not wear a communication device on her, Vaughn used a laser mic to communicate with her while in the compound. However, the walls of the estate were so thick that they could only communicate while she was near a window. Sydney found Bishop's computer and determined that the Valta was being held at Alameda Yards in container C0717. But Bishop returned before Sydney could leave the compound.

Since Sloane was instructed not to grab Bishop until the raid proved successful, Sydney did not want to blow her cover until they knew the outcome. Even though Vaughn had instructed her to get out immediately, she continued stalling Bishop until the raid went down.

Sloane forwarded the information to the CIA team. The assault team went in and destroyed the

Valta. But the mission went south and most of the team was killed. The team leader, Weiss, survived but was taken prisoner.

Bishop was alerted to the raid and the fact that someone had been on his server an hour earlier. Making the obvious connection, he took Sydney hostage. Vaughn and Dixon stormed the compound, but they were too late. Bishop and his men escaped through a tunnel under the building.

Bishop brought his two prisoners together while he tried to reason with his buyers, the Baden Liga. Though the situation was tense, Weiss was excited to learn that Sydney hadn't really left intelligence work. The excitement was somewhat tempered by the fact that their lives were in danger.

Marshall traced the frequency of Bishop's phone on the cellular network and came up with the location for the APO team to hit. Nadia and Jack joined the team as they infiltrated the building. At the same time, Sydney and Weiss managed to escape by working together and creating a distraction. As the team met up with the former hostages, Nadia killed Bishop in an extremely violent act. Her actions came under the false information that he had killed Derevko. Jack had told Nadia that lie.

LOCATION: **Andalucia, Spain**
ALIAS: **Sharlene**

OBJECTIVE: Obtain a viable sample of ICE-5

APO MISSION E405-A:

An American expatriate named Derek Modell contacted the CIA with an offer of a sample of a biological agent he had stolen from an arms dealer in Montenegro. The substance was called ICE-5. Sydney was sent in to meet with the exceedingly amateurish contact in an Algerian marketplace to buy a chemical weapon. After Modell had to be instructed where to go for the meet, Vaughn picked up a tail on the guy. In fact, several people were converging on the meet. Sydney demanded that he turn over the chemical, but in an ill-advised move, he had previously swallowed the container.

Sydney fled with Modell, while he complained that he was not feeling well. As they fought their way out of the marketplace, Modell doubled over in pain. Suddenly his leg cracked in two and split off, splintering below the knee.

Sydney and Vaughn carried him out. As they made their escape, Modell was shot in the back. On the bullet's impact, he exploded into pieces as if he were made of ice.

LOCATION: **Algeria**
ALIAS: **None**

APO MISSION E405-B:

It was believed that the biological agent Modell was transporting caused his bizarre death. The container housing the ICE-5 was not meant to be swallowed. It probably started leaking as soon as it hit his stomach. When he was tackled during the fight, the container suffered a complete rupture, spilling the chemical into his body. Early indicators suggested a synthetic bacterial agent that attacked and crystallized all moisture in the body. Considering that Modell had spent the previous five months as a relief worker at the Hospital Sava in Montenegro, they believed that ICE-5 was being developed there by a man wanted by almost every intelligence agency in the world: Fintan Keene.

APO was tasked to obtain a viable sample of ICE-5, since the one Modell had swallowed became inert after it had infected him. Sydney went into the hospital as a relief worker through the UK branch of Omnifam. The mission was simply for her to get in, get the ICE-5, and get out. Vaughn and Dixon offered support in the field while the rest of the team concentrated on preventive strategies to keep other organizations from obtaining ICE-5 before APO.

While at the hospital, Sydney witnessed a man brought in suffering from the effects of ICE-5. Sydney was working with a nurse named Kiera MacLaine, who clearly recognized the effects of the chemical. MacLaine followed the patient to an off-limits area that required a swipe card and a code to access. Sydney easily obtained the code by watching MacLaine, but she needed to get the swipe card.

Vaughn entered the hospital in the guise of a flirtatious priest needing some stitches due to a bar fight. He managed to lift the swipe card and hand it to Sydney. As Sydney went off to the secure section, he continued to distract MacLaine. As she worked on Vaughn, Fintan Keene came in for a not-so-private conversation, during which Vaughn realized MacLaine was Keene's sister.

Sydney went into the secure area and discovered that Keene was testing ICE-5 on human subjects. She also found pressurized canisters, indicating that he had found a way to make the chemical airborne. Released into a city, the chemical could cause deaths in the tens of thousands. There were fourteen tanks in the lab, being prepped for a buyer in Damascus. APO needed to shut Keene down, but the three-person unit of Sydney, Vaughn, and Dixon was simply not enough for the necessary tactical mission.

Since they needed to get to Keene by more covert means, Vaughn used his growing friendship with MacLaine—whose real name was Megan Keene—as their in. Knowing she was already conflicted about Keene's actions, Vaughn had to convince her to move against her brother.

Vaughn bonded with MacLaine at a bar, sharing his personal story of how he knew what it was like to feel trapped by a past he could not escape. He told MacLaine of how he had been forced to kill his wife, Lauren. Even though he was doing what he had to do, he said, the act still haunted him. He then offered to help MacLaine break free of her brother.

MacLaine agreed and they went back to the hospital. At first it seemed like she was going along with the plan, but she alerted Keene to the deception out of misplaced family loyalty. Keene was about to inject Vaughn with a syringe full of ICE-5, when he came up with a better idea. He told his sister to do it. MacLaine was about to follow through with it when Sydney burst into the room.

During the ensuing fight, Keene grabbed the hypo full of ICE-5 and used it as a weapon. Thinking he was about to attack Vaughn, Keene turned and accidentally injected the chemical into his sister. As MacLaine died, she told Vaughn that she forgave him for doing what he had to do.

Keene was then taken into custody and all samples of ICE-5 were acquired by APO.

LOCATION: Montenegro
ALIAS: Relief worker from Omnifam

OBJECTIVE: Infiltrate Liberty Village and retrieve the prototype HPM device

APO MISSION E409:

An electromagnetic weapon was stolen from a warehouse in Kostroma. The device was a prototype HPM mechanism with repeatable core and an amplified radius. In layman's terms, it was an electromagnetic

pulse (EMP) that could destroy electronic equipment and melt circuitry in everything within a ten-mile radius. With the repeating core, it could be detonated multiple times, meaning one could black out Los Angeles and then take down San Francisco in the same day.

It was believed that Yuri Korelki, a former KGB officer currently with ties to an extremist

group known as the October Contingent, had the device. German authorities picked up a man and a woman attempting to smuggle weapons through a customs checkpoint. Subsequent interrogation revealed them to be Dimitry and Alyona Tabakov, suspected Chechnyan mercenaries. Under duress, they disclosed that the October Contingent had made back-channel overtures toward them to join the group. Sydney and Vaughn were sent in posing as the mercenaries to infiltrate the October Contingent, identify the group's objective, and retrieve the electromagnetic weapon.

Considering the high-risk nature of their infiltration, the only method of communication with APO was through a wristwatch with burst transmission capabilities. In case of emergency, they would receive an abort code through the watch.

Sydney and Vaughn made contact with Yuri—who went by the name Tom—and were surprised to learn that they were expected to pose as Americans. They were given new American identities as David and Karen Parker and taken to "Liberty Village," (officially known as Training Sector 56-B). It was a prototypical American suburb in the middle of Russia.

Liberty Village was a former government operation used to train Russian agents on American lifestyle for infiltration and deep-cover assignments. Sydney and Vaughn were instructed that their main objective of the moment was to pass as Americans with other members of the team. "Tom" informed them that they would be tested as they went. If they passed, they would be accepted into the organization. If they failed, they would not survive.

The first test was simple: negotiating a welcome party in their new home, passing themselves off as a loving couple. Using the wristwatch, Sydney sent images of the party guests to APO. There the guests were identified as foreign operatives with a laundry list of crimes. The October Contingent was obviously up to something big. This was substantiated when Sydney went out for a run and confirmed that the village had a strong paramilitary presence containing a perimeter with armed guards, rotating patrols, and heavy surveillance.

Their first morning in Liberty Village, Sydney and Vaughn were tested in a scenario where they had to pass as Americans while buying a convertible. Though it seemed like a simple enough task since they were, in fact, Americans, there was a surprise element. At the end of the transaction, they were expected to fight over the car with another couple who were new to the village. And they weren't expected to haggle, either.

Sydney and Vaughn were handed pieces of a gun that Vaughn had previously been told to practice assembling. The other couple, however, was given a head start. The two couples fought through the showroom using bullets and the very convertible itself as weapons. Sydney and Vaughn won the fight, but the wristwatch was damaged during the scuffle. They lost their only means of communication with APO.

Now that they were welcomed into October Contingent, Sydney and Vaughn were told they were moving to Chicago, where they were to get jobs at the Pierce Financial Investment Firm. Their goal was to get access to the company's servers, as the other team members would be doing at banking and investment firms across the United States. October Contingent was planning to use the EMP device on the New York Stock Exchange. By having access to America's investment firms during that time, they could redistribute massive amounts of wealth into their own accounts.

At the same time, the mercenaries Sydney and Vaughn had been impersonating were moved to a maximum-security prison. Unfortunately, the order was sent over an unsecured line that the October Contingent was monitoring. Fearing discovery, APO sent the abort code to Sydney and Vaughn. They did not receive it because the watch was broken.

Sydney and Vaughn came under attack. They managed to fight their way out of the house with the electromagnetic pulse and used the device against the Liberty Village defenses, bringing down a helicopter in the process. With all the electricity out in the village, they still managed to escape. They were extracted from the area with help arranged through a contact of Jack's. Afterward the Russian government took down the October Contingent for good.

LOCATION: **Moscow, Russia**
ALIAS: **Alyona Tabakov, a Chechnyan mercenary**
posing as Karen Parker

OBJECTIVE: Identify and dismantle the Nocturne project

APO MISSION E406-A:

While undercover teaching English in Amsterdam, CIA agent Nancy Cahill began to hallucinate in front of her class, soon growing so terrified she took her own life. Formerly an agent in Langley's narcotics task force, her most recent psych evaluation had reported nothing of note. Her husband, Jason, was also an agent. He hadn't checked in with his handler in three weeks.

Sydney and Jack were sent in to the Cahills' apartment to recover all evidence of their affiliation with the CIA, while the rest of

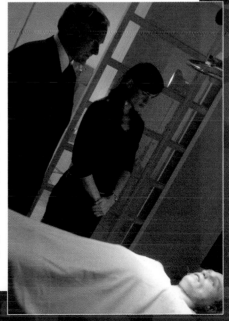

the team back-traced their recent activities to find out what might have happened. Sydney found a secret room and what appeared to be the body of Jason Cahill. As she explored the room, the "body" sat up. Cahill attacked her, biting Sydney in the neck. Jack was forced to shoot Cahill to protect his daughter.

LOCATION: **Amsterdam, Netherlands**
ALIAS: **None**

APO MISSION E406-B:

Sydney was examined and her scans were clear of any infection. Autopsies showed that the Cahills had come in contact with a drug that affected their nervous systems, enlarging the pineal gland, which regulates sleep cycles and body temperature. APO's Dr. Jain confirmed that an acute melatonin imbalance has been known to induce uncharacteristic behavior, including extreme acts of violence.

The team was tasked with locating the substance the Cahills had come into contact with and finding out who manufactured it. While the team met, Sydney went home to rest, but she could not sleep. At first she was reluctant to believe that she was experiencing a delayed reaction to the drug, even though she was beginning to hallucinate.

Marshall reconstructed the Cahills' records to learn that they had met with a contact in Bucharest known as the Count. His real identity was Andre Sterescu, and he regularly supplied the Cahills with new drugs for their investigations. They had another meet set for the following night. Sydney joined the team to make that meet, even though Dixon had warned Sloane against allowing her to return to active duty so soon after the strange attack.

En route to the meet Sydney began to exhibit signs that worried her father and Vaughn. She continued with the mission and made contact with Sterescu, revealing that the Cahills were dead and leading him into an increasingly agitated discussion. He recognized the effects of the drug she described, referring to a group known as JHP.

Sterescu tried to flee, but Vaughn intercepted him. Sterescu eventually revealed his history with the Cahills, noting that he was hired to keep an eye on Jochem Hasdeu Pharmaceuticals. His job was to steal documents and other items. One such item was a synthetic narcotic known as Nocturne.

During the interrogation Marshall contacted Sydney, warning that the biological agent did have an incubation period. She was infected by the drug and it was currently altering her brain chemistry.

Sydney broke down in front of Sterescu, Jack, and Vaughn, fearing that she was losing her mind. Sterescu admitted that he had given Cahill an old sample of the drug, which was being developed to try to create soldiers who could function around the clock without sleep. Sydney's symptoms were unfortunate side effects. He did not know where the drug originated, other than that it was from Prague. Sydney's condition deteriorated quickly and Sloane ordered her to be taken to a hospital in Rome.

LOCATION: Bucharest, Romania
ALIAS: An associate of the Cahills

APO MISSION E406-C:

Weiss and Nadia realized that Nancy Cahill's last words included a clue to the identity of the company that manufactured the agent. It was made by the Grapping Group in Prague. Jack believed there might be an antidote. So instead of going to Rome for treatment, the team headed for Prague to hopefully find a cure.

As Sydney's condition worsened, Vaughn infiltrated the company and found that there was an antidote. At the same time, Sydney attacked Jack out of irrational fear and fled the surveillance van. Vaughn found her, but she was inconsolable, announcing that she had killed her father.

Sydney attacked Vaughn, but Jack—who was not dead—had previously removed all the bullets from the gun she had obtained. Vaughn subdued her and gave her the antidote. Sydney experienced a full recovery; Interpol raided the offices of the Grapping Group and dismantled the Nocturne program.

LOCATION: Prague, Czech Republic
ALIAS: None

OBJECTIVE: Obtain stolen sample of Black Thorine

APO MISSION E404-A:

Sydney kept watch as Vaughn met with a contact who informed him that the Russian government was developing Black Thorine. They had actually been able to distill ten milliliters of the explosive, which was enough to fill a small vial. But that vial was stolen. Vaughn's contact, Anatoly Grodsky, found a routing number to his superior's account, into which a great deal of money had recently been deposited. It was believed that Grodsky's superior had aided in the theft of the highly dangerous explosive.

The development of Black Thorine violated twelve treaties between the United States and Russia. It was an undetectable explosive that could level a city block with only one drop. Ten milliliters was more than enough to do substantial damage.

LOCATION: **Irkutsk, Russia**
ALIAS: **Bartender**

APO MISSION E404-B:

The Russians were stonewalling the American government, refusing to acknowledge that Black Thorine existed, much less that it had been stolen. In the meantime APO was able to trace the routing number Grodsky provided. Boris Tambor, a Russian oil magnate who had recently gotten into arms dealing, had deposited two million euros into the account of Colonel Nikolai Vaskov. Tambor was booked into a hotel in Monte Carlo. He was known to have a penchant for gambling, going to the high-stakes poker table every night at nine. The team was sent in to surveil Tambor's hotel room and get in and out with the information on Black Thorine.

The plan was to go in and access Tambor's laptop and PDA when he went out for his nightly game. However, he did not stick to his schedule that night, preferring to remain in his room to watch the soccer match of a team he owned. Based on the contents of the room, which the team had under surveillance, Sydney and Nadia had determined that he had a female companion. Considering that Tambor would rather spend the evening watching soccer instead of spending it with her, Sydney and Nadia surmised that the woman might be a way in.

Against Sloane's orders, they tracked the woman, Bridget, to the hotel bar. Undercover as two similar high-society women, they befriended Bridget and gained access to the room. Under Tambor's eyes, they impressively managed to clone the computer's hard drive as well as the PDA.

LOCATION: **Monte Carlo, Monaco**
ALIAS: **Falishia**

APO MISSION E404-C:

Marshall was able to break Tambor's encryption program to learn that the Black Thorine sale was going down in sixteen hours. The exchange was set to occur on Tambor's boat, anchored in protected waters of the Black Sea off Turkey.

Marshall provided a schematic of the vault in the captain's office. Through research on Tambor's recent purchases, Marshall determined that the man actually had a safe within a safe. The outer safe would not be a problem; however, the inner safe would be more difficult to crack. For Sydney to access the time-synchronized lock that randomized the combination every sixty seconds, she needed to read the LCD of a key card on Tambor's person.

Sydney and Nadia requested to go on the mission to finish what they had started. Sloane initially wanted to refuse the request, because it would appear that he was rewarding their going against orders. Though Nadia had apologized for ignoring him on the mission in Monte Carlo, Sydney still refused to give him that satisfaction. Jack realized what was really going on, however, and he counseled Sloane not to get between the sisters, as it would not bring him closer to Nadia.

Sloane reluctantly allowed Sydney and Nadia to go on the mission. As they boarded the yacht, they noticed that a second boat, belonging to the buyer, was approaching. They did not have much time to break in and retrieve the Black Thorine. But that was not their only surprise. Sydney opened the safe to find that there was not just one vial of Black Thorine—there were ten.

Fearing discovery, Sydney was forced to shut the safe and hide with Nadia underwater, where they shared an oxygen tank. In the meantime the buyer, Leo Orissa, fired on Tambor's men in an attempt to take over his organization. Tambor tried to flee, but his girlfriend, Bridget, shot and killed him. She was working with Orissa.

Orissa was the head of a Russian crime syndicate whom Sloane had worked with while at SD-6. Upon hearing of the additional vials, the team reasoned that Tambor must have reverse-engineered the explosive in a lab. Considering that Orissa had killed Tambor and his men, he must have known where the lab was located. Sloane instructed Sydney to board the yacht again and he would feed her information over her comm. While she stalled Orissa, Nadia was to secure the Black Thorine.

Sydney did as instructed, surprising Bridget and Orissa by suddenly showing up on the boat. Once she told Orissa that she worked for Arvin Sloane, the man's attitude toward her suddenly became much more accommodating. She made an offer to Orissa, stating that it was one he could not refuse. To force his hand, Sloane provided Sydney with a reminder of a particularly violent episode in Sloane's past. Sydney used the example to convince Orissa not to betray Sloane. She even went so far as to add her own personal opinion of Sloane's malevolence.

Orissa accepted Sloane's offer and also provided the location of the lab in the Ukraine. Outraged that he had given the information so easily, Bridget shot Orissa and attacked Sydney. They both drew their weapons, but Sydney fired first, killing the woman. Nadia had secured the ten vials of Black Thorine, and the CIA located the lab and raided it to stop production of future samples.

LOCATION: **The Black Sea off the coast of Turkey**
ALIAS: **None**

OBJECTIVE: Capture Anna Espinosa and obtain the Dante Compound

APO MISSION E407-A:

Sloane's agreement with the CIA precluded him from participating in any missions involving certain operatives. He therefore informed the team that he had to temporarily step down as head of APO due to the fact that the next mission dealt with a person on that list. Jack Bristow was then handed full operational control of the unit for the length of this assignment. When asked why APO was given an assignment that Sloane could not work on, his response was that it involved a person with whom certain members of the team had had prior contact. The case was assigned to APO largely due to Syndey's past history with the target: Anna Espinosa.

Four days earlier the London listening post had intercepted chatter about a dead drop from a suspected terrorist group. Satellite surveillance picked up an image of Anna Espinosa. Up until that moment, she had been presumed dead following the fall of K-Directorate.

Intel indicated that Anna was about to make contact with an associate in Brussels. Sydney, Dixon, and Marshall were tasked to surveil the meet, given their familiarity with Anna's movements. They were to find out her assignment and, if the opportunity presented itself, bring her in.

Prior to the mission, Sydney sensed that Nadia was having a difficult time dealing with the entire Rambaldi mythos and her place in it. Hoping to help her half sister understand the situation, Sydney suggested they go for lunch. As the conversation turned to the prophecy, Sydney received a phone call at the hostess stand. It was Anna. She instructed Sydney to look back to her table. When Sydney did as instructed, she was surprised to see Anna with Nadia. A moment later, several laser targets locked on Sydney's chest.

Before leaving the restaurant with Nadia as her hostage, Anna made a request to her bitter enemy. She instructed Sydney to take the meet in Brussels posing as Anna. She was to retrieve a package from a man named Milos Sabine and deliver it to Anna. If she met her deadline, Nadia would be returned to her alive.

Sydney immediately flew to Brussels and met with Sabine. Believing her to be Anna, Sabine instructed her to kill a man named Willem Kreg and provide photo evidence of the corpse and his right index finger (which was Anna's signature) in order for Sabine to give her the package. Sydney had only forty minutes to return with the evidence.

Working quickly, Sydney went in as a prostitute and got Kreg to take her to his room. There she, Vaughn, and Dixon spared Kreg's life, but took his finger. She then returned to Sabine. In exchange for the evidence, he handed her a silver canister containing the last remaining sample of the Dante Compound, a super-rare phosphorus-based putty.

The compound was completely harmless on its own, but when mixed with certain nerve agents, it could mutate neurotoxins, causing them to self-replicate at an incredibly rapid rate. Jack asked Marshall to create a replica of the compound, but Sydney was concerned that Espinosa would spot a duplicate. With her sister's life in jeopardy, she convinced her father and Sloane to allow her to give Espinosa the real compound.

Marshall also suggested that Anna could be working for a fringe terrorist cell of former Covenant operatives known as the Cadmus Revolutionary Front (CRF). They had been trying to acquire the Dante Compound for over a year in an attempt to create a chemical bomb. Marshall then came up with the idea to contact Sark in prison to find out more about the CRF.

Sydney went to exchange the compound for Nadia. Surprisingly, Anna didn't even bother to confirm it was real, citing that she "trusted" Sydney. After Sydney handed it over, she couldn't control her rage against Anna. The two had a major smackdown in the middle of a high-end clothing boutique. They ended the battle with Sydney holding the compound and Anna holding the keys that would open the car Nadia was held in. The two exchanged items and left the store. Sydney found Nadia relatively unharmed, except for the fact that Anna had branded her with the mark of Rambaldi.

LOCATION: Brussels, Belgium
ALIASES: Anna Espinosa; prostitute

APO MISSION E407-B:

Vaughn interrogated Sark about the CRF, but received nothing more than the cryptic comment, "It has begun." Sark was much more interested in talking about Lauren's death, citing that he had been in love with the woman. Vaughn ended the conversation, since he was getting no answers from Sark. This was not a surprise, however, as they had a contingency plan in place.

That night APO operatives filled Sark's cell with an anesthetic gas, entered the cell as he slept, and injected him with a tracking device with a delayed activator. The tracker was also packed with a high-density explosive, just enough to blow his head off.

Sark was soon transferred to another facility, but an unidentified stranger—and agent of APO—broke him out and gave him transportation to the CRF. Sark's tracker went active and was picked up in

Johannesburg. Dixon led a team to take him, but it was a setup. Sark knew about the tracker. He then offered to help the CIA . . . for a price.

LOCATION: Johannesburg, South Africa

APO MISSION 407-C:

At the same time, APO picked up chatter about a meet scheduled between the CRF and Jan Vorich, an administrator of the Shillenost Chemical Labs in Estonia. It was assumed that Anna would participate in the meet.

Sydney and Nadia were sent in for observation only. During the meet they watched as Anna killed Vorich and took a tube of V/X gas. She now had the necessary component to activate the Dante Compound and turn it into a bomb. Sydney and Nadia were discovered by Anna's associate, Turner. But they would not be taken so easily.

Sydney went after Espinosa, while Nadia fought Turner. During the fight Nadia managed to get off a shot, killing Turner. As he lay dying, Nadia convinced him to confess CRF's plan.

Sydney continued through the construction site, searching for Anna. Thinking she had found her enemy, Sydney drew her weapon. When her target stepped into the light, it was revealed to be Nadia. As the pair realized their near-fatal mistake, Espinosa shot Nadia in the back and escaped.

LOCATION: Estonia
ALIAS: None

APO MISSION E408-A:

Knowing Sark would deal only with some-one he felt was his intellectual equal, Jack had him brought to APO to meet with Sloane. This was also in conflict with Sloane's agreement with the CIA, but Jack knew it was their only option. Sark willingly gave over information, along with an offer to infiltrate the CRF and retrieve the bomb. Then he named his price. He  wanted to visit Lauren's grave and see the body for himself. And he wanted Vaughn to open the coffin for him. Jack would not order Vaughn to do it, but Vaughn agreed that he would.

At the same time, Anna was discovered in Nadia's hospital. While Sydney and Weiss searched for

her, Anna entered Nadia's room and fired three deadly shots, then left. However, Sloane had anticipated the action and had Nadia moved. The shots were fired into a pillow. The comatose Nadia was then moved to the APO medical wing.

Marshall reviewed video from the construction site in Estonia and realized that Turner had told Nadia CRF's plan. The camera also caught that Anna overheard the discussion. That explained why she went after Nadia in the hospital. Since Nadia had the information needed to put an end to the CRF plan, Jack consulted Dr. Jain on the possibility of pulling her out of her coma early. Dr. Jain indicated that there was a high risk in waking Nadia from her coma prematurely, but Jack held that option in reserve if their other leads failed.

Sark provided the protocol to set up a meet with his former Covenant contact, Ushek San'ko. Since San'ko would be expecting Sark, he insisted on going in with Vaughn and Sydney to the meet at a club in Venice. Sark and Lauren had had a pre-existing weapons deal before the Covenant imploded. And since San'ko only knew Lauren's voice, Sark suggested that Sydney should meet San'ko while impersonating Lauren.

Sydney was forced to maintain the charade of the relationship between Lauren and Sark to convince San'ko to deal with them regarding the chemical bomb. It seemed a done deal until Anna intervened. She killed San'ko and fired into the club, causing a commotion. Sydney handcuffed Sark to a railing as she and Vaughn went after Anna. However, Anna doubled back and retrieved Sark.

Sydney wanted to use Sark's tracking device to follow them and capture Anna, but Vaughn insisted they blow the device. In the moments it took for Sydney to agree to go along with the plan, Anna was able to remove the device right before it blew.

LOCATION: Venice, Italy
ALIAS: Lauren Reed

APO MISSION E408-B:

As it turned out, Anna was not happy with the amount of money CRF paid her for her work. She saw the organization as weak, and intended to go into business for herself. When she saw Sark in the club, she sensed an opportunity for a partnership with another person similarly interested in the Rambaldi mythos. She then planned to contact CRF's buyer, Michel Guinot, directly to deal with him for the Dante Compound.

With their leads exhausted, Jack was forced to wake Nadia from her coma prematurely to find out CRF's plan. He passed the information along to Sydney, indicating that Anna was likely continuing with the mission on her own. Sydney's orders were to intercept the bomb and detain the principals. Marshall tasked a satellite to follow Guinot, who was on the move toward a property he owned. It was a graveyard in Venice.

Sydney and Vaughn went to the graveyard, where they made the ID. Anna and Sark were meeting with Guinot to sell him the Dante Compound. Combined with the V/X gas, it made for a powerful explosive. Sydney and Vaughn signaled for CIA tactical to come in. While the team was en route, they determined that Anna was about to escape and Guinot was about to leave with the bomb. This was not entirely the truth, but Sydney was not about to allow anyone else to take Anna in.

As Sydney and Vaughn made their move, Anna sensed they were there and fled. Sydney went for Anna, while Vaughn went for Guinot and the bomb. Guinot used the bomb case as a weapon, but it flung open and the bomb went rolling away. Just as it was about to drop and cause an explosion, Vaughn caught the bomb and took in Guinot.

Sydney caught up with Anna and the pair attacked each other brutally. Sydney was injured, but before Espinosa could strike a fatal blow, she heard an approaching siren. She and Sark started to flee, but Sark cut off her escape. Sark explained to Anna that he was betraying her because he had agreed to help the CIA. And he was a man of his word. The fight resumed and Sydney managed to get the upper hand. She had her gun on Espinosa, ready to pull the trigger, but she took the woman into custody instead.

In the end Nadia turned out to be fine. However, both sisters were still dealing with the revelation of Rambaldi's prophecy that one day they would battle each other and one would die. Sloane was glad to know his daughter was safe for the moment, but he was not quite prepared to forgive Jack for putting Nadia's life at risk.

LOCATION: **Venice, Italy**
ALIAS: **None**

OBJECTIVE: Recover the Blackwell Index and decoder

APO MISSION E410-A:

When the Alliance was dismantled, the CIA came into possession of a multitude of artifacts, files, and intel, including the Blackwell Index (named for Damian Blackwell, the head of the Gauss crime syndicate). Blackwell was believed to have compiled incriminating information on corporate heads, government officials, and common criminals in a master blackmail list that was encoded to a mobile terminal. Neither the Alliance nor the CIA had ever been able to utilize the index because it was encrypted using 4,096-bit encryption. Even with a supercomputer, it would take twenty years to decode. The index had recently been stolen from a CIA research lab in Sarajevo. Recent intercepts also indicated that the decoder disk had been located.

Blackwell's concealed base of operations had been identified and raided by French authorities, and he was arrested. Among the impounded articles was a minidisk that was believed to be the decoder. It was believed that the French did not know what they had found. French authorities refused to turn over the evidence, even though most of Blackwell's crimes had been committed on U.S. soil. APO expected that the thief who had stolen the index would go for the decoder next. When legal channels failed, the team was assigned to steal the decoder from the Paris prefecture. They were going to rob from the police.

Sydney, Dixon, Nadia, and Weiss were assigned the mission while Vaughn dealt with a personal family matter. Sydney, posing as an ecoterrorist, spray-painted a message on Weiss's SUV, which got her a free trip to jail. While she was in prison, the American Embassy supposedly sent a lawyer for her case. It was actually Dixon. Weiss tapped into the building surveillance and looped the feed in the interview room while Sydney slipped out to the evidence room, where she retrieved the disk. But an officer stumbled across her and sounded an alarm.

The team switched to Plan B for alternate extraction. Sydney was chased up the stairwell to the roof. With the police on her heels, she crossed the roof, heading for the ledge. Without missing a beat she jumped from the rooftop into a waiting helicopter with Weiss at the controls.

LOCATION: Paris, France

ALIAS: Amanda Peterson, environmental activist

CIA MISSION E410-B:

Unbeknownst to Sloane, Dixon had double-checked the mission intel and learned that Sloane did, in fact, have a lead on who had stolen the index out of the research station in Sarajevo. Sloane had contacted Miles Devereaux—former Alliance member and head of operations at SD-3—forty minutes after the index was stolen. It seemed that they finally had proof that Sloane was up to no good.

Dixon "borrowed" a micro-CD burner from Marshall's office, planning to make a corrupted copy of the decoder disk that they could give to Sloane while keeping the real one safe. Dixon went to Sydney for help. On one hand, Sydney was satisfied to know that her suspicions of Sloane were proving true and he was about to be caught. On the other, she hoped that she was wrong for Nadia's sake. Her sister had been growing closer to Sloane, and Sydney knew too well the hurt of being betrayed by the man.

While Sydney was in the evidence room in Paris, she stepped out of range of the surveillance camera so Weiss and Nadia did not see her duplicate the disk. Once they were back in the States, Dixon discovered that Sloane had been making calls from his home to a mysterious number in Brussels. Since the calls were routed through relay stations, the only way to find out whom he had been calling was by getting into the house and copying the encryption key from his secure phone. Sydney used her sister's birthday as a reason to suggest that Sloane open his home to her and a few selected guests. Sydney hated herself for using her sister in such a way but reasoned that it had to be done.

Although Nadia had not wanted to commemorate the day, she was glad to have a family that wanted to celebrate for her. That is, until she found out that Sydney had been using the opportunity to copy the phone's encryption key and send it to Dixon. Nadia did not turn her sister in, however, since Sydney claimed that she was doing this to hopefully prove Sloane innocent for a change.

With the encryption key in place, Dixon found evidence that Sloane was working with Devereaux to rebuild the Alliance. They immediately brought the information to Director Chase, who set up a mobile surveillance to track Sloane to the meeting in Brussels. Chase, Dixon, Sydney, and Nadia surveilled the presumed meet, but when they moved in, they found Sloane was alone. He was actually watching a live video feed of a meeting Jack was having with Devereaux.

Sloane had determined that the Alliance was regrouping. As the CIA would never allow Sloane to convene the Alliance leadership, he needed someone to bait them into the open. He approached Jack, who volunteered to go to the meet. Once Sloane explained the story, the team realized that Jack was about to hand over the decoder, unaware that it was a fake.

Devereaux was immediately suspicious of Jack when the decoder failed to work. Nadia was listening in to Sloane's conversation over the comm and heard of Jack's location. She started her car and headed for the meet. Devereaux refused to believe Jack's cover and was about to kill him when Nadia's car came crashing through the warehouse wall, rescuing him.

Dixon removed the tap on Sloane's phone and turned over the real decoder disk, only somewhat apologetic for his actions. Neither Sloane nor Chase pursued disciplinary action.

LOCATIONS: **Paris, France; Brussels, Belgium**
ALIAS: **None**

OBJECTIVE: Obtain the biometric targeting device

APO MISSION E411-A:

Sydney met with a man named Thomas Connelly to purchase a memory chip. But before the exchange was completed, Connelly was shot and killed. The shooter then grabbed the chip, but Vaughn managed to wound the man, which kept him from leaving. Knowing he had failed, the shooter pulled a knife and killed himself, apparently in the hopes that his death would protect his family from his employer, Sasha Korjev. APO retrieved the memory chip.

LOCATION: **Paris, France**
ALIAS: **Marie Gerard**

APO MISSION E411-B:

The information on the recovered memory chip confirmed that a biometric targeting device was being developed at a secure facility in Austria. Attached to a weapons system, the device would facilitate the targeting of an individual based solely on a DNA sample or a biometric scan. Sydney was sent in alone to Salzburg on a standard retrieval operation for the device.

The targeting system was stored in the sub-basement of Club Felice, which was owned by Korjev, as nightclubs are perfect fronts for money-laundering operations. The club security protocol was based on access cards, and Sydney would need Level-3 access to get into the lower levels of the building. Since the access card hardware was annoyingly hard to duplicate, she had to steal one from an employee. It didn't matter what level clearance card she took, because once she had the card she could swipe it through a mag-strip encoder that would reprogram it for full access to the building. She chose to take an access card from an American barback named Sam.

Once inside Korjev's office, Sydney learned that they had already moved the targeting device. The installation was complete, and it was field ready. In the meantime Korjev's security became aware of her presence in the secure area. The use of the stolen access card had alerted them to her presence.

A guard interrupted, but Sydney quickly got the upper hand. She forced him to reveal that the targeting device for the project, Operation Hawkeye, was being shipped out of Delongpre Shipping. Then she heard over the guard's walkie-talkie that security was going after the barback Sam, as she had used his card to access the secured area.

Feeling guilty for getting him into what amounted to a deadly situation, Sydney grabbed Sam to get him out of the club immediately. She was forced to reveal some of the situation while she saved him. Then she conscripted him for help with stopping the shipment. Sam, who had been looking for some adventure in his life, reluctantly went along and eventually joined in wholeheartedly, in spite of the fact that he was going to have to be put into Witness Protection afterward.

Sydney and Sam found the shipping yards and saw that a miniature UAV assault helicopter had been customized with the biometric targeting device. Once the chopper locked onto its prey, there would be no way to hide from it. Sydney, with a little help from Sam, infiltrated the warehouse where it was being stored. They were discovered inside, and the targeting device was set to kill Sydney.

A fight ensued, and Sydney managed to trick the device into thinking she was dead as she took out Korjev's men and retrieved the item. It was soon determined that they had taken out Korjev's entire operation in the process and that Sam would be safe to go home.

LOCATION: **Salzburg, Austria**
ALIAS: **Graduate of Buffalo State**

APO MISSION E411-B SECONDARY OP:

Since APO had confirmation that Sasha Korjev was involved, Dixon was tasked to locate the man's whereabouts and report to the CIA so they could handle the matter. Jack requested to take over the investigation, as he and Korjev had crossed paths in the past.

Jack later learned that a secondary mission protocol was to assassinate Korjev. He was uncomfortable with this but agreed to do it since he could get in close, whereas Dixon would have to do a distance hit. Sloane was concerned that Jack would not be able to make the kill, as it required acute emotional detachment. Jack assured him he would be fine.

Jack infiltrated Korjev's organization, where, following an initial misunderstanding with the guards, he was welcomed with open arms. Jack and Korjev had once worked together arming a rebellion and had become close friends. But Jack had suddenly disappeared when the CIA pulled him out. Korjev proudly declared that Jack had taught him almost everything he knew. But Jack was quick to remind himself that Korjev had turned his experience to criminal pursuits.

After meeting Korjev's wife and reingratiating himself with his old friend, Jack carried out his mission . . . and killed his former friend.

LOCATION: **Angola**
ALIAS: **None**

OBJECTIVE: Obtain the prototype Amplifying Glass

APO MISSION E412-A:

APO learned that the Belorussian Institute of Science had been developing a next-gen optical component called Amplifying Glass. When a laser pulse was fired through it, the glass magnified the laser's signal strength, boosting the laser pulse by a factor of ten thousand. That meant a simple laser, like the one used to play a CD, could be used to take a plane out of the sky.

APO had been tracking intel indicating that the Jakarta Faction wanted the lens. They had

employed freelance operative Cesar Martinez to obtain it for them. Nadia worked up a profile on Martinez. He had supposedly built his reputation with the execution of former Argentine intelligence officer Roberto Fox. Signal intercepts indicated that Martinez was assembling his team. The mission was to acquire the Amplifying Glass before Martinez.

The APO team attended a party at the Institute of Science in Minsk. Sydney was tasked to clone the PDA in the pocket of the architect of the building where the optical lens was stored. He always carried all of his project files on his PDA, which was encrypted with handwriting recognition software. Sydney pretended to be a fan of the architect, Ivan Saric, and asked for his signature to get the writing sample. Once Marshall cloned the PDA, they were able to get blueprints and security protocols for the new research facility. From there it was a simple matter of Nadia picking the pocket of one of the scientists to get an access card for the building.

As Sydney went for the lens, Nadia saw that Cesar Martinez was in the building, obviously making his play for the lens as well. Moments later an assault team crashed the party. Sydney was told to abort, but she suspected that she could make it before the assault team. She continued going for the lens.

As Sydney retrieved the Amplifying Glass, Martinez and his men cut off her escape. They were moments away from killing Sydney when Nadia interrupted. Sydney and the rest of the team listening were surprised to learn Nadia and Martinez knew each other. It was a fact that Nadia had covered up. However, it was also the reason why, instead of killing Sydney and Nadia, Martinez only tied them up and fled with the glass.

LOCATION: **Minsk, Belarus**
ALIAS: **Party guest**

APO MISSION E412-B:

Sloane was not happy that Nadia had withheld information that she knew Martinez from her youth. However, since Nadia did have a relationship with Martinez, she requested that she be allowed to contact him to retrieve the glass. Sloane instructed her to make an offer to Martinez and see if they could buy the glass out from under his initial buyer. She went in with Sydney and Weiss as backup.

Nadia made contact with Martinez and explained that she was in trouble with her employers because she could not deliver the glass and complete her mission. She easily convinced him to turn over the glass by playing on his feelings for her. Martinez agreed to give it to her as soon as she lost the tracking device on her so they could spend some time alone. She did as told.

Sydney and Weiss tried to keep a tail on Nadia, but they lost her. Sloane checked Martinez's holdings and surmised that he had taken her to the facility where they had been trained to be intelligence officers together. There Martinez and Nadia had a showdown. She confirmed that she had been the one to kill their mentor, Roberto Fox, because he was a traitor.

Following the revelation, Nadia and Martinez fought over the Amplifying Glass. Nadia managed to gain the upper hand and took him into custody with the Amplifying Glass.

LOCATION: **Buenos Aires, Argentina**
ALIAS: **None**

OBJECTIVE: Halt Third Faction attack

APO MISSION E416-A:

Sydney was sent to Cuba to meet with an unidentified contact working with a terrorist organization known as Third Faction. The pair met on the dance floor, right in front of the head of Third Faction, a man named Ulrich. For a fee, the contact offered information that Third Faction was planning a large-scale attack on a civilian target. He told her the information was on a hard drive in a locker in Los Angeles.

At the same time Dixon was in place at the L.A. train station with the locker in question. He retrieved the hard drive from locker 471 using a combination provided by the contact, which Sydney relayed via communicator. Once the exchange was complete, Sydney twirled off the dance floor, unaware that they had been made.

Sydney then met with her extraction contact. As he drove her to the airport, she noticed a red laser sight aimed at his head, but she could not warn him in time. A bullet tore through the rear windshield, killing the driver. Sydney was helpless in the backseat as the car swerved out of control and crashed, rendering her unconscious.

Unaware that Sydney had been compromised, Dixon gave the hard drive to a tech at APO, who began to download the information. Strings of code streaked across the computer screen, but something wasn't quite right. Before the technician could examine the files, the hard drive exploded.

Dixon pulled the technician from the room as a pathogen alert was automatically initiated. The offices of APO went into lockdown. As Dixon tried to revive the tech, he noticed strange blisters on the man's face and arms. Suddenly the man started convulsing violently, then died. As the body lay beneath him, Dixon noticed similar blisters on his own hands—he, too, had been infected.

In Cuba, Sydney regained consciousness in a cemetery, where Ulrich was threatening her contact. The contact was shot and killed right in front of her, but Ulrich had another, more sinister plan for Sydney.

LOCATION: Cuba

ALIAS: Cuban dancer

RPO MISSION E416-B:

After being rendered unconscious again, Sydney awoke to find herself buried underground in a coffin along with the dead contact. Ulrich had failed to take her cell phone, and she was able to use it to contact APO. She immediately warned them not to access the hard drive, but it was already too late.

APO was in lockdown protocol 4AC. The technician who had attempted to access the hard drive was dead and Dixon was in the infirmary. The hard drive had released a nerve agent into the offices, and the building had been placed in quarantine for thirty-six hours. With her coworkers in lockdown, and considering the secret nature of the black ops team, Sydney knew that the CIA could not send anyone to save her. But there was still one option available.

By pure luck, Marshall had been late for work that morning and was still outside the building. He was patched into Sydney's call and quickly sprang into action.

Marshall knew he could trace the radio frequency of Sydney's cell phone with a locator. Since he could not get one out of APO, he had to fly to Cuba and rig one up in a substandard electronics store. To ensure that there was a signal to trace, Sydney had to sever her connection with APO and temporarily turn off the phone to conserve the battery. Her limited supply of oxygen in the coffin left Marshall no room for error.

While in lockdown, the rest of the team was able to coordinate their research from base ops. Reports confirmed that ten canisters of Cyclosarin had been stolen from a warehouse in Morocco a week earlier. APO was hit with only a drop, equaling less than a gram. Third Faction had enough toxin to infect an entire city. Sloane ordered the team to use all resources available to them in the office to locate the target.

As she lay trapped in the coffin, Sydney realized that APO could ID her former contact. She took a picture of the man with her camera phone and sent it to APO. They checked his image against airport surveillance on inbound flights to Cuba to get a visual on the man's associates. APO could then track where the members of Third Faction had been coming from and—more important—where they were going. As the team at APO looked up the image, Sydney began repeating things she had already said. She was beginning to suffer from oxygen deprivation.

Marshall used his jury-rigged locator to find the Cuban cemetery where Sydney was buried. As he rushed into the huge graveyard, Sydney's cell phone battery began to die. Marshall was able to locate several freshly dug graves, but Sydney's battery cut out and he lost the signal before he could specify which one she was trapped inside.

Thinking quickly, Marshall instructed Vaughn via communicator on how to task a satellite to the location. He had Vaughn perform a thermal scan for a living body beneath the ground. Once the correct grave was located, Marshall raced there and dug Sydney out. The team watched via the satellite as Marshall pulled her limp body from the coffin. He performed CPR and saved her life.

LOCATION: **Cuba**
ALIAS: **None**

APO MISSION E416-C:

While Sydney was being revived, APO got a positive ID on her now deceased contact: Alex Rucker. The high-tech specialist had been recruited to Third Faction by Ulrich Kottor. When Ulrich's image appeared on Marshall's phone, Sydney confirmed that he was the man who had buried her.

The photo of Ulrich had been taken ten hours earlier at the Berlin airport. Ulrich operated out of a club in the city. Sydney and Marshall were tasked to infiltrate the club, find Ulrich's hard drive, and upload the contents to APO. Since Ulrich would recognize Sydney, the only way they could get close to him was by sending in Marshall.

Marshall went in posing as a man with information on another mole in Ulrich's organization. He used Jack Bristow as his cover name and did his best to adopt the persona of the hardened agent. Sydney fed Marshall information over the communicator to convince Ulrich that his third-in-command was setting him up. At the same time Marshall was wirelessly downloading information off Ulrich's hard drive. The problem was that the hard drive was connected to a network firewall. Everything that was being sent was encrypted.

At APO headquarters Vaughn was able to isolate the firewall and learned that it was in the basement of the club and that it was biometrically linked to Ulrich. They needed to get the man down there to disable it. Sydney instructed Marshall to threaten Ulrich at gunpoint, but Marshall's nerves got in the way while he tried to put together his cell phone gun. It accidentally went off, killing Ulrich.

The mission was not yet lost, however, and Jack got on the communicator. Since the biometric scanner was retinal, he instructed Marshall to remove Ulrich's eye so they could use it to access the firewall. Jack talked Marshall through the delicate operation. After a failed attempt, Marshall was able to remove Ulrich's remaining eye with the help of a spork.

As the suspicious guards looked in on their boss, Sydney went in with guns blazing. Together, she and Marshall went to the basement with Ulrich's eye and accessed the firewall. They obtained the location of the Cyclosarin bomb—Hong Kong—and alerted local CIA offices. The bomb was in downtown Hong Kong, and the Ministry of Security expressed its gratitude to Langley.

From the information Marshall downloaded, APO learned that Third Faction's operations extended far beyond initial estimates. They obtained information on hundreds of contacts throughout Europe and Asia. As APO was still in lockdown, the team—with a recovered Dixon—began sifting through the information in order to take down the entire organization. Meanwhile, Marshall returned home to his wife and son while Sydney waited at the train station for Vaughn.

LOCATION: Berlin, Germany
ALIAS: None

OBJECTIVE: Shut down Project Nightingale

UNAUTHORIZED MISSION E413-A:

While assisting Vaughn's ongoing investigation into locating his father, Sydney asked to use Jack's Level-6 clearance to access redlined files, searching for reference to the word "Nightingale," which had been found in Bill Vaughn's journal. To do this, she had to fill him in on Vaughn's suspicion that his father might still be alive.

Sydney found that Project Nightingale was the brainchild of Dr. Josef Vlachko, a molecular scientist. He had vanished twenty-five years earlier while under investigation for running unauthorized tests on human subjects. He took all records of Project Nightingale with him.

A year ago German mobster Hans Dietrich started branching

out into higher-risk investments like advanced weapons systems. He funneled a million euros to an encrypted bank account labeled "Nichtingall." His office was in Munich above a beer hall. Sydney figured he could get her and Vaughn to Nightingale.

At the same time, Jack reported to Sloane that Sydney and Vaughn were looking into something related to his and Sloane's ongoing investigation into Elena Derevko. Sloane wanted to shut Sydney and Vaughn down, but Jack suggested secretly using them to gather intelligence.

Sydney and Vaughn infiltrated Dietrich's operation via the beer hall. Sydney managed to get Dietrich alone in his office, where she forced him to open up his computer files to her and then knocked him out. Unfortunately, when she got to the file on Nightingale, she was prompted for a password. With Dietrich unconscious, Sydney was forced to rip out the computer's hard drive and take it. A bouncer interrupted, and she and Vaughn had to fight their way through the raucous beer hall to escape.

LOCATION: **Munich, Germany**
ALIAS: **Beer maid**

APO MISSION E413-B:

The intel from the hard drive indicated that Project Nightingale was active again, and Vlachko was running it out of an abandoned nuclear reactor in Siberia. The nature of the experiments was unclear, but they involved molecular science, altering human DNA. There was a list of more than a dozen human test subjects. All of them had died.

While Vaughn met with a mysterious contact, Jack tried to convince Sydney to bring the Nightingale case to APO. When Sydney and Vaughn reunited, Vaughn informed her what he had been up to. The unidentified contact had provided interesting information on Vaughn's investigation. Another agent had died the same day as his father. It was possible that the other agent's body had been used in Bill Vaughn's place. With that information in mind, Vaughn agreed to a deal with the unknown man. He would turn over a coil from the Project Nightingale machinery.

In a private conversation with Jack, Sloane noted that Vlachko had been off the grid for twenty years, and he was surprised to find the man through Sydney. Sloane intended to send in a strike force, but Jack convinced him to wait until Sydney brought it in, so she wouldn't think Jack had betrayed her. They would then draw up an ops plan that required him to go on the mission to interrogate Vlachko without Sydney or Vaughn knowing. They assumed Vlachko would lead them to Elena Derevko.

Vaughn brought Sydney up to speed about the coil while she filled him in on her father's suggestion.

He agreed to go to APO, but they would draw up a countermission to grab the coil for themselves. Since they wouldn't have time to duplicate the coil, they had to come up with a secondary protocol.

Considering that their plan for infiltrating Project Nightingale was complicated, Sloane noted that it needed to be a three-person team. Jack was assigned to join them, which complicated their countermission.

Once at the facility, Vaughn and Sydney split from Jack so they could get the coil while Jack overrode the security system. Jack took Vlachko hostage and questioned the man on Elena's whereabouts while he shut down security.

At the same time, Sydney entered the test chamber to retrieve the coil. A guard entered the control room, firing at Vaughn and taking out the control panel in the process. Vaughn subdued the guard with a tranquilizer, but the damage was done. The chamber had locked down and the reactor was coming online.

Vaughn connected Marshall to the facility's server, and the tech worked frantically to shut down the system before Sydney was hit with the deadly radiation. The only other way to shut it down was by removing the fuel rods from the core, but exposure to that kind of radiation would be similarly fatal. Marshall continued working to slow the countdown enough to give them time to corrupt the mainframe. It didn't seem like he would make it. But then, just as the countdown ended, Marshall's computer screen blanked out. There was a total system shutdown due to core corruption. Marshall had stopped the reactor.

Once things were settled, Sydney and Vaughn moved to Plan B, which required him to make it look as if he had overpowered her and taken the coil. Jack and Sloane did not believe it for a second, but they did realize his rash actions meant there was an unknown third party feeding him information and adding an unexpected element to the problem. Though Sydney and Vaughn's mission was a success, Jack was unable to get the information he needed from Vlachko.

After conducting a postmortem on the mission, Marshall realized that his actions had not stopped the countdown. Jack had gone in and pulled the rods, meaning he took in a fatal dose of radiation. When Marshall confronted Jack about his suspicion, Jack asked that they keep the secret between themselves.

LOCATION: **Yakutsk, Russia**
ALIAS: **None**

The Search for William "Bill" Vaughn

W hen Vaughn went to visit his sick uncle, a nurse at the convalescent home mistook him for his father, Bill. She said that Vaughn's uncle often spoke about Bill's visits, leading her to believe they had been more recent. Naturally, Vaughn explained to her that this would have been impossible because William Vaughn had died in 1979. The nurse, Rosemary, gave Vaughn a key to a bus station locker that was supposedly intended for Bill "when he came back." Inside the locker Vaughn found a journal belonging to his father. It was complete through 1982 . . . three years after he had supposedly died.

Vaughn later discovered that there was no nurse by the name of Rosemary at the home. The indication was clear: Someone wanted him to have the journal. Either his father was alive or someone wanted him to believe that.

The handwriting in the journal was a match for Bill Vaughn's script. The journal referred to various missions and someone code-named "Rover." The handle belonged to a former Special Forces agent named Frank Murdoch.

Vaughn met up with Murdoch in San Diego, and the man told Vaughn that he had met Bill in Argentina in 1982. Bill Vaughn was looking for men for a covert op regarding the Falklands conflict. They were supposed to lead a team of locals to secure a rebel position. The men were ambushed and Bill didn't even flinch. He simply told Frank to relax. Instead, Murdoch charged in to defend his men and Bill shot him in the back, paralyzing him. That was the last time Murdoch saw Bill.

Devastated by the revelation of his father's past actions, Vaughn told Sydney about the journal. Together they set about researching the classified missions named in the journal. Since Vaughn was reluctant to alert the CIA to his research by putting in an official request to see the operational archives, he managed to get the access codes from Marshall. However, there were some missions he could not verify. But Sydney was able to use a substitution cipher to break down the coded mission names into their proper headings.

Vaughn continued to decrypt the coded sections of the journal, finding an address in Lisbon. This led to Sophia Vargas, the woman to whom Bill Vaughn had given Nadia as a child. She told Vaughn that the only time she had met Bill was when he brought Nadia to her in Buenos Aires. Bill had been covered in blood. He said that Nadia was in danger and that others had been killed trying to protect her. None of that, however, explained why he had Sophia's current address in his journal. The only useful information she did recall was that Bill had referred to the name Nightingale while he was in her orphanage.

As Vaughn and Sydney attempted to research Nightingale, Vaughn received a call from an unidentified person. The voice on the other end of the phone instructed Vaughn to meet him at the Sherwood Library on UCLA's campus . . . alone. Vaughn went as instructed.

At the library, a note instructed Vaughn to inject an unknown liquid into his system. Vaughn agonized over the dangerous request. Fearing he would lose his chance to have his questions answered, he injected himself and was soon unconscious.

Vaughn woke to find himself paralyzed. A mysterious stranger told him the condition was only temporary. He then explained to Vaughn that he was interested in obtaining a transforming coil inside the experimental Nightingale system Vaughn had been researching. When Vaughn asked for more information on his father, the mystery man instructed Vaughn to look up a man named Philip Burke.

Vaughn discovered that Philip Burke had been killed in Laos in 1979, on the same day and in the same manner as Vaughn's father. Even more interesting was the fact that their dental records were identical, leading Vaughn to believe that Irina Derevko had killed Burke many years ago, not his father. Either the CIA didn't know the truth or they wanted people to believe William Vaughn was dead. Vaughn contacted the mystery man to tell him that he had a deal: Vaughn would retrieve the transforming coil.

OBJECTIVE: Secure a Rambaldi Manuscript

UNAUTHORIZED MISSION E414-A:

Vaughn met up with the mysterious stranger—now known as Roberts—in Paris, ostensibly to turn over the transforming coil. But Vaughn altered the deal. He would turn over the coil only after he was given his father's location. Roberts was not happy with the change in plan, but he allowed Vaughn to speak over the phone with his employer (though the person's voice was distorted).

The employer told Vaughn that the price for information had gone up, as Vaughn had not kept his end of the bargain to turn over the coil. However, the person also gave Vaughn a little something to keep him interested. Taped under the table at which Vaughn had been sitting was a *recent* photo of William Vaughn.

Vaughn was in.

Roberts took Vaughn to meet with his team: Jan, Gregor, and Sabine. Vaughn was introduced as Mike, a CIA operative going through a "transition." The group then told him the first part of their two-pronged plan. They were set to steal a cold laser housed in a heavily secure R&D wing of a private hospital in Bordeaux.

Vaughn and Sabine went into the hospital portraying a couple who had just been in a car accident. But when the doctor discovered that the wounds were fake, Vaughn and Sabine knocked out the staff and took the doctor's access card so they could get the laser.

However, while they were stealing the laser, a guard interrupted. Vaughn tried to fight the man off, but Sabine shot him to save the effort.

LOCATION: **Bordeaux, France**
ALIAS: **None**

UNAUTHORIZED MISSION E414-B:

The second phase of Vaughn's mission was entirely unexpected. Robert and his team were going to steal a Rambaldi manuscript from a two-car caravan out of Darmstadt. It was a CIA convoy.

Since the CIA outfits its safes with internal charges, the team knew that if they opened the safe without the proper access codes, the contents would be destroyed. Vaughn realized that this mission had been part of the plan from the start. There had been no intention of simply giving him the information after he provided the transforming coil. They needed him for the codes. After an internal debate over whether he was willing to betray the CIA, Vaughn agreed, so long as he was in control of the mission.

Vaughn noted that the truck would be heavily guarded with state-of-the-art surveillance. He insisted that every member of the team have radio frequency jammers. Once inside, Vaughn would bypass the safe's backup system while Sabine set up the cold laser to crack the safe. He insisted that they would not be firing their weapons on the job, as it was CIA protocol not to fire unless fired upon.

Vaughn and Sabine rode on street luges under a car driven by Roberts. When he pulled up to the armored car, they slid beneath it and used a butane torch to get them through the floor of the truck. The music from Roberts's car was so loud the CIA agents didn't hear them breaking into the truck, where they knocked out the guard inside. Once in the truck, Vaughn and Sabine broke into the safe and took the manuscript.

When the manuscript was secure, Gregor and Jan blocked the convoy, trapping the driver. They used a device emitting an electromagnetic pulse to render the electronic locks useless and trapped the CIA agents inside the truck. By coincidence, Dixon was in the lead car of the convoy. He had the driver turn back when he saw that something was wrong.

Jan ignored Vaughn's warning and fired on the CIA team. He received a shot in the chest in response. Vaughn and Sabine tried to escape, but Sabine was shot as well. On instinct, Vaughn fired at the shooter and hit him in the chest. It was Dixon. Luckily, the bullet hit him in his vest and there was minimal injury.

In that moment, however, Vaughn realized that his father would never betray his family and his country in the way that he himself had just done. Knowing that, Vaughn accepted that his father was really dead and planned to turn the transforming coil over to the DSR.

Roberts confirmed Vaughn's suspicions about his father and admitted that the entire plot was faked. Though this was all information Vaughn had previously surmised, there was one unexpected item in the confession—namely, the identity of their employer. According to Roberts, they were working for Arvin Sloane.

LOCATION: Darmstadt, Germany
ALIAS: None

OBJECTIVE: Locate and detain Arvin Sloane's doppelgänger

PERSONAL MISSION E414-C:

Unbeknownst to her family and friends, Nadia had been visiting Katya Derevko in prison, hoping to learn more about her mother. On the most recent visit, Nadia came with a gift of chocolate. Katya gratefully

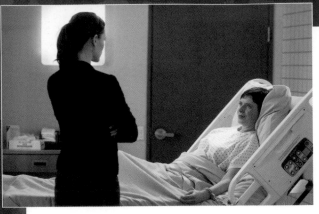

accepted and told a tale from her childhood as she nibbled on the candy. At the end of the story, she admitted that she was deathly allergic to chocolate and went into anaphylactic shock. She hoped Nadia would explain to Sydney that this was done to impress upon her the lengths to which Katya would go to see her other niece.

Sydney reluctantly visited the aunt who had tried to kill her at the Covenant dig site in Palermo. Katya explained that she had never intended to kill Sydney, adding that Irina hadn't been planning on it either. Katya continued, saying that before her sister was killed she sent a message to Katya telling her that someone was setting Irina up. Sydney didn't believe her aunt, but she also couldn't ignore the woman's information.

Following Katya's instructions, Sydney retrieved a music box with a secret message. The music box produced a pattern of light that revealed a string of numbers. Sydney used those numbers to access a file on the banking records of the man hired to kill Sydney: Kazu Tamazaki. The files not only exonerated Irina but also provided the identity of the real person behind the hit: Arvin Sloane.

LOCATION: Los Angeles, California, USA
ALIAS: None

APO MISSION E415-A:

After Sydney shared the news with her father, Jack went after Sloane. He threatened to kill his former friend, who supposedly set him up to kill Irina Derevko. But Sloane reasoned that, based on the logic of the situation, the setup made no sense. The only reason Sloane would have created such a ruse was to get closer to Sydney, and both men knew that would never happen.

Sloane returned to APO under tense suspicions. Since Roberts was in custody, Sydney suggested

they have him ID Sloane, but Roberts said that Sloane wasn't the man who hired him. He did add that his "Sloane" was a reasonable facsimile.

Sloane tasked the team with locating the man who had apparently been impersonating him. Roberts was interrogated, but his knowledge of the organization for which he was working was limited. Sydney suggested using Roberts to set up a meet, giving him the transforming coil and putting him in play. Once the exchange was made, they would track the coil back to the fake Sloane. Roberts was reluctant to agree to the plan because the fake Sloane was so dangerous. He eventually agreed, after securing a promise that he would be guaranteed immunity

from all his crimes and, more important, put into protection. Roberts then got in touch with his employer's number two man, Carter. They agreed to meet at a Los Angeles hotel.

Prior to the meet, Sydney and Nadia patched Marshall into hotel surveillance. Jack and Sloane observed with Marshall at APO while the rest of the team kept watch at the hotel. Instead of Carter, a third-party contact approached, leading Roberts into a glass elevator. As the team watched the elevator rise on the video, Sydney followed Roberts and saw Sloane's double descend in another glass elevator. It was at that moment that the real Sloane understood his counterpart's plan. The evil doppelgänger was going to cut the wire to the elevator. Unfortunately, the realization came too late for Roberts and the unidentified contact. A small explosion severed the elevator cable, sending the car crashing into the basement. Roberts and the contact died on impact, and Carter retrieved the coil from the wreckage.

LOCATION: Los Angeles, California, USA
ALIAS: Flight attendant in hotel bar

APO MISSION E415-B:

After reviewing the previous mission, Sloane concluded that the imposter most likely believed he was the real Sloane. The man was seen only briefly by Sydney and surveillance cams, and even though he was not an exact duplicate, he was enough like the real Sloane to be unnerving. Suspecting that the fake's goal was related to Rambaldi, the real Sloane considered removing himself from the case, but Sydney insisted that he stay on. He was their

best shot at anticipating the double's next move. Sydney was forced to ask him to go back to the hunt for Rambaldi against his—and Nadia's—better judgment.

Dixon accompanied Sloane to the DSR facility (Project Black Hole), where Sloane pieced together the double's plan. The man they were looking for was attempting to construct an energy source; in essence, a massive battery with which the team was quite familiar. Sloane reasoned that the construction would require an engineer with a specialty in nuclear physics and an advanced knowledge of quantum electrodynamics. It didn't take long to determine that a Dr. Margaret Sinclair was missing and presumably working with the fake Sloane against her will.

Sloane knew that the device could not be built without other necessary components, including a substance known as Xanthium 242. He contacted a former associate in Sicily who dealt in such illicit chemicals. Apparently "Arvin Sloane" had placed an order for an unprecedented amount of Xanthium. The real Sloane asked the contact to hold the order, promising to pick it up personally.

Sloane went to Sicily and met with his contact, Ignacio. Sloane made it clear that he had not made the initial order; rather, it was someone posing as him. Ignacio was immediately fearful for his participation in the plot, but Sloane assured the man he was not to blame. Ignacio then told Sloane the shipment was intended to go to Santiago, Chile. Sloane intended to fulfill the order himself.

LOCATIONS: **Nevada; Sicily, Italy**
ALIAS: **None**

APO MISSION E415-C:

Sloane led the team with the delivery. They split into two groups to retrieve the doctor and secure the lab. Sydney insisted that she was going with Sloane, which he claimed he was going to suggest as well.

The fake Sloane realized they were under attack and ordered Carter to secure the building. Meanwhile, Sydney attached a lock descrambler to the hangar entrance, but it was moving too slowly. After the first two letters, "J-A," appeared on the screen, Sloane suggested she try the name "Jacquelyn" but did not explain further. The code name worked. They accessed the building and found another large version of the Muller Device like the one she had seen destroyed in Taipei.

Sydney wanted to destroy this device as well, but Sloane said they should simply dismantle it, as it could lead them to the others involved in the plot. Sydney did not agree. The discussion was cut short when Dixon called over the communicator, informing them that his team had been cut off. Sydney had to go for Dr. Sinclair. After a moment of hesitation, she went to rescue the doctor, leaving Sloane alone with the device.

As Sloane waited, Carter approached him, believing him to be the boss. Carter was quite surprised to learn the truth. Sloane briefly questioned Carter, shooting the man in the kneecaps when Carter said he worked for Arvin Sloane. The fake Sloane had promised Carter that he "could live forever" with the help of Rambaldi's plan. This outraged Sloane, who saw it as a bastardization of the true belief of

Rambaldi. Sloane bludgeoned the man to death, claiming that immortality was simply a rumor. Sloane's anger was not over the plot to impersonate him. He simply could not forgive the man for the corruption of Rambaldi.

Sydney rescued Sinclair and secured the facility. Meanwhile, Nadia found her father, bathed in blood, standing over the dead man's body. Though he told her it was over, the look in his eyes said otherwise.

LOCATION: Santiago, Chile
ALIAS: None

OBJECTIVE: Recover the stolen Hydrosek water contaminant

APO MISSION E417:

An emerging terrorist group known as the Beograd Faction bombed the Indonesian embassy in Copenhagen. It was their fourth major attack in recent months. Though some assumed it to be their first overtly political act, the organization claimed no ideology and made no demands or pronouncements, leaving the true motivation for the bombing unclear.

Langley was desperate to acquire intel on the Faction and had previously placed undercover agent Thomas Raimes within the organization. Two weeks earlier Raimes had warned Langley of the impending attack in Denmark, but he never followed up with the details. He had also missed his last four meetings with his handler. It was assumed that Raimes had either been caught or killed.

In one of his last communications, Raimes provided the identity of the head of the group as Milos Kradic. Echelon intercepts indicated that Kradic had a meeting set at a location in Amsterdam. Dixon and Vaughn were sent to run surveillance. If Kradic showed, they were to neutralize him and take him into custody. It did not take long for them to locate Kradic, but they were surprised to see that Raimes was alive and still in Kradic's company.

Dixon and Vaughn were tasked to shadow the men. They managed to get Raimes alone for questioning, hoping he could explain why he went out of contact and didn't provide the intel to stop the embassy bombing.

According to Raimes, Kradic was a very suspicious type. Raimes had feared that if he warned Langley, Kradic would be on to him. Kradic was after a new weapon developed by the Indonesians. It was a water contaminant known as Hydrosek, and it could wipe out whole ecosystems. Raimes had allowed fifteen people to die because he feared that if he was caught contacting the CIA, Kradic would have him killed and still come away with the Hydrosek.

The embassy bombing was crucial in Kradic's plan to acquire the Hydrosek. Kradic was trying to determine the location of the chemical. According to standard embassy evacuation protocol, in the event of a breach all confidential intelligence was transferred to off-site servers. The explosion triggered those protocols and Kradic intercepted the outgoing data.

APO's new mission was to obtain the Hydrosek. To do this, they put Raimes back in play but switched Dixon with a computer hacker contact named Liam Halsey. The man was scheduled to meet Kradic for the next phase of the plan. At APO Sydney and Nadia performed a computer search to locate Halsey in Amsterdam. Vaughn intercepted the man and forced him to provide information that Dixon used so he could infiltrate Kradic's organization pretending to be Halsey.

After passing a test to confirm his identity, Dixon was welcomed into the group as Halsey. Kradic showed Dixon a dozen lines of encrypted code that needed to be deciphered. En route to the objective, Dixon was made, based on a supposedly intercepted communiqué.

Seeing no other out, Raimes led Kradic to believe that he was Dixon, effectively giving up his life. As Kradic was about to kill Raimes, Dixon stepped in to finish the job, shooting Raimes in the chest but managing to avoid any major arteries.

Sydney joined the mission as the team arrived in Vienna for an exchange in which Kradic would take possession of the Hydrosek. Posing as a club waitress, Sydney slid Dixon a gun while they waited for the delivery. Sydney and Vaughn were on surveillance and saw two men arrive with a case carrying the Hydrosek. At the same time, a man put an empty glass on Sydney's tray. She noticed that something was wrong with the glass and warned Vaughn to take cover. She then managed to dump the glass before it exploded.

Several other bombs exploded around the room as an unknown third party went for the case. Sydney intercepted the man and the case went sliding to Vaughn's feet. As Kradic's man went for Vaughn, Dixon shot the man, revealing himself as one of the good guys. Kradic fired back as he retrieved the case and fled the club.

Dixon went after Kradic with Vaughn in pursuit. They followed Kradic down to the sewers of Vienna, where he threatened to drop a capsule of Hydrosek into the water supply. As Kradic began a rant, Dixon shut him up with a single bullet, then called in a hazmat team to gather the remaining Hydrosek. The team returned to APO with a drawing of the unidentified man who had placed the bomb on Sydney's tray.

File Note: Outside of this mission, Nadia welcomed a visiting Sophia Vargas, the woman who raised Nadia in the orphanage. When she arrived, it was clear that Sophia had been beaten. She explained that the bruises came from people searching for Nadia. Sophia claimed that she had not revealed any information and had come to find Nadia and to hide in case the others came back. Sloane conducted a quick background check, which only seemed to prove that Sophia was willing to go to great lengths to protect Nadia. However, during their reunion Sophia presented Nadia with a bugged necklace. As it turned out, Sophia was really Elena Derevko.

Elena was the one who had leaked the information that APO had a mole in Kradic's organization. She was also able to confirm that APO had managed to take possession of the Hydrosek and that they had a drawing of her associate, the unidentified man who placed the bomb on Sydney's tray.

Elena arranged to have her associate

access Nadia's secured laptop and pull the location of the Hydrosek. She and her associate accessed the facility, killing several guards, and stole the Hydrosek. Elena then killed her associate because he had been made.

LOCATION: **Amsterdam, Netherlands;**
   Vienna, Austria
ALIAS: **Waitress**

OBJECTIVE: Locate Dr. Atticus Liddell

APO MISSION E418:

Jack Bristow had been missing for several days. Unbeknownst to APO, he was experiencing hallucinations tied to the radiation poisoning he had received in Mission E413-B. Jack believed he was being treated for the sickness by a former contact, but he was really acting on his own, not truly aware of what he was doing.

Sydney and Vaughn visited Jack's apartment (a first for both) and were forced to pick the lock to break in when no one answered the door. Inside they found notes indicating that Jack had been monitoring his vital signs. They also found bloody tissues and syringes in the bathroom, along with numerous medicine bottles with the labels removed.

Using the medication found in the apartment as a starting point, Sydney went to Marshall for help in determining the truth behind her father's condition. When she realized that Marshall knew more than he was letting on, she forced the full story out of him. Sydney was brokenhearted to learn that her father had sacrificed his own life for hers. Marshall told her that there was no treatment as far as he could tell and that whatever doctor Jack had been seeing must have been lying. At the same time, Jack was picking up a dangerous chemical for the "treatment" his supposed doctor suggested.

APO was able to track Jack to the Los Angeles warehouse district. Sydney and Vaughn raced to the site to find Jack alone among the homeless. He was living out a hallucination in which he was receiving treatment from an American doctor named Liddell whom he had extracted from Russia in 1981. As part of the delusion, Jack injected himself with poison, but the doctors at APO managed to get it out of his system. However, Jack continued to believe that it was 1981, back when he was husband to Laura and father to a young Sydney.

Sloane tracked Jack's doctor's name back to Dr. Atticus Liddell, who had developed a radical thesis for treatment of genetic mutations twenty-five years earlier. In 1981 he left the United States to pursue his theories, working with patients devastated by an undisclosed nuclear accident in the Soviet Union. But it being the Cold War, the Soviets believed him to be a spy, which he was. Jack extracted Liddell before the Russians could kill him, and he gave Liddell a new identity. Considering that Jack's handler was now dead and neither man had documentation of the highly classified mission, the only way to find Liddell was to get the information from Jack.

Because in Jack's mind it was still 1981, it would be almost impossible to get him to give the information freely. But when Jack mistook Sydney for Laura, Sloane came up with a different tack. With Jack's condition, normal regression therapy was deemed unlikely to get the information they needed. Sloane suggested that there might be a way to convince Jack that he was actually back in 1981.

APO quickly replicated the former Bristow home, and Sydney played the role of her mother to try to get the information from Jack. They even hired a young actress to play a six-year-old Sydney. During the odd reenactment, Vaughn called, pretending to be Jack's old handler looking for information on where they were moving Liddell. Jack was reluctant to give the information, but he eventually went with the facade, providing the intel—in code.

As Marshall worked to break the code, Jack continued the hallucination, explaining to Laura that his handler, Grady, had just phoned with a mission. Apparently Jack had previously told his wife that he was a spy. Sydney managed to get Jack to reveal that Liddell had been taken to Finland. Marshall then ran a biometric of Dr. Liddell against the databases of the Finnish passport offices and medical licensing board to get the man's current information.

As Jack continued to relive his past, he told Laura that he was going to give notice when he returned. He was tired of missing out on their daughter's life and was going to leave the CIA. Sydney could barely contain herself when she learned that her father had intended to give up his livelihood for her.

Sydney came to realize that it was about two weeks after Jack returned from Finland that Irina was extracted from her assignment and faked Laura's death. With Jack planning to leave the CIA, his usefulness had been coming to an end. The subsequent revelation of her betrayal was ultimately what kept him in the CIA.

After Jack was sedated, Sydney journeyed to Finland, where she found the doctor and pressed him to help her father.

LOCATION: **Los Angeles, California, USA;**
   Helsinki, Finland
ALIAS: **Laura Bristow**

OBJECTIVE: Locate Elena Derevko and prevent her from fulfilling Rambaldi's vision of the future

APO MISSION E419-A:

The Sloane imposter reappeared when a rare orchid was stolen from the Monte Inferno Monastery in Umbria. The monks had been using the orchid in a Rambaldi formula to breed aggression out of a variety of highly venomous bees. It was believed that the orchid had chemical properties that heightened receptivity in the neural pathways. Satellite photos confirmed that the same man the APO team had encountered in Santiago was involved with the theft of the orchid and the murder of forty-five monks.

Jack and Sloane knew that another version of the Muller Device had been used to agitate the bees into killing the monks.

Sydney suggested a way to find the fake Sloane: by offering the Rambaldi texts known as the Vespertine Papers for auction. The texts referred to the orchid but were rumored to have

been destroyed during World War II. The APO team leaked dummy intel that the lost papers had been found among the monks' belongings and used some loaned DSR documents to set up the auction.

Dixon and Nadia went into the auction house in Paris as Marc Mullens from the Carolina Institute and Felicity Hardwick, his authenticator. Marshall and Vaughn watched from a surveillance truck, but Sydney stayed behind, fearing the imposter would recognize her from Santiago. Over video feed, Sloane recognized the regular Rambaldi players in attendance . . . with the exception of an unknown woman. He assumed that she must be the one working for the duplicate Sloane. When the woman stopped bidding, Sloane realized it was because she was going to recover the papers through other means. Meanwhile, backstage her associate had removed the tracking device from the papers and made off with them.

The team gave chase on both the papers and the woman. During the chase, the team stopped a delivery van and found the fake Sloane in the back clutching the papers. They brought him in.

LOCATION: Paris, France
ALIAS: None

APO MISSION E419-B:

Back at the offices of the APO unit the second Arvin Sloane claimed to be the real one. He even possessed information that only the real Sloane could know. Additionally, his supposedly unique brain pattern was identical to Sloane's.

Marshall recalled working on a project at SD-6 that dealt with brain imprinting and engram encoding. Calvin McCullough, the head of the Psychological Warfare and Operations Division, oversaw the initiative called Project Brainstorm. Its purpose was to explore experimental technologies to aid in interrogation and brainwashing to create sleeper agents and transfer memories from one subject to another. The "clone" was programmed to be Sloane in every way.

McCullough managed to evade capture when SD-6 fell (thanks to a tip from Sloane) and had obviously continued the experiments. Sloane knew how to find his former associate, and Jack put Dixon and Vaughn on the case. The men found McCullough in Buenos Aires and attempted to interrogate him. However, McCullough feared his current employer more than his past one and killed himself, providing hardly any answers.

Meanwhile, the imposter agreed to talk . . . but only to Sydney.

The Sloane clone indicated that his endgame had to do with an application for one of Rambaldi's formulas re-engineering the evolution of the species. The fake Sloane indicated that the overall plan had to do with human nature itself and the vanquishing of "evil" for the ascendancy of "good." The plan partly involved genetics and bioengineering to create a way to "mutate" or change people into more evolved and less aggressive beings. Of course, the process could be used to instigate aggression as well—as proved with the bees.

The fake Sloane revealed that it would be only a matter of administering the formula to the general population, where it would quietly alter brain chemistry, exponentially expanding humanity's capacity for qualities such as empathy and harmonic coexistence. It could easily be added to drinking water, food supplies, and inoculations against disease—many of the same items Sloane's Omnifam organization had already distributed across the globe.

The real Sloane admitted that he had used Omnifam to introduce a combination of substances into water supplies around the world. His intent had been to create a more peaceful species and breed aggression out of the population. Without the flower he failed, because he attempted to artificially manufacture the orchid's nectar. But now the imposter had the orchid, and since the other substances were already in the water supplies, all that needed adding was the nectar. Somewhere between three and four hundred million people had already drunk the infected water and could be susceptible to the mental alteration. It would be just as easy to breed aggression into them all.

Using McCullough's files, Marshall learned that SD-6 had performed detailed brain scans of Sloane that were uploaded into the subject. The unknown man's belief that he was Sloane ran deeply. The only way to get information on the orchid was to shock him out of his belief and split him off from the dual persona so his real personality would assert itself. The best way to do that was by reliving a deeply traumatic event . . . in Sloane's past. Since the clone would resist hypnotic regression, Sloane had to go through the procedure himself so they could use the information on the clone.

Using McCullough's technology, Marshall could record Sloane's memory and upload it into the clone. Sloane suggested that they begin with Jacquelyn, the code name he guessed the clone had used in Santiago.

The APO team then watched as Sloane mentally relived events with his wife Emily from thirty years earlier. It was a time when they were going to have a child, a girl named Jacquelyn. But the baby was stillborn.

Once he recorded the painful memories, Marshall used them against the clone. Within moments, the programming began to break down and the clone revealed that the orchid was at a warehouse in

Lugano, Switzerland, at 43 Passeo Mantello. But something went wrong with the procedure, and the personality split drove him mad right before their eyes.

At the same time, Jack and Sydney learned there was a problem with the real Sloane. He refused to come out of his newly created happy memory of living with Emily and their newborn daughter. Marshall was reluctant to force him out of the memory, considering what had happened to the clone. The only possible way out was to guide him back to his current life. And the only one able to do that was his living daughter, Nadia. She succeeded in bringing him out of his dream state.

LOCATIONS: Los Angeles, California, USA;
Buenos Aires
ALIAS: None

APO MISSION E420-A:

Shortly after Nadia's friend Sophia said she was leaving Los Angeles, the CIA conducted a raid on APO, looking for Rambaldi items stolen from the DSR. Unbeknownst to the APO team, five DSR agents were dead and several Rambaldi artifacts were gone. At the same time, Director Chase had a team at Sydney's home looking for Nadia. Records showed that she had overridden the DSR security system earlier that evening using her secured laptop.

Though Nadia denied having anything to do with the break-in, she also admitted that no one else had access to her computer. But when the search team found a microtransmitter in the necklace Sophia had given Nadia, a horrible theory began to reveal itself. Jack and Sloane believed that Elena Derevko was behind all the recent events and that she had been hiding in plain sight for years as Nadia's former caretaker, Sophia Vargas.

Looking over what had been stolen from the DSR, Sloane believed that Elena now had all the components to assemble the Rambaldi artifacts for her evil purposes.

Knowing this, Sloane and Nadia realized that the one place Elena had to go was to see a Rambaldi follower by the name of Lazlo Drake. He was the man who had what amounted to the instruction book for Rambaldi's endgame. Sloane admitted that in Elena's hands the results would likely be an apocalypse.

Knowing the manuscript made him a target, Drake lived off the grid, constantly moving. Nadia tracked him through a billionaire financier named Grayson Wells, who backed most of Drake's early research into Rambaldi. Although Sloane was forbidden from participating in cases dealing with Rambaldi, he was most likely the only one who could get the necessary information from Drake, so he continued to oversee the mission as the team went in.

After Wells was tracked to Cannes, Sydney moved in, posing as a wealthy jewelry shopper to get his attention. Wells took the flirtatious bait and grew even more interested when he saw the Eye of Rambaldi "tattooed" to her hand. Once they retired to a hotel room, Sydney tied up Wells and got Drake's information from him. She communicated with Sloane, who was back in L.A., and told him that he wasn't going to see Drake without her. They would meet at the Solana Airfield outside Mexico City.

LOCATION: **Cannes, France**
ALIAS: **Pretentious jewelry shopper and Rambaldi follower**

APO MISSION E420-B:

Sloane did not want to wait for Sydney, but she refused to give him any more on the location until they rendezvoused in Mexico. They arrived at Drake's mobile home together to find the man dead. Elena had beaten them to Drake. She had the instruction book.

Sydney found a security camera that had taped Drake's encounter with Elena. But just as the recording was about to reveal Elena's location, Sloane sedated Sydney and took the tape. When she regained consciousness, Sydney reported in that they had been betrayed. As she was heading for home, Sloane contacted her to apologize. He had only attacked her because he wanted to keep her safe and warned that she shouldn't follow him. The situation was too big for anyone other than him alone to stop.

LOCATION: **Mexico City, Mexico**
ALIAS: **None**

APO MISSION E420-C:

Sydney and Jack separately realized that Katya Derevko was their only link to finding Elena. As such, Jack reluctantly went to speak with her in the detention center. He promised that he would do everything in his power to gain her freedom if she provided information that led to Elena. Before she provided the requested intel, Katya had one last surprise for Jack. She informed him that Elena had been gathering Rambaldi artifacts for years under her front organization—the Covenant.

Katya told Jack that she could help him find Elena, but Irina had been the only one who knew how to stop their sister. Unfortunately, that information died with her.

Katya then provided intel leading APO to Elena's base of operations: a decommissioned chemical facility in Prague. Vaughn and Marshall were able to pinpoint the location based on declassified KGB files, and thermal satellite imaging confirmed that the base was active. Sydney went to Prague to meet

up with the team, unaware of the fact that Sloane was already there. He had apparently joined Elena on her quest.

The team entered the facility authorized to shoot to kill. They split up to cover the building. On the search for Elena, Dixon saw something he had not expected. Elena's men were loading a familiar captive into a truck. Before Dixon could report the discovery, Sloane entered the scene, holding a gun on his former employee. The two men were in a standoff as Sydney and Nadia raced to their position. But they were too late. Before either man could end the face-off amicably, Elena shot Dixon and left him for dead.

Dixon survived and regained consciousness in the hospital. His only request was to speak to Sydney. It was his first chance to report on the identity of the prisoner he had seen with Elena's men.

It was Irina Derevko.

LOCATION: **Prague**
ALIAS: **None**

APO MISSION E421-A:

Marshall was able to recover some images from the DSR security tapes that had been wiped clean. The tapes revealed one of Elena's men as a former Covenant agent named Lucien Nisard. Jack recognized the name and had Marshall log on to Sloane's computer so he could get into the Blackwell list (which Marshall believed had been turned over to the CIA proper).

At the same time, APO was getting reports of an accident in Russia, but officials weren't giving details. Satellite footage of the city of Sovogda showed that the Russians were coordinating a military perimeter around it. A hacker Marshall knew sent raw footage of the incident, showing chaos in the streets around a giant red ball, part of a huge version of Rambaldi's Muller Device. The ball was at least six city blocks in diameter.

Though the Russian government claimed it was an industrial accident and was keeping a tight lid on information, word was leaking that the residents of Sovogda were experiencing mass violence, aggression, and the inability to reason. The APO team assumed that Elena and Sloane had infected the water supply with the chemical properties of the orchid to make the residents of the city susceptible to the Muller Device. Based on past experience, Marshall hypothesized that if they could not shut down the device properly, they'd risk a dangerous toxic event the equivalent of draining primary coolant from a nuclear plant . . . times ten million.

The only way APO knew to shut down the device was by finding Irina Derevko—if she was even really alive. And their only lead for that would have to come through using the information Jack had obtained on Elena's former associate Lucien Nisard.

Sydney and Vaughn went into a club in Ibiza posing as a sexually adventurous couple interested in Nisard. They took him into the bathroom, where the amorous meeting took a sudden, violent turn. When Sydney threatened to reveal the sordid details from Nisard's file on the Blackwell Index, the man hardly minded at all. He believed the end of the world was coming. In light of that, some embarrassing information wasn't much of a threat.

At the same time, Marshall wirelessly downloaded information from Nisard's PDA. While going through the information, he came across a reference to Project Helix in the files. Under duress, Lucien eventually gave up some information. He revealed that Elena had found the Helix protocol and used it with one of their followers to create a double of Irina. That woman had volunteered for the assignment to fool Jack Bristow, knowing she'd be murdered. Nisard finally confirmed that Irina was alive.

LOCATION: **Ibiza, Spain**
ALIAS: **Party girl**

APO MISSION E421-B:

Sydney and Vaughn learned that Irina had been taken to a remote location in Tikal. While Vaughn secured Nisard for extradition and transport, Sydney met Jack and Nadia in country to extract Irina. Jack waited at the exfil point as Sydney and Nadia took a boat downriver to the camp. En route Nadia asked if they could wait to tell Irina the truth about Nadia being her daughter. Sydney agreed to allow Nadia the time.

Together the sisters infiltrated camp and found Irina being held in a small underground bunker. Irina was badly beaten and nursing bruises from the months of torture she endured in her sister's captivity. The guards attacked as Sydney and Nadia tried to get their mother out of danger. But the women fought back and escaped to the waiting boat, then they reunited with Jack.

LOCATION: **Tikal, Guatemala**
ALIAS: **None**

APO MISSION E421-C:

Since she knew how to stop the Rambaldi device that she had been tortured into helping build, Irina insisted that she accompany them to Sovogda to stop Elena. Jack had their plane redirected to that location. Irina went to change into clothing that Nadia had thoughtfully brought along for her. As Nadia tenderly passed her mother the bag of clothing, Irina realized the true identity of the young woman. With barely a word, Nadia confirmed that she was Irina's daughter and the two shared a long-awaited reunion.

Director Chase learned of the rescue mission to retrieve the fugitive Irina Derevko and had the plane diverted to Los Angeles. There, the plane was boarded by U.S. marshals intent on taking Irina in.

When the team returned to APO, Sydney convinced Director Chase to let them proceed with Irina. Failing any other options, the Russian government was planning to destroy the device in an air strike, which would surely lead to disaster. The Russians refused to listen to the United States and even moved up their timetable.

The only option for the APO team was to parachute into the city and rendezvous with a DSR team already in place. Understanding the gravity of the situation, Chase allowed Irina Derevko to take part in the mission.

En route to Sovogda, the APO team learned that the Russians had moved up the air strike. The team only had four hours to locate Elena and Sloane and stop their plan. Not knowing what may lie ahead, Vaughn pulled Sydney aside on the transport jet to speak to her privately. He explained that he had planned another trip to Santa Barbara, where he intended to propose on the beach as he had wanted to do four years earlier. Considering what they were about to jump into, he did not want to risk something happening before he could ask her to marry him. Sydney was moved, but she did not give him her answer right away, telling him to save the proposal for after the mission when they could be together on that beach.

The team of Sydney, Jack, Vaughn, Nadia, and Irina then dropped into Sovogda to find the streets littered with dead. When the DSR team failed to meet at the rendezvous point, they followed a signal from the DSR's transponder. It led them to a severed hand holding the transponder, which seemed to be all that was left of the team.

At the same time, Director Chase was in Washington working with a coalition to convince the Russians to stop their bombing mission. The Russians, however, weren't buying the threat.

At APO Marshall and Weiss schemed to slow the Russians from launching their attack on the device. Knowing the Russians needed the MILSAT satellite network to vector their bombers, Marshall believed he could shut it down if he got into the secure system (even though such an act would be a violation of numerous international laws). To get into the system they would need an access code, which only a Russian military official would have. Taking a page from his bosses' playbooks, Marshall suggested consulting the Blackwell Index.

Marshall and Weiss dug up some interesting dirt on Russian deputy defense minister Karkov and managed to get what they needed in a phone call. Once they had access to the satellite network, Marshall discovered an encrypted broadcast connected to the Russians' network. Elena Derevko was broadcasting a signal over the closed network.

Meanwhile, the on-site team contemplated their next move among the remains of the dead DSR team. As they took in the situation, a man stepped out of the shadows. It was Brodien, the man Sydney had used during the staged CIA mission that led to her public resignation from the organization months earlier. He was the lone surviving member of the DSR team.

Brodien informed them of what he had already learned: Tranq guns would not work on the infected Russians. It took only six of the infected to kill the well-trained DSR team. The Russians then turned on each other when they believed there was no one left to kill. Brodien said that there were still hundreds, if not thousands, of infected roaming the streets.

The municipal water supply was tainted with Rambaldi's formula, and the device over the city was broadcasting a subaudible frequency off any spectrum. Anyone in the radius of the signal who drank the water had been psychologically altered. According to Brodien, there was no way to reverse the infection. Six months earlier the DSR had run the scenario. It was theoretical, but the only thing that stuck no matter the variables was that once a person was infected, there was no cure. The only way to deal with the infected was to kill them.

The epicenter of the device was four miles northwest from their initial position, hovering over the Oransky building. This suggested that the control center for the device would have been located on the rooftop of that building. Even though the DSR had already taken out the city's power grid, the device continued operating.

According to Irina, the device had been modified to run off an internal energy source. They needed to get to the control center to cut off that source. With all the streets blocked from gridlock, the only way to get there was through the subway system. The team was going to have to jump an emergency battery system to power up a subway car. Considering the pitch-black tunnels had only one way in and out, it was not going to be an easy mission.

As the team went for the subway, they came under attack from an infected man and Brodien was killed. The team was forced to leave the body behind as they rigged a subway car. Their options were limited: Once the car started, it could only be stopped at the track switch for Oransky station. They had no manual control over the brakes.

While working on the line switches, Nadia and Sydney split up. Sydney finished and returned to the subway car, but a group of infected came after Nadia as she completed her task. Once she finished setting the last green light on the tracks, the subway car started inching forward. Nadia made a run for the car as the infected gave chase.

Sydney reached out for her sister. Nadia's hand was barely in Sydney's grasp when an infected person sideswiped Nadia. Sydney could only watch in horror as the subway car picked up speed and left her sister behind with the infected.

The subway car carrying Sydney, Vaughn, Jack, and Irina continued down the tracks toward the destination. It came to a hard stop at Oransky station, where Sloane was waiting with a half-dozen armed guards. But by the time they hit the station, they were surprised to see that Sloane had already taken out every member of Elena's assault team.

Though the APO team was not thrilled to see him, Sloane reminded Sydney that he had never been disingenuous with her regarding his plan. He had aligned himself with Elena to put an end to her plan . . . alone. He would have completed the task himself, but Elena had built in a series of security measures and he didn't have the time to finish his work. Moving forward, Sloane laid out his plan.

Elena had secured herself in a bunker beneath the Oransky building. Sydney and Vaughn were tasked to open a communications line to APO, because they would need Marshall's assistance in deactivating the device. Jack was then ordered to take point. As Sloane was about to give Irina her orders, Jack grew tired of listening to the man . . . and decked him.

The team then made contact with APO, and Marshall informed them that he had found Elena's signal imbedded in the Russian satellite system. She was preparing to use the Russian satellite network to broadcast the frequency worldwide, so that everywhere the water had been primed with the Rambaldi formula would experience the same horrors as the town of Sovogda. But that wasn't all. The instant the

Russians scrambled their bombers, the satellite network would go online and broadcast her signal. That gave the team only about twenty minutes to get to the roof of the building to deactivate the device and prevent the end of the world.

Marshall sent the building blueprints to them as Jack told Weiss to contact Chase so Washington could alert foreign leaderships to begin preparations. Jack then tasered Sloane awake and ordered him to help get them into the building. Once they reached the roof, Irina would cut power to the relay and reverse ionization. Aside from the damage caused from impact, the water that would be released would be rendered harmless. But when Sloane informed her that Elena had reconfigured the wiring, Irina told him to take her to her sister instead.

At the same time, Nadia managed to evade the infected, but she was caught by one of Elena's men and brought to her aunt. When Nadia refused to go along with the plan, Elena injected her with infected water.

Before the team split up to enact their parts of the plan, Sydney paused for a private moment to accept Vaughn's recent marriage proposal. He placed the ring on her finger and they shared a passionate kiss before Vaughn and the rest of the team went to the bunker to find Elena. Sydney then made her way to the roof to shut down the device, but she was stopped by the infected Nadia.

Having secured Elena, Jack and Irina insisted over the communicators that Sydney take her sister out so she could deactivate the device. But Sydney couldn't do it. The sisters fought, and Sydney managed to get the upper hand, rendering Nadia unconscious but alive. As Sydney went to work on the device's circuit board, she had to choose between two colored wires to cut. Only Elena knew the correct answer.

Jack threatened to infect Elena with the tainted water if she didn't tell him which wire to cut. She eventually relented, telling him to have Sydney cut the white wire. Irina immediately shot her sister in the head and then instructed her daughter to cut the blue. As Sydney went to shut down the device, Nadia regained consciousness and attacked. As she choked the life from Sydney, a shot rang out. Sloane had shot his own daughter to stop her from killing Sydney.

Vaughn arrived and helped the wounded Nadia into the elevator while Sydney cut the blue wire. Moments later the device deactivated and the red ball let loose a torrent of water. Vaughn, Nadia, Sloane, and Sydney reached the bunker just as the water hit. The building was destroyed, but the team survived.

In the aftermath, Nadia's vitals were stable, but she was being kept under sedation until an antidote could be found for her condition. Jack had allowed Irina to escape as they awaited medical transport and evac. Before she left, Irina told Sydney that she had fulfilled Rambaldi's prophecy and taken down the greatest power.

LOCATION: **Sovogda, Russia**
ALIAS: **None**

Mission Accomplished?

After returning to the states, Sydney and Vaughn were heading on a ride up the coast to fulfill their long-awaited weekend in Santa Barbara. En route they decided that with Nadia still unconscious and all that had happened in recent weeks, it would be easiest just to elope on the beach. But before they could go through with the ceremony, Vaughn decided that it was time he finally came clean with Sydney.

To lighten the mood, Sydney joked that she could handle anything as long as he didn't tell her he was a bad guy. But the look on his face was not what she expected. His reply was, "It depends on who you ask."

Vaughn began to explain that his secret went back a long time . . . before they met. In fact, he said, it was the reason they met. He claimed that it wasn't an accident that he was the person at the CIA when she came in with her story about SD-6. He then said that his name wasn't actually Michael Vaughn . . . but an SUV slammed into their car before he could say anything more.

OP TECH MANUAL

SURVEILLANCE>>

DESIGNED BY MARSHALL FLINKMAN

LIPSTICK GRID CAMERA >>

Takes photos and measures space in three axes from one vantage point. Inside the lipstick tube are two lenses with a short-pulse laser and grid analyzer. The technology assembles images based on GPS and creates a blueprint of any building, accurate to the centimeter. The camera has a maximum capacity of forty-two photos. (MISSION J535-A)

Pearl Necklace Recording Device: The microphone is located in the pendant. The pearls are made of fiberglass to allow better transmission of the vibration from the wearer's larynx to the electronic mic. **(MISSION E632-A)**

Parabolic Microphone: Hidden in a travel pouch, the microphone has a laser transmitter that works in a three-hundred-yard radius with a low-frequency tantalum wind filter to eliminate unwanted sounds below 150Hz. **(MISSION E633-B)**

Pen Telescope: A telescope disguised as a pen that expands to view significant distances. **(MISSION E633-B)**

Thermal Glasses: Green-tinted sunglasses that allow the wearer to see though walls. **(MISSION E635-A)**

X-Ray Device: Small enough to be hidden in a woman's purse, this device not only scans the contents of a subject's pockets, but can also read information off key cards within two feet to create a duplicate. **(MISSION E636-A)**

Sunglass Telephoto Camera: Built into "superswank" pink sunglasses, the camera works in silent mode. Press on the arm of the sunglasses to focus the telephoto and snap pictures. **(MISSION E639-A)**

<< BUGGED RING
Designed to look like the fraternity ring belonging to Brandon Dahlgren. The ring carries a recording device. (MISSION E643-A)

Nonlethal Radioactive Isotopes: When ingested by a subject, these nonlethal radioactive isotopes can be tracked through the particle decay via satellite in geosynchronous orbit. (MISSION E650)

Bugged Phone Wire: Planted inside the wire that connects the phone to the wall, the bugged wire is a universal system, so the programmer only needs to know in which country the phone is located to adjust it. (MISSION E652-A)

<< LIP GLOSS MINICAMERAS
The lip gloss tube contains three miniature video cameras with a compressed air ejector. (A fourth camera had to be left out so there would be room for the lip gloss.) Flip open the back of the tube and the ejector will shoot a camera that will embed itself into ceiling tiles. The lip gloss comes in pistachio flavor. (MISSION E656-A)

Millimeter Wave Reading Glasses: Spectacles that allow the wearer to see objects hidden in clothing. (MISSION E663)

Cloaked Bug: Operates on an MD14 data adapter that cloaks the signal to bug sweepers. It works on a burst transmitter, periodically sending the recorded data to a receiver. (The bug also bears the Superman crest with the initial "M" soldered in the center of the circuit board.) (NOT MISSION RELATED)

Subdermal Tracking Device: A tracking device that is injected under the skin. (MISSION E668-A)

Passive Subdermal Tracking Device: This version can avoid detection from electronic sweeps because it does not become active until after a set time. (MISSION E669-A)

Digital Camera Sunglasses: The camera is wirelessly connected to a memory chip, and a plastic ballpoint pen acts as a shutter release. (MISSION E303-A)

Laser Microphone: The mic is set in a man's ring and is used for eavesdropping by targeting specific subjects at a distance. (MISSION E304-A)

Lipstick Transmitter: Located on the base of the lipstick tube is a transmitter with adhesive on the back so the user can tag an item to be tracked. The lipstick comes in peach. **(MISSION E304-A)**

Necklace X-Cam: Miniaturized X-ray camera hidden in a necklace. It scans a person's underlying bone structure and facial construction. The information is sent to a PDA that has been programmed to identify fractures, scar tissue, and implants of anyone who has undergone plastic surgery. **(MISSION E306-A)**

RFID Tracker: A PDA that can home in on a radio frequency identification chip. However, if the specific frequency the chip transmits at is unknown, the tracker must be set to cover a broad spectrum and could be set off by certain microwave ovens. It can track a signal for fifty yards. **(MISSION E306-B)**

HIDDEN CAMERA >>
A video camera with infrared capabilities set inside a fake rock.
(MISSION E313-A)

Network Sniffing Sunglasses: Searches for a specific wireless network. Once the network is found, the user presses a button on the arm of the glasses to send a message to the corresponding PDA. **(MISSION E318-A)**

Wristwatch Scanner: A watch that can scan pages of text and uplink to the operations center. **(MISSION E319-B)**

Laser Microphone: This microphone can both project and listen in to conversations at great distances. When projecting a voice, it sounds like the person is right next to the subject. The microphone does need to be aimed directly at the subject, however, and it cannot work through thick walls. **(MISSION E403-B)**

Multipurpose Wristwatch: When activated, the watch can home in on the electromagnetic core of an EMP device. It is also capable of burst transmissions of audio and video. The watch can also receive simple codes, such as an abort code to scrub a mission. **(MISSION E409)**

Millimeter Wave Camera: Allows user to read a combination off a key card with an LCD screen through a person's clothing. The camera can be suction-mounted to glass. **(MISSION E404-C)**

Compact Camera: A camera designed to look like a woman's makeup compact. **(MISSION E640-A)**

Lipstick Voice Recorder: A recording device hidden in a lipstick tube. **(MISSION E640-A)**

Flash Memory Card: A 512-megabyte memory card that is compatible with an SD-6 digital camera. **(MISSION E643-A)**

Delay Transmitter: Installed in SD-6's phone wire, the device causes a delay, allowing the CIA to control what SD-6 hears with their bug. **(MISSION E652-A)**

COMPUTER ACCESSING EQUIPMENT>>

DESIGNED BY MARSHALL FLINKMAN

Rhine-Kom

Hana Theisemuncher
NetzÜberwachungsprogramm   Telefon: 37-2-555-2183

<< BUSINESS CARD HACKING DEVICE
When placed on top of a computer monitor, the transmitter overrides the CPU so the network thinks the user is the system administrator. The user can then manually override the company firewall to allow for a transfer of files. (MISSION E634-A)

Remote Hard Drive Reader: Placed on or near a computer hard drive, it literally sucks information off the hard drive into an internal flash ram. It can record up to forty gigabytes of information in less than two minutes. **(MISSION E638-A)**

Razor-Prism: The prism can cut into any fiber-optic cable without disrupting the data stream, allowing the user total access to a computerized security system. **(MISSION E643-A)**

Cell Phone with Flip-out Keyboard: The phone allows the user to upload and corrupt a maser operating system. Pressing "1" on the keyboard connects the user with the operations center technician, who can access the system and corrupt it. A copy of the corrupted version can be stored on a flash memory card in the phone. (MISSION E307-A)

Low Frequency Wi-Fi: This device can scan and clone a PDA kept inside a subject's pocket. Since the working radius is only a couple of feet, the user must get close to the subject for the device to scan. (MISSION E412-A)

Cigarette Case Hard Drive Reader: The flash drive inside this cigarette case automatically begins the transfer of information once the user is within a two- to three-foot range of a computer. (MISSION E416-C)

DESIGNED BY CIA TECHS

Lighter: A USB flash RAM drive for storing computer information, disguised as a lighter. (MISSION E640-A)

STEALTH TECHNOLOGY>>

DESIGNED BY MARSHALL FLINKMAN

Cigarette Lighter/RF Scrambler: The RF scrambler can disrupt any video signal for a 420-yard radius. It requires a twenty-volt cell, which only gives four minutes of charge. (MISSION J535-A)

Video Scrambler: This round silver metal box can be used to scramble the video camera in an elevator. Once it is attached to the elevator controls, the user gives a quarter of a clockwise turn to activate the device. (NOT MISSION RELATED)

Alarm Override: A microchip-controlled box used to override alarm systems. (MISSION E634-B)

Tactical Cold Suit: This formfitting suit can shield the wearer's heat signature from cameras that read body heat. (MISSION E667-B)

Directional Sound Projector Wristwatch: A device that projects a prerecorded message that only the person the watch is aimed at can hear. (MISSION E670-A)

<< ANTI-EAVESDROPPING WRISTWATCH
A watch that emits a high-pitched squeal for ninety seconds to block any listening devices. A blinking red light indicates when time is up. (NOT MISSION RELATED)

EMP Grenade: Place the grenade into an electrical outlet and twist counterclockwise to release an electromagnetic pulse that causes a brief outage in a building's electrical system. (MISSION E303-B)

<< REMOTE CONTROL CAR WITH OPTICAL CAMOUFLAGE

A miniature remote car with a surface covered in microfilaments that interpret the UV waves generated by the surroundings to make the car blend in. It can be guided by remote control and pass undetected past security cameras to a central alarm control that can then be deactivated using an internal modem. The noise output is .04 Dbs, which is inaudible to human ears. The car can be separated into a telescoping camera hidden in a lipstick tube, and the car body can fit into a makeup compact. (MISSION E307-A)

Security Override: An override that can corrupt a security system, locking all guards in their respective sections. (MISSION E308)

Latex Mask: A skintight mask to make the wearer look like Lauren Reed. (MISSION E322-A)

Voice Modulator: A device that allows the user to disguise his or her voice. (MISSION E322-A)

Signal Jammer: Designed as a pen, the device provides sixty seconds of false radio interference to cover up monitored conversations. (NOT MISSION RELATED)

LOCK PICK/ENTRY TOOLS>>

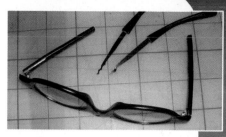

LOCK PICK GLASSES >>
These glasses hide a lock pick and tension rod within the arms
of the frames. (MISSION E631-A)

SAFECRACKING WATCH >>
This watch decodes a safe-locking device. As the digits appear on the watch face, the user turns
the dial to the correct numbers to gain access to the safe. (MISSION E635-A)

Cell Phone Biometric Sensor: A cell phone that can lift a fingerprint off any smooth surface, digitize it, and then create a latex duplicate to fool fingerprint scanning technology. There is
only enough latex in the device to create one duplicate. **(MISSION E638-A)**

Laser Lock Pick: A device that burns out the lock so an object, such as a safety-deposit box, will
pop open. **(MISSION E638-B)**

Key Card Descrambler: The hotel-style key card unscrambles the Jericho key card system
found on the Semba Island resort, among other hotels. It can be easily hidden within a cell phone
with a false back. **(MISSION E639-A)**

High-Resolution Scanners: Built into a pair of red-tinted sunglasses, the scanners work up
to a distance of about thirty feet, although certain lighting systems can disrupt the signal. The user
must make direct contact with the subject to scan his eyes. The glasses link wirelessly to a base station that produces a silicon and fluoropolymer compound, creating a set of contact lenses to fool a
retina scanner. **(MISSION E640-A)**

Makeup Compact Vault Code Scrambler: Placed
above a vault's locking mechanism, the compact will scramble
the code to prevent access. **(MISSION E641)**

ELECTROMAGNETIC CLAMP >>
A clamp that can break through the magnetic seal on a secured
door. (MISSION E643-A)

Standard Pick Kit: A kit that contains all the tools necessary to break into assorted locks. (MISSION E644)

Cardiac Event Recorder: Built into a ring, the device can read heartbeat signatures when pressed against any part of a subject's body that produces a pulse. The ring transmits ECG data to a cell phone that enables a secondary agent to fool a biometric sensor into a false identification, taking several seconds to record and transmit. **(MISSION E650)**

<< CELL PHONE SAFECRACKER

Based on the principle of outlaws using stethoscopes to open safes, this technology is built into a cell phone with a cone attachment. After the cone is placed over the dial, the user presses 7-9-3 on the phone's keypad (which spells "Syd") and the cone will amplify the tumbling mechanism through the phone. The numbers scroll on the cell phone's screen until it finds a match. Once the numbers are lined up, the user manually turns the dial to open the safe. (MISSION E653-A)

<< ELECTRONIC SKELETON KEY

A key that is designed as a medal from a Russian army uniform to access the FAPSI library. Each medal opens a different lock: The Order of Bravery accesses the top floor; the Order of Zhukov, First Class, opens the technical library; and the Order of Merit provides access to the automated selection retrieval system. (MISSION E655-A)

Acid Pen: A pen that emits acid through the tip that is able to eat through glass. **(MISSION E668-B)**

X-Ray/Stethoscope Safecracker: Designed with sonogram technology, the safecracker is hooked to a USB laptop with software that manipulates the voltage to crack the safe's encryption algorithm. The "stethoscope" part monitors the locking mechanism using imaging and audio cues. Once the safe's keypad is rewired and the probe is attached, the software will do the rest. **(MISSION E304-B)**

Lipstick and Perfume Acid Combination: Two halves of an acid mixture are stored in a lipstick tube and perfume bottle. With the "lipstick," the user traces out a line on whatever object she wants to open, then sprays the "perfume" over the lipstick line and the resulting chemical reaction can burn away metal. **(MISSION E310-B)**

Choker/Voice Recorder: A microphone in the choker records a subject's voice and transmits it back to a voice construction software program to build a password using the syllables and phonemes in the subject's speech patterns. **(MISSION E317-A)**

Magnetic Wand: This wand turns the tumblers of the lock on a safe from the inside. **(MISSION E319-A)**

Tie Clip Retinal Scanner: A tie clip that can record a subject's retina and uplink it to a PDA so the image can be used to open a security door that requires a retinal scan. **(MISSION E320-A)**

Wax Overlay: Worn on the hand, the wax piece can lift a palm print while shaking hands. The print can then be used to open a biometrically locked safe. **(MISSION E403-A)**

Retinal Recorder: Inserted into the lenses of a pair of sunglasses, the recorder duplicates the image of a person's retina. The lens can then replay the image to fool a retina scanner. **(MISSION E403-A)**

Laser Lock Pick: Housed within a watch face, the laser lock pick can be used to access a locked server. The wearer simply turns the watch bezel to adjust the laser. Warning: The watch does have a problem with overheating. **(MISSION E403-B)**

Mag-Strip Encoder: Pull away the backing of this fake pack of cigarettes to reveal the encoder. Once an access card is swiped through the encoder, it will run an analysis on the access control algorithms, extrapolate clearances, and reprogram the card to give full access to a secured building with varying levels of security clearance. **(MISSION E411-B)**

DESIGNED BY CIA TECHS

Lipstick Safecracker: A safecracker disguised as a tube of lipstick. **(MISSION E644)**

Lock Pick and Tension Wrench: A combination pick-wrench used to open locked doors. **(MISSION E653-B)**

Heat-Sensitive Shirt: A shirt that can read and record fingerprints for accessing print-sensitive locks. **(MISSION E651)**

TRANQUILIZING AGENTS>>

DESIGNED BY MARSHALL FLINKMAN

<< RING SEDATIVE INJECTOR
This fashionable ring can hide two doses of a powerful sedative that can knock a person out on contact. The sedatives can also be put into a cufflink. (MISSION E631-A)

Perfume Atomizer: The container is filled with a mild sedative that can be sprayed in the face of a subject. (MISSIONS E638-B AND E644)

High-Intensity Strobe Light: Built into a snapshot camera, the strobe light is capable of rendering subjects unconscious. Specially treated sunglasses can block the effect. (MISSION E647-A)

Wristwatch Tranquilizing Spray: One twist of the chronograph dial emits a tranquilizing spray. (MISSION E654-A)

Briefcase with Halothane Gas: Press two times on a button on the handcuff attached to the case to activate the gas, which then sprays out of the rubber stoppers on the bottom of the case. (MISSION E657)

Anti-Anesthetics: A mixture including synthetic caffeine that is taken right before the administration of anesthesia (such as halothane gas) to prevent sedation. (MISSION E657)

Scopolamine: A drug that can be administered in a mild dose, the effects of which last for five minutes so the subject reawakens thinking he merely dozed off. (MISSION E661-B)

<< HIGH-INTENSITY PULSED STROBE LIGHT
The digital projector emits a pulse strobe that flashes at the same intensity as human brain waves. The subjects experience a period of three minutes as if they are in a daydream. The user must wear a pair of sunglasses that are time-synchronized with the pulses so he or she will not be affected by the light. (MISSION E662-A)

Lapel Microphone: A mic that emits a burst of tranquilizing spray in the opponent's face. The trigger is located on an accompanying video camera. (The camera also has a compartment for storing a gun.) **(MISSION E668-B)**

Lipstick Sedative: One kiss with this sedative-laced lipstick will render the victim unconscious. Must be used in conjunction with rubber strips to protect the wearer's lips from the sedative. **(MISSION 402-B)**

Tranq Shooter: Disguised within a fountain pen, the tranq gun has a laser sight to ensure a direct hit on the victim's vagus nerve for immediate action. **(MISSION E410-A)**

DESIGNED BY CIA TECHS

TRANQUILIZER-TIPPED NEEDLE >>
A needle, coated with a tranquilizing agent, that can be worn in the hair. (MISSION E658-B)

WEAPONS>>

DESIGNED BY MARSHALL FLINKMAN

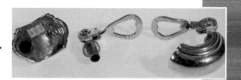

EARRING EXPLOSIVE >>
A minigrenade hidden inside an earring. (MISSION E641)

MAGNETIC SHAPE CHARGE >>
A device that can penetrate two meters of armored steel and fire a secondary tear gas munition for disabling guards inside an armored truck. (MISSION E661-A)

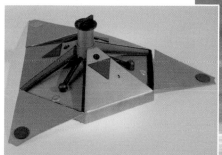

M-79 Grenade Launcher: This launcher can be rigged to fire canisters of chloroform. (MISSION E661-A)

Explosives Sniffer: The sniffer works like a normal tracking device, but it detects various compounds of Semtex, dynamite, and plasma within one hundred feet of the explosive. **(MISSION E314-B)**

Cell Phone Gun: The cell phone breaks apart into a stock, barrel, and trigger. The gun has a two-bullet magazine. The user needs to take extra care when assembling the gun, as it could accidentally go off and kill someone. **(MISSION E416-C)**

DESIGNED BY CIA TECHS

Explosive Cell Phone: A mobile phone that is packed with plastic explosives. **(MISSION E649-A)**

Heckler & Koch P-11 Underwater Pistol: This pistol holds five rounds of tranq darts and fires in virtual silence. **(MISSION E658-A)**

Exploding Necklace: If the wearer attempts to remove the necklace, layered with C-4, while it is armed, she will break the circuit and it will detonate. The explosives can also be triggered by a remote detonator. **(MISSION E659-B)**

Red Mercury Charge: A charge that contains a mechanical fuse. **(MISSION E651)**

ASSORTED ITEMS>>

DESIGNED BY MARSHALL FLINKMAN

<< SONIC WAVE EMITTER
Hidden inside a normal-looking Spanish peseta coin, the emitter synchronizes with the resonance frequency of glass within a range of one meter to shatter the glass. The remote trigger for the device is implanted in a pen. (MISSION E632-A)

Backpack Parasail: A parasail built into a backpack as a safety precaution. **(MISSION E645-A)**

Infrared Pulse Emitter: Built into an earring, this device emits an infrared pulse invisible to the naked eye. The pulse is easily recognized by IR-capable contacts, which were SD-6 SOP for high-visibility brush passes. **(MISSION E647-A)**

SOUND CANCELING DEVICE >>

Metal device worn on an armband to perform active noise control by emitting an out-of-phase audio signal that cancels out any sounds within a hundred-foot radius. Intended for use against audio sensors that pick up any sounds above 5 Dbs. (MISSION E648-B)

Metal Detector: A device used to find a safe. **(MISSION E653-A)**

HYDRAULIC LUGE >>

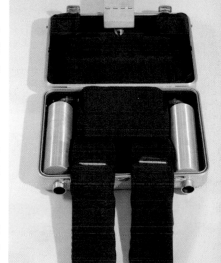

The high-performance hydraulic luge can go up to speeds of 150 mph and has the ability to cover two miles in less than twelve seconds. The luge is designed to be hidden inside a briefcase. (MISSION E654-A)

High-Glide Tactical Parachute: The parachute is compressed into a man's suit jacket along with a hyperextending tandem sling. **(MISSION E662-B)**

Artful Dodger: A ring with a sharp half-inch spike in it that cuts through clothing to aid in pickpocketing. It was named for the character in the book *Oliver Twist*. **(MISSION E663)**

KEVLAR BALLS >>

Designed as a countermeasure to a lethal response system, the balls can be sent into a room with motion-activated machine guns to attract firing and repel the bullets until the guns run out of ammunition. (MISSION E313-C)

Neoprene Hot Suit: Worn to protect a person from excessive temperatures, like those found in a steam vent. **(MISSION E316-B)**

Superadhesive: When this powerful glue is sprayed on glass the glass will break, but not shatter. The broken pieces will remain in place, to be rolled up like paper and put aside. **(MISSION E401-C)**

Weight Compensator: Can be used on an alarmed sword pedestal that is weight sensitive to ten milligrams. The compensator's two arms are placed at either side of a weight-sensitive rack holding the item (such as a sword). The damper arm of the device is then slipped down onto the base. The damper will increase pressure on the base as it lifts the item, matching the weight and pressure of the item as it is removed. Though the compensator failed twice in tests, it worked perfectly in the field. **(MISSION E401-C)**

DESIGNED BY CIA TECHS

Lipstick with Homing Beacon and Waterproof Cache: An amphibious tracking device that can be used on land or underwater. **(MISSION E648-B)**

<< FRICTION DECELERATOR
Used in conjunction with a high-tension wire, the decelerator works as a braking system when descending at a fast rate of speed. **(MISSION E653-B)**

Laser Torch: A laser used to cut through glass. **(MISSION E653-B)**

Catapult: An air ram catapult used for vaulting over high fences. **(MISSION E565-B)**

<< PROPULSION JETS
These jets can be strapped to a swimmer's legs to permit him or her to swim at speeds as fast as five knots underwater. **(MISSION E658-A)**

MISSION KEY

SEASON 1

EPISODE	ORIGINAL AIRDATE	MISSION
"Truth Be Told" Written and Directed by: J. J. Abrams	9/30/01	J535-A, J535-B
"So It Begins" Written by: J. J. Abrams Directed by: Ken Olin	10/7/01	E631-A, E631-B
"Parity" Written by: Alex Kurtzman & Roberto Orci Directed by: Mikael Solomon	10/14/01	E631-B (Countermission) E632-A, E632-B
"A Broken Heart" Written by: Vanessa Taylor Directed by: Harry Winer	10/21/01	E632-B, E633-A, E633-B, E633-C
"Doppelganger" Written by: Daniel Arkin Directed by: Ken Olin	10/28/01	E633-C, E634-A, E634-B
"Reckoning" Written by: Jesse Alexander Directed by: Daniel Attias	11/18/01	E634-B, E635-A, E635-B
"Color-Blind" Written by: Roberto Orci & Alex Kurtzman Directed by: Jack Bender	11/25/01	E635-B, E636
"Time Will Tell" Written by: Jeff Pinkner Directed by: Perry Lang	12/2/01	E636, E637-A, E637-B

EPISODE	ORIGINAL AIRDATE	MISSION
"Mea Culpa" Written by: Debra J. Fisher & Erica Messer Directed by: Ken Olin	12/09/01	E637-B, E638-A, E638-B
"Spirit" Written by: J. J. Abrams & Vanessa Taylor Directed by: Jack Bender	12/16/01	E639-A, E639-B
"The Confession" Written by: J. J. Abrams & Daniel Arkin Directed by: Harry Winer	1/6/02	E639-B, E640-A, E640-B
"The Box Part 1" Written by: Jesse Alexander & John Eisendrath Directed by: Jack Bender	1/20/02	E641
"The Box Part 2" Written by: Jesse Alexander & John Eisendrath Directed by: Jack Bender	2/10/02	E641
"The Coup" Written by: Alex Kurtzman & Roberto Orci Directed by: Tom Wright	2/24/02	E643-A, E643-B
"Page 47" Written by: J. J. Abrams & Jeff Pinkner Directed by: Ken Olin	3/3/02	E643-B, E644
"The Prophecy" Written by: John Eisendrath Directed by: Davis Guggenheim	3/10/02	E645-A, E645-B
"Q&A" Written by: J. J. Abrams Directed by: Ken Olin	3/17/02	E646

"Masquerade"   4/7/02   E646, E647-A, E647-B
Written by: Roberto Orci & Alex Kurtzman
Directed by: Craig Zisk

"Snowman"   4/14/02   E647-B, E648-A, E648-B
Written by: Jesse Alexander & Jeff Pinkner
Directed by: Barnet Kellman

"The Solution"   4/21/02   E649-A, E649-B
Written by: John Eisendrath
Directed by: Daniel Attias

"Rendezvous"   5/5/02   E649-B, E650
Written by: Erica Messer & Debra J. Fisher
Directed by: Ken Olin

"Almost Thirty Years"   5/12/02   E651
Written and Directed by: J. J. Abrams

SEASON 2

EPISODE	ORIGINAL AIRDATE	MISSION
"The Enemy Walks In" Written by: J. J. Abrams Directed by: Ken Olin	9/29/02	E651, E652-A, E652-B
"Trust Me" Written by: John Eisendrath Directed by: Craig Zisk	10/6/02	E653-A, E653-B
"Cipher" Written by: Alex Kurtzman-Counter & Roberto Orci Directed by: Daniel Attias	10/13/02	E654-A, E654-B
"Dead Drop" Written by: Jesse Alexander Directed by: Guy Norman Bee	10/20/02	E654-B, E655-A, E655-B
"The Indicator" Written by: Jeff Pinkner Directed by: Ken Olin	11/3/02	E656-A, E656-B
"Salvation" Written by: Roberto Orci & Alex Kurtzman-Counter Directed by: Perry Lang	11/10/02	E657
"The Counteragent" Written by: John Eisendrath Directed by: Daniel Attias	11/17/02	E658-A, E658-B
"Passage Part 1" Written by: Debra J. Fisher & Erica Messer Directed by: Ken Olin	12/1/02	E659-A, E659-B

"Passage Part 2"   12/8/02   E659-B
Written by: Crystal Nix Hines
Directed by: Ken Olin

"The Abduction"   12/15/02   E661-A, E661-B
Written by: Alex Kurtzman-Counter & Roberto Orci
Directed by: Nelson McCormick

"A Higher Echelon"   1/5/03   E662-A, E662-B
Written by: John Eisendrath
Directed by: Guy Norman Bee

"The Getaway"   1/12/03   E663
Written by: Jeff Pinkner
Directed by: Lawrence Trilling

"Phase One"   1/26/03   E665-A, E665-B
Written by: J. J. Abrams
Directed by: Jack Bender

EPISODE	ORIGINAL AIRDATE	MISSION

"Double Agent" 2/2/03 E664-A, E664-B
Written by: Roberto Orci & Alex Kurtzman-Counter
Directed by: Ken Olin

"A Free Agent" 2/9/03 E666-A, E666-B
Written by: Roberto Orci & Alex Kurtzman-Counter
Directed by: Alex Kurtzman-Counter

"Firebomb" 2/23/03 E666-B, E667-A, E667-B
Written by: John Eisendrath
Directed by: Craig Zisk

"A Dark Turn" 3/2/03 E668-A, E668-B, E668-C
Written by: Jesse Alexander
Directed by: Ken Olin

"Truth Takes Time" 3/16/03 E669-A, E669-B
Written by: J. R. Orci
Directed by: Nelson McCormick

"Endgame" 3/30/03 E670-A, E670-B
Written by: Sean Gerace
Directed by: Perry Lang

"Countdown" 4/27/03 E671-A, E671-B, E671-C
Teleplay by: Jeff Pinkner
Story by: R. P. Gaborno
Directed by: Lawrence Trilling

"Second Double" 5/4/03 E672-A, E672-B
Teleplay by: Crystal Nix Hines
Story by: Breen Frazier
Directed by: Ken Olin

"The Telling" 5/4/03 E673-A, E673-B, E673-C
Written and Directed by: J. J. Abrams

SEASON 3

EPISODE	ORIGINAL AIRDATE	MISSION
"Conscious" Written by: Josh Appelbaum & André Nemec Directed by: Ken Olin	11/30/03	E309
"Remnants" Written by: Jeff Pinkner Directed by: Jack Bender	12/7/03	E309, E310-A, E310-B, E310-C
"Full Disclosure" Written by: Jesse Alexander Directed by: Lawrence Trilling	1/11/04	E311
"Crossings" Written by: Josh Appelbaum & André Nemec Directed by: Ken Olin	1/18/04	E312
"After Six" Written by: Alison Schapker & Monica Breen Directed by: Maryann Brandon	2/15/04	E313-A, E313-B, E313-C

"Blowback"   3/7/04   E314-A, E314-B
Written by: Laurence Andries
Directed by: Lawrence Trilling

"Facade"   3/14/04   E315-A, E315-B
Written by: R. P. Gaborno & Christopher Hollier
Directed by: Jack Bender

"Taken"   3/21/04   E316-A, E316-B, E316-C
Written by: J. R. Orci
Directed by: Lawrence Trilling

"The Frame"   3/28/04   E317-A, E317-B
Written by: Crystal Nix Hines
Directed by: Max Mayer

"Unveiled"   4/11/04   E318-A, E318-B
Written by: Monica Breen & Alison Schapker
Directed by: Jack Bender

"Hourglass"   4/18/04   E319-A, E319-B, E319-C
Written by: Josh Appelbaum & André Nemec
Directed by: Ken Olin

"Blood Ties"   4/25/04   E320-A, E320-B
Teleplay by: J. R. Orci
Story by: Monica Breen & Alison Schapker
Directed by: Jack Bender

"Legacy"   5/2/04   E321-A, E321-B, E321-C
Written by: Jesse Alexander
Directed by: Lawrence Trilling

"Resurrection"   5/23/04   E322-A, E322-B, E322-C
Written by: Jeff Pinkner
Directed by: Ken Olin

SEASON 4

EPISODE	ORIGINAL AIRDATE	MISSION
"Authorized Personnel Only Part 1" Written by: J. J. Abrams Directed by: Ken Olin	1/5/05	E401-A, E401-B, E401-C
"Authorized Personnel Only Part 2" Written by: Jeff Melvoin Directed by: Ken Olin	1/5/05	E401-C, E402-A, E402-B
"The Awful Truth" Written by: Jesse Alexander Directed by: Lawrence Trilling	1/12/05	E403-A, E403-B
"Ice" Written and Directed by: Jeffrey Bell	1/19/05	E405-A, E405-B
"Welcome to Liberty Village" Written by: Drew Goddard Directed by: Kevin Hooks	1/26/05	E409
"Nocturne" Written by: Jeff Pinkner Directed by: Lawrence Trilling	2/9/05	E406-A, E406-B, E406-C
"Détente" Written by: Alison Schapker & Monica Breen Directed by: Craig Zisk	2/16/05	E404-A, E404-B, E404-C
"Echoes" Written by: Josh Appelbaum & André Nemec Directed by: Daniel Attias	2/23/05	E407-A, E407-B, E407-C

"A Man of His Word" 3/2/05 E408-A, E408-B, E408-C
Written By: Breen Frazier
Directed By: Marita Grabiak

"The Index" 3/9/05 E410-A, E410-B
Written by: Alison Schapker & J. R. Orci
Directed by: Lawrence Trilling

"The Road Home" 3/16/05 E411-A, E411-B
Written by: Josh Appelbaum & André Nemec
Directed by: Maryann Brandon

"The Orphan" 3/23/05 E412-A, E412-B
Written by: Jeffrey Bell & Monica Breen
Directed by: Ken Olin

"Tuesday" 3/30/05 E416-A, E416-B, E416-C
Written by: Drew Goddard & Breen Frazier
Directed by: Frederick E. O. Toye

"Nightingale" 4/6/05 E413-A, E413-B
Written by: Breen Frazier
Directed by: Lawrence Trilling

EPISODE	ORIGINAL AIRDATE	MISSION
"Pandora" Written by: J. R. Orci & Jeff Pinkner Directed by: Kevin Hooks	4/13/05	E414-A, E414-B, E414-C
"Another Mister Sloane" Written by: Luke McMullen Directed by: Greg Yaitanes	4/20/05	E415-A, E415-B, E415-C
"A Clean Conscience" Written by: J. R. Orci Directed by: Lawrence Trilling	4/27/05	E417
"Mirage" Written by: Steven Kane Directed by: Brad Turner	5/4/05	E417, E418
"In Dreams . . ." Written by: Jon Robin Baitz Directed by: Jennifer Garner	5/11/05	E419-A, E419-B
"The Descent" Written by: Jeffrey Bell Directed by: Jeffrey Bell	5/18/05	E420-A, E420-B, E420-C
"Search and Rescue" Written by: Monica Breen & Alison Schapker Directed by: Lawrence Trilling	5/26/05	E421-A, E421-B, E421-C
"Before the Flood" Written by: Josh Appelbaum & André Nemec Directed by: Lawrence Trilling	5/26/05	E421-C

TRAVEL LOGS

TRAVEL LOG

AGENT >> Sydney Bristow

YEAR >> PRE-01

Siberia — SD-6

Paris, France — SD-6

Lisbon, Portugal — SD-6

Corsica — SD-6

Memphis, Egypt — SD-6

Former Yugoslavia — SD-6

Peru — SD-6

London, England | SD-6
Oxford, England | CIA

Paris, France | SD-6
| CIA

Madrid, Spain | SD-6
Malaga, Spain | CIA

Morocco | SD-6
| CIA

Las Vegas
Nevada, USA | SD-6

Buckingham
Virginia, USA | SD-6
| CIA

Los Angeles, California, USA | SD-6/CIA
Santa Barbara, California, USA | unauth

Positano, Mexico | SD-6

Havana, Cuba | CIA

São Paulo, Brazil | SD-6
Rio de Janeiro, Brazil | CIA

Argentina | SD-6
| CIA

TRAVEL LOG

AGENT >> Sydney Bristow

YEAR >> 01

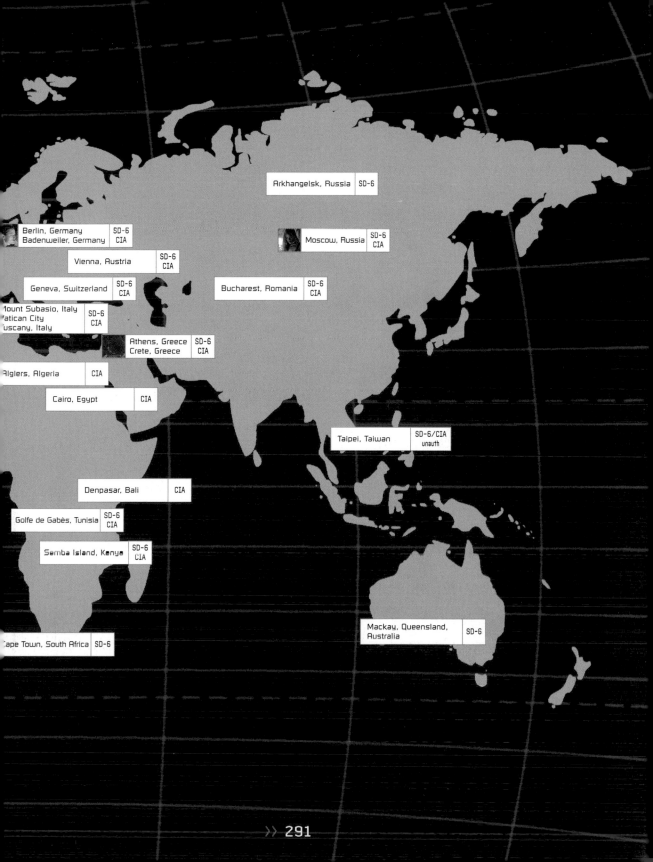

Arkhangelsk, Russia | SD-6

Berlin, Germany | SD-6
Badenweiler, Germany | CIA

Moscow, Russia | SD-6
CIA

Vienna, Austria | SD-6
CIA

Geneva, Switzerland | SD-6
CIA

Bucharest, Romania | SD-6
CIA

Mount Subasio, Italy | SD-6
Vatican City | CIA
Tuscany, Italy

Athens, Greece | SD-6
Crete, Greece | CIA

Algiers, Algeria | CIA

Cairo, Egypt | CIA

Taipei, Taiwan | SD-6/CIA
unauth

Denpasar, Bali | CIA

Golfe de Gabès, Tunisia | SD-6
CIA

Semba Island, Kenya | SD-6
CIA

Mackay, Queensland, Australia | SD-6

Cape Town, South Africa | SD-6

TRAVEL LOG

AGENT >> Sydney Bristow

YEAR >> 02

London, England | SD- CI

Nice, France
Marseilles, France | SC
Cap Ferrat, France | C:
Paris, France

Saria, Spain | una
Port of Barcelona, Spain | C:
Over the Atlantic

Washington, DC, USA | unauth

Rabat, Morocco | SC
| C

Los Angeles, California, USA
Mojave Desert, California, USA | CIA

Mexico City, Mexico | SD-6
Guadalajara, Mexico | CIA

Cayo Concha,
Dominican Republic | CIA

Panama City, Panama | CIA

Cartagena, Colombia | CIA

Buenos Aires, Argentina | CIA

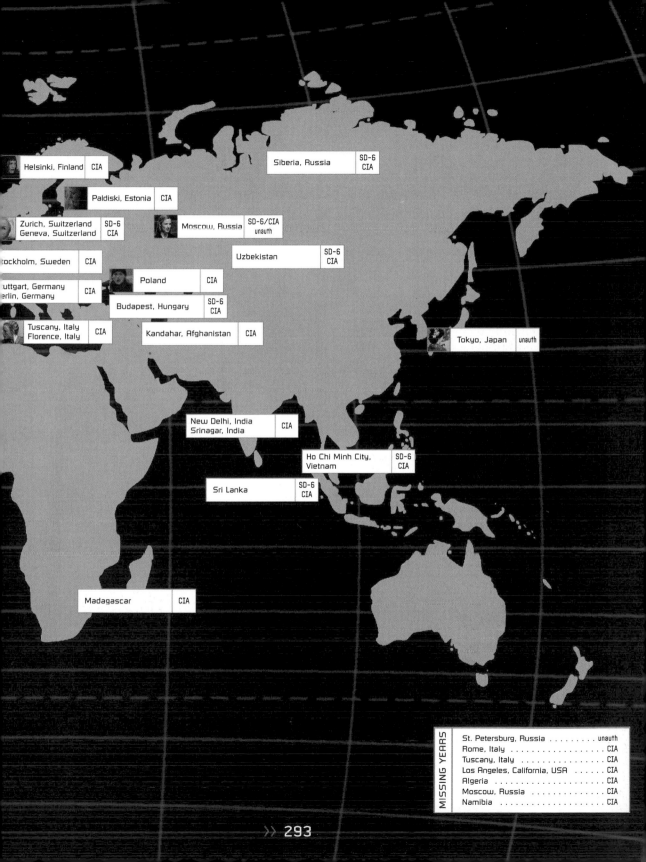

Helsinki, Finland | CIA

Siberia, Russia | SD-6 / CIA

Paldiski, Estonia | CIA

Zurich, Switzerland | SD-6
Geneva, Switzerland | CIA

Moscow, Russia | SD-6/CIA
unauth

Stockholm, Sweden | CIA

Uzbekistan | SD-6
CIA

Stuttgart, Germany | CIA
Berlin, Germany |

Poland | CIA

Budapest, Hungary | SD-6
CIA

Tuscany, Italy | CIA
Florence, Italy |

Kandahar, Afghanistan | CIA

Tokyo, Japan | unauth

New Delhi, India | CIA
Srinagar, India |

Ho Chi Minh City, | SD-6
Vietnam | CIA

Sri Lanka | SD-6
CIA

Madagascar | CIA

MISSING YEARS

St. Petersburg, Russia	unauth
Rome, Italy	CIA
Tuscany, Italy	CIA
Los Angeles, California, USA	CIA
Algeria	CIA
Moscow, Russia	CIA
Namibia	CIA

Vancouver, British
Columbia, Canada | CIA

Belfast,
Northern Ireland | CIA

Wisconsin, USA | unauth

New Haven,
Connecticut, USA
Washington, DC, USA | CIA
unauth

Seville, Spain
Pamplona, Spain
Saragosa, Spain | CI

Lisbon, Portugal | CIA

Nevada, USA | unauth

Los Angeles,
California, USA | CIA
unauth

Cienfuego, Cuba | CIA

Sonora Desert, Mexico
Mexico City, Mexico
Nogales, Mexico | CIA

Patagonia,
South America | CIA

TRAVEL LOG

AGENT >> Sydney
Bristow

YEAR >> 03

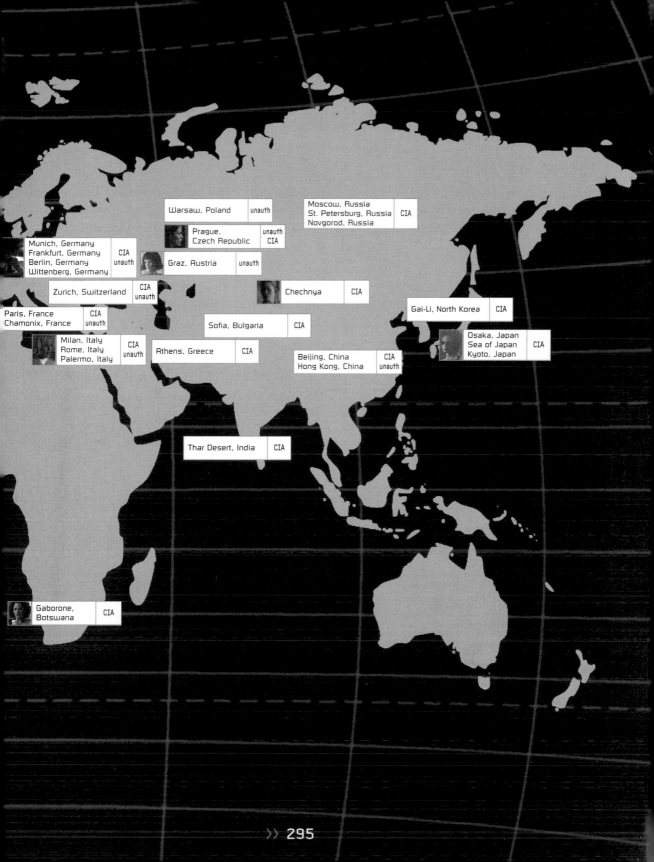

Warsaw, Poland | unauth

Moscow, Russia
St. Petersburg, Russia | CIA
Novgorod, Russia

Prague,
Czech Republic | unauth
CIA

Munich, Germany
Frankfurt, Germany | CIA
Berlin, Germany | unauth
Wittenberg, Germany

Graz, Austria | unauth

Zurich, Switzerland | CIA
unauth

Chechnya | CIA

Gai-Li, North Korea | CIA

Paris, France | CIA
Chamonix, France | unauth

Sofia, Bulgaria | CIA

Osaka, Japan
Sea of Japan | CIA
Kyoto, Japan

Milan, Italy | CIA
Rome, Italy | unauth
Palermo, Italy

Athens, Greece | CIA

Beijing, China | CIA
Hong Kong, China | unauth

Thar Desert, India | CIA

Gaborone,
Botswana | CIA

Amsterdam, Netherlands | APO

London, England | APO

Andalucia, Spain
Ibiza, Spain | APO

The Bahamas | APO

Algeria | AP

Los Angeles,
Santa Barbara,
California, USA | APO
personal

Tikal,
Guatemala | APO

Cuba | APO

Mexico City, Mexico | APO

Rio de Janeiro,
Brazil | APO

Buenos Aires,
Argentina | APO

Santiago, Chile | APO

TRAVEL LOG

AGENT >> Sydney Bristow

YEAR >> 04

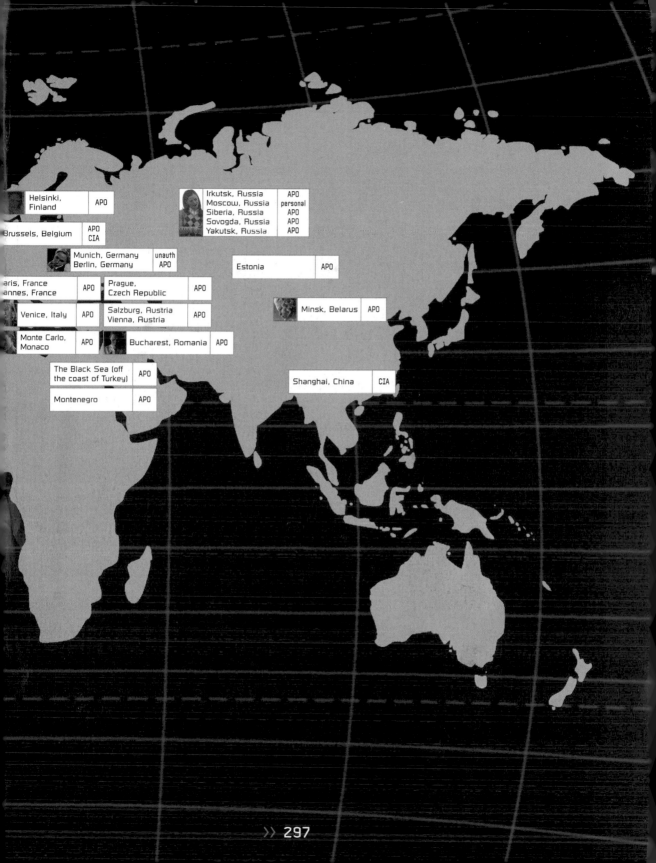

Helsinki, Finland — APO

Brussels, Belgium — APO / CIA

Irkutsk, Russia — APO
Moscow, Russia — personal
Siberia, Russia — APO
Sovogda, Russia — APO
Yakutsk, Russia — APO

Munich, Germany — unauth
Berlin, Germany — APO

Estonia — APO

Paris, France — APO
Cannes, France

Prague, Czech Republic — APO

Minsk, Belarus — APO

Venice, Italy — APO

Salzburg, Austria — APO
Vienna, Austria

Monte Carlo, Monaco — APO

Bucharest, Romania — APO

The Black Sea (off the coast of Turkey) — APO

Shanghai, China — CIA

Montenegro — APO

ACKNOWLEDGMENTS

With much appreciation to J. J. Abrams and the cast and crew of *Alias* for making one of the most original (and most intricately plotted) series on television. And special thanks to Patrick Price for starting me on the journey (and then abandoning me); to Tricia Boczkowski for her guidance (and ability to split her time evenly between this and that *other* episode guide she was editing); and Emily Westlake for always being there when everyone else was mysteriously out of the office (except for the one day I actually came to visit). Additional thanks to everyone else who contributed so much to this book, especially Pierluigi Cothran, Melissa Harling, Yaffa Jaskoll, Jennifer Pricola, Lili Schwartz, and Wendy Wagner.